Eye of Re

Amy Sumida

Contents

More Books by Amy Sumida

The Godhunter Series(in order)
Godhunter
Of Gods and Wolves
Oathbreaker
Marked by Death
Green Tea and Black Death
A Taste for Blood
The Tainted Web

Series Split:
These books can be read together or separately
Harvest of the Gods & A Fey Harvest
Into the Void & Out of the Darkness

Perchance to Die
Tracing Thunder
Light as a Feather
Rain or Monkeyshine
Blood Bound
(Eye of Re)
My Soul to Take
As the Crow Flies
Cry Werewolf
Pride Before a Fall
Monsoons and Monsters
Blessed Death

In the Nyx of Time
Let Sleeping Demons Lie
The Lion, the Witch, and the Werewolf

Beyond the Godhunter:
A Darker Element
Out of the Blue

The Twilight Court Series:
Fairy-Struck
Pixie-Led
Raven-Mocking
Here There Be Dragons
Witchbane
Elf-Shot
Fairy Rings and Dragon Kings
Black-Market
Etched in Stone
—Complete Series—

The Spellsinger Series
The Last Lullaby
A Symphony of Sirens
A Harmony of Hearts
Primeval Prelude
Ballad of Blood
A Deadly Duet
Macabre Melody

The Spectra Series
Spectra
A Gray Area

Erotica
An Unseelie Understanding

Fairy Tales
Happily Harem After Vol. 1
Including:
The Four Clever Brothers
Beauty and the Beasts
Pan's Promise
Wild Wonderland
The Little Glass Slipper
Happily Harem After Vol. 2
Including:
White as Snow
Awakened Beauty
Twisted
Codename: Goldilocks

Historical Romance

Enchantress

*Pronunciation Guide in the
back of the book.*

Get a free gift when you subscribe to Amy's Newsletter:

http://google.us11.list-manage.com/subscribe?
u=398603e0fc6b3876340e37356&id=3abd32edce

Chapter One

Ah; the joys of pregnancy. Well, the joys of supernatural pregnancy. I smiled as I rubbed a hand over my massive belly and my son, Rian, shifted against my touch. We had become psychically connected, and I could sense his every emotion. For the moment, he was only a mass of feelings, a burgeoning life forming around a god soul and a faerie essence. He didn't have thoughts the way that we do but if he had, I was pretty sure that I'd be able to hear them. It made me wonder if we would continue our mental connection after he was born. For now, I knew my child to be generally peaceful but when I got upset, it could cause him to react violently. So, I had to be very careful to keep my cool these days. And for a dragon, that statement becomes literal.

"Leave her be!" Trevor's growl echoed out to me from the hallway.

Trevor, my beautiful werewolf Prince and alpha lover. He could be a little overprotective. More so now that I was pregnant. I don't know how many times I'd caught him snarling at someone because they weren't looking at me or talking to me in the right way. The right way being soft and gentle because a pregnant dragon-sidhe needs to be coddled; insert hysterical laughter here.

"She deserves to know," Odin argued.

Now, Odin and I had history. I had been his wife in a past life, and I was about to become so again. Actually, I was going to marry all four of my non-fey lovers. I was already married to my faerie husband or he would have been included. Don't judge me; it's a lioness magic thing. I need a lot of lovers or my lioness goes into heat, and I accost any male within range. I'm serious. Stop laughing.

Odin is also one of the more level-headed lovers I had, so I was instantly curious about what he thought I should know. I grimaced and pushed myself laboriously up in the lounge chair I'd been relaxing in, out on our bedroom's balcony. The Sun had been gently warming my bare legs and there was a light breeze scented with sweet grass swirling through my hair. It had been perfect, and Rian and I had been enjoying the peace immensely.

"I von't allow her to involve herself in zis," Kirill added his voice to the argument.

Kirill is a Russian Intare; a black werelion with a sexy as hell accent and an even sexier body. He's also mine, all mine; bwahahaha. Except that meant that I'm also his, and he, even though he isn't my alpha lover, is still an alpha male and takes my welfare seriously. He, like Trevor, had become even more serious about it since I'd gotten pregnant. Even though the child was Arach's—the aforementioned fairy husband—and would actually be living in Faerie as the long-awaited Prince of the Fire Kingdom.

"What in the name of all the gazillion Gods is this about?" I snarled and wobbled to my feet. Graceful is not an option when you're at the beach ball stage of pregnancy.

"I'm telling her," Fallon's voice now.

Fallon is not one of my lovers, he is, however, one of my good friends and a high-ranking Intare. Oh, by the way, the Intare are my werelions. I say mine because I hold the magic that sustains them. I'm the Lion Goddess and it's that same magic that turns me into a polyamorous pregnant woman. Soon to be a polygamous un-pregnant woman (we're waiting for the baby to be born before we get married). We all live in Pride Palace, a huge palace in my African-esque territory within the God Realm. There are a little under eighty male werelions, but I'm the only female. It's a sort of reversed pride.

Actually, no; that's not so true anymore. Fallon married my good friend Samantha. Samantha is a Froekn—werewolf—just like Trevor. Together, Fallon and Sam had Zariel, the first naturally born Intare... and the second lioness in the Pride. There may or may not be problems with her one day because of that. But I'm hoping that her part of the twisted future I'd seen recently wouldn't pan out. She was my niece in a way, and I loved her very much. I didn't want to have to kick her out of the Pride.

Back to the matter at hand. My bedroom was on the top floor of Pride Palace. It's a I'm-in-charge-so-I-get-the-best-room thing *and* a tactical thing. You could only get into my rooms through a narrow hallway after going past five Intare-filled floors. The bedroom door was shut against that very hallway so I couldn't see the men who were arguing but as I made my way into the bedroom, I could hear a shuffling sound coming through.

"Let him go, Kirill," Odin snapped.

"Nyet," Kirill snapped back. "I'm Ganza, I decide vhat ve tell our Tima."

"Just because you're the highest-ranking Intare, it doesn't mean you can withhold pertinent information from our goddess," Fallon said reasonably.

Fair point there.

"Da, it does." Kirill wasn't feeling reasonable evidently.

"Does it now?" I yanked open our bedroom door and scowled at the scene in the hallway.

Odin and Trevor stood near Kirill and Fallon. Kirill had Fallon's neck in a vise. My Ganza looked up at me and abruptly shoved Fallon away from him like a playground bully caught in the act.

"You do *not* get to decide what I hear or don't hear," my lioness, wolf, and dragon teamed up against Kirill in an alien growl. "Whether you're my Ganza or my husband! Which, may I remind you, you *aren't* yet."

Fallon shot Kirill a smug look, and Kirill punched Fallon in the face with a casual, sideways maneuver that was so fast that I barely tracked it. Fallon went down like a boxer with a glass jaw, and I gaped at the mass of his crumpled body. Fallon's a big guy, and I had a feeling that he'd be lying there until he woke up. *I* sure as hell wasn't going to carry him down to his wife.

"Kirill!" I screeched.

"Vhat?" Kirill shrugged. "Zere vas bug on his face."

"A bug?" I lifted a brow as I simultaneously glared at him.

"On his face." Kirill nodded. "I killed it."

"You gonna punch me in the mug too?" Odin grimaced. "Cause I'm still going to tell her. I learned long ago never to keep things from my wife."

"Not mug; *bug*," Kirill insisted.

"Mug is another word for a face," Trevor explained as he gave Kirill's shoulder a pat.

"Someone had better freakin' start talking right now!" I shouted, and my lovers went as still as a band of meerkats sensing a predator.

"Anubis has invited all of us to a party," Odin said softly.

"A party?" I blinked.

"Yes," Trevor nodded.

"You're all upset because of a party?" I clarified.

"Party in *Duat*," Kirill growled, his lion coming out clearly in his voice.

"So?" I frowned. "It'll give the Intare a chance to visit their dead brothers. It's very nice of Anubis to invite us."

"If it's even *his* idea." Trevor's jaw clenched.

"Whose idea would it be if not..." I trailed off as I finally understood why they were so tense. "Re. You think Re has persuaded Anubis to host a party in Duat so that he can what; abduct me? Woo me? Hypnotize me with his beauty?" I waved my hands around my face mockingly. "You guys do know that I'm *pregnant*, right?" My hands went down to my huge stomach. "I don't think the Egyptian Sun God is going to be interested in shagging a woman who's obviously carrying another man's child."

"Why not?" Odin cocked his head at me. "We are. I think you're beautiful pregnant."

"Yeah, but you guys love me," I huffed. "Re doesn't. All Re has are some hazy dreams about a future that will never happen. He's not masterminding an abduction with the help of another man who once did actually think he loved me."

"Another man who abducted you," Trevor pointed out. "You can't trust Egyptian Gods. Just look at those damn jackals. It's not right."

"Da." Kirill gave a mock shiver. "Creepy."

"Just because Anubis' jackals have main forms which are animal instead of human, it doesn't make them creepy," I protested. "Just a little dumb."

"And vicious," Trevor added. "They'd have no problem abducting you if Anubis told them to."

"Anubis has moved on," I protested. "Ever since his dip in the fountain, he's become much calmer. And saner. Less inclined toward stealing unwilling women."

"Zen he may not mind helping Re." Kirill circled back to his main argument.

"You've all lost your damn minds over this Re thing," I huffed at them. "This is silly. I haven't even heard from Re since that day."

"You mean the day he vowed to have you despite the fact that you're already taken?" Trevor narrowed his eyes at me. "You never got around to speaking to him like you said you would."

"He did not vow to *have* me," I grumbled. "And I haven't spoken to him because when I finally had the opportunity to do so, too much time had gone by without any contact from him. If I approached him now, I'd look stupid. Re's my friend. He probably just needed some time to cool down and think things over. To realize that dreams don't make a relationship and that a relationship between us wouldn't work anyway."

"I agree." Odin nodded.

"You do?" I looked at him in surprise.

"Even if he were to try something," Odin said, "we can handle one little sun god."

I frowned at that. Smack talk always preceded trouble.

"You do know that Re is the head of the Egyptian Pantheon, don't you?" Trevor narrowed his eyes at Odin.

"He is?" I looked back at Trevor.

"Yeah, I know that," Odin huffed. "So what? He doesn't

actually pull the Sun across the sky."

"Re uses boat," Kirill corrected. "Apollo is sun god vith chariot."

"I know." Odin rolled his eyes. "It still amounts to carting a burning star across the heavens, whether you pull it or carry it in a boat."

"I don't zink it's actually in boat," Kirill mused.

"Oh, who cares?" Odin snapped.

"The point is; Re's stronger than Anubis and that damn jackal-headed asshole didn't have any problems capturing Vervain," Trevor growled. "In fact, he made *her* go to *him*."

"I was a lot weaker then," I interjected. "And he had stabbed me with that soul sucking dagger of his."

"But you're pregnant now," Kirill added. "Baby makes you unstable."

"Not so unstable that I can't kick someone's ass." I looked at Kirill pointedly. "In fact, I'm more likely to do so now."

"You may kiss my ass, Tima." Kirill shook his massive shoulders out and flicked his long, black braid back. "As long as you don't go to Duat."

"I said kick, not kiss." I chuckled despite myself.

"Vhatever you vant." Kirill gave me a sexy grin.

"It's just a party," I whined, unsure if I was whining because I wanted to go to the party or wanted to take Kirill up on his ass kissing... er, I mean, ass kicking offer.

"If we go, it will be with all of the Intare, and I'm not letting you out of my sight." Trevor glared at me.

"Fine." I shrugged. "I don't think Anubis will mind all the

Lions coming. He probably expects it."

"At the first sign of fishiness, you will be escorted away by one or all of us. Agreed?" Trevor went on.

"All right," I said and sighed. "If there's even a single anchovy on the buffet table, we're outta there."

"I still don't like it," Kirill mumbled.

"You can have the first shot at him if he tries anything," Trevor offered, and Kirill began to smile.

Kirill's sapphire eyes sparkled as if Re were strung up before him and someone had handed him a bat and told him it was pinata time. It was kind of terrifying... and really damn sexy.

I know; I have issues.

Chapter Two

So, I may have mentioned that I was getting married to four men at once. My mother was thrilled. Not because of the four men thing but because she'd known about my unique situation and assumed that she'd never get to see me walk down the aisle. She had been the only mother whose opinion I'd considered when I'd said yes to the unusual marriage proposal. I'd never thought about my lovers' mothers, mainly because Azrael was the only one who still had one living.

Azrael is lover number four; the Angel of Death, who had once carried my soul to Hvergelmir, the Viking Well of Souls, because Odin had begged him to. Odin wanted to be able to bring my soul back from death, and he couldn't have done so without knowing where it was. So, Az had put me in the Well and when he did, he touched me. Touched my soul. He knew me more intimately than any other living person. And the really amazing bit is that he loves me anyway.

What was even more amazing was that his parents; Lucifer and Holly Morningstar, otherwise known as Satan and the Holy Spirit, were both thrilled that we were getting married. Holly wanted to be a part of the process, and Azrael wanted his mother to be happy. So, even though I was immensely preggers, and I could use my magic to transform anything within my territory into whatever I wanted—including a wedding gown—I had to go dress shopping with my mom and my soon to be mother-in-law.

It was Hell. Figuratively speaking. In fact, a couple of the Hells I've been to would have been preferable to dress shopping in my condition with Azrael's mother. Not that she's a bad person. On the contrary, I love Azrael's mom and normally, I would have loved the way she shopped. But under present circumstances, it was just exhausting.

First of all, we were in New York City, a place I've never wanted to go to but where Holly insisted we must if I wanted to find the absolute perfect dress. I told her all I really had to do was find a picture of a gown I liked, and I could transform a twig into it, but she said a bride needed to have the full experience and should never make her own wedding dress, no matter how easy it was for her to do it.

So, we traced to California to pick up my mother and then traced her over to New York City with us. My mom wasn't used to tracing yet and the experience of traveling through the Aether as a thought-form was still a little unsettling for her, but I think she found it vastly preferable to sitting on a plane for hours. I know I did.

We stepped out of the Aether and into an alley a few shops down from the bridal boutique Holly had insisted on. The boutique took up a six-story slice of a length of buildings. I say *length* because I truly couldn't determine where one building ended and the next began; they were all connected in one long line. The simple white lettering on the black, shiny storefront said: Pronovias, and I'm sure it was the best of the best, but I'd never heard of the place. The entire front of the store, from first floor all the way up to the top, was glass windows; showcasing beautiful wedding dresses in the simple way that only really expensive stores could manage.

Holly looked immaculate in her red linen suit (she'd taken to wearing red more often now that she's married to Luke) but my mom and I weren't quite up to her level of pristine polish. Oh, we were dressed nicely—I love my fashion—

but no one could compare to the Holy Spirit in her full, shining glory. So, when we walked in the door, it was Holly who instantly commanded attention. The fact that she'd been their client when she married Luke, helped as well.

"Ah, Mademoiselle Esprit!" A very pretty man with dark hair, graying just slightly at the temples, rushed over to kiss Holly on both cheeks.

"And now, I'm in a RomCom," I whispered to my mother, and she giggled. "How cliché can they get?"

"It's not Mademoiselle Esprit anymore, Andre." Holly pushed teasingly at the man's shoulder. "I'm Madam Morningstar now."

"Andre. Madam," I mouthed at my mom, and her face started to get red from her efforts to contain her laughter.

"Yes, yes." Andre gave a little shrug. "But you will never look like a Madam."

"He doesn't know the half of it," I again murmured to my mother.

"This is my son's fiance." Holly swept an elegant pale hand back at me, and I was instantly enveloped in French gay kisses and a light cloud of expensive cologne.

"Oh, cherié, you are lovely!" He looked back at Holly with a delighted smile. "Isn't she lovely?"

"Of course, she's lovely." Holly slid her arm through mine. "My son is a hell of a catch; he wouldn't choose an ugly woman."

"*Hell* yeah; he's a catch," I said with a chuckle.

"I'm sure he is." Andre's expression turned a bit naughty as his gaze fell on my belly. "And I see he's been busy."

"They won't be getting married till after the baby is

born." Holly slapped Andre's arm playfully. "You and I both know how long it can take to find the perfect dress, though, and we wanted to start now. We have her approximate measurements from before the pregnancy."

"Very wise," he agreed. "We'll use those measurements for now and then measure again after the baby comes. When is the wedding going to be?"

"April," I said immediately.

"Wonderful!" He clapped his hands. "I love Spring weddings. And will you be shopping for your entire trousseau here?"

I just blinked at him.

"Oh, yes, she will." Holly smiled, and Andre beamed.

"Champagne!" Andre clapped his hands and started heading back into the shop.

An elegant woman sitting behind the reception desk jumped up and ran off.

"Yep, RomCom." I cast my mother a look and grabbed her hand before Holly and her cliché cohort could whisk me away. "Do you think someone will show up to try and persuade me to marry him instead of Azrael?" I laughed.

"Or maybe all of your fiances will show up," Mom whispered back. "That would blow Andre's mind."

"Or make him jealous." I snickered.

We were led to a swirling, wide, curlicue staircase with low, marshmallow-colored walls encasing it so it looked like one of those perfectly curled ribbons on a Christmas present. Honestly, I was happy to leave the main floor, which was too modern for my taste; glass or mirrors coating everything while the entire wall behind the reception desk was made up of flat screen monitors playing scenes from fashion shows and images of stunning women in stunning dresses. I felt like a whale among mermaids.

We came out onto the second floor and were led back into a dressing room. Maybe I shouldn't call it a room, it was more like a suite. When I'd said this was a Romantic Comedy, my words had been truer than I'd thought. It turned out that this was the room they used in like *every* movie with a wedding gown shopping scene in it. Andre made sure to inform me of this.

There was a wide expanse of pale wood floor with a square gray carpet in the exact center and a square, cream, padded... I don't know what you call it; perhaps a huge ottoman? It was big and puffy and meant to be sat on and it was in the exact center of that carpet. Then, placed directly across from each other, were floor-to-ceiling mirrors set into simple, wood, box frames. On the wall between the mirrors stood a rack devoted entirely to wedding gowns.

"Now"—Andre looked me up and down—"we shall determine what your style is. Madam Morningstar, the measurements if you please."

Holly instantly produced a small piece of white paper with my previous measurements scribbled across it.

"My style?" I blinked at Andre.

"Yes, style." He looked me over. "I see that you are not unfamiliar to fashion but it's hard for me to determine what your style is, what mode you prefer. I don't know if this is the sort of dress you wear normally or if it's a pregnancy outfit."

"Oh." I looked down at my loose cotton dress and then helplessly at my mother.

She just shrugged. My mom is the type of woman who wore fanny packs. I'd finally bought her a Gucci fanny pack because if she was going to wear one, I at least wanted it to be a nice one. I'm a woman who adores fashion, but I'd never had the time to invest in becoming an expert. So, as far as my style was concerned; I wore whatever I thought was pretty.

"Well, I think I'd like to go classic but romantic; perhaps Vera Wang or Dior? Or maybe Marchesa; I love Marchesa. Do those ladies make wedding apparel?"

"Oh!" Andre swooned. "Thank heavens, it *is* only a pregnancy outfit. By simply breathing the word Marchesa, you've made it absolutely clear that you're a woman of taste. I know exactly what to show you."

"Andre," Holly said imperiously. "Bring out the Elie Saab, if you please."

"Oooh!" Andre fanned himself with a limp hand. "Truly?"

"There's no limit today." Holly nodded. "My son's bride will have the best."

"I won't have to try anything on, will I?" I looked down at my belly.

"Oh no, my darling," he assured me. "We have models to do the actual work. All you have to do is sit here and drink your champagne..." His stare landed on my belly. "Oh no, no, no! How horrid of me." He turned to holler down the stairs. "Make that sparkling cider, Sherie!"

Chapter Three

Halfway through the fashion show, I excused myself to use the restroom. I knew exactly where it was because that was something you learned to make yourself aware of the further into your pregnancy you got. I hobbled down the stairs and went straight to the elegant bathroom at the back of the building. It was more like a bathroom you'd find in an expensive home than in a business. There was only one toilet, no stalls, and so the door itself locked.

On my way out, I ran into a solid chest which pushed me back into the room. The click of the lock sounded, and I looked up into Re's gorgeous face. I stumbled away in shock and gaped at him. He looked wonderful, as usual; his dark brown hair swept back into a ponytail, showcasing the way it shifted to blond in streaks as well as putting the dramatic angles of his face on stark display. His skin was deeply tanned but it looked much lighter due to its golden shimmer. It looked as if he'd dusted himself with real gold powder but it was actually natural, the shimmer was within his skin.

The golden gleam highlighted the curves of his muscular chest, glimpsed through the V neck of a light blue, thin sweater, and his muscular thighs were hinted at by subtly-clinging black trousers. I looked away from his distracting body to his even more distracting face. Thick eyebrows, a shade darker than his hair. A strong jaw with a hint of stubble. High cheekbones like a supermodel. But his regal nose didn't look so noble now, resting as it was below worried, golden eyes.

"Vervain." Re reached for me, and I backed further away.

"Re, what are you doing here?" I demanded.

"I needed to see you without all of your men around," he explained quickly and reached for me again.

"How did you even find me?" I stepped back once more. This time, the wall stopped me.

"I am the Sun God, Re," he huffed. "I see all."

"You saw my posting on Facebook, didn't you?" I groaned.

I should have known better but it was rare that I had any kind of news I could share with my human friends and family, and I wanted desperately to be able to bask in the joy of my wedding like a normal woman.

"It doesn't matter how I found you," he said imperiously. "Here we are, and we need to talk."

"Yes, we do." I sighed. "I should have called you and had this talk awhile ago, but I hadn't heard from you, and I thought you'd gotten over me."

"Gotten over?" He blinked. "You're the one who keeps visiting me, Vervain."

What do you mean?" I gaped at him, totally forgetting that I'd gone along with Re's assumption that the memories were just dreams playing out between us.

"Are you seriously going to stand there and act as if you haven't been coming to see me every night in the Dream Realm?" He shook his head in disbelief.

"I..." I floundered.

"And now you want to shy away from me?" His voice lowered to a husky tenor as he eased forward, placing his hands on the wall to either side of me. "You're driving me mad, Lala," he whispered into my ear then lowered his lips to the rapid pulse in my neck. "The dreams are fantastic, but I wake disappointed, longing for the feel of your flesh."

"Um, I need to explain something." I angled away from him.

"Yes." Re dove lower, and I felt his breath sliding into my cleavage. "Explain to me how you did that thing with your teeth. It was miraculous."

My eyes went wide in horror as I simultaneously shivered. What had I done with my teeth? No; don't go there, Vervain.

"Whoa now. Take a look down, Romeo. I'm not in a condition to be romanced," I said breathlessly. Yes, as in barely breathing. I couldn't help it, the man was sex on a stick; he made me want to lick him like a popsicle.

"You weren't pregnant last night." He spun me around and draped me over a little side table that held a basket of hand towels.

The towels went flying as my belly conquered the tabletop, and I leaned into the wall. Re was immediately pressed up tightly against me, hands sliding down my sides until he got a hold of the hem of my dress. He slid his fingers beneath it and edged them forward, trailing them up the front of my thighs as he pressed his hips up into the curves of my ass.

"Re!" I hissed. "Stop!"

"Oh, so it's all right for you to sexually assault me in my dreams, but I can't touch you in real life?" He growled in my ear. "Who do you think you're playing with, little girl? You can't just toy with me every night and then pretend there's nothing between us. You've had me *every* night," his voice vibrated across the delicate skin on the back of my neck. "And now, I will have you."

"I never actually had you." I sighed and leaned my forehead to the wall.

"Haven't you?" His breath was hot on the hollow of my collarbone.

Then his lips replaced it and the scent of burning frankincense wafted into my nostrils. I breathed in deep and groaned.

You might think that a pregnant woman has no sex drive. I mean; why would she? Nature has accomplished its goal, you're now well and truly with child. Why would it continue to give you urges to make more babies? Who knows why Nature does what she does? She's one crazy bitch... and she's rather randy too.

Or maybe that was just me.

The feel of Re's hands skimming further up my thighs, leaving hot trails on my skin, sent me reeling with desire. I wanted to do things with him, right there in that bathroom, that shouldn't be done in public. Much less one floor down from my mother and soon to be mother-in-law as they looked over possible wedding gowns for me. That thought snapped me out of my lust haze, and I grabbed at Re's questing hands.

"Back away from me, Re," I said firmly. "Please."

"Damn it, Vervain!" Re pulled away and ran a hand angrily through his hair, yanking it out of its ponytail. Thick strands fell around his frustrated face. "Why are you doing this to me? I thought we were friends."

"We are friends, and I'm not trying to do anything to you," I said. "Look, I was hoping I wouldn't have to explain this, but I'm not visiting you in your dreams."

"You know damn well that you are!" Re narrowed his eyes until they turned into golden slits.

"No, I'm not." I took a deep breath. "I've recently been to the future."

"What?" That threw him.

"My daughter came back in time, using my Ring of Remembrance"—I held up the ring for him to see—"to warn me that I'd made a terrible mistake. She couldn't tell me what I'd done, she could only take me forward and show me."

"You went into the future?" He gaped at me.

"And it was bleak." I nodded. "I was dead, which was the only reason I could travel forward. But that wasn't the worst of it. I won't go into the details, but I found that the turning point was Odin. Odin had been overtaken by the personality of the body I'd put him into, and this Griffin persona took over and prompted him to leave me."

"Odin left you?" Re shook his head and leaned against the counter.

"And I let him," I confirmed. "That's where everything went wrong. I had to come back and fix my relationship with Odin. I saved him from Griffin and it saved my future."

"And how does that affect my dreams?" He frowned.

"It doesn't." I waved away the question. "In that twisted future, I'd lost a lover and needed to find a new one."

"Me." Re gaped at me. "I was that lover, wasn't I?"

"Yes." I sighed. "I spent some time with you there, and you told me about our life together. Somehow, during that conversation, you shared your memories with me, and I was able to experience them."

"And then you what; brought them back to me?" He cocked his head.

"I think I may have." I swallowed past the dry lump in my throat. "I'm sorry I deceived you and let you believe I was coming to you in your sleep. I thought it would be worse if you knew we had something real together in a time that would never happen."

"What if I still want something real with you?" He whispered.

"I can't, Re." I sighed. "You're incredible, and I'd love to be with you, but I can't."

"Why not?" He looked genuinely confused.

"Because I'm about to give birth to my husband's child," I ground out. "And after that, I'm going to marry four more men. Do you not see how another man in my life is not an option?"

"No." He lifted his chin. "Actually, it seems very much like an option."

"I need five men." I groaned in frustration. "Five, Re, and that's what I have right now. With five, the Intare magic is satisfied and the magic is the only reason I take multiple lovers. Now, I'm about to exchange vows with those lovers and swear that it will only be them for the rest of our lives. I can't add another man to the arrangement."

"Things change." Re eased forward and his palm went to my cheek. "Hearts change. Your men will understand. They have before."

"It's not about understanding or even my heart." I shook my head, dislodging his hand even though the feel of it on my cheek seemed natural.

"Tell me then." Re brushed his lips across mine. "What is

this about?"

"It's about boundaries." I pushed him away gently. "I'm sorry I crossed them with you. I didn't do it on purpose, and I hope you'll forgive me."

"Vervain." His jaw hardened. "You just told me that these dreams I'm having of you are actually memories. That means that we share them. How could you have experienced what I did and yet stand there so unaffected?"

"I am *not* unaffected," I whispered.

"Then—"

"Did you tell Anubis to host a party?" I changed the subject and cut him off.

"What party?" His eyes skittered away.

"That's it; I'm not going," I declared.

"Blast it, Vervain," he growled. "Fine. You want me to leave you alone? I'll leave you alone. You want to deny what's between us? Go ahead; deny it. Take a good look at me and tell me that I mean nothing to you. Then go home and lie in bed tonight and say it again to yourself. Say it over and over." He came in close once more. I could feel the heat of his skin and smell that fiery frankincense. I almost missed his next words. "Say it until you believe it and then, when you feel strong enough," he slid his cheek against mine and whispered in my ear, "think about how I'll be spending the night with another woman. Touching her, when I could be touching you. Tasting her, when I could have been relishing the taste of you. Fucking her, when I could have been sinking my cock into you."

I shivered as he pulled away, and he saw it; saw it and smiled.

"The party, Re." I steadied myself. "Are you behind it?"

"Go to Anubis' party, Vervain." Re rolled his eyes. "Since my presence bothers you so much; I promise I won't be there."

"Really?" I pressed.

"You're good, Godhunter." He grinned wickedly. "Maybe up in my top five. But you're not *that* good. I'll be over you as soon as I've got another woman beneath me."

He left with a smirk.

"Well, you didn't have to be so mean about it," I muttered.

Chapter Four

"Please make her stop," I groaned to Azrael when he walked in.

We had spent all afternoon in the bridal boutique and it wasn't nearly as bad as I'd thought it was going to be. The Elie Saab, as Holly had called it, was the most amazing gown I'd ever seen. It was hauté couture and would have to be made special for me but once I saw it, I didn't care. Holly was right; it was perfect.

Thousands of crystal beads had been hand sewn onto snow white silk, radiating up and down from the waist in sparkling lines. The main portion of the beads were champagne gold with fringed stripes of shimmering silver at the bodice, waist, and near the full hem. The beads covered nearly the entire dress, stopping only about a foot before the hemline to show off the silk tulle beneath. Andre had assured us that it could be created in bone white to accommodate a more traditional taste and that the beads could be done in any colors we wanted. So, we ordered the dress. I decided against the bead covered veil, which Andre had said would require a handful of bridesmaids to carry behind me. Instead, we chose something more sedate with just a beaded comb to hold it on.

I nearly fainted when he read the total. Let's just say it was more than I'd pay for a really nice car. Holly whipped out a black American Express card and paid not only for the dress but also for my entire trousseau, which was a package deal that had a whole bunch of extras Andre was just throwing in because Holly was spending so much damn money. My mother just gaped at Holly, as did I.

"I feel bad," Mom had whispered to me. "I wanted to help pay for something."

"Don't feel bad and don't pay for *anything*," I whispered back. "That's the Devil's wife. They've probably got more money than God. Literally."

"I heard that," Holly called over her shoulder then smiled brilliantly. "And we do. Jerry isn't even half the business man Luke is."

So, yes, that bit was fun. But then we'd gone back to Azrael's home in Shehaquim, and Holly started bombarding me with questions on everything from lettering on the invitations to the flavor of the cakes... as in multiple. What the hell was a groom's cake? Didn't we just share a cake? I mean, wasn't that the point of getting married? To share things? And, even worse, each groom had to have his own cake. As if he'd be eating it all by himself. Then again, knowing my men, maybe they would. Big appetites there.

Holly had wanted us to go to her house, but I refused to make my mother walk through Hell. The Garden of Eden, yes. Hell, absolutely not. As it was, my mom was passed out in the living room. She'd made the mistake of drinking a glass of sacred wine to settle her nerves and it had gone straight to her head. Which meant that I was alone with the wedding-crazed Holy Spirit.

Until Az walked in, that is.

"Mom, what are you doing to Vervain?" Azrael sighed and sat down beside me. "We expected her home hours ago."

"I'm just going over the necessary details," Holly said sweetly.

"I saw Vervain's mom sprawled across the couch. What happened to her?" Az asked.

"She had some wine," Holly said.

"I was in the bathroom," I added.

"Mom," Azrael chided Holly. "You need to remember that she's human."

"I know." Holly sighed. "But Darlyne's fine. She can come home with me."

"I'm going to say this one more time, Holly." I held up a hand. "I'm not leaving my mother in Hell for the night."

"Oh, please." Holly rolled her eyes. "Our home is lovely."

"And it's *in Hell*," I reminded her. "She'll have to literally walk through Hell to get there. Nope, not happening. And let me just say that it's Luke's fault for not allowing people to trace into his home."

"Well, the Devil can't have people just showing up in his living room whenever they want," Holly huffed. "What if he was doing something devilish?"

"Like rearranging the furniture?" I rolled my eyes.

Luke is more Martha Stewart than Master of Sin.

"Mom, enough." Azrael slid his hand around her waist and helped her to her feet. "It's time to call it quits for the day."

"And night." I sighed.

"You've worn out Vervain." He waved a hand to me. "And you know she has both fey and goddess resilience. That's a lot of wearing out."

"Well, she's pregnant," Holly said defensively.

"Yes, exactly." Azrael looked pointedly from my belly to Holly.

"Oh!" Holly clamped her hands to her mouth. "I'm so sorry, Vervain. I guess I wasn't thinking about how exhausting it gets when you're pregnant. I went through some rather stressful pregnancies myself. Did I ever tell you about the War in Heaven?"

"Another time, Mom." Azrael hurried her out the door.

"Goodnight, Vervain," she called back to me.

"Goodnight!" I called and then sighed, sliding down into my seat.

"I'm so sorry." Azrael rushed back in. "What can I do? Do you want a back rub? A foot rub?"

"Not unless you want to bring on labor." I sighed deeper.

"What?" He blinked.

"There are pressure points in the feet that can make a woman go into labor." I gestured at my feet, which actually weren't all that sore, considering. "My mom could probably use a back rub, though." I laughed.

"I'm going to carry her up to a bedroom." He started to get up. "I told the others that you'd probably stay the night. We can trace her home in the morning."

"Yeah, that sounds good." I yawned. "Hey, before you go, I need to tell you something."

"What is it?" He sat back down.

"I saw Re today," I said simply.

"What? Where?" His eyes went wide and angry.

"At the bridal boutique," I said. "It's okay, we talked, and I think he's going to back off now. He promised he wouldn't be at Anubis' party."

"Are you sure we can trust that?" His eyes narrowed.

"He got a little bitter and told me he'd be over me as soon as he had another woman beneath him." I chuckled. "I don't think that will take too long, and I don't think he'll show up at the party either."

"Well, bitter is better than determined," Azrael said in relief. "I still think we need to be careful with him."

"All right." I gave another yawn. "I'll tell the others about it tomorrow."

"Good." He stood again. "I'll go put your mom in a spare room." He stopped and turned to me. "Did she see Re? Did *my* mom see him?"

"No, he waited till I went to the bathroom." I rolled my eyes. "And I didn't tell them."

"Good." Az nodded as he left the room. "Let's keep it that way."

"Indeed." I leaned my head back in my chair and closed my eyes. I was asleep before he got back.

Chapter Five

Shopping for my wedding dress had been fun but when I got back to Pride Palace, I realized that it would have been more fun if I could have tried on the dresses. Then it occurred to me that I'd have to come up with yet another dress to wear to Anubis' party... and this one would have to be maternity wear.

I spent the morning flipping through fashion magazines for pregnant women, trying to come up with a design that wouldn't make me look like balloon. I ended up on the floor in the library's sitting room, pictures of beautiful, pregnant models spread around me. My belly was so big now that it pushed my legs apart when I sat and my boobs had gotten bigger too, going from Double-D to Double-WTF. They bulged over the mass of my belly as if they wanted to fall off and roll away. I wanted to roll away with them. I was looking more like the prehistoric fertility version of a goddess than the Greek love goddess I was supposed to be.

I felt ugly and fat and swollen and tired, and I didn't think I wanted to go to a party anymore. Maybe I'd stay home and just roll around the floor until someone felt sorry for me and threw some food in my mouth. I could bark like a seal and clap my hands for more.

That's when I began to cry.

Oh, and they were ugly tears. The sniffing, hiccuping, snot-nosed variety. I couldn't reach the tissue box on the table so I tried to wipe my nose with a magazine page. It crumpled against my face and only made things worse. I pulled it away and the poor pregnant woman in the picture glared at me angrily.

"Oh, screw you," I snapped at her and balled her up so I could throw her across the room. Then I gave up and just wiped my nose with my sleeve.

"Tima?" Kirill walked in.

Why is it that whenever I look my worst, some gorgeous guy walks in? Kirill was dressed in worn jeans and a button-down gray shirt. It brought out the jewel tones in his eyes and made his ass-length hair look blacker than sin. His forearms bulged beneath rolled up sleeves and the top two buttons of his shirt were undone, giving a tempting glimpse of smooth, muscled chest. He looked like a fantasy come to life.

I started crying again.

"Tima!" Kirill rushed over, coming down to the floor beside me. He slid a hand along my neck and another across my belly to pull me against him. "Tell me," he said simply.

"I'm fat!" I wailed.

"You're not fat; you're pregnant," he corrected gently as he smoothed the hair back from my wet face. "And you're beautiful. Even vith crying, you're still beautiful."

"You *have* to say that," I whined. "Look at me." I pulled away from him and gestured at my belly and boobs. "I'm gross. Like a giant ball with limbs. Not even a ball, a ball is smooth at least, I'm all bubbly. I can't go to the party looking bubbly."

"Ah, so zis is about party." He gathered me up easily, despite my bulk, and draped me over his lap. One large hand went to my cheek and settled me against his neck. I fit there perfectly. I swear, his neck was made for my face to nuzzle. "You vill look amazing at party, and ve all vill be proud to valk in beside you."

"Stop lying to me." I sniffled. "I'm staying home. It's settled."

"Stop zis right now," he chided sweetly. "You have baby in belly and zat is beautiful. You're a goddess of life right now, a true vision of fertility and love. You're stunning. So magnificent zat it hurts to look at you sometimes. I can't vait for moment when you carry my child." His hand laid over my stomach and rubbed gently while a wistful expression crossed his face.

"She's going to be amazing." I sniffled, some of his words finally working their way past my insecurities.

"Lesya," he whispered and smiled wide. "The defender of man."

"Is that what it means?" I wiped my eyes.

"Just like her mother." Kirill nodded. "It's Russian. I must have picked it."

"You must have," I agreed. "It's a wonderful name."

"Tell me more about her," he urged. "Vhat vill she look like?"

"Like you," I said immediately. "She has... *will have* your hair, though it's wavy like mine, and she'll have your beautiful eyes." I stopped to touch his cheek. The more I spoke of Lesya, the calmer I got. As if I needed to remember why I was going through this. "She'll be tall like you too, but she'll have my nose and the shape of her face will be closer to mine."

"I love your nose." He kissed the tip of said nose and sighed happily. "She vill be beautiful."

"Definitely beautiful." I slid my arms around him and

snuggled closer. "And brave. You should have seen her stand up to Zariel."

"Stand up to Zariel?" He pulled away and looked down at me in confusion.

I'd forgotten that I hadn't told the men about Zariel's betrayal. I'd thought it was bad enough for me to hold a non-existent future against her; I didn't want them to do it too.

"She was fighting Lesya for the Pride," I confessed.

"Nyet!" He growled.

"You helped Lesya stand up to her, but Zariel took advantage of my death and abused several Intare," I went on. "She used their past damage against them and made them subservient again."

"Zariel?" His eyes looked wounded. "Nyet."

"Yes, Zariel." I sighed. "Our little lion princess turned on us. I'm trying hard not to hold it against her. And I've been debating whether I should tell Fallon or not. I'd decided to tell him but now, I'm reconsidering again."

"Vhat good vill it do?" Kirill looked away sadly. "A father vill never believe such zings of his child. Leave zat future vhere it belongs; in your past."

"Why don't I just come to you whenever I have any kind of problem?" I teased.

"I don't know." He grinned. "But you should."

"Yes, I should." I leaned forward into his kiss and forgot about being fat or feeling ugly. In Kirill's arms, I was always a love goddess.

Chapter Six

I was floating in the pool in front of Pride Palace, my belly bulging out of the water like a buoy, when a tingling emanated from my son inside me. I opened my eyes and found myself floating in a river instead of our natural-looking pool with its little waterfall. Shock flooded my limbs, and I jerked upright, treading water as I scanned my surroundings.

It was dark, full night, but firelight came from somewhere behind me. Before I could turn to see the source, a boat floated silently up to me. It was flat-bottomed and very simple in design, but I wasn't paying too much attention to it. Its occupants were way more interesting.

Humanoid but definitely not human. More shadow than flesh, they consisted of condensed darkness. That thought would have frightened me once but after creating the Dark Fey and helping them find their balance, I didn't fear the Darkness anymore. So, I didn't even flinch when one of the shadow people leaned forward to speak to me.

"Beware of the Eye of Re," the shadow spoke even though he didn't have a mouth.

"Who are you?" I demanded.

"I am no one." He straightened. "Nothing but magic and shadows. An ushabti, made to serve."

"Serve who?" I frowned. "Re? What has he done? Why should I be wary of him?"

"I serve the dead," the hollow voice continued. "And it is not Re whom I warn you of."

"No, just his eye," I muttered.

I was about to ask him what exactly was wrong with Re's eye, when he, the boat, and the whole dang river disappeared. I found myself back to floating in my pool. I was so shocked that I fell beneath the surface and came up sputtering.

"Vervain!" Thor was standing at the edge of the pool, looking as if he was about to jump in.

"I'm fine!" I held up a hand. "Just help me out, please." I waved toward the shallow end of the pool.

"All right." Thor met me there then reached down and helped me up the steps of the pool. "Are you sure you're okay?"

"I'm fine." I nodded but my hand trailed to my belly.

What the hell was that? Was it a vision or a hallucination? Had Rian given it to me or had someone sent it to me? And what was wrong with Re's eye that I had to be wary of it? Damn it; I hated prophecies.

"Vervain?" Thor peered into my face with concern.

"Sorry." I waddled over to a little iron dining set and sat my wet butt down on a metal chair. "I just had some kind of weird vision."

"A vision?" Thor took a seat beside me.

"It was probably the fried pickles I had for lunch." I shook my head. "Never mind that. What are you doing here? Is everything all right with you?"

"I'm well." Thor sat back in his seat as he placed a manila folder down on the table. "I just wanted to bring this over for you."

"What's this?" I nudged the edge of the folder open with a wet finger. It looked like bank papers.

"I sold Ull's law firm," Thor said. "Then I put the money in a trust for him. The account is in your name. You may use the money for his upbringing or save it and give it to him when he gets older. I'll leave that up to you."

"Thor." I scanned the pages in surprise. "There's almost twenty million dollars here."

"It was a very successful law firm." Thor nodded.

"No kidding." I laughed and closed the folder. "Thank you for taking care of that for him. I wouldn't have thought of it."

"I'm his father," Thor said and frowned. "I was his father."

"Thor." I leaned forward and took his hand. "You will always be Ull's father. This life will be Rian's but that doesn't mean he won't know you or who you were to him."

"Thank you for saying that." He cleared his throat. "I couldn't bring myself to sell his homes so I just hired a company to maintain them until Ull... I mean; Rian, is old enough to decide whether he wants them or not."

"I'm sure he'll appreciate that," I said gently. "I'm also sure there will come a day when he'll want to know about his old self, and his personal things will help with that."

"Then you're not upset?" Thor lifted a brow.

"Of course not." I eased back into my seat. "But I'd like you to have the maintenance companies send me the bill. It should come out of this account instead of your pocket."

"All right, I'm okay with that," he said. "Vervain, I don't remember if I've said this yet but thank you for bringing him back to us. Even if it isn't in the way I would have liked. It's so much better than him being born to some random family. We may never have found him again."

"He's safe now." I laid a hand on my stomach. "That's what's important. And no matter what name he bears, deep down, he'll always be our Ull."

"I miss him so much." Thor took a shaky breath. "We were close; closer than father and son."

"I know," I said softly. "And that kind of bond will surely be carried into his new life."

"Do you really think so?"

Rian shifted inside me, edging closer to Thor, and I knew exactly what he wanted. I took Thor's hand and laid it on my belly. Thor's eyes widened as I felt Rian lean into that hand, as if he was laying his head into Thor's palm.

"Ull," Thor whispered brokenly.

Then Thor laid his cheek against my stomach and cried, but I think they were happy tears. Tears of relief. I don't think he had truly accepted that my son carried Ull's soul inside him until that very moment. Even if he had, he'd believed that Ull wouldn't remember him in this new life. Thor had mourned his son, thinking that he would never have Ull back as he'd once known him. Even though that was true, and Thor would never see Ull again, he now knew that his son remembered him. When Rian was born, Thor would have a second chance, a second life with the man we both loved.

I held Thor there and hugged him as he hugged our son; once his and now mine. There was a time when I'd thought about having children with Thor. But that was a long time ago, and I'd believed that our chance had passed. Funny how our daydreams sometimes come to life in unexpected ways and at unexpected times.

Chapter Seven

Only two weeks later, it felt as if my belly had grown five inches. I made a face at myself in my full-length mirror. Maybe it wasn't so bad. I turned to the side and slid my hands down the chiffon silk, cupping them beneath my belly before releasing the pale blue folds. I'd chosen a Grecian style gown with swaths of silk falling from gold, lion head clasps at my shoulders. Layers of thin silk gathered over my breasts to form a deep V and show off my significant cleavage. Directly beneath my cleavage, right above my belly, a gold band held the silk together. From there, it draped in wispy elegance around me, just over the tips of my gold Valentino heels.

"You look spectacular." Trevor whistled as he came into my dressing room.

"Says the sharp dressed man in my doorway." I looked him over appreciatively.

Trevor always cleaned up well, even though his best look was rough and a little dirty. He had a pale blue dress shirt on that matched my dress perfectly and black designer slacks. Shiny leather shoes peeped out beneath the cuffs. His unruly dark curls had been slicked into order so they formed attractive waves down to his nape. He'd cut his hair recently so it wasn't quite as wild as normal, but Trevor could never look perfectly civilized. His wolf came through in the way he held himself, as if he were on the verge of attack even when he was relaxed. It showed in his smile, which became almost feral sometimes. And most of all, it peered right out of his lupine eyes. Werewolf Prince was the perfect title for him.

"Vhich sharp-dressed man are you talking about?" Kirill sauntered past Trevor and struck a pose, setting his hands casually in his pant pockets.

"Oh." My eyes widened.

Kirill had gone for a full suit; black on black, with a slim, pale blue tie for a spot of color. His hair was pulled back into a low ponytail, making it appear short from the front and bringing out the angles of his face. Although his lion heart was just as wild as Trevor's, Kirill didn't exude the same ferocious appeal. His allure was more subtle, seeping in slowly, like scented oil massaged on skin. You meet him and think; wow, he's attractive. But then five minutes later, you realize he's addictively gorgeous. The kind of charisma-infused appeal that keeps pulling you back without any effort at all. You end up staring at Kirill because there simply is no other option.

I think it had to do with the twist my magic had put on his lion instincts and the fact that Kirill had been born a human prince, son of Peter the Great. He exuded the confidence of a man who was secure in both his place in the world and his attractiveness. He was powerful but too satisfied to be ambitious, deadly but too reserved to display it, and strikingly handsome but too modest to use it to his advantage. A lion, born to be king but content to let his queen rule so that he could do what truly made him happy; protect her.

"Are they voguing?" Azrael asked Odin as they strode into the large (thank goodness) dressing room.

Azrael was wearing an angelic shirt; one enchanted to split around his wings. It was a wrap style that should have looked feminine but on him, it was pure wicked masculinity. It fell in a deeper V than my bodice, showing off an obscene amount of thickly sculpted chest. Midnight black, the shirt played up his sinister new facial hair; a goatee which gave his angelic face a villainous twist. The only thing that saved him from looking like sin incarnate, were his slacks. They were the same sky blue of my dress.

Odin had apparently got the pale blue memo too, but he'd upped the ante. He was dressed completely in the color. However, he'd also gone totally Norse. He wore a heavy cotton tunic with leather pants. Yep, even the leather was baby blue. A black belt wrapped his waist with an elaborate sword hanging from it and on his feet were black boots. He was the tallest of my men and had the thickest build, as you'd expect of a Viking god. But he didn't look barbaric, not even with his shoulder-length hair and full beard. Hid deep walnut hair had golden highlights and his beard was neatly trimmed but what really gave him a civilized appearance was the gleam in his color-shifting eyes. He stared out at the world as if he'd been studying it for centuries but still wanted to learn more. I guess, at heart, Odin was really more of a scholar than a warrior. Of course, that didn't mean he wasn't capable of kicking some ass.

"I think I'm going to faint." I fanned my face dramatically. "Why don't we just stay home and have dinner in bed?"

"Uh-uh." Azrael gave me a devilish grin. "You talked us into this party, and we all got dressed up for it. We even color coordinated. We're going."

"All right." I laughed. "But I don't know whose arm to take."

A flurry of movement erupted and suddenly both of my arms were claimed. Kirill, who had been closest to me, had the left, and Azrael got the right. I just shook my head and let them lead me out while Odin and Trevor fell into line behind us, grumbling.

Chapter Eight

"I haven't seen this many people here since..." I trailed off as I realized what I was about to say.

"Since I abducted you and had a Ball to present you as my trophy?" Smooth and low, Anubis' voice slid over me, and I turned to see the God of the Dead smiling at me regretfully. "I hope I haven't forever ruined any chance of you enjoying Duat."

"Not at all." I went forward and gave him an awkward, pregnant-woman hug. "The ballroom looks amazing... as usual."

"Thank you." He smiled sweeter as he nodded and the little gold beads in his straight, ebony, shoulder-length hair clicked together. "All of you are most welcome." His oil slick eyes shifted to include my men before settling on me again. "I've invited my entire pantheon tonight. You've met most of them, Vervain, but I doubt you'll remember."

"I was a little stressed the last time." I gave him a small smile.

"Yes." Anubis sighed deeply. "Hopefully, this time you'll be able to focus more on enjoying yourself and socializing. Still, may I be so bold as to ask you for a dance later?"

"Nyet," Kirill said immediately, and my other men shifted together behind him in support.

"You can't blame a god for asking." Anubis chuckled and held up his hands. "Your lions are waiting to see you." He motioned to a section of the massive room where the souls of my dead Intare waited, looking completely corporeal. "They've been excited for days."

"Their brothers have been too." I nodded at the group that was already being enveloped in lion hugs by their living brothers. "Thank you, Anubis." I laid a hand on his arm. "It was nice of you to invite us."

"As long as the invitation truly came from you," Trevor added.

"What does that mean?" Anubis frowned.

"They think that this was Re's idea," I said in a low voice.

"Re?" Anubis frowned deeper. "Why would he want me to invite you, in particular?"

"He didn't tell you?" I blinked in shock.

"Tell me what?" Anubis' eyes narrowed. "What did he do now?"

"Nothing." I shook my head. "It's a long story but basically, I've recently had some trouble with the future."

"The future?" Anubis' angry look went blank.

"I had to use my ring to go into it and change a few things." I took a deep breath and then forged ahead. "I had lost Odin and needed a new lover. You were married, so—"

"I was married?" His face turned hopeful.

"Yes." I stopped to smile. "I told you, you just need to be patient and keep looking for her."

"You did tell me that," Anubis' eyes softened. "And I am still looking, though maybe not patiently."

"Anyway." Azrael rolled his eyes and came up beside me.

"Anyway," I slid Az an irritated glance before going on, "I ended up with Re."

"You *what*?" Anubis went back to being angry.

"It's all in a future that will never happen," I assured him. "I changed it."

"Then why is it an issue?" He asked shrewdly.

"Because Re somehow remembers it," Odin answered grimly. "And he's determined to steal our woman."

"*What*?!" The jewel tones over Anubis' black irises started to swirl.

"Can we all just relax please?" I huffed. "I saw Re recently, and we've worked it out. He's going to leave me alone. He promised that he wouldn't even attend this party."

"Well, that explains why he's not here," Anubis growled, his eyes shifting around the ballroom. "Even though he was the one who suggested this party; said we needed to liven things up around here. I thought nothing of it."

"Did he tell you to invite Vervain?" Trevor went on.

"No, but he'd know I would." Anubis went back to searching the room. "I don't like this. Re can be tricky. He'll keep his word, he always does, but swearing to not attend the party isn't the same as swearing to not show up in my palace. He could still be lurking around here somewhere. Don't go anywhere unattended, Vervain. I'm going to have some jackals search the palace and grounds for him. If he's here, we'll find him."

"Darling, what's upset you?" Anubis' mother, Nephthys, had sashayed up silently. Her voice was as melancholy as usual but it had nothing to do with her emotions, she was simply the Goddess of Mourning and couldn't help it.

"Nothing, Mother," Anubis said instantly. "I've just re-membered something that I need to take care of. Will you do me the courtesy of introducing Vervain and her fiances to the family?" He kissed her cheek and hurried off.

"Of course." She frowned after her son and then trans-ferred her dark gaze to me. "Vervain, you are blossoming."

"Thank you, Nephthys." I gave her a hug. "It's good to see you."

"You as well, darling." She sighed. "I just wish it were my grandchild within that belly."

"Um." I glanced at my suddenly snarling men and gave Nephthys' hand a pat. "Why don't we go and meet everyone?"

"Oh, yes." Her eyes slid out to the crowd. "You at least recall meeting my husband, Set?" She asked as she waved a hand in the direction of Anubis' father.

"Oh, yes." I cleared my throat. "I don't need a repeat of that."

"He is rather boorish sometimes." She gave a light laugh. "Ah, how about Isis and her husband, Osiris?" She indicated a stunning Egyptian couple who were talking with my friend Horus.

"They attended Odin's funeral." I glanced back at Odin. "Horus said some very touching things about you."

"That was nice of him," Odin brightened. "I hope his par-ents recognize me in this new body."

"Sweetheart." I laughed. "You look exactly the same. Well, except now you have two eyes again."

"Yeah." He huffed a laugh. "That's magic for you."

"I'm afraid, I don't remember actually meeting them at the funeral, though," I admitted. "I was a little distraught."

"Let's change that then," Nephthys offered as we made our way through the crowd.

"Vervain!" Ma'at, Anubis' sister, came up on my left and grabbed me.

Ma'at looked magnificent; pearly hair done up in complicated curls and dark skin dusted with opalescent powder. A gown of deep green silk flowed around her, a step away from being scandalously sheer. Ma'at is supermodel thin and was very graceful, twirling into her mother's embrace after hugging me.

"Mother, what are you doing with Vervain?" Ma'at asked Nephthys.

"I'm going to introduce her to Isis and Osiris," Nephthys said.

"Oh, no; not them." Ma'at rolled her eyes. "They'll monopolize Vervain as soon as they get their hands on her. You know how Isis is with magic-wielders. Best to leave them for last. Come this way, Vervain; I have something better in mind."

"Actually, I think I'd like to speak with Isis and Osiris. It's been a long time since I've seen them." Odin edged away. "If you don't mind, love?"

"No, go ahead." I kissed his cheek, and he started off in their direction.

"Who are you intending to introduce her to?" Nephthys frowned at her daughter.

"The Twins of course." Ma'at smiled broadly.

"Oh!" Nephthys looked relieved, which made me wonder who she thought her daughter was going to take me to. "Yes, she'll love them."

"The Twins?" I asked as Ma'at led us to the side of the room.

"Here we are." Ma'at waved her hand at a couple of strikingly beautiful Egyptian women.

The first had tawny-gold hair flowing in waves down to her rounded rump. Her eyes were deep chocolate brown and her skin was a pale gold. Elegant fingers, tipped in vicious looking talons, curled at her sides and when she smiled, her full lips parted to reveal a set of fangs. She was wearing a gold, slinky gown, and she filled it out way too well.

Next to her stood a more subdued beauty. This woman had pitch black tresses and deeply tanned skin which seemed to mute the harsh color of her hair. Her body was sleek but still curved in the right spots. I knew this because she was wearing a skin tight, black, mini dress. Golden cat eyes smiled at me before the grin reached her lips and revealed that she too had fangs.

"Sekhmet, Lion Goddess of Healing and War"—Ma'at waved at the golden goddess—"and Bastet, Cat Goddess of War and Protection"—another wave at the dark lady. "I'd like you to meet Vervain, Goddess of Lions, Love, and… what is it now, Vervain?"

"The Moon." I chuckled. "I know; even I get confused sometimes."

"Ah yes; the Moon," Ma'at went on. "She's also the Queen of the Faerie Fire Kingdom *and* my dear friend."

"This is the one Re saved from Anubis?" Sekhmet lifted a brow and looked me over.

"Well, he helped but it was more Ma'at who rescued me

than Re." I shot a quelling look at my guys, who had immediately tensed at the mention of Re. "But it's all good now; I don't hold a grudge towards Anubis. He's provided an afterlife for my lions and that goes a long way toward making up for things."

"That's wise." Bastet held out a hand to shake mine, and I noticed that she had claws too. "It never does you any good to hold a grudge. Especially against gods who could be powerful allies. Plus, you never know why people do the things they do. Perhaps they have a good reason, but you just can't see it at the time."

"Yeah, Anubis had a good reason; he wanted my woman," Trevor growled.

"Trevor," I whispered. "Please."

"Sorry," he huffed.

"No, don't apologize, handsome," Sekhmet purred. "I like a feral man."

"You did catch that I'm taken, right?" Trevor narrowed his eyes at her.

"I didn't say I wanted to bed you." She clucked her tongue at him. "Just that I like you. Down, Boy."

"Oh my damn!" I exclaimed and laughed at Trevor. "She just put you in your place." I reached out and shook her hand. "It's nice to meet another lion goddess."

"Yes, it most definitely is," Sekhmet agreed. "We cats gotta stick together."

"I guess I deserved that." Trevor sighed and held out his hand to Sekhmet too. "My apologies."

"Again, I say; do not apologize. Not ever. It's a waste of words." She grinned at him and shook his hand.

"Anyway." I cleared my throat before I started to laugh again.

"I can be feral," Aidan, one of my Intare, declared from his spot against the wall, a few feet down from us.

"Mmm." Sekhmet looked him over thoughtfully. "I'll bet you can. And I happen to love lions."

"And I happen to have been searching for a lioness lover." Aidan waggled his black brows at her. "Care to dance?"

"Love to." She licked her lips and took his hand.

"Oh, you were so right," I said to Ma'at. "I like them both."

"I knew you would." Ma'at nodded.

"Well, I guess my services aren't needed." Nephthys kissed my cheek. "Have fun, my darlings. I'm going to find my husband before he insults someone more powerful than himself. Again."

"Good idea." Bastet gestured behind us, and I turned to see Set talking to a tall man with a regal and stern face.

"Oh, dear." Nephthys hurried off.

"Who's that?" I asked Bastet.

"Ptah," she said and shared a look with Ma'at. "Sekhmet's husband. He's a bit volatile and carries this scepter that can do unpredictably powerful things."

"Sekhmet's *husband*?" I asked and looked over to where the lion goddess was dancing with my lion.

"Oh, they have an open marriage." Bastet waved a hand. "You're not the only lioness who likes multiple lovers."

"Oh, all right then. As long as Aidan isn't getting himself into trouble." I sighed in relief. "Let me introduce you to my fiances. This is Trevor, Azrael, and Kirill."

"A pleasure." She nodded to them but kept her claws to herself, so different from her sister.

"Wait." I looked back and forth between Bastet and Sekhmet. "You're twins?"

"Fraternal." Bastet laughed. "Not that it would matter; the magic made us as we are."

"How stupid of me." I rolled my eyes. "Of course."

"Not at all," Bastet said graciously. "We've been in these forms for so long that even we forget that they aren't our original bodies."

"Oh." I grimaced. "I'm so sorry, but I need to use the restroom. It comes on me suddenly sometimes. Please excuse me."

"I need to go too. I'll accompany you," Bastet offered.

"Just like human women." I giggled, and Bastet giggled along, sliding her arm through the crook of mine.

We began to head for the ballroom door, and my men followed behind us.

"I think we'll be okay, gentlemen." Bastet stopped to look back at them in surprise.

"We're on high alert, I'm afraid," Trevor explained. "We can't let Vervain go anywhere unattended."

"She's not unattended; she has me," Bastet huffed. "And my claws are just as sharp as yours, Froekn Prince."

"What's wrong?" Sekhmet was suddenly beside us, trailing Aidan.

"Vervain's men won't even let her go to the bathroom by herself," Bastet reported to her sister in a horrified tone.

"Shut up!" Sekhmet laughed, waving her hand as if it was ridiculous.

"No, I'm serious," Bastet insisted.

"I'll be okay," I whispered to my men.

"Look, I'll go along as well," Sekhmet offered. "Then she'll have two war goddesses with her, and may I just say that we both kick ass... *major* ass. She'll be perfectly safe, I promise."

"What about our dance?" Aidan pouted.

"We'll dance again later," Sekhmet purred and drew a claw down Aidan's cheek. "I promise."

"Okay then." Aidan gave her a goofy grin.

"Well." Trevor frowned and exchanged looks with Kirill and Azrael.

"I guess it's all right,." Azrael looked worried so I gave his hand a squeeze.

"I think we're getting a little paranoid," I said. "I'll be fine."

"All right. Five minutes," Trevor finally said.

"I'm not making any promises," I teased. "You know how it goes with pregnant women."

"TMI, honey." Sekhmet waved her long nails in my direction. "Come on, let's go."

"Should I go too?" Ma'at asked.

"I think we're good," Sekhmet said and laughed. "Really people, she's pregnant, not the President of the United States. There aren't snipers out there."

"It's okay." I shook my head at Ma'at and left the ballroom with the feline goddesses.

Just us cats, sticking together.

Chapter Nine

The bathroom wasn't far away from the ballroom but when I was finished, I came out to find Bastet on high alert.

"What is it?" I looked around the empty hallway.

"We heard something strange." Bastet stared off in the direction of the Hall of Two Truths. "Sekhmet went to investigate."

The Hall of Two Truths was where Anubis, Ma'at, Thoth, and this goddess/thing called Ammut, judged souls. I'd once been forced to sit beside Anubis' gold jackal throne there, chained to his side. He would pull the heart from a soul and judge it. If it was worthy, it could go through the Golden Gates of Aaru to make it's way through even scarier, demon-guarded gates and, hopefully, get to some sort of paradise where it would live happily ever after in the presence of Osiris.

It was not somewhere I wanted to go hang out in after hours, as it were. Or ever, for that matter. It didn't exactly hold the best memories for me. I shivered as one of my memories of Ammut surfaced. Her hodgepodge body reminded me of the Hidden-Ones so it wasn't her form that bothered me. It was how she ate the hearts of the evil souls. How can a soul have a heart? Well, just like with my dead lions, souls in Duat are substantial. So, it was a very real, very juicy heart that I'd watched Ammut devour and it was a memory I didn't want to relive.

"We can go back and tell Anubis about it," I offered.

Then we heard a scream which was cut off abruptly, and I reacted automatically; running in the direction from which it came. Granted, I couldn't run very fast, and Bastet ended up racing ahead of me. When I reached the Hall, it was to find it completely dark. Still, I didn't have a problem with the dark, what with my triple threat of lioness, wolf, and dragon. I could clearly see Bastet kneeling over a body at the far end of the room. I rushed over.

"Is she all right?" I asked as I saw that the body was Sekhmet.

"Yes, she's fine," Bastet whispered. "Please forgive us, Vervain. What we do, we do out of love for our father."

"What are you talking—" before I could finish, Sekhmet lurched up and snatched the Ring of Remembrance off my finger as Bastet pushed me from behind. I screamed as I tumbled over Sekhmet. The golden gates leading to Aaru opened up and swallowed me whole.

I rolled forward into the dark and was surprised when I landed softly. I heard the slam of doors behind me and stood up to see the gate shut tightly. There didn't even appear to be a seam between the doors on this side of the gate. Still, I launched myself at the barrier, pounding my fists fiercely.

"Damn you nasty pussies!" I shouted. "Open these doors!" Rian reeled inside me suddenly, and I felt his anger rising up my throat. "Easy now," I soothed him and stepped back. "We can't lose our heads."

"You cannot go back," an eerie voice spoke behind me, and I jerked around.

I stood on the banks of a river, at its source actually. It began just twenty feet or so in front of me, bubbling up from underground. Soft, dry sand covered the ground and above me, a twinkling expanse of stars hung in the night sky without a moon to rule them. I shivered when I saw that. I didn't like it when the Moon was dark; it made my magic uncomfortable.

Beneath that moonless sky, standing right before me, was an ethereal looking woman. She gestured behind her, where a pair of sleek wooden boats waited in the water, bobbing gently in the bubbling froth. They were tied to a little dock with a simple rope. Beyond the boats, the river led to a narrow gate set into stone walls. The walls extended out to both sides as far as I could see. Sharp spearheads topped them and thick wood doors sealed the gate, stopping up the water like a dam and causing it to slowly rise along the banks. Daunting yes but not as daunting as what surrounded the gate.

Guarding the gate were huge, hooded snakes; one with his head at the top and one at level with the water. They were breathing a constant stream of fire right in front of the doors. The fire didn't look normal either; it sputtered and sizzled, sparking blue in spots. An acidic smell filled the air, and I realized why the fire looked so strange.

"They're venomous, aren't they?" I asked the spirit before me as I edged closer to the river.

"You cannot go back," she said again. "The only way is forward. Welcome to the Watercourse of Re." She turned, walked across the dock, and stepped into the boat.

"The Watercourse of *Re*?" I growled. "I thought this was the gate leading to Aaru? Did Re put you guys up to this? Where is that shiny bastard? I'm going to kick his golden ass!"

"Heteptiu, followers of Re are welcome on the Mesektet." She held her arms wide to indicate the boat she was standing on. "But the followers of Osiris must journey to Sekhet-Aaru and pass through the twenty-one gates." She indicated the other boat.

"I don't want to get on either boat," I grumbled.

She said nothing, just stared at me as if I hadn't said a word. And waited. She waited in a really creepy, patience-of-the-dead sort of way.

"How are we getting through a closed, snake-guarded gate?" I asked her, but she continued to remain silent.

I had no choice, I had to go forward and there was no way I was going through the twenty-one gates of Sekhet-Aaru. I assumed those were the demon-guarded gates which the poor worthy souls had to pass through before they found Heaven. So, I took a deep breath and followed the creepy woman, stepping onto the Mesektet boat and heading to the prow, where she stood.

"Fine, take me to Re," I snapped. "Come on, get this damn boat moving."

She turned to face the snake gate and the boat began to glide forward. The woman barely paid me any attention as we floated calmly toward the monstrous reptiles. I cocked my head and admired the streams of their fiery breath. It was so bright that the light carried all the way to the shore.

"Fire doesn't bother me, you know," I said to the silent specter. "And I'm both a faerie and a goddess so I'm immortal. Even if they are spitting venom, they won't hurt me. I just don't understand how we're going to get those big doors open. You wanna give me a hint?"

Nothing.

"I could change into a dragon and give them a push," I offered. "That would probably do the trick."

More nothing.

"My fiances will be looking for me," I warned her. "They'll find you and your stupid Re boat. It would be in your best interest to help me get back to them."

"You cannot go back," she intoned again. "Ur-nes awaits. You shall be given herbs and grains of the field, water of life, and great pleasure. Look forward to your glorious afterlife."

"Wonderful. Herbs, grain, water, and pleasure, what else could a woman want?" I rolled my eyes but then something occurred to me. I stuck my hand out, right into her, and nothing happened. My hand went right through her body, and she didn't react at all. She did waver a little bit though. "What are you?" I frowned. "You're not a soul because here, souls are solid. You're like what a human would think a soul would look like. A fake ghost. A faux phantom."

"I am Heka, Goddess of the Word," she intoned. "I shall open the way for you."

"Uh-huh," I narrowed my eyes at her. "Where exactly are we going?"

She just stared straight ahead. I was going to push her for more answers but while I had been watching her, we had sailed so close to the gate that I could feel the heat of snake breath on my cheeks. My dragon twisted inside me, wanting to come out and bask in the flames. I pushed her down resolutely. I had no idea what this place was all about or what would happen if I played in the fires of Aaru. They could be magic fire that somehow managed to incinerate even a dragon. Those damn Egyptians were weird... and tricky. Especially the cat ones, evidently.

Inside me, my son was shifting in agitation again, sensing my distress. I laid a hand over my belly and tried to calm him before he went dragon-baby ballistic. We'd faced tougher things than a few monstrous snakes. Hell, we were snake gods in a way, we could get through this. No problem. He seemed to agree with that and settled down to let me handle things.

Then the spurious spook at my side called out something weird in Egyptian, and the snakes shut their mouths.

The venomous fire ceased, and the snakes eased back as the wood doors swung open (don't ask me how the wood managed to keep from being burned). The water that had been building up behind the doors was now released, and we flowed through the narrow passage on the crest of a wave. I glanced up at the reptile in repose above me. His eyes were closed peacefully, probably enjoying himself a well-deserved nap after all his huffing and puffing.

"Welcome to Ur-nes, where Re is Lord," ghost girl said. "Here you will find your pleasure." She waved her hand to the right, and I looked over to see six intimidating men standing on the shore, each of them holding some sort of weapon. The sky was dark in this region, but they stood in the light of several torches. "The Gods of Grain and Seasons will see you to your new home."

In front of the Gods of Grains and Seasons bobbed a long, thin boat but it remained tied to the dock there. No one approached it or made any move whatsoever. They just stood and stared at me as if I was an interloper who didn't belong on their damn river. They were obviously not about to see me to my new home.

"What the hell is wrong with you guys? This is like a strange, screwed up, Disneyland ride," I growled. Then I shouted to the six gods on the shore, "I didn't ask to be here, you know!"

I turned away from the unresponsive gods in a huff, crossing my arms over my belly. Heka had gone back to staring straight ahead and the boat was continuing down the river. Maybe I had to keep going with her, even though she'd pretty much told me to get off the boat. I looked towards the other shore for a clue.

There were a few boats docked there. They didn't have masts or rudders so I guess they were just rafts, not boats, and they were full of shadowy human forms. I knew those forms; those shadow people. I walked toward the railing in a daze, the vision I'd had in the swimming pool coming back to me.

"My baby is psychic," I whispered as a chill went down my spine. Rian shifted inside me, and I rubbed my belly as I spoke to him. "It was you, wasn't it, Rian? You gave me a warning. Too bad your mother was too dumb to understand it."

Then a full sized boat emerged from the center of the rafts. It was large and loaded with people, their oars slipping into the water steadily to push the boat forward. Someone stood at the prow and although I couldn't make out his face, I was familiar with his arrogant stance. I growled, now knowing for certain that Re was behind this conspiracy. Trevor and Kirill had been right; the party had been a means of getting me into Duat so those cat twins could toss me through the Gates of Aaru.

Which meant... was Re their father? Bastet said they were doing this out of love for their father. Oh, what did it matter? The last time I'd been stuck in Duat, things hadn't gone so well for me but this time it would be different. Because this time I was a dragon, and dragons didn't put up with this kind of malarkey. I was going to make those monster snakes look like helpless worms and turn their sun god into burnt toast. In fact, I might just feed him to his own snakes. How's that for poetic justice?

I looked away from the approaching boat, trying to get control of my anger. I was way too close to my due date to let myself get this upset. I didn't want to go into labor early and end up giving birth outside of Faerie. So, I crossed my arms and stared forward petulantly along with Heka, the ghost girl. That's when I noticed that we were approaching another gate which was guarded by yet another pair of hooded fire snakes. Again? I was distracted momentarily by the irritating reptilian repetition—creativity is very important to me—and so was a little surprised when the thud came, indicating that Re's boat had come abreast of ours.

"Hello, Lala," Re said as he jumped down next to me.

"Hello, dead man," I snarled back.

"Now, Lala." He held up his hands placatingly.

"Don't call me that!" I slapped Re across the face, and he stumbled back. "How dare you! You're abducting me? Seriously? I defended you. They told me I shouldn't come to Duat, that you would try something like this, and I told them that there was no way you would do anything to hurt me. We've fought battles beside each other. You're supposed to be my friend."

"I'm not going to hurt you," he said gently. "I spoke out of anger the other day. I didn't mean any of it. I was just so upset that you didn't share my feelings, that you could have experienced all of what I had and not love me back. As soon as I returned home, I realized that you must *not* have experienced what I had. That somehow, you had carried a link to those memories but not the memories themselves. I knew that I had to try one last time, to talk to you about what I saw. It was amazing, Vervain, and I can't give up without at least trying to share that with you."

"So, you got a couple of pussy cats to shove me through the Gates of Aaru?" I growled.

"My daughters," he confirmed my suspicions. "They did it for me. Because I needed to get you here, to my home, someplace where you couldn't run away before I had a chance to tell you everything." He waved a hand towards the shore he'd come from. "Please, just hear me out."

"They took my ring; the one my father left me!" I glared at him.

"I asked them to," he confessed. "I knew you could use it to leave. Don't worry, they'll bring it by later tonight, and I'll return it to you. You have my word. Now, please, Vervain."

"Uh, let me think about it... no." I stared at the snakes instead of him.

"Vervain, you don't want to go through those gates," he warned me. "There are monsters beyond them. It's dangerous."

"I think I'll manage." I shrugged.

"Not here you won't." Re grabbed my arm. "Here you won't manage anything without my help."

"That's convenient." I glared at him.

"It's why I brought you here," he admitted. "But I promise I will see you home safely. Just have dinner with me, listen to me talk about what I've seen in my dreams, that's all I ask."

"Dinner and conversation?" I lifted a brow. "That's it?"

"That's it," he promised.

"You could have picked up a phone to ask me to dinner," I grumbled.

"And you would have said no." He gave me a sad look. "Please, it's just a few hours of your time. Is that really too much to ask when it was you who brought these memories back to me, in the first place?" He held his hand out to me, and I gave a deep sigh.

"Just dinner." I put my hand in his.

"Thank you," he whispered and pulled me against his chest.

"Hey, now." I pushed him back.

"I need to help you into the boat." He nodded toward his

ship. It was a bit higher than the one we stood on and the only way aboard appeared to be by a rope ladder. It would be awkward to climb that in my condition.

"Fine," I grumbled, and he lifted me into his arms with a satisfied smile.

A man was waiting at the railing, and Re passed me up into his grasp before climbing the rope ladder. The man seemed human, and he immediately put me down and stepped away from me, keeping his eyes cast down. As soon as Re was in the boat, the other men began to row, taking us back to shore.

Re led me to a luxurious couch set on the deck between the rowers and helped me sit before taking a seat beside me. He was silent the whole way, probably didn't want to push his luck, and I had nothing to say either. I just sat there, trying to keep my cool so my unborn son didn't decide to roast everything in sight... and trying to figure out if that would be such a bad thing.

Boy, the Egyptians sure do know how to throw a party.

Chapter Ten

An Egyptian chariot waited on the shore for us, all gold with depictions of the Sun molded into it. It had two wheels with an open back; one of those stand-in affairs made for one or two passengers. It was hitched to a single white horse, and Re helped me into it, showing me where to hold before he took the reins and drove me deeper into his territory. As we got further inland, the sky lightened a little. Though it was still night, it wasn't that heavy, dismal darkness that shrouded the river. I was able to make out rolling fields around us, bordered by sheer mountains in the distance.

In the middle of it all loomed a grand Egyptian palace with a two-story colonnade. The columns were painted in bold colors with gilded accents. They stood out against the stark white of the walls behind them. Tall braziers burned on either side of the stone steps that led up to the veranda, illuminating the colored columns with wavering light. We rode right to those steps, where a man waited to collect the chariot. Re passed him the reins without a word, and the man bowed deeply.

"Welcome to my home, Lala," Re said as he led me up the steps and onto the wide colonnade.

"When do we eat?" I snapped.

"Momentarily." he laughed. "Please try and enjoy yourself just a little. You'll be returned to your lovers soon enough. Aren't you just the least bit curious about my home?"

"Re, just get on with whatever you have planned." I sighed. "I don't want to be here, and you know it."

"As you wish." His expression hardened, and he took my arm more firmly, leading me through the tall, elaborately outlined doorway.

We strode down hallways lined in more lotus topped columns. Luxurious rooms spread out to either side of us, but we continued on, past a grand stone staircase and straight into the heart of the palace. Finally, we came to a dining hall; a long and narrow room with a single table stretching its length. A feast was laid out at one end and group of people stood along the walls nearby. Re led me down to where platters full of steaming food waited. The aroma of roasted meat, fresh baked bread, and sauteed vegetables filled my nose. My stomach rumbled, and Re grinned.

"I'm glad you're hungry." He pulled out a chair for me before taking the one on my right, at the head of the table.

"Just feed me, Seymour" I grumbled.

"Immediately, my goddess." He chuckled and snapped his fingers.

The slew of servants rushed forward and began filling our plates. I inhaled deeply as a golden plate laden with stewed meat, warm flatbread, and roasted vegetables was set before me. There was a bowl filled with pieces of chicken in thick gravy and also a dish of olives placed around my main plate and then a glass of something red went nearby.

"It's just juice." Re waved at the goblet.

"You and I both know that doesn't matter," I huffed. "This baby's not going to be hurt by a little alcohol."

"Well, just the same." He shrugged. "Children should be cared for even before they're born."

"Go on, Re" I said as I took a bite and then groaned in delight.

"With what?" He asked innocently.

"Your spiel," I huffed. "You have me here; now say what you wanna say."

"All right." Re put his glass down and his expression went serious. "I didn't want to fall in love with you, Vervain. I didn't want to be a part of your complicated life or be counted as one of your numerous lovers. But we connected, we shared things, and since you don't remember the sharing, I want to tell you about it now."

"Perhaps it would be best to just forget it all, Re." I reached out a hand and touched his fingers gently. "There's a faerie spell for that. I can just take it away."

"I am *not* forgetting!" He snatched up my hand and held it to his stunning face.

Even in the midst of this frustrating situation, I couldn't keep from admiring him. He was just that beautiful. And I knew his heart was even more beautiful. Re was kind and generous and he'd been a good friend to me. He just wasn't thinking clearly at the moment. Love and lust can do that to you; make you behave like an imbecile. I, above anyone else, knew that, and I tried to remember it, tried to remember that Re had been there for me. He had helped me get through my time with Anubis, and he'd gone to war beside me... a war that had nothing to do with him and everything to do with me. The least I could do was give him some respect and hear him out.

"All right," I said and gently pulled my hand away.

"I can't stop seeing you beneath me, above me, all around me," his voice lowered to a dangerously sexy tone, and I began to rethink the whole hearing him out idea. "Your face is everywhere I look. Even, no, *especially* when I close my eyes. There you are; taunting me, saying such sweet things to me. Your words are worse than your face; they seduce and enthrall."

"Damn it all!" I swore and looked away. "I'm so sorry, Re. I thought you'd forget me on your own but now, I see that I should have helped you. Maybe if I had, you would have been able to move past this already."

"No." He leaned close, and I found myself caught in his golden stare, caught in the scent of burning frankincense wafting from his tawny hair.

Those long-lashed bedroom eyes lured me in, turning my thoughts into traitors. I couldn't help it; sex practically oozed from him. It was in every angle of his face and every curve of his body. Re lifted an elegant hand and candlelight glinted in the golden shimmer on his skin.

I was caught like a snake; hypnotized by the light as he laid a warm palm against my face and whispered, "I'm in love with you and it's not something I can move past."

"You're *not* in love with me." I broke the charm and pulled away. "The future Re is; the future Re who will never be."

"How much of those memories did you see, Vervain?" Re pressed me. "Tell me the truth."

"Enough." I swallowed hard and looked away.

"Months worth?" He continued. "Weeks? Days? Hours? How much?"

"I'm not sure exactly." I frowned. "But it was enough to see that we loved each other."

"No, not nearly enough," he was whispering again, his voice dripping over my skin like melted butter. "If you *had* seen enough, I wouldn't have had to abduct you, you would have come on your own."

"I saw the amazing chemistry we had together." I sat back, away from him, and put a hand to my belly. His eyes drifted down to it and then darted to the side. "Yes, Re, I'm pregnant, in case you've forgotten. With another man's child. A dragon's child, in fact. How can you even look at me with lust?"

"Because I love you." He brought his gaze back to mine resolutely; dropping it pointedly to my belly before bringing it back up again. "Because you will not always be pregnant. You will have the baby, and then I will have you."

"No." I sighed deeply. "I don't love you, and you only think you love me. Those memories aren't really yours. They never had the chance to be made."

"Of course, they're mine." Re gaped at me. "How can you not understand? I may not be headed down the same path, but I lived it once, and you brought back a connection to it. You gave me the memories, and what are we, if not our memories? Why do we love people, if not for the past we've shared with them? And how do memories from a non-existent future differ from memories of the past?"

"But I don't love you," I said again and watched him wince. "How can I not feel the way you do, if these memories are true?"

"Because you haven't had the right perspective." His expression hardened once more and suddenly started to go blurry.

I blinked and swayed. His hand shot out and steadied me.

"They were *my* memories, you see? You need to relive your own," Re said.

I swayed again, and he got up, pushing back my chair so he could lift me out of it.

"What are you doing?" I felt the words slur on my tongue. "What did you *do*?" I knew that feeling, that weightless, blissful apathy. "Did you give me Net?!"

Re lifted me into his arms and carried me out of the room.

"Just a little." His face was going in and out of focus for me. "Enough so that I don't have to fight you when I cast the spell."

"Where did you even get Net?" I blinked in confusion. "Hades kicked Pasithea out of the Underworld and destroyed all the poppies."

"Do you really think she didn't have some poppy seeds stored for a rainy day?" Re shook his head at my naivete.

"Wait... what did you say about a spell?" I tried to be concerned, but I just wasn't. Nothing seemed to matter except the wonderful lassitude stretching through my limbs.

"I'm casting a spell on you." Re laid me down on something soft and then his face filled my vision. "I am the greatest of the Egyptian Gods, Lala. The creator. I have many spells at my disposal and if you can't remember me, then I will make you remember." He laid a gentle kiss on my forehead and chanted, "Tudhkar lana."

Over and over, he spoke those words as his eyes began to brighten. They went so bright that I had to close my own against their radiance. As soon as I did, something shot into me, some kind of burning connection. Perhaps it connected me with my future self, the one who would never be. Maybe, somewhere in the web of time, she had been waiting, languishing in stasis, just for an opportunity like this. A chance to share her past with me. Whatever it was, the memories of my evaded future surged into me and sucked me down.

"Beware the Eye of Re," I whispered.

Chapter Eleven

For one brief second, I knew I was trapped in memories, and I looked down in horror to find that Rian was gone; I wasn't pregnant. But then even that small knowledge faded and the memories I was never meant to have took over and became all too real.

"Are you okay?" Kirill found me hiding in a corner, and he blocked my view of the rest of the ballroom with his body.

"No," I whispered, afraid to even speak too loud.

Any sort of emotion might throw me into a tailspin... a lust-spin. Ever since Odin had left, my lioness had begun to get restless. It started with just a little ache in my gut then had progressed slowly into this all-consuming need that would tingle through my limbs, making me weak until I fed it with sex. That was fine and all, my husbands were more than happy to comply, except the need didn't go away entirely. Even after giving into the lust, it would still be there, coiled in my belly and waiting to strike again.

Kirill knew exactly what was wrong; I didn't have enough lions in my pride. I know, that sounds silly when I have over a hundred of them now, but the pride my lioness was concerned about was the one we made totally ours; my lovers. I was now one lover short of making her happy and when Mama Lioness isn't happy, no one's happy.

"Hold onto me," Kirill whispered. "Press yourself

against me; let her feel another Intare."

I did as he instructed and the beast inside me eased back just enough for me to think; to get a little control. I exhaled roughly against Kirill's crisp, white, dress shirt and then pressed my ear to his wide chest so I could hear the pounding of his heart. His lion heart. The lioness gave a little possessive purr and eased back further. I was okay; I could do this.

"Is she all right?" Trevor came in beside us and behind him was Azrael, his midnight wings spread out a little to hide us even further from any curious stares.

We were at a wedding in Duat, the Egyptian Underworld, and no one wanted to make a scene. I, especially, didn't want to ruin the day for Anubis, who had finally found his bride and was blissfully happy. She was an amazing woman even though she was technically a demon. I, of all people, would never hold that against her. I had some very good friends who were demons. Azrael's father was kind of their king.

"She's gaining control but it von't last," Kirill whispered back to the others. "We have to do something about zis, right now!"

"What?" Trevor huffed. "You want me to go around the wedding reception and find a bunch of guys she can interview in this corner? I don't think this is the place for that, and I'm not sure I'm even up to the task."

"This is what we signed up for," Azrael said gently. "All of us knew Vervain has these needs. We have to support our wife."

"I know that," Trevor snapped. "It doesn't mean I have to like it or have to be the one hunting down her new lover."

"You'll be fine as soon as ve find her someone ve like," Kirill said reasonably. "Intare magic vill ease your jealousy."

"Yeah, as soon as we spend the night with the guy," the tone in Trevor's voice was enough to tell me he was rolling his eyes.

"Please stop arguing," I ground out and turned to face them. "You're getting her excited again."

My lioness loved a good fight, especially if it was her men fighting over her. Oh, yeah; that was popcorn time for my big cat. She'd relish the display but then she'd expect to reward the winner, and I couldn't deal with that at the moment.

"I'm sorry, Minn Elska." Trevor leaned in and laid his forehead against mine. "This whole thing has upset me. That bastard Odin leaving and now this. I hate seeing you hurt."

"I know." I lifted my face for a kiss. "Don't worry, I'll be okay. Just give me a little air. I'm drowning in beautiful men." I smiled and pushed gently at his chest.

"Not enough of zem." Kirill sighed. "You must choose, Tima, and soon."

"Um, pardon me." Re, the Egyptian God of the Sun, and a close friend of mine, slid into view. "Am I interrupting something?" His golden eyes swept our group.

"Not at all." I smiled at him and then glanced away.

Re had the kind of appearance that could be devastating to stare at too long. Like the Sun itself, his was a dangerous beauty that had the potential of doing you lasting damage. On this night, in particular, he was wearing a loose linen shirt, cut at the neck to reveal a modest amount of deeply tanned skin, which nonetheless looked pale from the metallic gold shimmer laid over it... a natural shimmer which couldn't be washed away. Though it might be fun to try.

His body was ballet dancer beautiful, with sleek muscles that made him look as if he could lift you over his head one-handed. His lips were pouting full, lips for kissing, and his golden eyes were kept from fading into the rest of his golden glow by extra long, ebony lashes that gave him that sated, I-just-had-sex look. The only thing even partially normal about Re was his hair; a sedate chestnut brown, but even that showed brilliant blond highlights when the light hit it. He was sex incarnate and not at all the kind of man I needed to be around at the moment.

"Would you like to dance, Vervain?" Re asked, his voice in that low tone reserved for bedrooms. He wasn't doing it on purpose either; he just talked like that.

My lioness lifted her head in interest.

"Um, I..." I frowned and faltered.

"She vould love to." Kirill gave me a little push, and I stared back at him in horror. "Tima," he growled and looked at me pointedly. "Dance vith him."

"I would love to," I said gaily to Re and took his hand. "Thank you for asking."

The Sun God frowned a little in confusion but escorted me to the wide dance floor in the middle of the Venetian style ballroom. The place was done up exceptionally gaudily tonight, with swaths of shimmering white fabric hanging on the mirrored walls, held in place by draping bouquets of flowers. A banquet table laden with food was set up against one wall at the far end of the room. It stood near the bar and a multitude of round dining tables waited before it. Beyond them, I could see the manicured gardens of Duat through the glass panes of French doors that led out to the balcony.

Above me hung enormous crystal chandeliers, spreading their sparkles all over the marble floor. One draped over the exact center of the dancing area that Re led me to. Around the edges of the dance floor, seating areas with elegant gilded couches and chairs gave relief to gods who'd danced or drank too much. Liveried werejackals maneuvered through them carrying silver trays full of champagne flutes. I took a deep breath as Re took my waist, and I tried to calm the rising tide of lust that he was churning.

"What was all that about?" Re asked me as he started to lead me around the floor. "And why are your husbands staring at me like that?"

"Oh, Gods." I rolled my eyes and looked at him. "I'm so sorry, Re. We've been having issues ever since Odin left, and I'm afraid you look like a good solution to them."

"What issues?" He was immediately concerned. "I'm happy to help you in any way I can."

"Oh, you do not want to say that." I laughed.

"Vervain, what is it?" His voice went low and stern. "Tell me."

"My Intare magic. You know; the one that makes me take multiple lovers?" I swallowed roughly.

"Yes." He frowned deeper.

"I'm one lover short," I said simply.

"Oh." His face smoothed out. "Oh!" He stopped dancing entirely and stared at me in shock.

"I know." I chuckled. "Don't worry; I'm not gonna take you at your word and demand that you help me in any way that you can."

"Oh, thank goodness." Re sighed. "No offense, Vervain, but I have no interest in being a part of that." He waved a hand at my husbands, and I laughed harder.

"I know." I looked up at him and found myself staring. The lioness roared inside me and my grip on his shoulders tightened.

"Vervain?" He leaned closer. "Do I need to take you back to them?"

"No," the word ended in a purr as I held his gaze longer than I'd ever dared.

It was my lioness taking over. She liked him, boy did she like him, and she had no intention of letting him get away. At least not without a fight.

Re took a long, deep breath, his chest lifting my clenched hands, and stared back at me. For once, I wasn't intimidated by his beauty; I saw the man beneath all the glamor... and he looked just as amazing as the mask. I was caught by it; the concern in his eyes, the kindness in his heart, and the strength in his soul. Whoa; why had I never looked before? Maybe because I didn't want to see any of that; I had enough wonderful men in my life. Till now, that is.

I don't know what Re saw in me. Whatever it was, it had him lifting his palm to my face, and I shivered from the heat of it. The tips of his fingers trailed up into the hair at my temples and the lioness inside me growled, thrusting me forward against his chest. Re caught me, his arms sliding tighter around me as dancing couples continued to twirl around us as if nothing unusual were happening.

"Vervain, I..." Re let out a shaky breath and then gave an even shakier laugh. "I think I've just discovered how you attract so many men."

"Son of a succubus," I growled and looked away. "Did I do something to you? I'm so sorry if I did. Sometimes with the combination of the Love and Lust magic along with the Lion, I can't control myself and I—"

"Vervain." His hand had never left my cheek, and he used it to turn my face back to him. "I am the Creator God of the

Egyptians, the most powerful Sun God in existence. You don't have to worry about enchanting me. At least... not with your magic," his voice went low.

"Re, you don't want to start anything with me, remember?" I said gently.

"No, I don't," he whispered. "But you're the first woman in a thousand years to look at me as if you really saw me. Just now, Vervain. Your eyes, they focused on me; *me*, not this visage my people dreamed up. Tell me what you saw... please."

"You know what I saw," I whispered. "But Re, I didn't have to look at you to see it. I already knew what kind of man you are."

"No, you didn't," he insisted. "You suspected, but you didn't know until right now. So, please, do me the courtesy of being honest."

"I saw courage and horrible guilt." I sighed. "I saw a heart that's full of love without the relief of someone to give it to. I saw loneliness and yet vibrant joy. You're supremely grateful for all that you have but you still want more and that wanting makes you feel ashamed. There's a deep well of kindness in you and a fierce need to see justice done. Even against yourself. A fighter *and* a lover; that's what I see in you."

"By all that's holy!" Re exclaimed. "Who are you, Vervain? How did you see all of that in one look?"

"Some of it was simply an affirmation of what I already knew and the rest was recognition of things I myself have felt." I swallowed hard and glanced over to where my husbands waited, watching both hopefully and dejectedly. They didn't want this, of course, they didn't, but they wanted me healthy and happy, and I, or rather my lioness, wanted more. Just like Re.

"I don't think this dance was such a good idea after all,"

Re murmured as I looked back up at him.

"I understand." I gave him a small smile. "I hope you find someone to give all that love to, Re."

"Thank you, Vervain." His hand finally slid away from my face, and he backed away from me, leaving me standing in the middle of the dancers, alone in the crowd.

I sighed and started to make my way out when a hand took mine and twirled me around.

"Morpheus!" I exclaimed and laughed.

"I heard you have a thing for men with wings." Morph waggled his brows at me.

Morpheus. I hadn't even considered the Dream God. We'd had a brief flirtation, and by that I mean; he tried to make me his underworld bride, despite my violent protests. Hmm, kinda like Anubis. I slid a look over to where Anubis sat with his new bride. He glanced my way and gave me a huge grin. Oddly enough, I was close friends with both Anubis and Morph. But did I want to get closer to Morpheus? Part of me kind of cringed at the idea. Morph had become like a brother to me and sleeping with him might feel incestuous. No; I don't think I wanted Morph to be my next lover but that didn't mean I couldn't dance with him.

I smiled up at Morpheus and let him whisk me around the floor; his wings a beautiful backdrop to his boyish face. As we danced, I glanced around the room and caught Finn's calculating stare. Finn. Just like with Morpheus, there had been an attraction between us once. But that was mostly on Finn's side. Still, I realized that I might have more options than I'd originally thought. Maybe this wasn't such a bad place to look for my new lover after all.

Chapter Twelve

Shivers skittered over my skin, tremors shook my limbs, my hands clenched into fists, and I cried out in need.

"It's okay, Tima," Kirill whispered. "I'm here. Trevor's here. Ve vill help you."

And they did. They pushed back the rising lust with their hands and their tongues and their teeth and their whole bodies. With everything that made them men and made them mine. It was so much pleasure, my Lust magic came to life and pulsed out of me in waves of rosy rapture.

But it still wasn't enough.

"Just kill me now!" I cried in frustration as I lay between my two exhausted husbands.

"Minn Elska." Trevor flopped an arm over my stomach. "Just try and relax. Breathe through it. I promise; we'll find you someone soon."

"Maybe I should go back to Faerie." I exhaled roughly. "I miss Rian and Arach, and the distance might help."

"Distance from us?" Kirill gave me a chiding look. "It's your magic vhich does zis, Tima, not ours."

"I know." I rubbed at my temples with frustrated fingers. "I just can't think in this state. My body feels as if it's full of electricity and it's frying my brain. I'm going insane, and Rian always calms me. I need to see my son. He's three-years-old now, he knows something strange happens when I leave."

"You're back in seconds. He may suspect, but he doesn't know for certain," Kirill reassured me. "Even if he did, he vould understand."

"You know you can't go back until this is settled," Trevor said gently. "I'm sorry but you can't. Think about what could happen if you were in Faerie like this? You wouldn't have time for Rian anyway, you'd be too busy trying to keep yourself satisfied with just one man."

"Yeah, all right," I grumbled. "It would be bad."

"You just need to pick someone." Trevor sighed. "How hard can it be to choose a lover?"

"I don't want to just settle on someone." I groaned. "*We* need someone whom we all can live with. Someone I can love, not just have sex with, and someone whom all of you will at least respect."

"I know but maybe finding someone to tide you over wouldn't be so bad." Trevor laid his head in the crook of my neck and promptly fell asleep.

I couldn't blame him, this last round had lasted all night, and even werewolf princes need their rest.

"I don't want someone to tide me over," I grumbled down at the sleeping wolf. "Then I'd have to break up with him and go through all of this again."

"Come, Tima." Kirill was still holding onto consciousness but just barely. "Let's make some coffee. I vill stay up vith you until Azrael gets home."

"Okay. Thank you." I sighed and let him help me out of bed.

Trevor just flopped onto the pillow behind me and

started snoring.

Kirill picked up my silk robe from the floor beside the bed and wrapped me in it, giving me a sweet kiss on my cheek before padding across the carpet nude. He headed to our little kitchenette, which was only about twenty feet from the bed. I just stood there and admired the view, especially enjoying the way his braid swung across the tight curves of his ass. I shook my head roughly and looked away.

"Baby," I groaned. "You need to cover yourself."

Kirill shot a smug look over his shoulder and then headed up to his bedroom instead of to the coffee maker. "Fine but you make coffee zen," he called back to me.

"Da," I mimicked him as I watched him climb the stairs. His ass looked even better when he climbed stairs. "I make coffee zen." I dropped the accent and went to do just that, giggling a little. "What is zen coffee anyway? Decaffeinated maybe? Or would it actually be tea?"

"Tima?" Aidan's voice came through the intercom on the wall. I turned on the coffee pot and headed over to it.

"Yes?" I asked as I pressed the button to speak.

"You have a visitor," Aidan said crisply. "It's Re."

"Re?" I squeaked and clutched my robe like a startled southern belle.

"Yeppers." Aidan laughed. "He looks kinda anxious and —" his voice cut off abruptly and when he came back on, he sounded more reserved. "I mean, he seems completely at ease. Ugh... well, what did you want me to say?" The sound cut off again, and I started to smile. Then Aidan came back on with a voice like a British butler, "The Sun God, Re is here to see you, Tima."

"Yeah, I got that." I chuckled. "Send him up. Wait!" I

looked over at the sprawled form of a naked, snoring were-wolf in my bed. "No, take him into the library sitting room. I'll meet him there. And ask him if he'd like a cup of coffee."

"The Sun God, Re would like a cup of coffee with cream and two sugars please," Aidan intoned.

"Okay." I had to release the button to laugh. I pushed the button again and did my Julia Child impersonation, "Tell the Sun God, Re that I will bring him his coffee."

"Right-O, Tima," Aidan laughed. "Toodle-pip!"

"Re is here?" Kirill came up behind me, dressed in jeans and a T-shirt which read: *Lion Lovers will make you Purrrrr.*

"Oh, come on," I griped and waved a hand at his shirt. "Now, you're just rubbing it in."

"I couldn't resist." He chuckled. "And I will rub more into you later. But, Re is here? Zis is good?"

"Maybe." I shot a glance at Trevor. "Do you mind waiting here while I see him? Aidan's taking him to the library."

"Nyet, it's fine." He went to pour himself some coffee and then stopped suddenly. "In fact, I zink I vill take nap instead."

"Okay, honey." I went forward and gave him a kiss. "I'll see you later... and I'm going to hold you to that rubbing."

"Good luck vith ze Sun God, Re." Kirill grinned and headed to bed.

"Thanks." I poured two cups of coffee and added sugar and cream. As I left, I mumbled to myself, "I'm gonna need it."

The whole elevator ride down to the library, my stomach did flip-flops. Why was Re here? What did he want? And why was I so damn nervous about it? He was my friend, there shouldn't be any weird feelings between us. Still, I'd been deeply affected by our exchange the other night and maybe it was just the lioness magic, but I'd been thinking about him. A lot.

The gilded cage of the old fashioned elevator opened, and I stepped out onto the second floor of Pride Palace. My hands started to shake, and I had to stop and settle myself before stepping into one of my favorite rooms in my home. The library was my sanctuary, with its high, warm, wooden shelves filled with cherished books, the collection of my paintings hanging on the walls in gilded frames, and the thick Persian rugs covering the floor. Reading nooks with heavy tables, comfortable chairs, and desk lamps nestled in corners, and the balcony had lounging chairs that offered yet another pleasant place to read.

"Aunty V!" Fallon's six-year-old daughter, Zariel waved at me from a table to the left of the door. "Uncle Aideen said I gotta go away right now because you gonna see the Sun God, Ta."

"Sorry, Vervain." Samantha, Zariel's mom, giggled from her seat beside her daughter and gave the little girl an affectionate pat. "It's Uncle Ai-*dan*, honey and Re, not Ta."

"Not like *tadaah*?" Zariel jumped off her seat and held out her arms as if she'd just performed a magic trick. Her hazel eyes were bright with glee and her dark curls bounced around her round face.

"Tadaa! It's the Sun God!" I laughed and played along.

"See, Mommy?" Zariel looked back at Sam.

"It's Re, Zeezee, Raaaah," Sam drug it out, "not Ta." She sighed. "V, you're not helping."

"Okay, okay." I held up my hands in surrender. "Your mother's right, Zariel; his name is Re but there actually is an Egyptian god whose name sounds like Ta but it's spelled P-T-

A-H so it's got like a fast P sound at the beginning."

"P-taaadaah!" Zariel did her presentation again, and I chortled as I picked her up and swung her in a circle.

"You are my favorite little lion girl, you know that?" I asked her, and she nodded solemnly. "Good, now go with Mommy so I can talk to the Great Tadaah."

"Vervain!" Samantha huffed as she picked up the books they'd been reading. "You'll make her incorrigible."

"*Make* her?" I huffed and put Zariel down. "Accept the truth, Sam; she's already there."

"In-cure-ra-gible!" Zariel shouted and ran out of the library.

"That too." Sam rolled her eyes and followed at a much slower pace.

"Gods, I miss Rian." I sighed as I stepped into the sitting room, which was just off to the right side of the library.

"It's a delightful age," Re agreed, and I stopped short in the doorway as he continued. "How old is your son now?"

Re was dressed casually, in loose jeans and a button-down blue shirt. The ocean color made his eyes seem warmer, closer to Trevor's honey-brown, and the resemblance pulled an automatic response from me. It was like a trigger for my heart. But the rest of Re was so much different from Trevor and had other parts of my anatomy responding.

The ends of Re's sleeves were rolled and pushed up over his corded forearms, showing off a sprinkling of pale blond hair which seemed to add another layer of sparkle to his golden skin. At the end of those forearms were a pair of elegant hands; wide palms with long fingers and short, buffed nails. I started imagining what he could do with those hands and had to give myself a mental shake and lift my gaze quick. But that only brought me to the breadth of his chest and his strong shoulders so I continued up even further. His shoulder-length hair was pulled back into a ponytail carelessly, making him look like a model on a smoke break. Strands of the chocolate-colored hair had come loose and one hung down his cheek, bringing my attention to his full lips.

I started to lose focus.

"Vervain, are you all right?" Re came forward and took the coffee cups from me.

That was probably a good idea; my hands had begun to shake.

"Do you have to look like that?" I whined as I focused my eyes on his with supreme effort. "I'm in a horrible state here, you know? I just wore out two of my husbands having lunatic lioness sex, and I'm still not satisfied. I'm walking the edge, Re, and your gorgeousness does not help! You're like a beautiful abyss, and I'm teetering right over you. *Teetering!*"

"I'm sorry." Re chuckled as he put the cups down and came back to me. "Come and sit down, Vervain." He helped me to one of the couches and sat beside me. "I thought I'd dressed down. I don't know what else I could have done."

"Perhaps... oh, I don't know," I mused, "*not* show up at my house?"

"I couldn't stay away," he whispered and my gaze shot to his face. His golden eyes were really warming now, brightening until they were molten hot.

"What?" I gaped at him. "I thought you said you didn't want to be a part of my crazy love life?"

"I didn't." He grimaced. "And then I saw you dancing with other men. I didn't like it."

"That makes no sense." I frowned. "I'm married to five

men. You know this is exactly what you'll have to put up with if you get involved with me so why would that reaction make you interested?"

"I think I may be able to accept that you have five husbands," Re said. "I wasn't jealous of them. It was the men who could potentially *become* your next husband who bothered me. Perhaps because I'd so prematurely taken myself off that list."

"What are you saying?" I gaped at him.

"I'm saying that I went home and laid in my empty bed and thought of you." Re's hand went to my cheek. "I wanted you there beside me and try as I might to think of someone else, there was no other woman whose image I could hold onto. Your face constantly replaced theirs."

"I think you should take more time to think about this, Re," I tried to be reasonable despite the roar of my lioness vibrating through my limbs. She saw our prey within our grasp and all she wanted to do was pounce. I clenched my fists and tried my best to control her urges.

"You don't have a lot of time, do you?" He countered, looking me over carefully.

"Do not make this decision because you simply want to help me." I took his hand from my cheek and held it.

Re looked down at our joined hands and when he lifted his gaze, it lingered on the gap in my robe. Right, I'd forgotten that I was wearing only a robe. I really was losing my mind. And the insanity kept getting worse because instead of closing the robe, instead of pulling my hand away and putting some distance between us, I just met his hot stare with my own. It simply wasn't fair to tempt Re further. I knew it was wrong, but I still found myself leaning towards him.

"This isn't about helping you," he whispered right before his lips touched mine.

Sweet burning love, I felt as if I were on fire within seconds. It was a good thing my dragon gave me an affinity for flames because without it, I think Re's passion would have reduced me to ashes. I flung my arms around his neck and pulled him to me if I were a teenager in the back of her daddy's car with her horny boyfriend. Re rumbled low in his throat and yanked me onto his lap, pushing my legs apart and placing himself intimately against me.

I flung my head back as a growl of triumph rushed out of me. The sound startled me back into some sanity, and I took Re's face in my hands to stare hard at him. I wanted to tear his clothes off and rub myself all over that glittering body of his, but I knew I'd hate myself for it later. This was not my husband or even my lover. Re wasn't mine, not yet, and I wouldn't make him so without full disclosure.

Oh, damn the disclosure.

His eyes were full of desire, and he was rubbing himself against me in lazy hip circles that were threatening to turn me into a trollop. His full lips were parted, waiting for me to slide my tongue between them, and I just didn't have the strength to resist. I covered his mouth with mine, tangling my tongue with his before pulling back to bite and suck at his wicked lips. Re moaned and started to spread my robe. Cool air hit me and brought back reason once more.

"Damn it all!" I cursed and pulled away.

"You come back here, right now!" Re demanded as he reached for me.

"No." I stood just out of his reach and held a finger up in his face. "We're not going to make this decision like this. You need to know exactly what you're getting into."

"Hopefully"—he stood, looking predatory—"it's those

little red lace panties."

"Oh, wow." I gaped at him. "Did you really just say that?"

"Well *you* were just riding me as if I were your only horse to Paradise," he flung back.

I started laughing and then his face broke into a smile.

"As if you're my only horse to *Paradise*?" I repeated in disbelief.

"It just came out." He laughed and ran a hand over his hair.

"I want you really bad." I sat back down. "And I think it's clear that you want me too. That's great, and if I didn't care so much about you, I would snatch you up before you could change your mind."

"But you *do* care about me?" He lifted a perfect, thick brow.

"I do," I confirmed. "And you don't deserve to be misled. I'm not just looking for a quick tumble, Re. I'm looking for someone who's going to stick around."

"I know that." Re leaned forward. "Didn't I say as much?"

"Yes, but you were reacting to jealousy and lust. That can make men behave unreasonably," I reasoned. "Many a woman has used that trick, but I won't use it on you."

"I've been reasonable for most of my life." He shook his head. "Maybe it's time to be a little reckless. I want this. I want you, Vervain."

"But for how long?" I gave him a little smile and pushed him gently away from me. "If you were Intare, I could be assured of your loyalty but you're not. I'm not your goddess, and I can't demand fidelity from you."

"And that's what you want?" He narrowed his eyes at me.

"Absolutely," I declared. "All of my husbands are faithful to me, and I am faithful to them."

He gave me a skeptical look.

"I know it sounds strange but it's true." I shrugged. "I wouldn't be here with you, if I didn't have their full consent. That's my way of being faithful. I don't have sex with anyone but them. Not if I can help it, at least." I grimaced, thinking of Toby. Unfortunately, Toby was happily married now and wasn't an option for me. "If a new man is added, they must approve of him first. So, in my opinion, this isn't cheating."

"But you'd expect me to sleep only with you." He sat back and studied me.

"Yes. I know it seems unfair but my beasts are very territorial." I shook my head. "Even if I wanted to allow my men to have other women, I don't think my animals would allow it. Look what my lioness is doing to me just so I'll give her another lover. I don't want to think about what she'd do if she thought I was sharing them. Then there's my dragon. The number of our lovers doesn't matter to her, but she's very possessive of what we make ours. I've learned that it's best not to fight her if I don't have to. Can you imagine pissing off a dragon?"

"Actually, I can." Re grimaced. "But let's not get into that. I won't commit to that type of arrangement."

"I completely understand," I said as internally, my lioness roared an angry denial.

"Not without first dating you," he went on to my great surprise.

"What?" I blinked in shock.

"I want to date you," Re repeated. "I want a preview of how it can be between us, and I want a few conditions to our arrangement."

"Conditions?" I lifted a brow.

"Yes." He inhaled deeply and then went on, "First, the dating. It will be between you and I only. I want to get to know you before I get close to your husbands."

"Okay." I blinked some more.

"And I want sex," he said blandly. "I want to know how every part of our relationship will be and the sex will be a big part of it. I want it before I commit to this, and I want it soon. I know that may seem as if I'm just trying to bed you, but I assure you, it's with the intention of creating something lasting between us. We need to know if we're compatible before this goes further."

"I think we'll be compatible." I rolled my eyes.

"There are things about me that you don't know." Re held up a hand in warning. "Private things that may make you revise that statement."

"Okay." I swallowed past the sudden dry lump in my throat.

"There will be no holding back," he continued. "I want to know everything about you, and I want to be able to share myself with you."

"Sounds good," I said. "What's the catch?"

"Once we've decided if this will be a long term thing," he said gently, "then I want my own time with you. I know about your magic and how it works. I know I need to sleep surrounded by your other men so that I can accept them and this situation. I will do that if I must but then I will expect you to make time to be only with me. I need some kind of an illusion that I have you to myself or it won't work for me... lioness magic or not."

"Re." I smiled and took his hand. "How do you think we make it work? The men each have their own bedroom but they also have separate places that are purely theirs. Well, Kirill shares Pride Palace with me so his private place is just a little waterfall we like to go to, but Trevor has a cabin in our mountains, and Azrael has Shehaquim. Then Arach, of course, has all of Faerie to himself. He really needs that illusion you're talking about and when I'm around him, I try not to mention the others at all. I even take off my wedding ring." I lifted up my hand with its gold band.

"Really?" He blinked in surprise. "How do you find the time for all of this?"

"The Ring of Remembrance." I held up my other hand and showed him the ring my faerie father had left me. The clear cabochon glowed in the room's low light, and Re stared at it, entranced. "It allows me to jump back in time, to remember and re-experience things, but I've found a bit of a loophole. Time in each realm is a separate thing and in order to relive it, I must have been there living it to begin with. If I go back into a time and realm which I have never experienced, then I'm able to function in it freely. This means that I can leave the Faerie Realm and go back to the moment I left the God Realm without losing any time here. Then I can go right back to the moment I left Faerie and pick up where I left off there. Which is the only reason I can leave Rian there; he doesn't even know that I've left."

"So, you leap back and forth in time and as long as your lovers are in different realms, you can be with them constantly?" He grasped it fast.

"Yes," I went on, "and I use it to go on dates with my husbands here by jumping back and forth from the God Realm to the Human Realm."

"So, for example, you could go on a date with Trevor in the Human Realm and then go back in time to the God Realm and reuse those same hours with Azrael in Heaven?"

"Yes, exactly," I said.

"Well, look at that," he said and smiled. "This may work after all."

Chapter Thirteen

"I don't think this is going to work after all," Trevor said just hours after Re had left... with the promise of returning for me that night.

I had told Re that I needed to talk to my husbands before I made any kind of decision, even if it was only to date. Turns out, I'd been right to be wary.

"It *must* vork," Kirill said firmly.

"We don't need another stubborn alpha male who's going to make demands of our wife," Trevor growled. "It's bad enough with the Lizard King."

"I think a wuss would be much worse," Azrael said reasonably. "We wouldn't be able to count on him to defend her and that's the whole point, isn't it? The lioness magic wants a strong mate to help protect the Goddess. A beta male isn't going to do the trick."

"I think Azrael's right." I shrugged. "I danced with a few guys who would fall into that beta category, and I didn't feel anything. In fact, my lioness yawned at one point."

"See?" Kirill waved a hand toward me.

"Well, what gives Re the right to make demands?" Trevor tried again.

"Uh, the fact that we need him?" Azrael continued in his calm tone.

"We don't need him." Trevor snarled.

"Ve do, my friend." Kirill laid a hand on Trevor's shoulder. "Ve need him. Zis is right man, I know it."

"So, we just give in?" Trevor looked at Kirill as if he were stabbing him in the back.

"Nyet," Kirill said gently. "Ve are not giving in, ve are luring in. Most men don't vant zis. I know it seems shocking now but try and remember vhat it vas like before Vervain. You vouldn't have shared voman. Re is like zat now."

Trevor frowned and pondered. Then he lifted his gaze to Kirill's and nodded.

"All of you get private moments with me," I said. "That's what he'd be getting. There would just be more moments for him right now, while we get to know each other during a trial period."

"It's the trial period that bothers me the most," Trevor admitted. "What if he's just doing this so he can sleep with you, and then he leaves you at the end?"

"Then he's a fool," Azrael said and chuckled, "because if he isn't already half in love with our wife, he will be after spending just one day with her undivided attention."

"Fair enough," Trevor huffed and looked over at me.

"I don't think Re's that kind of man," I said. "If he was, I wouldn't be attracted to him."

"True." Trevor sighed.

"And this is Re, we're talking about." Azrael grimaced. "If he wanted to have sex with a beautiful woman, the hardest part for him would be deciding on which one or how many."

"There's that," Trevor huffed and came to sit beside me on the bed. "All right, Minn Elska, go on your date and do what you need to do with the Egyptian. If I'm completely honest, I'm a little relieved that I won't have to try and satisfy you tonight."

"Nyet, you shouldn't have said zat." Kirill rolled his eyes as Azrael inhaled sharply.

"Brother"—Az laughed—"you realize I will hold those words against you for eternity."

"Watch it, bird man," Trevor growled. "Two swipes of my claws and those wings are mine."

"Dogs." Azrael snorted. "Always barking up the wrong tree. If this bird actually came down and paid those empty threats any attention, you'd be wolf-kebabs in seconds."

"Bring it on, Son of Satan," Trevor growled.

"Anytime, Son of a Bitch," Azrael shot back.

"Zat vas not right," Kirill tsked, but I wasn't sure who he was chiding.

"Watch it or I'll go *Son of Sam* on you both," I snarled.

"My mom wasn't a bitch, just an asshole," Trevor snapped.

We all paused and looked back and forth between each other before bursting into laughter.

Chapter Fourteen

Re took me home for our first date, as in his home territory inside Duat. I had no idea that Gods lived beyond the Gates to Aaru; the gates which guarded a horrifying path that only the worthy souls were "lucky" enough to travel. Those worthy ones had to confront monsters and pass through several more gates before they were purified enough to be in the presence of Osiris... who also happened to live in Aaru.

Re's territory was just beyond the first gate (well, second if you counted the golden gate in the Hall of Two Truths). But we didn't need to go through any gate to get there, we just traced. Yay, no confronting monsters for me. Not that I minded monsters, it was just that I already had to walk through Hell to visit my in-laws; I didn't want to have to do it to visit a lover.

Re led me out of an empty, stone, tracing chamber and through grand, airy hallways with high ceilings held up by Egyptian columns. They were painted brightly, with lotus petals forming crowns at their tops. Smooth sandstone swept beneath my feet and simple Egyptian furniture posed on it; very elegant but not really my taste. I liked lush and plush; a lot of pillows and thick carpets. Things that made an environment comfortable. The hard wood furniture looked decidedly *un*comfortable.

We went up a wide, white staircase with gold handrails to the second floor. From there, we went into a library/

office which was decorated much more to my liking. A large wooden desk dominated one end, surrounded by floor-to-ceiling bookshelves full of both books and interesting pieces of art. A maroon and gold rug laid on the floor and a couple of chairs upholstered in brown leather sat over it. A small table stood between the chairs and behind them, were more bookshelves. The smell of leather and old paper permeated the air. I breathed deeply as we passed through the room and went out onto a balcony.

The wide balcony took more than a few strides to cross it and reach its low railing. I glanced right and left; it seemed to circle the top floor of the palace. Mostly empty, the space in front of us held only a few potted palms and two wooden chairs. I guess Re didn't want anything to detract from the spectacular view.

Low, rolling, grass-covered hills languished before us with grand, smoky-violet mountains soaring up behind them. A sparkling river ambled through the terrain and groups of palm trees added a texture. A few cream-colored stone buildings glistened beneath the bright sunlight and snow white birds flew above it all with long trailing tails flowing behind them like ribbons.

"Beautiful," I whispered.

"Thank you." Re smiled at the scene. "It's simple but I love it."

"Whose homes are those?" I pointed at the buildings.

"The Spirits of the Corn," he said.

"Spirits?" I questioned. "Well, as long as they're not *Children* of the Corn."

"The horror film?" He cocked his head at me.

"Oh, well done, you." I nodded in appreciation. "I didn't

expect you to be up to date on human pop culture."

"I have a lot of time on my hands." He grimaced. "The Egyptians think I spend all day pulling the Sun across the sky and then spend all night dead, floating through the Underworld to be reborn in the morning. It doesn't exactly leave me with a lot of work to do."

"And would you do it?" I lifted a brow at him. "If they did expect something from you that you could actually do?"

"Of course," he huffed and pulled himself up as if offended. "They're my people; I owe it to them."

"Good to hear." I nodded approvingly. "Well, you totally lucked out. Azrael spends a lot of his time collecting souls, and he used to take care of Shehaquim too, but Michael's been taking over for him a lot lately. Like you, Michael doesn't really have much to do so it's not a big deal for him to watch over the Third Heaven."

"I don't know," Re mused, "I think it might be nice to have a purpose. Or at least some way to contribute."

"Well, what about these spirits?" I asked. "What do they do? Can you help them?"

"They're basically caretakers; they watch over the land and handle the servants," he said and frowned. "I don't think they'd like my interference."

"The servants?" I lifted a brow.

"I told you"—he slid a smirk my way—"I'm kinda a big deal in Egypt."

I burst out laughing.

"Seriously though," he went on, "my people sometimes ask to serve me instead of lazing away in their afterlife across the river."

"Interesting choice." I cleared my throat.

"Well, they don't actually do any work." He shrugged. "They each have a few ushabti to command. My followers, they're called Heteptiu, they just kind of oversee what needs to be done and in exchange, they get to be close to me."

"Ushabti?" I lifted a brow.

"Ushabti are kind of like golems I guess," he seemed to ponder it a moment before he continued. "When a person dies, his family creates little clay statues which they imbue with magic and entomb with the body. This energy follows the soul into the afterlife and becomes an ushabti, a magical shadow person, who performs any labor which needs to be done for the soul."

"Humph," I huffed. "That's a nice perk but still, these souls serve you here forever?"

"Devotion"—he shrugged—"it's a wondrous thing."

"No kidding." I looked away, thinking of all the devotion given to me and how lucky I was to receive it.

"I know this is going to seem weird for a first date"—he took a deep breath—"but I want to introduce you to my daughters. They're very important to me. In fact, one of their titles is; The Eye of Re."

Something clenched anxiously inside my belly, but I had no idea why. I pushed the strange sensation away and lifted a brow at Re, "One of *their* titles?" How can they, plural, be an eye, singular? And *your* eye to boot?"

"They both hold the title." He grinned. "Egyptians tended to hand out numerous traits and titles which then had to be shared. Sekhmet and Bastet were born twins, but they developed into goddesses separately. Still, I'm their father and because of our connection, they were given similar magics.

Though Sekhmet is fiercer than her sister, more prone towards war, where Bastet is calmer and more protective without being so aggressive. As a father, I hate to say such things, but Bastet is kinder, more loving, and she's my favorite."

"You can't help but have a favorite," I said gently. "We all get along better with certain types of personalities and our children are no exception. With such differing temperaments, it makes sense that one would appeal to you more than the other."

"Yes, I think you're right," he agreed. "Thank you. That makes me feel a lot better."

"Gods can be human too." I gave him a grin. "Besides, it's not as if you love Bastet more than Sekhmet... wait a minute." I cocked my head at him. "What about their mother? Are we going to have to deal with a scorned woman? Scorned women are the worst."

"No, not scorned. She's deceased," Re said softly.

"I'm so sorry." I touched his hand gently. "I've known that pain."

"Yes, I know you have." He smiled sadly. "I was at Odin's funeral. I saw how broken you were. I remember thinking to myself that you still had other lovers, that you shouldn't be so destroyed by the death of one. But it's like with my children, isn't it? Loving more than one man doesn't lessen anything, it doesn't thin the love out or water it down in any way."

"Sometimes I think it makes the love stronger. As if the more men I love, the harder I try to be sure that all of them are happy, that no one goes wanting, and the effort makes me focus on them so much that I can't help but love them even more." I stopped and chewed my lip. "Does that make any sense?"

"Yes." Re nodded. "When we lose sight of our partner's

needs, we lose sight of the love we have for them. I think that's why a lot of marriages fail and then later the couple reconnects. Their time apart makes them miss each other and refocus on what had drawn them together, to begin with. Then, suddenly, they're back in love. The heart is a muscle like any other; it must be exercised to stay strong."

"Exactly." I exhaled on a low laugh. "I love all of my husbands deeply, more than life or fire or breath. When Odin died, that love threatened to destroy me but, at the same time, it was what saved me." I went on slowly, breathing deep through the painful memories. "I wanted to lie down beside him on that boat and just let the life drain out of me, but I couldn't. I had Trevor to think about; he would die with me. And Kirill, who would lose his sanity along with the rest of my lions. And Azrael, who would go back to being the reclusive Angel of Death, ever comforting the grieving but never comforted himself. And, finally, Arach, whose race would die out without me."

"Sounds as if you have a lot on your shoulders," he whispered. "But perhaps that's a good thing."

"How's that?"

"You have a lot to live for and without all of it, you would have died," he said simply. "You would have given up and gone to the grave with Odin. Instead, you picked yourself up and went into the Void after him. You brought him back."

"And maybe I shouldn't have," I whispered, my mind straying to Odin as it often did lately.

Was he happy? Did she make him smile? Laugh? I missed his laugh and his peacock-colored eyes. But he didn't have those eyes anymore, just as I didn't have him anymore. People always say heartache gets easier, that it lessens with time, but I've found that when you truly love someone, the pain never goes away. It gets buried, pushed down and ignored like any other pain the body learns to live with. And just like a constant backache or headache, as soon as you give it any thought, heartache is right back with you, as strong as it ever was.

"Don't say that." Re's hand covered mine on the stone railing. "Life is always a blessing, even if we're not allowed to be a part of it. You loved him, and you brought him back. That's miraculous, Vervain. Don't belittle it with bitterness. Give him this life fully, to make of it whatever he will. That's true love, isn't it? Limitless and without conditions."

"And it's easier said than done." I smiled through the heartache his words revived.

Re was right; Odin's soul was his own and his life was his own. I shouldn't lament him living it just because he'd chosen to do so with someone else. How bitchy was that?

"It's devastating to lose a spouse," Re said. "Whether it's to death or desire. I didn't think I could go on either when my wife died but I had to, for our children. Lusaset gave her life to save our daughters during the fall of Atlantis. I could hardly dishonor her sacrifice by giving up. I had to take care of them; see them safe."

"You really do understand," I whispered.

Re had gone through something very similar to what I had. His wife gave her life for their children, and Odin had given his life for me. Then both Re and I had to push past our grief to take care of the other people we loved.

"I do." Re swallowed visibly and looked out, across the wind-bowed stalks of grass. "I built this place for them and for Lusaset's memory. Then I became the kind of man women want but never love. I think I did that for her as well; kept my heart separate from my body."

"That can't be true," I denied. "Yes, you're amazingly beautiful but that should only encourage women to love you."

"Women don't love men as beautiful as me," he said and shrugged. "I'm the kind of man you fantasize about and perhaps have an affair with, but I'm not the man you want to father your children or share your life with."

"I guess it might be too much for some women," I mused. "When your lover is so much more attractive than you are, you begin to worry that they'll look elsewhere."

"Precisely." He nodded. "No one can live under that kind of stress. It turns rational women into paranoid stalkers and love into bitterness."

"That's something I had to deal with early on." I shrugged. "A human among Gods; I never could come close to matching their beauty. Even after I got Aphrodite's magic and got a little help in the looks department. I had to accept that what I had inside me was more important to them. That this face didn't matter so much as my magic and my heart."

"You shouldn't discount your physical appeal so easily." He gave me a sexy grin. "There are different types of beauty and different types of people to appreciate them. I appreciate yours very much."

"Thank you." My cheeks warmed as I looked away self-consciously.

"Are you blushing?" Re leaned his face into my view. "Did I make the Godhunter blush?"

"You know you did." I nudged him away with my shoulder. "And it's not exactly a huge surprise."

"All a part of my persona." Re waved a hand over himself and then sobered, looking back to me. "Which you saw right through."

"Anyone could if they'd only look a little deeper," I said as I did just that. "You have little lines of blue in your eyes," I breathed out the words.

"Blue which no one sees." He blinked slowly. "Because no one has looked at me like you do."

"Surely your wife did." I swallowed hard and tried to look away, but I couldn't. The gold of his eyes was like the shine off a hypnotist's watch.

"Yes, but I didn't look like this then." He glanced down, breaking the spell.

"Oh, wait... so, you're an original," I whispered. "Right, you said Lusaset died during the fall of Atlantis."

"Yes, of course." Re looked back at me immediately. "You do know that I founded this pantheon, don't you?"

"No." I blinked in surprise. "I thought perhaps Isis and Osiris did. I know they fled Atlantis with Odin and Thor."

"Isis and Osiris?" He laughed. "Vervain, Isis is my Great Granddaughter."

"What?!" I felt my eyes go round. "No way."

"Yes." he laughed at me. "She's a twin too; sister to Nephthys."

"She's Nephthys' sister?" I pulled back in dawning horror. "But that would mean that both Horus and Anubis are your..."

"Great Great Grandsons." He nodded. "I was lucky enough to have quite a lot of my family survive Atlantis."

"God damned long lived Gods!" I snarled. "You do know that I've been with Anubis, right?"

"You do recall how we met, *right*?" He countered and gave me an exasperated look.

"I've slept with your great great grandson!" I whimpered. "That's gross. I'm already guilty of sleeping with a father and his son, I don't know if I want to do great great grandpa and grandson. Oh Gods, I think I feel a little sick."

"Two greats in there, Vervain." Re shook his head. "That's a bit far down the family tree."

"But still!" I accused. "It's the same tree."

"Yes." He laughed. "Is that going to be a problem?"

"No." I calmed down. "I guess not. It's not as if I was even with Anubis by choice. You just surprised me."

"Is it Anubis?" He asked shrewdly. "Do you have feelings for him?"

"No, it's not that." I ran a hand through my hair nervously. "A relationship between Anubis and me would be impossible, even if he hadn't just gotten married. My husbands would never accept him because of what he did, and I just don't love him like that. I care about him as a friend but not as a lover. Honestly, it's hard to love someone who once raped you, no matter how much he now regrets it."

"I understand," Re said gently. "So, it really is just the lineage that upsets you." He thought it over. "Most of your men are quite a bit older than you, aren't they? I'd think you'd be used to this sort of thing by now."

"This sort of thing?" I gaped at him. "Age is not an excuse for a lack of morality."

"It's not immoral and you know it," he chided. "Actually, the Egyptians used to marry their siblings."

"Ugh, they're worse than the British Monarchy." I made a disgusted face.

"Well, in their defense, they thought they were imitating their Gods." Re shrugged. "They believe that Isis and Osiris were twins; lovers in the womb."

"That's really disturbing," I muttered. "As a mother, the idea of my twin babies having sex inside me is enough to send me screaming into a padded room."

"Well, it's impossible, of course," Re said. "Nature does have reasons for everything she does, and there's no reason to give a fetus a sex drive. Besides the fact that sexual organs wouldn't be developed enough to function within the womb."

"Okay, let's stop talking about this please." I swallowed back the bile rising in my throat. "Impossible or not, the thought is disgusting."

"Sexuality is ever altering among mortals," he went on smoothly. "It was only with the birth of science and its genetic proof that siblings should not procreate that such things fell out of practice."

"Oh, great." I rolled my eyes. "We're still on incest."

"I'm not talking about fetal sex anymore." He smirked.

"Okay, please just stop." I held up a hand. "I get it; you're older and wiser and more philosophical than I am. Kudos, bravo, accolades, and all of that. Just stop."

"Yes, I'm quite a bit older than you." He chuckled. "And now you know how long it's been since I've loved a woman."

"That's why I saw the loneliness," I suddenly sobered.

"I'm surrounded by love." He sighed. "I have a huge family who supports me, followers who worship me everyday, and women who quite literally fall at my feet."

"You could have left that last part out," I grumbled.

"But I don't have the love I truly desire," he went on, sliding his hand over my cheek. "And for the first time since Lusaset died, I have hope that I may have found it."

"Well, you sure don't hold back, do you?" I leaned into him, surrendering to the need to kiss him, and his warmth slid around me, making me forget just how ancient this god was. And who he was related to.

"Will you meet my daughters?" He asked after we slowly leaned away from each other.

"Of course," I said immediately.

"I believe you've met them before... and the rest of my family." Re grimaced. "But it was at the Ball Anubis held when you were his prisoner."

"So, I probably don't remember them." I nodded. "Let's just never speak of what happened between me and Anubis. As in never ever again."

"Agreed." Re nodded as he led me back into the palace.

We went down to the first floor and into a dining room that was almost as large as the dining hall of Pride Palace. It was bright and airy, with tall windows open to let in a cool breeze. Gauzy curtains flowed in that breeze, basking in the scent of lotus, jasmine, and rose like a woman in her bath. A wood table ran down the length of the room, its numerous legs carved with ram heads and gilded gold. Wide, throne-like chairs with low backs topped by gold lotuses on each end sat around the table. Two women already sat in a couple of those chairs, down at the far end of the room. A host of servants stood near them, waiting with pitchers of wine and serving utensils. A few of them came forward when they saw us and re-moved golden domes from the platters of food on the table.

"Here are my lovely girls!" Re smiled wide and held out his arms.

The women got up and rushed forward to hug him, one to either side. They stared at me over his shoulders. The one on the left was a golden goddess, similar in coloring to her father except her hair was golden blonde and her skin wasn't pale because of a gold shimmer over it, it simply was that color. Her eyes were rich brown and full of fierce scrutiny. On Re's other side was her sister, who didn't look like her twin at all. This one had ebony hair and skin as tan as Re's was beneath his shine of gold. She had his gold eyes but they boasted slit pupils, like a cat's, and they were regarding me with innocent interest.

Re pulled out of their hug and turned to me. "This is Sekhmet," he introduced the golden one. "And this is Bastet," his hand waved to the dark one. "Girls, this is Vervain. I know you've met her before, but you'll have to forgive her for not remembering."

"It was a horrible moment for you," Bastet said gently and came forward to shake my hand. Her hand was tipped with claws, and I saw the point of fangs behind her lips as she spoke. "I wish I could have done something to help you."

"But you handled it well." Sekhmet nodded approvingly as she came forward to shake my hand too. She shared her sister's traits of claws and fangs. "I was impressed with your grace under such circumstances... and you handled Anubis like a pro. Well done."

"Thank you." I nodded back; not sure if that whole *pro* thing was really a compliment. "It's nice to meet the both of you."

"We're delighted that Father has finally shown an interest in someone for more than just a dalliance," Bastet said plainly.

"But perhaps not so delighted about *your* situation," Sekhmet added. "Jealous maybe"—she smiled wickedly—"but not delighted for my father. I think he deserves his own woman."

"Understandable." I chuckled. "And nothing is set as yet. This is just about us getting better acquainted."

"As acquainted as you got with Anubis?" Sekhmet lifted a brow.

"Sekh!" Re snapped.

"Oh, come on, Dad." She rolled her eyes. "We all know she didn't want to sleep with Anubis. I was only teasing. You told me yourself that she used his attraction against him."

"Perhaps it isn't the kindest decision to tease a woman about being raped," Bastet said chidingly to her sister. "Or to blab about what Father told us in confidence."

"Perhaps not." Sekhmet sighed. "I'm sorry, Vervain. Sorry, Dad."

"It's all right," I said. "Just please don't bring that up again."

"Never again." Re added with a wink at me.

"I promise." Sekhmet drew an X across her chest with one, long, crimson painted talon.

"Thank you." Re sighed and gestured at the table. "Shall we eat before Sekhmet says something else insulting to the Godhunter?"

"Definitely!" Sekhmet laughed and plopped into a chair.

Chapter Fifteen

"Well, that was a grueling first date." I glanced at Re as he escorted me upstairs, away from the dining hall and his interrogating daughters.

"That was just dinner." He laughed and pulled me in tighter to his side. "You wanted me to be aware of what I was getting into, and I wanted to give you the same courtesy. Most of my family doesn't have the time to visit with me, but my girls come by often. If you become a part of my life, you'll be a part of theirs as well."

"I get it," I said. "I just wasn't prepared for a family dinner so soon."

"I know this is fast, but you don't have the time for me to get to know you slowly." He opened a tall door and led me into an spacious bedroom. "We need to figure out if we are compatible as soon as possible."

I stopped short in the doorway and stared. Compatible. Right. So, this was what he meant by that whole *private things* comment.

The first thing that caught my eye was the round bed which dominated the far end of the room. Beneath it, a gold sun lay embedded in the white stone floor with spokes radiating out from it sharply in all directions. Around the bed, silk curtains draped down in luxuriant swaths from golden hooks in the ceiling, and snowy silk sheets, a gold velvet comforter, and enough pillows to stock a harem sprawled across the bed. The mattress itself looked big enough to sleep eight and was set far enough away from the wall to make determining head from foot nearly impossible. I was used to big beds but this was ridiculous for just one man. Unless he was used to entertaining multiple lovers.

I swallowed convulsively, my pulse starting to race. You'd think I'd be okay with the idea of sex with multiple partners, but I rarely slept with more than two of my husbands at a time. There were exceptions to that, but they were saved for special occasions, like Valentine's Day, when no one wanted to be left out, and when I was short a lover and turning into a nymphomaniac. At heart, I was an old fashioned girl, believing that sex should be between two people who loved each other. I didn't want to think about Re romping around in his round bed with a bunch of wild women. It made me nervous.

But not as much as the rest of the room.

To the left of the bed rose a semi-circular area filled with... well, I'm not sure what to call it all. In the very center of the dais there appeared to be a golden throne. If it had been anywhere else in the palace, I might have disregarded the throne but the bedroom seemed an odd place to hold court, and Re wasn't exactly a king. He did have a narcissist vibe going, though, so I wouldn't be too surprised if he were into being worshiped in the bedroom as well as in the rest of his territory.

But the throne wasn't the strangest piece of furniture. Off to the right, a gold swing hung from chains set into the ceiling. It was strangely shaped; circles of gold holding a curving seat between them. The seat scooped forward, with a low back and ledges set against the sides; too low to be armrests and too high to be footrests. I wandered over to it and touched the cool metal, giving it a little push. An image of how I'd be positioned if I sat on it came into my head, making me blush and turn away.

I headed behind the throne and over to the other end of the terrace where gold ribbons hung from loops in the ceiling. They fluttered in the light breeze that drifted in through an archway on my right that opened onto the balcony. I brushed my hand through the wide lengths of swirling fabric, wondering what they were used for. At least they had subtlety on their side. The rest of the items on display were much more obvious. Like the gold stripper pole set in an open area behind the throne.

I gave the pole only a cursory glance. Although its purpose was obvious, it wasn't as shocking as the items before me. A golden oak wall unit had shelves on top and drawers beneath, with a wide ledge dividing the two. There were some books on the shelves, most of the titles including the word *sex*, but mainly, there were items on display. Beautiful cut-crystal bottles made their multi-colored liquid contents seem exotic. They seemed safe enough but right before them laid a golden tray holding an assortment of objects, most of them phallic. I know you're thinking that I should just call a spade a spade, or in this case, a dildo a dildo, but I don't think that's what all of them were. There were quite a few whose shape had me confused.

Another shelf had a display of vibrators, some with their own stands as if they were pieces of art. In fact, each shelf had its own little light to illuminate the objects. Jewels glittered in that illumination; jewels set into little golden clamps that were held together by a thin chain. Next to those were golden mannequin heads wearing masks of silk and leather. They stared at me with their shiny eyes.

I felt Re come up behind me as I pulled a drawer open. Inside waited an assortment of clothing that didn't look appropriate to wear in public. Most of them were missing their crotch. I cleared my throat as I picked up a piece of fur and discovered that it was a glove. What would you... oh, right, not everyone had shifter lovers available to them. Yeah, I could understand the fur thing.

Then I opened another drawer and found a collection of instruments and gadgets that had my eyes widening. I picked up a stainless steel contraption and frowned over the leather straps connecting it. It looked like some sort of brace, with silicone coating two sides.

"It's uh." Re smiled nervously. "That helps with fellatio."

"It does?" I turned it around in my hands, still not able to figure it out.

"You put it over your head"—Re gestured to the leather straps—"and the steel bars hold your mouth open. The silicone guards the teeth so your partner can be more, um... aggressive with you."

"Ah." I laid it back in its place, shutting the drawer and then leaning against it for good measure.

This gave me a perfect view of the wall directly across from us. My pulse began to race... and not in a good way. I don't know how I'd failed to notice it before, I guess I'd been too distracted by everything else to see the open length of wall with gold manacles embedded into the stone. There were pairs of them set at floor level and some much higher; high enough to draw someone's arms above their heads. The manacles gaped open at their hinges, like the mouths of predators waiting for new victims, and there was more than one set of them. Three sets of manacles all in a row. Three!

Bondage had kind of lost its appeal for me awhile back but manacles, especially golden ones, really upset me. They reminded me too much of Anubis and it was sort of ironic that I found them in Re's bedroom. I took a shaky breath and looked away; straight up into a mirror. There were multiple gold-framed mirrors, set at different angles around the ceiling, giving me all kinds of interesting perspectives of the erotic playground.

"God damn freaky Egyptians Gods," I whispered as I turned back to face the rest of the room.

I looked back toward the bed and realized that the gold hooks holding all the pretty silk around it, were thick and appeared capable of holding something much heavier than cloth. Another glance at the floor revealed small metal loops hidden within the rays of the sun and a crevice in the floor which circled the bed. Near the back, a suspicious gold post stood. There was a handle on top of it. What the hell was that for?

"Vervain?" Re stepped in front of me, blocking out the sight of the astonishing bed.

"You're a perv!" I accused him.

"A bit of one, yes." He gave me an apprehensive smile. "This is what I wanted to show you. Do you think you can handle my tastes?"

"I don't know." I slipped around him and stepped down from the terraced area. "Do I have to sign a contract before we have sex?"

"What?" He followed me.

"It's like *Fifty Shades of Gold* in here." I waved a hand behind me at the particularly disconcerting area.

"Oh." He chuckled as his expression cleared. "Uh, no, there are no contracts, and I don't want to hurt you in any way. I just like pleasure... both giving and receiving."

"Who doesn't like pleasure?" I looked back at him. "But this is a little extreme."

"Says the polyamorous love goddess." He gave me a cocky look.

"I know." I held up a hand. "And I admit, I've been adventurous. But before anything happens between us... no chains, Re. I can't stand being chained."

"I..." Re swallowed hard and nodded. "I understand. Look, this isn't about dominance or submission for me. I'm neither a sadist nor a masochist. I don't need you tied up and helpless or begging me for mercy. It's just about finding ways to magnify the joys of the sexual experience, and I hope I can show you what I mean by that."

"I hope so too," I whispered.

"Pleasure." He took my hand. "A love goddess should be fine with exploring all forms of it."

"I should be, yes." I tried to breathe through the rising tide of lust that suddenly hit me. I wasn't sure if it was my Lust magic or my Lion. Maybe it was both. They could be ganging up on me; I wouldn't put it past them.

"But?" Re led me to a set of low couches off to the right side of the room.

It was a less lusty side; just a sitting area in front of another wide arch which led to the wrap-around balcony. A fireplace was set flush into the wall, looking a little strange within the Egyptian architecture. Still, it was hardly the most startling addition to the room so I barely spared it a glance.

"But this feels like cheating," I confessed as I took a seat. "I don't know why but all of these... extras just makes it feel more so."

"Are you being unfaithful?" He asked earnestly. "Because we don't have to do this. We've yet to cross a line that can't be uncrossed."

Re had leaned forward to speak and it brought his beautiful face too close. I inhaled sharply as my control broke and my lioness took over. With one move, I pushed him back onto the couch and his shocked eyes met mine briefly before I set my mouth to his. I felt him go hard between us in an instant, ready to take everything I gave him, and his arms circled me almost violently.

Tongues twirling, hands grasping, clothes tearing, Re lifted me and carried me to that garish bed. We fell through the curtains, and I landed on top of him. Half of my clothes were already gone, and I yanked the rest away as I bit at his lips, growling low in my throat. Enough with the waiting, enough wanting. The hunt was over; it was time to claim my kill and feast.

I reached between us and tore Re's pants away. Yep, just like that. You'd be surprised what a lioness in heat can do. The pants shredded, and I tossed the remnants aside as Re inhaled sharply. He stared up at me with wide eyes, hands lifting to slide over my stomach and then up to my chest. He was gentle for a bare second before his fingers clenched and kneaded at me deeply. It was the perfect response to my predator, and I cried out, lifting my head as the magic lifted inside me.

Lion blended with Lust, and I fell on him wildly, reaching between us to grip his shaft and direct him home. We both cried out in completion as he slid inside me, and I set my hands to his chest to start the tribal tempo that would truly complete us. Fingers digging into his golden skin, I pounded against him as the light of lust filled me. A blushing pulse, starting inside my chest but spreading with every touch, every heartbeat. It grew stronger and stronger, deeper in color and intensity, until it lifted up and hovered beneath my skin.

Everywhere I touched Re, or was touched by him, my skin lit up in response. A crimson glow of magic seeking contact. It seeped into him, collecting until it burst up through his skin and rushed back into me through our joined lips. Re groaned as Lust tingled through our tongues, but I knew it wasn't stopping there. The magic surged back down into me and entered him again through my sex, sending ripples of pleasure down my thighs. Back up again it went, creating a circle of sensation that grew more powerful with each pass.

Re shouted in pleasure as the magic reached its apex and exploded out from us in the form of thousands of little stars. They hung suspended above us for a moment and then gently rained down on our skin, sending little jolts of ecstasy singing through us wherever they landed. I inhaled sharply through the rush of power it gave me and when I opened my eyes, it was to see Re glowing with the same magical charge. My Lust magic was a very generous lover, it created a power surge from sex but it always shared. Yet even with that tantalizing energy filling me, I fell onto Re's chest, unable to hold myself up any longer. I was sated for the first time in months and that super-seded any sexual high.

I breathed roughly against Re's skin, soaking in the relief he'd given me, and basked in the delicious lethargy that finally filled my limbs. My lioness purred in my belly, satisfied at last. This was what we needed, *this* with *him*.

Then my eyes flew open in shock as I felt him harden inside me. I pushed up enough that I could look into his face. Re was flushed, his lips swollen from my violent kisses but still parting for more. A sheen of sweat covered his brow, collecting in his golden strands of hair and, as I watched, his eyes filled with heat. The gold warmed then brightened, lightening to sunlight. Something inside me responded to it and began to shine back... and it wasn't my Lust. It was my Moon, and he recognized it immediately.

"Rise again, Sweet Moon," he whispered. "Rise for your lover, the Sun. Take my light and make it your own. Shine for me."

Re slid his hands around my hips and pulled me up his chest. My eyes widened when he settled my sex over his mouth. I clutched at the silk hanging before me and wrapped the lengths around my wrists to steady myself. As his tongue touched me, a heat seeped through it and into me. No, not heat; light. Sunlight filled me, surging up through that intimate connection to meet the moonlight inside me. They blended together and burst from body, setting my skin to glowing again. I ground myself against his face greedily, and Re pulled me closer; sucking on that special spot before licking, thrusting, and laving me expertly. And this was only the beginning.

All through the night, the Moon glowed, but it was the Sun God who rose over and over, filling me with his light and his body and the pleasure they both gave me until I passed out within his arms.

Chapter Sixteen

I woke up before sunrise, just as the sky was starting to lighten, and opened my eyes to see Re's face on the pillow beside me. He looked almost normal in that half-light, with those metallic eyes shut and his striking features softened by sleep. But he wasn't normal; he wasn't human, and neither was I. Not entirely. If I had been, I wouldn't be lying there, pondering why I felt so guilty. I wouldn't be there at all. So, why was I feeling guilty?

"Because one woman shouldn't have all this," I whispered and turned away from Re. "What am I doing?"

I hung my head in my hands and replayed the previous night in my head. Flashes of golden skin beneath my hands; beneath my lips. Glowing eyes staring up at me from between my thighs. Re's beautiful face at my breast; sucking and biting. On hands and knees, staring back over my shoulder to see golden muscles clenching as Re pounded into me savagely. His face strained with rapture. The sound of his release echoing through my mind to this present and making me shiver in need. He had called my name.

"I don't even recognize myself. I don't want to do this." I stood and blinked at the rising Sun, streaming in through the arched balcony doors. Then I looked over at his collection of sex machines, furniture, and accouterments. "I don't want this," I said to them, almost in accusation, even though we hadn't used any of them. "I don't want to be this woman."

I picked up my clothes and pulled them on before I rushed from the room and down the wide staircase like Cinderella fleeing the Ball. As I passed a sitting room, I heard Bastet call out to me, but I kept going; heading straight for the tracing room down the hall. It was a small room, as most tracing rooms are; its only purpose was to let people in and out of a territory... and I wanted out. Right now. *Get me outta here!* I rushed inside and called out the chant to take me home.

In seconds, the magic took hold of me, changing my solid form into mere thoughts, and I went hurtling through the uniting realm of the Aether. I emerged in the tracing room of Pride Palace, taking a huge gulp of air into my freshly reformed lungs. I stood there a moment, panting in panic, though I wasn't sure why. It wasn't as if Re was going to chase me home and even if he did, he wouldn't try and drag me back with him to strap me to his love wall. I'm sure he'd respect any decision I made. And yet... my heart was pounding in fear, my hands shaking and my legs trembling.

"Minn Elska?" Trevor's hands were suddenly on my arms, and I was falling forward into his embrace.

I began to cry violently, and he pulled me in closer, rubbing my back soothingly. He didn't even ask what was wrong, just picked me up and carried me back into the elevator he'd stepped out of.

I cried the whole ride up to the top floor, and he made gentle sounds of reassurance while nuzzling my face with his own. Wolf instincts. It was exactly what I needed. My own wolf huffed in satisfaction, rising to reconnect with Trevor as I breathed in his spicy musk. Slowly, I began to get control of myself and reason seeped back in.

I shouldn't have this luxury. I shouldn't get to break down on Trevor. He didn't deserve it, and I didn't deserve him. Of all the people in our combined marriage, I was the one who had the least to complain about. How dare I cry because I slept with another man? It was stupid and immature. I sniffed and swiped at my face angrily as he stepped out of the elevator and carried me into our bedroom.

"I'm sorry, Honey-Eyes," I whispered. "I'm okay now."

"No, you're not," he said resolutely and carried me past our bed and through the French doors that led into the Butterfly Garden. He knew how much it calmed me to be out among the sweet flowers and gliding butterflies. "I know this isn't what you wanted. I know you think it should just be you and me, that marriage is between two people only, but this isn't what we were handed. You hold a magic that comes with conditions, and if I want to hold you, I have to deal with those conditions... and I *do* want to hold you."

"I know," I whispered. "And it's completely unfair of me to be upset by this. You guys have the short end of the stick."

"I don't care what end of the stick I have"—Trevor grinned down at me as he continued to carry me down the pebbled path towards the clearing in the middle of the garden —"as long as you're holding the other end."

"Da, me too." Kirill came up behind us. "It vill become easier, Tima. You know zis is hardest part."

I sighed and laid my head on Trevor's shoulder, looking up at the sky revealed through the mesh covered latticework of the garden's roof. The Sun was climbing higher and my precious butterflies were out, flitting from bloom to bloom and adding their vibrant colors to the rest of the visual concert. Nick leapt out of the underbrush, and I tapped Trevor to let me down as my gray tabby cat ran over to us.

"Hey, baby," I whispered as I sank onto the soft grass beside him.

I filled my fingers with his striped fur, and he climbed

into my lap and began to purr. The Butterfly Garden was calming but nothing eased my tensions better than a purring cat. A cat in the lap is the best therapy. Well, then again; perhaps there is one other thing that calms me. I smiled as my men settled down beside me, and I was surrounded by love.

I leaned into them and with the scent of roses and jasmine heavy in the air, a rumbling cat in my lap, and their arms around me, I felt the peace of home settle over me. I wished that I could stay there with them and not have to wreck this happiness. Just lie back and watch the butterflies as I languished in love with them. What a life.

"If you don't vant Re, ve vill find someone else." Kirill stroked his fingers through my hair and started rubbing my scalp. "It vill be okay."

"You will *not* find someone else!" Re declared as he strode up the path.

All three of us gaped at Re as he set himself right before us and stared hard at me. Nick jumped up and ran off into the bushes as Re continued.

"You and I shared something wondrous last night," he said. "Something beyond sex. We touched more intimately than I've ever experienced. My sun melded with your moon, Vervain. That's not something you run away from."

"I was consumed by my lioness," I whispered. "It won't be like that again."

"The hell it won't," Re huffed and went down on one knee before me, taking my hand. "That wasn't just your lioness and it wasn't just our magic. It was *us*; you and me together. No toys or tricks or anything but you and me. Do you know how rare that is for me? I want that again, and I *will* have it, Vervain. I'm not going to let you hide from me because it scared you."

"It didn't scare me!" I sat up straight, my hackles instantly rising in response to the challenge.

"Yes it did." He smirked, knowing full well he was using playground tactics to get his way.

"I'm not scared of anything that happened last night." I stood up and dropped Re's hand so I could glare down at him.

"I think you are." Re stood to face me and his smile settled into a determined line. "I know *I* am."

"What?" I faltered.

"I'm scared, Vervain," he admitted. "Because what we had was so incredible, just one night of it, that more of the same might make me an addict; a slave to the pleasure you alone can give me. That kind of weakness can destroy a man, even a god."

"Then why are you here?" I asked simply.

"Because it would be both cowardly and foolish to let go now," Trevor answered for him as he stood to slide an arm around my waist.

Kirill got up as well, his arm winding around me from the other side so that the three of us faced Re as one unit.

"She is vorth ze veakness," Kirill added. "In end, she makes you stronger."

"Yes, I think you're right," Re said without taking his eyes off me. "Come back with me, Vervain. Let's see where this takes us."

My husbands looked down at me, waiting for me to decide before they gave their support either way. It was their love that helped me reach out and take Re's hand. Before he pulled me forward, I angled myself up to kiss Trevor and then Kirill. Their arms slid away and their palms went to my back, gently easing me towards Re.

That kind of love was so hard for me to understand, even holding the magic of love inside me. I could never have encouraged one of them into the arms of another woman. But in that moment, I didn't feel guilty for having their devotion; I felt lucky. Really damn lucky.

As I walked out of the garden holding Re's hand, I knew it was true. It may make me a greedy bitch, but I was grateful for their love, and I was hoping to find more of the same.

Chapter Seventeen

"Where are we going?" I asked as Re led me from his tracing room and then out of his palace.

"I thought we'd take a stroll around my territory," he offered. "I don't show it off very often."

"No time for sightseeing when you bring a lover home?" I teased.

"I generally don't allow them to stay very long after the screaming is over," he said simply.

"After the screaming is over?" I laughed. "Who are you?"

"The Sun God, Re." He stopped to pose with hands on his hips, looking off into the distance.

"Really? Cuz you kinda look like Peter Pan right now." I rolled my eyes. "I don't know whether to laugh at your ego or smack you silly for it."

"You can do either." He shrugged. "Both suggestions make me happy."

"You're obnoxious," I said but smiled anyway.

"In-cure-ra-gible." Re nodded.

"Oh, sheesh," I huffed.

"Come here." He pulled me down a gravel path. "I want to show you the Watercourse."

"The water horse?" I lifted a brow.

"The Water*course*." He laughed. "It's the river the souls travel down on their journey to paradise."

"Oh, yay," I said in a monotone.

"There are snakes," he promised with lifted brows. "Big ones that breathe fire."

"Fire-breathing snakes?" I was instantly interested. "Those are my peeps!"

"Yes." He chuckled. "I guess they are. Come on." He took my hand, and I followed along like an excited toddler.

The sky started to darken the further down the path we went until, finally, it looked like the middle of the night. The middle of the night in the middle of nowhere. But then I saw the glow of firelight, enough of it to brighten the darkness and lead our way to the shore. Re took me down to a sandy beach, and we stood there, staring out across a wide river.

On our side of the river there were boats; several flat-bottomed raft-like vessels carrying shadowy humanoid shapes and one large craft done in an Egyptian style. On the other shore there were six men, staring across at us sternly. They each lifted a hand in salute, and Re lifted his in return.

"Those are the ushabti I told you about. They remain aboard the rafts until they're needed." Re indicated the shadowy forms crowding the rafts, and I frowned at them. They seemed familiar, almost in a deja vu way. But then Re waved at the men across the river, and I let it go. "And those are the Gods who look after my followers."

"You can't look after your own followers?" I lifted a brow at him.

"No, I'm much too important for that." He winked at me. "Besides, I've already provided them with a beautiful kingdom to inhabit, I don't think I should have to look after them as well."

"Uh-huh." I focused back on the river.

The river didn't really go anywhere, so I guess it was really a lake. Or maybe you could call it a dammed river —dammed, not damned—since massive walls stood at both ends, stretching out to the riverbanks and cutting off the flow of water from both directions. The walls on our left went on endlessly through Re's territory on both sides of the river, but the walls on the right angled away, forming a box. I would have called it a building but it didn't seem to have a roof.

What it did have was a doorway; a passage that was right over the water but completely covered by tall, wooden doors which extended down into the river. The walls on our left had a similar passage, narrow and tall, with wooden doors barring the way, but they also had a pair of hooded snakes guarding them. Snakes as big as I was in dragon form... and they were breathing a constant stream of fire.

"Why is the fire sparking like that?" I waved at the snakes.

"They're venomous too," Re said proudly.

"Nice." I grinned and glanced back at the snake-free gate on our right.

"Within those walls lies the first country beyond the Gates to Aaru." Re waved his hand at the walls I'd been contemplating. "Duat is considered to be a separate country within our connected territories and the gate provides passage for the worthy souls to get from there to here. It's similar to a tracing room except you can only trace to one place and it's a one-way ride."

"Interesting. So, you can only travel down the river, not up it." I returned my gaze to the snakes. "Are there more of these gates further down?"

"Several more," he confirmed. "Each gate opens onto an-other country of Aaru, or sub-territory if you'd prefer. I rule a couple of them but Osiris and Isis have the largest. They need it for the souls. There are also some other gods living here; Sokar, Khepera, and Apep... he's a snake-shifter, you'd probably get along well with him."

"Snake-shifter? Like a naga?"

"Similar." Re nodded but then the gates on our right opened and a sleek boat glided through on a rush of water. He waved towards it excitedly. "This is what I wanted to show you. The Heteptiu souls have arrived."

"Really?" I looked towards the boat curiously.

The boat had a simple design; sleek as the old Egyptian crafts were. There was no sail or oars but it still kept gliding down the center of the river, straight towards the snake gate. I could only assume that the rush of the previously dammed up water must have helped to carry it along. Either that or it was magic. Whatever the case, the boat moved onward, carrying solemn passengers. Some of them spotted us and word spread. Soon, they all stood at the railing, crying out to us.

"What are they saying?" I glanced up at Re.

"Oh, the usual." Re waved at them casually. "Hail Great Re, that sort of thing."

"Go figure." I rolled my eyes. "No wonder you're so full of yourself. Do you come down here every day just so you can hear them worship you?"

"No," he huffed, obviously offended. "I don't have to come here for that. I have servants, remember?"

"I'm going to slap you really hard," I warned him. "Be-cause you're obviously in need of a wake-up call or an intervention or something. This is ridiculous!" I pointed at the crying souls. As in literally crying, some of them were sobbing in joy to see their golden god.

"I think it's quite wonderful," he protested.

"Of course, you do." I grimaced. "You're the Sun God comma Re. Re, the Great and Powerful. Re, the God of Chippendales. Re the Head of the Egyptian Pantheon. Re—"

"I'm sorry, what was that last one?" He asked with a smile.

"The Head of the Egyptian Pantheon?" I asked innocently.

"No, the one before that," he insisted.

"The God of Chippendales." I sighed. "Come on, I've used that joke on you before."

"But being compared to male strippers never gets old." He laughed.

"Please tell me you're not the one who dances around that stripper pole in your bedroom," I begged.

"No, of course not," he scoffed. "I don't need a pole to pose with while I strip."

"That's a relief." I sighed.

"The fact that my body is being revealed is entertainment enough." Re smiled wickedly.

"You know, I have to tell you; I've met a lot of egotistical gods, but you take the cake." I shook my head. "And that says a lot."

"What kind of cake?" He lifted a dark brow. "Can I have it *and* eat it?"

"Knowing you, it would be one of those giant cakes with

a half-naked woman popping out of it." I snorted, ignoring his eating comment.

"Only if you'll consent to be that woman." He licked his lips as if he could already taste the frosting.

"Not happening," I muttered but then movement caught my eye.

As we'd been talking, one of the six gods standing on the other shore had rowed out to the soul boat on a large raft. The souls had left their boat for the raft and now, they were being rowed to the shore.

"Where are they going?" I asked Re.

"To the afterlife I've provided for them," he said and sighed. "Haven't you been listening?"

"But wait." I frowned, trying to remember what I'd heard of the Egyptian afterlife. "I thought they had to pass through a whole bunch of gates before they got to their afterlife?"

"That's only for the followers of Osiris." Re grimaced. "Just past those gates"—he waved towards the snakes—"is Osiris' Kingdom. His souls take another boat into it and they're met by a minor god, Akhabit. He leads them toward the Twenty-One Gates of Sekhet-Aaru, each one guarded by demons. They have to pass through the gates to get into Sekhet-Aaru, the Field of Reeds."

"Okay, so some of the souls come here and the rest go into Osiris' Kingdom. I assume there are more god territories past that. But where exactly does the river lead?" I inquired.

"To Hell," he answered soberly. "After that, it's cut off by the Aether, forced underground to return to its head and recirculate."

"The Aether?" I blinked in surprise.

"There's a gate at the end of Aaru and going through it is like touching a tracing point. You'd be launched directly into the Aether, a situation which wouldn't be so great for a human soul but is rather convenient for us gods."

"You're not worried about the souls making it that far?" I asked.

"They're met and guided by gods so there's little chance of that happening." Re shrugged.

"Wait... Hell?" I frowned. "I thought the evil souls got eaten by Ammut and destroyed. Isn't her name *the Destroyer*?"

"Yes, but she's actually a connection to Hell," he explained. "A physical gate. When Ammut consumes a heart, she takes a piece of that soul into herself and transports it to our version of Hell. The piece serves as both an anchor and a lead, pulling the rest of the soul to it. Unworthy souls don't get to ride either boat."

"Through the mouth of a goddess and straight into Hell," I mused. "That's horrifying."

"I didn't come up with it." He shrugged.

"Yeah, yeah; I know." I sighed. "It's all the humans' fault. Us and our crazy imaginations."

I looked back at the empty soul boat and saw that it wasn't actually empty. There was a ghostly figure of a woman standing on deck. Ironically, souls don't look like ghosts. In the God Realm, souls could appear as solid as a living person if they were joined to a god. If not, they were invisible. This woman did not look solid and yet she was still visible. But she was very wispy, her long hair trailing back into vanishing ribbons as she stood at the prow. Then the boat reached the gate, and the ghost lady called something out in Egyptian. The snakes stopped spewing flames and slid back, the doors opened, and the boat sailed through on a rush of water.

"What was all that about?" I asked Re.

"Every gate in Aaru, be it one of Osiris' twenty-one or those on the Watercourse, can be opened by the correct words." Re grimaced. "But that's a lot to remember and even those Egyptians who've remained true to the old religion don't often recall them all. Personally, I believe that if you're judged worthy by Ma'at, you should get your afterlife. I'm not into testing the good souls, like Osiris is."

"So, what did you do?" I prompted.

"I created Heka, Goddess of the Word, to lead my followers through the gates." He grinned sheepishly. "She's a magical hologram, programmed with specific greetings, trigger words to respond to, and instructions to impart. She speaks the proper words at each gate so the souls can just relax and sail through."

"That's nice of you." I watched the snakes slide back into place. "But why so many gates if your souls stay here and Osiris' get off in the next territory?"

"The Watercourse isn't meant for just the souls," Re said. "This is the journey I am supposed to make every night; lying dead in a boat."

"What?" I lifted my brows. "That's a little macabre."

"You're right! It absolutely is; enough of this!" Re declared and took my arm. "Time for more pleasant pursuits."

"Already?" I lifted a brow. "I thought we'd spend a little more time talking first."

"Not *those* pursuits." He laughed. "I want to introduce you to the Spirits."

"Oh." I nodded sagely. "Yes, the Not-Children of the Corn."

"Yes, them." Re slid his gaze over to me as we walked, and I held it.

It struck me then how easy it had become to look at him. Now that I knew I could have him, his beauty was no longer a taunt. I could simply enjoy it... though perhaps I should try to do so surreptitiously so I wouldn't add to his astounding ego.

We came to a sprawling collection of buildings in the middle of an orchard. Several varieties of fruit hung from the trees and beyond the orchard, fields of barley and wheat undulated like water. They made a gentle shushing sound when the breeze picked up. It was calming, as was the scent of ripening fruit, and I found myself smiling. Re led me up a crushed stone path to the front steps of the main building, and I glimpsed a vegetable garden going around the side. We went to the front door.

"Where's the corn?" I asked Re as he knocked.

"It's in the back," a woman said as she opened the simple, white door.

I flinched, startled. "What were you doing; waiting right behind the door?"

She was a tiny thing, and I'm only five-foot-three so that says a lot. She barely reached my shoulder, but she had a huge presence and an even bigger smile. Her teeth were shockingly white against her coffee-colored skin and the look in her dark eyes matched the warmth of her grin. Pale yellow hair hung down her back nearly to the floor in a thick braid. She had on a bright white tunic, belted with a golden cord.

"I saw you walking up," she confessed. "I'm Besa." She held her hand out to me, and I shook it.

"Vervain," I said. "Nice to meet you."

"Come in, please." Besa waved us inside. "I'll fetch my sisters."

Besa wandered off while Re led me into a comfortable living room. Woven rag rugs sprawled over hardwood floors with overstuffed couches upholstered in floral fabric over them. Lace doilies laid beneath crystal baskets and a stack of wood waited beside the fireplace. Not at all what I was expecting from Egyptian spirits.

There was a bit of a commotion from the back of the house with the sounds of exclamatory voices. I frowned at Re, but he just shook his head with a smile. Then two women rounded the corner into the living room with Besa trailing after them. They both had the same coloring as Besa; dark skin and eyes with that pale, butter-colored hair. They were also dressed the same; in white tunics and gold belts.

"He does have a woman with him!" One of the new ladies exclaimed.

She was much taller than Besa; willowy thin and graceful with her gestures. Her hair was up in a bun on top of her head, emphasizing her angular features.

"He sure does!" The last woman peered at me as if I were a rare plant, her dark eyes wide and her little mouth starting to hang open.

She was of a height somewhere between the other two and her features seemed to be a blending of the tall one's angles and Besa's softness. She had a sharp nose with rounded cheeks. Her hair hung free so that I could see how fine the strands were and how wispy. The lifted a little in the breeze like fluff... or cornsilk. That was it; they had cornsilk hair.

"And this is shocking?" I asked them.

"You don't know the half of it, honey." The tallest one walked forward and stuck her hand out at me. "I'm Tepu-yn and this is my sister, Nepra. Are you really the Godhunter?"

"Word travels fast." I shot a look at Re as I shook her hand.

"Servants talk." Tepu-yn shrugged. "So it's true?"

"Yes, it's true," I confirmed.

"The same one Anubis captured?" Nepra came forward.

"No, the *other* Godhunter Anubis captured." Tepu-yn rolled her eyes.

"Does everyone have to bring that up?" I grumbled.

"Nepra," Besa chided. "She's right; that was rude."

"I just wanted to know." Nepra pouted.

"It's only of note to us because that was when Re first met you," Besa explained. "And we recall his interest from back then."

"It's surprising that he has waited so long to bed you." Tepu-yn nodded and took a seat across from us on one of the couches.

"And this conversation just keeps getting better," I groaned.

"Ladies please." Re held up his hands. "I didn't bring Vervain here to be harassed. I just thought you'd like to meet her."

"Since she's the first woman in ages who's held your interest for longer than a night?" Nepra asked.

"In ages and ages," Besa added.

"As in since we've known him," Tepu-yn said. "What did you do to him?" She leaned towards me conspiratorially. "Was it something with your tongue?"

"Tepu!" Besa smacked her sister in the arm.

"What?" Tepu-yn growled. "It's a valid question."

"Was it?" Nepra took over.

"Um." I looked to Re for help, but he was too busy trying to hold back his laughter. "I don't believe so."

"Our magic blended," Re finally was able to speak. "It was phenomenal."

"Your magic?" Besa blinked and looked at me. "What do you hold that would blend with the Sun?"

"The Moon," I said soberly.

All three women inhaled in delight and sat back to smile at us.

"Absolutely," Tepu-yn said.

"Perfect," Besa added.

"You were meant for each other," Nepra surmised.

"There are other sun gods," Re chided them.

"None like you," Besa huffed.

"And other moon goddesses," I added.

"None that have held his interest." Nepra shook her head.

"Well, it's rather soon to say that I've *held* his interest." I chuckled. "It's only been a couple of days."

"Didn't you hear me say he's been captivated by you since Anubis had you?" Besa asked with lifted brows.

"What?" I looked at Re for confirmation, but he was busy giving Besa an irritated scowl. "Is that true?" I demanded his attention.

"You're an interesting woman." Re sighed. "But I could hardly seduce you after Anubis mistreated you so horribly.

It would be taking advantage of a vulnerable woman, and I'd never do that."

"And I had all my other men," I noted.

"That too." He took a deep breath and looked back at the Spirits. "If I'd known you were going to divulge all of my secrets, I wouldn't have brought her here."

"Hardly a secret," Tepu-yn huffed.

"That you found her attractive," Nepra finished.

"You like strong women," Besa said and nodded. "It's not surprising that the Godhunter would pique your interest."

"But what is surprising," Tepu-yn started again.

"Is that you're *still* interested," Nepra added.

"Even though she has multiple lovers." Besa turned to me. "He's never been the jealous type, but we think that's more due to apathy than ego."

"Well, he's not lacking in ego either." I grimaced, and the women laughed.

"Exactly why we're so surprised," Tepu-yn declared.

"If you're important enough to bring here," Nepra mused.

"Then you're important enough to possess," Besa concluded. "And be possessive with."

"Could you please cease your efforts to embarrass me?" Re sighed. "You know it won't work."

"Hmm." Tepu-yn pondered the Sun God, Re. "I think he's up to something."

"He's *always* up to something," Nepra agreed.

"He's never up to anything." Besa rolled her eyes.

"Which means that he's so bored, he's probably up to something this time."

"*Are* you up to something?" I asked Re with twitching lips.

"Yes," he admitted instantly. "I'm trying to lure you into my life by introducing you to my friends. Unfortunately, they're acting like ninnies at the moment."

"Ninnies?!" Tepu-yn gasped.

"Uncalled for!" Nepra exclaimed.

"Unacceptable!" Besa declared.

"I like them." I nodded.

"Oh, we like you too, Godhunter." Besa instantly turned a warm smile in my direction.

"You're lovely," Nepra added.

"With wonderful taste in men," Tepu-yn agreed. "But watch out for this one." She pointed at Re. "He's sneaky. Too much time on his hands you see."

"Idle hands are the Sun God's playthings." Besa nodded.

"That's not the saying." Nepra grimaced.

"She changed it to fit, you ninny." Tepu-yn shook her head at her sister.

"Yes, these are my friends." Re sighed as if it pained him to admit it.

"Please call me Vervain," I said to them, and they all beamed at me in delight.

Chapter Eighteen

"I had fun. Thank you for introducing me to them," I said to Re as we walked back to his palace.

"They're very entertaining," he agreed. "And, you're welcome. I'm glad you enjoyed them."

"Do you have any other children?" I asked suddenly. "Or only the Twins?"

"I have a son too." He gave me a small smile. "Shu, God of Air. He doesn't visit very often, though."

"Makes sense," I said, "a sun god having an air god for a son."

"He married Tefnut, Goddess of Moisture," Re went on as he took my hand. It was an unconscious gesture, and I slid into that easy companionship as we headed into his palace and up the wide staircase to his bedroom.

"Moisture and Air." I gave a huffing sound of agreement. "That makes sense too. And I assume that they had children?"

"Oh, yes," he confirmed and closed the door behind us. "They are whom most of the main pantheon stems from. Teftnut and Shu had Nut, Goddess of the Sky, and she married Geb, who became God of Earth. Nut and Geb had Isis and Nepthys, whom you know already."

"Isis married Osiris and had Horus." I nodded.

"Yes." Re started swinging our hands a little. "They had three daughters as well, but they perished in the fall of Atlantis."

"Yeah, Thor told me. How awful to lose your children." I sympathized with Isis and Osiris but my thoughts were actually with Horus.

The loss of his sisters and his lover had made Horus standoffish with women, but he'd slowly warmed to me and now we were close friends. Hekate was helping him loosen up even further, and I was so relieved that Horus had finally found love.

"It *was* awful," Re went on. "For all of us." I gave his hand a gentle squeeze and he smiled down at me before continuing, "You know also of Nepthys and Set, how they married and had Anubis and Ma'at."

"So, you actually had most of your family with you when you left Atlantis," I observed.

"Yes." He nodded. "We were very lucky. It was pandemonium during the fall. Our family was separated at one point. I'd thought we'd lost Isis, Osiris, and Horus, but Odin saved them."

"Yes, I heard about that too," I whispered.

"Horus and Thor were close friends," Re added. "I'm glad they've kept their friendship strong for so long."

"I guess your family tree isn't as branched as it could be," I mused, trying to steer away from talk of Odin or Thor. "You could have had hundreds of great great grandchildren by now."

"Gods tend to go slowly on the procreation thing," he said. "You have a few children and that's it usually. As far as Horus and Anubis, well, you know of their issues, and Ma'at always looked after her brother. She never made time for a husband or children."

"Fenrir sure didn't go slowly." I chuckled. "That guy went crazy."

"Well, he was creating his own army, not just a family," Re pointed out and led me to the bed. "Fenrir did what he had to do to survive, and I understand that. You'll also recall that he left Atlantis long before it was destroyed."

"Forced from it, you mean," I corrected.

"Yes." Re's jaw clenched. "That was... a tragedy."

"He's a pretty great guy." I tried to still my wildly beating heart as I perched on the edge of the bed. Here we go. Would it be as good as the last time? Or had that been a fluke?

"You didn't sleep with him too, did you?" Re lifted a brow at me.

"What?!" I was shocked out of my apprehensions.

"I'm teasing." Re laughed as he eased towards the odd gold pole right beside the bed. "You're so sensitive about lineage."

"I'm sorry if I don't want to keep it *all in the family*," I huffed.

"Stay right there. I want to show you one more thing." He pulled the handle on top of the pole and a grinding sound started coming from beneath the bed.

"You can save some for later, you know?" I teased as I glanced around me in curiosity.

"The Sun is setting; I can feel it," Re said as he took a seat beside me.

Then the bed began to spin upward.

"What in the world?" I put both hands to the mattress

and stared at the floor.

The circle of stone beneath the bed was turning, lifting like an unwinding screw. My eyes shot up to the ceiling as the curtains around the bed shifted aside, and I saw that a circle shaped panel had descended, split in half, and then slid out to the sides. We continued to rise through that opening until we emerged on the roof of Re's palace; the gold floor piece sliding seamlessly into the hole in the ceiling. Which I guess was now the floor.

"I like to come up here to be alone sometimes," Re said softly.

"But you're not alone." I lifted a brow.

"I know." Re gave me a little smile. "This is the first time I've ever wanted to share it with someone."

"Thank you." I took his hand, and we looked out across the flat stone roof towards the setting Sun.

There was no railing up there, nothing to impede our view. Just three hundred sixty degrees of the Kingdom of Re. The falling Sun bathed the polished stone beneath us with its glow and turned it into a shimmering cloud, making it feel as if we were suspended in the sky. It was spectacular.

The fields were painted deep rose and pumpkin spice, turning them into a sunset sea. Grass bent in the breeze like waves coming in to shore and birds flew across the scene, dipping their feathers into the colors of the sleepy sun. Re eased back on the bed behind me so he could slide his legs around me and pull me in close to his chest. His arms came around my waist and his chin laid gently on top of my head. I could feel his heartbeat against my back and the scent of burning frankincense surrounded me. I closed my eyes for a second and when I opened them, the bright colors were gone, muted into the cool tones of twilight.

Something lifted inside my chest with happiness; my Moon. Now that my lioness was appeased, I could feel my other magics more intensely. It's like having a backache and getting a massage to work it out. As soon as your back feels better, you find that another part of your body hurts. You just never realized it was in pain because you were too focused on your back. Well, my backache was gone and now, I could feel other parts of me again.

The Moon knew that this was her time, her moment to shine. The Sun was a vain, glaring thing; demanding attention and respect like a king. But the Moon was his queen, and she had no need for such displays. Her beauty was more gentle; a soft, guiding light. Perhaps she didn't cause the fruit to swell upon the bough or the grain to sprout upon the shaft of wheat, but she did inspire the poets to write and the sweethearts to swoon. Her smile lured more men than Cleopatra; more than Helen of Troy, or even Aphrodite. More than any woman who has ever lived. She brings mystery to the night and leads lovers to their beds, creating life in her own seductive way.

"Your kingdom is mine now." I smiled wickedly back at Re as I threw a hand out and released the moon magic.

I'd inherited several aspects of the moon magic from Atahensic. One of them was Illusion and that was what I used to change the landscape. An ancient forest sprouted before us; trees taller than any on Earth. In the center of it, pennants flew, proclaiming that the High King was home in the Castle of Eight. Beyond the faerie forest, a mountain range appeared, tongues of lava oozing down it, bordering the carvings of Castle Aithinne. Then a golden dragon launched itself into the air and flew across the sky.

"Marvelous," Re whispered as he watched the flight of the dragon.

"I thought you might like to see Faerie." I shrugged.

"This is what Faerie looks like?" Re's eyes darted over the landscape.

"That's the Forgetful Forest." I indicated the massive trees. "And beyond it is Castle Aithinne, the border of the Fire Kingdom and my home."

"It's beautiful," he whispered. "You're not just the Queen of Fire, you're Queen of Illusions, my little Lah. And I have a feeling that you'll claim much more than my kingdom."

"Lah?" I let go of the illusion, allowing his world return to normal as I turned to him. I ignored the rest of what he'd said, it made me too nervous to think about.

"It means *moon* in Egyptian," he explained.

"But isn't there already a god named Lah?" I lifted a brow at him and smiled.

"There was," he mused. "But he died and was replaced by Khonsu."

"Then you can't call me Lah; the name already belongs to someone else." I thought about it and then declared, "Call me Lala. I love how silly it sounds. All of my other titles are so serious, even the romantic ones."

"Lala it is." Re leaned down and sealed our silliness with a kiss and then we let the Moon lure us together with her light.

Chapter Nineteen

"You wanna tell me what the throne is all about?" I asked as we descended into Re's bedroom... or maybe I should call it a boudoir.

"The throne?" He frowned as the ceiling halves clicked into place above us.

"The big golden chair over there." I pointed to his naughty nook.

"Oh!" he laughed. "That's not a throne, it's a sex chair."

"Of course it is." I rolled my eyes. "How did I not catch that?"

"It's quite comfortable." Re smiled wickedly. "Why don't you climb on it and let me give you a massage?"

"Said every frat boy to every girl they've ever gotten in their room," I scoffed.

"Just relax, Lala." He loved the new nickname and it made me smile.

Re used that moment of weakness to lure me over to the big golden throne... I mean; the sex chair.

It wasn't solid metal after all but had soft cushions covered in gold vinyl. Re pulled some levers and lowered the back of the chair flat then pulled some more and lifted the foot.

"It's a La-Z-Boy of love!" I laughed.

"It's for those moments that get too messy for a bed," he said and smirked. I was about to say something nasty when he went on, "Such as an oily massage." He slid around my back and started unzipping my dress. It slid to the floor with a whisper but when he went for my bra, I turned to grab his hand. "A massage is better without clothes," he said and smiled innocently.

"Yeah, I bet it is," I huffed and let him take off my underwear.

"Thank you." he stole a quick peek down my body before helping me onto the flattened chair.

I stretched out on my stomach and tried to relax as he fetched one of the bottles off a shelf. Re poured golden oil out into his palm and then rubbed his hands together. The scent of almonds drifted over to me. I closed my eyes as he set his hands on my back. He was damn good too; working at knots I didn't know I had. Soon, I'd forgotten where I was and what I was lying on. I was totally relaxed.

And that's when the pervert struck.

Re started to adjust the chair. A sliding maneuver with a lift had me kneeling; the back of the chair bent into an L. My knees were on the seat, and I was still lying across the back but that didn't last for long. I started to get up and protest his obvious ploy, but Re's hand went to the small of my back as his knees slid onto the wide seat between my own. My legs shifted apart as he eased forward, and I inhaled sharply as his hands slid beneath my belly and up to knead my breasts. Re pulled me up against his chest and continued to massage me as he set his teeth to my neck.

I was a goner. I don't even remember most of what happened after that. Just the slide of oiled flesh, the knead of expert fingers, and the scrape of teeth. I do recall the way he pushed me back down and told me to hold on, setting my hands to the top of the chair. What I'd previously thought were just carved adornments were actually handles. I held on, and Re slammed his cock into me violently. But no matter how forceful he got or how much I bucked back into him, that chair held firm. The angle was perfect and the cushions were thick enough that I was never uncomfortable. By the end, I was a convert. I liked the chair.

Much later that night, we made it back to the bed... after showering off all the oil. We were intimately enjoying each other once more—licking each other languorously as we laid on our sides—when a woman walked in. We probably wouldn't have even noticed her if she hadn't come to the foot of the bed and spoken to us.

"I apologize for the interruption, but you haven't answered any of my calls, you bad boy." She smirked as she enjoyed the display.

We had jumped apart in shock as soon as she'd spoken and I'd scrambled to the head of the bed beside Re and pulled the covers up to my neck; as one does when caught in flagrante delicto. Re, however, sighed when he saw who it was, and simply settled back onto the pillows without even bothering to cover his nudity.

"I haven't responded because I'm rather busy." He waved a hand towards me, and I gaped at him in horror.

"I see that." She licked her full lips and looked me over. "She seems to have a talented tongue."

"You have no idea." Re smirked.

The woman was a Hindu goddess but, oddly enough, I'd never met her before. I say oddly, because I've met hundreds of them and fought hundreds more. Well, Demigods, not Gods exactly, but still. It was strange that I didn't recognize her.

She looked strong; muscular arms shown off by a red cropped top and a hard stomach showing above her low-slung, flowing skirt. She had deep, golden skin and probably looked perfect next to Re. Long obsidian hair hung in a thick braid down her back and the eyes scrutinizing me matched the color of her hair exactly.

"Who is this?" I looked to Re for an explanation.

"Vervain." Re waved a hand at the woman. "Durga. Durga, meet Vervain. You may know her as the Godhunter."

"The Godhunter?" Durga looked even more interested, coming to sit on the edge of the bed. "Well done!" She glanced at Re then back at me. "We've never met, but you're friends with my daughter; Sarasvati."

"Sara's your daughter?" I sat forward in surprise.

"Yes." Durga smiled wide. "And she thinks very highly of you. You've been a good influence on Brahma."

"Hardly," I huffed. "Brahma doesn't listen to anyone but Sara."

"More so now that he's friends with you," Durga insisted. "So"—she looked from Re to me—"care if I join in? I have talents to offer." She held out her arms and six more appeared, taking up her entire torso. She wiggled her fingers as she stuck her tongue out at me... a very long tongue.

"Uh." I felt my eyes go wide.

"Are you up for it?" Re lifted a brow at me.

"Up for it?" I immediately snapped out of my shock and snarled at him. "No; I'm not up for it, you asshole."

"Wait," he said and frowned. "You're not even open to having another woman in bed with the both of us? You can have all of your husbands, but I can't even have one woman to *share* with you?"

"Well, that's not fair." Durga pouted.

"No; it's not fair," I agreed as I slid out of the bed, taking the sheet with me. "And I told him how unfair it would be *before* I slept with him."

"So, it's okay because you told me?" Re snapped. "You didn't tell me we couldn't at least share a woman together."

"I thought it was a given when I told you that I *don't share*!" I snapped back.

"Oh, I like her, Re." Durga sighed in delight. "She's fiery."

"You have no idea," I said in a low voice.

"Oh, my darling"—she laughed—"but I do. I know all about your dragon nature. It's very exciting. Would you mind shifting for me?"

"Yes; I do mind!" I growled and turned back to Re. "Obviously, this was a mistake. I thought you could commit yourself to one woman but, evidently, you can't... which is totally fine. Do your thing! Rock the super god bed and your adjustable sex throne." I waved a hand at the chair. "I'll be more careful in my next choice... and more *clear*."

"Damn it, Vervain!" Re crawled out of bed and started to come forward. "There has to be some middle ground we can reach. Be reasonable."

"Reasonable?" I huffed. "I'm talking about commitment. I know it's a weird situation, but I'm faithful to my men, and they're faithful to me. No one gets into bed with us who isn't a part of that commitment."

"So, you'd be okay with another woman as long as I committed to her too?" Re shot back.

"No!" I screamed. "Were you not paying attention? This isn't a fair arrangement. I'm sorry but that's just how it is. I told you about my beasts. We're possessive and unreasonable and there's no middle ground for us. This is me; take me or leave me. In fact, I'll save you the hassle and leave you!"

I turned around, wrapping the sheet around myself like a toga, and walked out. Re didn't follow me.

Chapter Twenty

"We have a problem," Trevor said as I walked into our bedroom. Then he saw what I was wearing and frowned. "More than one, evidently."

"You could say that." I grimaced.

"What happened?" He pulled out a chair from our little dining set, and I slid into it, folding my sheet around my legs.

"Durga walked in on us having sex and tried to join in," I said.

"Durga?" Trevor blinked.

"Durga is Sarasvati's mother," I said blandly.

"What was Sara's mother doing at Re's palace?" Trevor sat down beside me.

"What do you think?" I gave him a look, and his eyes widened. "Re hadn't been returning her calls so she came for a visit and found us in a... private moment. And this is after he implied that he didn't sleep with women more than once."

"Oh, no," Trevor whispered.

"Yep," I took a deep breath. "And it gets worse."

"No." Trevor gaped at me. "He didn't."

"Oh, yes he did," I confirmed.

"He wanted her to join you?" Trevor was mortified,

bless his little, loyal, wolf heart.

"Yep." I nodded.

"Nyet," Kirill said from behind us. "He vill die."

"It's fine," I waved Kirill into a seat. "He's right; this situation isn't fair. I understand why he thought he could at least have another woman if he shared her with me."

"That's not who you are." Trevor frowned. "Did you even discuss sex before you had it?"

"Not really." I sighed. "I guess I should have mentioned that I'm not bisexual, but I didn't think I needed to after I told him I expected him to be faithful. I thought all that was kinda self-explanatory."

"I guess not." Trevor grimaced.

"Ve vill find someone else." Kirill stroked my shoulder gently and leaned down to kiss my cheek.

"At least you've had something to tide you over," Trevor offered. "It buys us a little time."

"Yeah; you're right." I was suddenly sad.

The anger was wearing off, and I was remembering all we'd shared. It wasn't much in the scheme of things but it still seemed like a lot at the moment. I had thought that I'd finally found someone to take Odin's place in my heart and now, I had to start over. But maybe that was where I'd gone wrong. No one could take Odin's place. I would forever have an emptiness inside me that belonged to him, and I needed to come to terms with that before I could move on.

"Oh, damn it," Trevor growled. "You have feelings for him already, don't you?"

"I'll get over it." I waved it away resolutely. "Now, what were you going to tell me when I first walked in?"

"Are you sure you want to deal with this now?" Trevor asked with a concerned look.

"I'm happy for a distraction," I admitted.

"All right." Trevor shared a grim glance with Kirill. "Things have heated up in Afghanistan again, and we believe we know who's responsible for it."

"Who?" I asked, my heartache instantly shoved aside.

"A trio of gods," Trevor began. "The first is Gish, he's an Afghani war god."

"And zen zere's Qaus," Kirill added. "He's Arabian, God of Veather and Rainbows."

"Rainbows?" I couldn't help a small smile. "Is he also the God of the Gays?"

"Nyet," Kirill said seriously, making me roll my eyes. "He is closer to Zor, vith zunderbolts."

"Zunderbolts and lightning, very, very fright—" I stopped singing when I saw their faces. "It had to be done," I whined. "Come on, it's funny."

"I vish you'd stop making fun of my accent." Kirill sighed deeply.

"Really?" I was instantly contrite. "I'm so sorry, sweetheart. I thought you didn't mind. I—" Then I saw his lips twitch. "Damn it, Kirill!" I slapped him. "You had me worried."

"I know you zink accent is sexy." He smiled smugly. "Your teasing is actually flirting."

"Okay, good," I said. "So, moving on; who's the third god?"

"It's a goddess," Trevor took over. "She's the supreme goddess of the Kafir. Her name is Disani."

"Like the bottled water?" I tried very hard to keep a straight face.

"I zink zat's Dasani," Kirill said.

"Close enough." I waved my hand. "Oh, this is just perfect!" I exclaimed. "I'll need to prepare a list of insults before we go after them."

"Vervain," Trevor groaned.

"What?" I huffed. "I hate being unprepared, especially when there's such good material to work with."

"Gish wears a quiver that has a rainbow sling," Trevor admitted. Like pulling off a Band-Aid, I think he wanted to get it all out there at once.

"Wait." I blinked in shocked delight. "One is the God of Rainbows and the other *wears* rainbows?! Oh, it's a Christmas miracle!" I clapped my hands.

"It's not Christmas." Kirill frowned.

"It's a saying." Trevor shook his head at my lion.

"Let's see." I tapped my lips with a fingernail. "Rainbow Twins. Yes, yes; that's good." I got up and started heading towards the intercom. "Rainbow Brite? Oh, I like that. But the water thing; I think I'll have to go watch some Dasani commercials for that."

"Minn Elska?" Trevor called.

"Yes?" I turned around.

"What are you doing?" He asked.

"Telling whoever's on duty downstairs to text the Squad," I said as if it were obvious. "We need to have a meeting."

Chapter Twenty-One

"Damn Isis," Pan growled. "Horus, tell your mother to stop killing Arabs."

"It's not my mother," Horus snapped, "as you very well know."

"And she's not killing Arabs," I added with a chuckle. "That's a Cure song, by the way. ISIS is *a group of* Arabs."

"Horus, tell your mommy to stop stirring up the Arabs," Pan corrected.

"I'm going to stir up your intestines with a fork if you don't stop talking about my mother!" Horus' metallic eyes, one gold and one silver, glinted with menace.

Looking at Horus now, I wondered if he'd inherited the golden eye from his great great grandfather. I knew the myths spoke about Horus' right eye being connected to Re, and that was Horus' golden eye. His left eye, the silver one, was supposed to be connected to the Moon. Then there was that whole Eye of Re/Eye of Horus thing. From what I'd read, they were interchangeable, basically the same thing; an amulet of an eye adorned to represent a hawk's eye—yes, those weird swooping lines were meant to imitate the way a bird's eye looks—and was used for protection. But Re had told me that both of his daughters were also called *The Eye of Re*. It was damn confusing. How many eyes could one god have?

Then again, now that I think about it, some myths portray Azrael as covered in eyes and tongues. He's also supposed to have four faces and four thousand wings. Now, I ask you; how would that even be possible? Four *thousand* wings! Where would they all attach? Unless they were teeny tiny wings. But the eyes? That's just gross. How would he sit down? I swear, sometimes I think people make stuff up without considering how they would actually work. I've come across quite a few descriptions of ridiculous forms which humans have tried to give their gods. Thank goodness the Gods don't have to follow the myths precisely.

"Oh, you're so hot when you get angry," Horus' girl-friend, Kate, AKA Hekate, said and brought me out of my eye-ball musings.

Hekate knew Horus so well—had him wrapped around her little finger—and easily dissipated his anger with her smile. I was ecstatic that he'd found her. Or rather, *she* found *him*. Kate had been the one to practically club Horus over the head and drag him home by his short hair.

"Thank you." Horus slid an arm around Kate.

He was dressed in a suit, and she was in Goth nightclub wear. They looked ridiculous sitting together but yet perfect somehow.

"Can we get back to the more pressing matter?" Thor asked. "I'd like to get home at a reasonable hour."

"Is that you or your wife talking?" Blue smirked.

"As if it's any different for you," Thor shot back, turning Blue's smirk into a scowl.

"I *choose* to go home early." Blue straightened the cuffs on his black, cotton, dress shirt. "It just happens to coincide with her desires."

"Soooo," I drawled, "what are we going to do about

this?"

"What did your man on the inside say again?" Hades asked Trevor.

Hades didn't have to get home anytime soon. His wife, Persephone, was sitting right next to him.

"He's not my man on the inside," Trevor huffed. "He's a froekn who happened to be traveling through Afghanistan."

"Why?" Teharon asked with genuine concern.

Teharon's a healer, and I'd rarely seen him behave in an unkind manner. His girlfriend, Karni Mata, is almost as sweet as he is, but she's the Goddess of Rats and that tends to put people off. Not Teharon, though. He loved her more than anything.

"Sightseeing," Trevor said simply.

We all stared at him in shock.

"He's a werewolf." Trevor shrugged. "War isn't a big deal for us. In fact, it can be the equivalent of an amusement park."

"Valid point," I conceded.

"He spotted Gish and recognized him," Trevor went on. "So, he followed him. Dave wasn't on the inside, just in the right place at the right time."

"Great," Morpheus, AKA the Greek God of Dreams, ran a hand through his short, ebony hair. "And he heard Gish talking to his cohorts about instigating a war. So what? Gods do that all the time."

"And we try to stop them," I reminded him.

"I know," Morph huffed, crossing lean muscled arms over his chest. "What I meant was; why is this so alarming? Why is *this* time special enough that we need to act on it immediately?"

"Did you miss the part where I said they were working both sides?" Trevor asked. "How the Gods are helping to supply weapons to both ISIS and the Afghan National Army?"

"So, we stop their arms dealings?" Morpheus asked.

"No, that won't do much good," Thor mused. "They're intending on causing a battle of such gigantic proportions that it destroys both armies. A plan like that will have backup plans. There will be numerous suppliers, I'm sure."

"Where's the attack going to be?" I asked Trevor.

"Kabul," he said, "where else?"

"I don't know." I rolled my eyes. "I'm not an expert on Afghani cities... Afghan cities... Afghanistan cities... whatever."

"Definitely not an expert," Horus muttered.

"They're slowly infiltrating both armies," Hekate observed. "I've heard that the Afghan National Police force is dirty; quite a few of them are drug users and a quarter of them quit every year."

"They're not the only dirty ones," Brahma added, stroking his close-cropped beard thoughtfully. "The Afghan National Army has high officials who regularly take bribes or otherwise use their position to enrich themselves."

"ISIS would be harder to infiltrate," Teharon said. "Those are people who are acting out of strong beliefs."

"Religion." I shook my head.

"These are extremists," Blue protested. "They're not true followers of Islam."

"Yeah, I get that," I agreed. "Still, religion is at the base of this."

"Is it?" Blue mused. "Or is it about power and oppression?"

"Things you know all about." Hades smirked at Blue.

"Well, isn't that the pot calling the kettle Blue?" I shot back before Blue could get mad.

"Fair enough." Hades lowered his dark shades so he could wink at me, giving me a glimpse of Hell through the brown-tinted window panes of his irises. Cheeky bastard.

"Can we get back to stopping mass destruction?" Thor sighed.

"Let's," I agreed and looked at Trevor. "Does Dave know where Gish is now? And does he have any other information that could help us?"

"He's been keeping an eye on them for us." Trevor huffed a laugh. "I think he's having fun; it reminds him of the days when we were assassins."

"Good times." I grimaced.

"Wolves need to hunt," Trevor said unapologetically. "It's in our blood."

"So, we'll know where to find Gish," Thor got us on track again. "But you said Gish mentioned two others; Qaus and Disani."

"Qaus is working with ISIS, Gish with the Afghan Police, and Disani is serving as a go between," Trevor explained.

"Makes sense." Thor nodded. "Qaus is Arabian."

"God of the Gays," I added with a straight face.

"Excuse me?" Thor frowned at me.

"Ignore her," Trevor said. "We're having issues with finding a replacement for Odin, and Vervain has gotten twitchy."

Thor swallowed roughly and looked away.

"Sorry." Trevor grimaced. "I wasn't thinking. I know you must miss your father."

"He left a lot more than Vervain's bed," Thor rumbled, casting me an angry glance.

"Yes, he did." I leaned across the table towards Thor. "And we know that; of course, we do. This is a personal issue I'm having—"

"*We're* having," Trevor corrected.

"A personal issue *we're* having." I shot an exasperated look at Trevor. "And we're not going to let it interfere with the God War. I'll be fine."

"Da, but Re is fool." Kirill shook his head.

"Re?" Horus straightened in surprise.

"Yes, Re," I said and sighed. I'd been hoping to not have to address this at all since it now looked as if Re wasn't going to be a part of my life... at least not in that way.

"He was being considered for..." Horus looked as if he was choking.

"For her next lover." Kate gave him a pat on the back. "Ease up, Sweetheart; it's just sex."

"Not vith Vervain, it isn't." Kirill grinned.

"Girl, you gotta tell me your secret one of these days." Kate chuckled. "What is it; lined in gold or something?"

"Well, that would make sex uncomfortable," I shot back, and she laughed harder. "I think they'd run screaming."

"Re is my grandfather!" Horus exclaimed, sending Kate a quelling look.

"Oh, damn!" Hekate gaped at me. "You were gonna sleep

with Horus' grandpa?"

"Have you met Re?" Persephone waggled her brows at Hekate.

"Good point, girl." Kate leaned over to fist bump Persephone. "That man is like a woman's wet dream."

"Technically, Re's his great great grandpa," I corrected. "And I *did* sleep with him."

Horus started to make strangled noises.

"Damn!" Hekate hooted. "You go, girl!" She reached across the table to fist bump me next.

Horus started to turn red.

"Relax." Kate knocked him in the shoulder. "We're gods, it's not as if she were screwing a wrinkly old man."

"He's still my grandfather," Horus spoke in a strained whimper.

"Great great grandfather," Kate corrected. "Two greats equals a lot of space."

"And by the way, Brahma"—I looked over at the Hindu god who was completely fascinated by the conversation —"your mother-in-law is a freak."

"Are you referring to her ability to manifest multiple arms or her sexual appetite?" Brahma cocked his head at me.

"Yes." I nodded, and he laughed uproariously.

"Could we perhaps move on from Vervain's gold-plated vagina and Brahma's sexually deviant mother-in-law?" Thor asked dryly, making everyone burst into more bouts of laughter. "Come on, people; this is serious."

"You just said the words *gold-plated vagina*." I pointed at Thor. "You are now officially part of the silliness."

"I am not!" He pulled himself upright.

"So much silliness." I shook my head as we all continued to laugh.

"Look what you've done," Blue accused Thor. "Now, we'll both be home late which means that neither of us will be having sex tonight."

They sighed together, doomed men, and the rest of us laughed harder.

Chapter Twenty-Two

I didn't expect Kabul to be cold.

"Why is it snowing?" I whined as I stoked my internal temperature up to such a high degree that I started steaming. The Gods around me huddled closer.

"Because it's Winter." Thor rolled his eyes. He had no problem with the cold. Damn Nordic giant. He was like a yeti without fur. A hairless yeti.

"But I thought Afghanistan was a desert." I looked around the snow-covered streets and then up to the snow-capped Hindu Kush mountains that surrounded Kabul. "Deserts are supposed to be hot, aren't they? It's definitely not supposed to snow in the desert."

"Ve are at high elevation," Kirill explained.

"Oh, damn; you're handy to have around!" Kate sighed as she eased into the circle of gods gathered around me as if I were a space heater. I guess I kinda was. "I understand why they all love you," she went on. "In fact, I think I'm in love with you now. Will you marry me, Vervain?"

"Shut up!" I laughed. Snow melted as I passed over it, and we ended up walking through puddles but the heat was worth it.

"I can't help it." She slid closer. "Cold makes me crazy. I'm an Underworld goddess; I like it hot."

"So do I." But then I frowned and looked over at her. "The Greek Underworld isn't hot."

"Tartarus is." She smirked wickedly.

"True enough," I agreed, remembering my one journey through the actual Greek Hell, which laid beneath the Underworld; a sort of Under-Underworld. That was one place I hoped to never visit again.

"Here's where Dave is staying." Trevor led us off the slushy street and up a wide path.

The cement walkway had garden plots running down the center and along its sides but all the plants were covered in cloth for the Winter. Still, it was pretty and halfway down it, the space opened up to a fountain filled with frozen water and snow. It was like walking through the gardens of some magnificent French palace in the dead of Winter.

A hotel loomed at the end of the frozen path. Made of a creamy beige stone and boxy, it looked luxurious yet subdued. As if it couldn't decide whether to be a shopping mall or a five star hotel. But the sedate stone exterior hid a Middle Eastern wonderland. I gaped as we walked into the lavish lobby to be immediately greeted by a well-dressed member of the staff. He welcomed us to the Kabul Serena Hotel and then directed us through the lobby, barely eyeing our strange group.

Still rather boxy, the lobby was much more elegant than I'd expected. Several massive, crystal chandeliers hung from the wood-beamed ceiling and lots of comfortable couches had been scattered around to lounge on. We walked past arches that soared over intricately patterned stone floors and inhaled the aroma of exotic food as we made our way to the elevators. I turned down the heat as soon as we entered and was quite comfortable as I stepped into the spacious elevator that was big enough to fit us all.

We went up to Dave's floor, casting impressed looks at each other. Then we padded down a thick carpet, through a softly-lit hallway to his room. Dave answered our knock immediately, as if he'd been standing there waiting for us, and waved us into his suite. The Middle-Eastern décor continued there but in a more sedate, hotel room fashion.

Modern furniture upholstered in richly patterned textiles lazed about, made even more luxurious by the beautiful carvings done in all the wood accents, like the headboard and the border around the large window. The view through that window was spectacular but it was the room itself that we all stared at in shock. It wasn't nearly the nicest hotel room I'd ever seen, kind of modest in size and without a balcony, but it was far better than I'd been expecting to find in Kabul. And everyone seemed to share my opinion.

"Now, I see why you're vacationing here," I said to Dave.

"Though why you chose this time of year is beyond me," Horus grumbled.

"Reduced rates." Dave shrugged. "Plus, we wolves don't mind the cold."

"This isn't just cold." Hades sniffed. "This is Arctic. This is frigid. This is—"

"Hell?" I asked with a smile.

"Indeed." Hades lifted his dark brows. "Though I think Helheim would be a more accurate description."

"That's uncomfortably true." Trevor grimaced.

Helheim was named after its ruler, Hel, who also happened to be Trevor's Aunt... who had once attempted to keep him trapped in her cold castle of the dead. Yeah, it's as bad as it sounds.

"It's not that cold. I've been to the Arctic and it's much

173

colder," Dave said and then motioned us to the large bed, where he'd laid out a bunch of photographs. "Here's where Gish and his group have made their headquarters." He pointed at a nondescript building. "There are about sixty men there, no biggie, but I hope you've come up with some kind of plan because starting a god fight in the middle of downtown Kabul isn't such a good idea."

"I could always go dragon on them," I offered.

"No!" Everyone shouted.

"Joking." I laughed and held up my hands in apology.

"We don't know what kind of explosives they have in there," Dave added. "One wrong breath and you could take out the entire city of Kabul all by yourself."

"I said I was joking," I huffed.

"Did you get anything on where the other two gods are hiding?" Trevor asked Dave.

"Yeah; Qaus has ISIS with him at a location deep in the mountains," Dave said. "I tracked Disani back to another spot in the desert. That seems to be the gods' personal stronghold."

"We'll have to split up so we can attack both armies at the same time," Thor said. "We can't risk one god warning the other."

"Good point," Blue agreed.

"But how are we doing this?" Dave asked.

"I can sneak into the building and put all of the humans to sleep," Teharon offered. "No one has to die."

The room went quiet again.

"Teha," Karni Mata slid her hand over Teharon's, the nickname sounding so exotic on her lips. "Leaving them alive may not be the best decision. They have been tainted by greed and anger."

"That doesn't mean they can't recover from it." Teharon frowned at us. "These are innocents; humans manipulated by Gods. Are we really just going to slaughter them?"

"Teharon is right," I said. "Killing these people would be wrong and would accomplish exactly what these Gods want."

"Death." Hades nodded. "We kill these people and it will only make the Gods stronger. They'll take the deaths as sacrifice."

"So, we need to find a way to get to the Gods without injuring their followers," Pan mused. "That's going to be difficult."

"And we'll have to destroy their weapon stores," Finn added, his voice lilting with just the touch of an Irish accent.

"Maybe Teharon putting the humans to sleep isn't such a bad idea," I said.

"But he can't be in two places at once." Torrent lifted a blond brow. "And we need to attack both gods at the same time."

"Torrent"—I cocked my head at the Internet God —"could you unmake the magic that's been cast on the humans?"

"You mean the influence these gods have impressed upon them?" Torrent blinked in surprise and then thought about it. "I think I could, if it really is a magical influence, but I don't know how long it would take or how close I'd have to get to unmake the magic. Plus, I'd have to unmake each spell individually."

"Do you think there are individual spells cast on each person?" Artemis asked her boyfriend. "Or do you think they did a blanket spell of influence? These people probably didn't need a lot of encouraging, just a little nudge to choose these Gods to lead them."

"Hmm," Torrent considered. "If that's true, I could probably undo it from a distance. Magic cast upon a group of people tends to ripple out in an effort to keep everyone within its grasp."

"Okay," Thor said decisively. "Torrent, we need you to go with a group into the mountains and attempt to neutralize the enchantment. Teharon can go with the other group who will handle the Afghan Police here in Kabul, and he will attempt to put as many of the humans to sleep as possible."

"And what if I can't unmake the magic?" Torrent asked nervously.

"Why don't we have Torr try to do his thing first?" I suggested. "We'll keep in communication with each other and only attack if Torr manages to undo the spell. If he doesn't, we meet back here and brainstorm a new plan."

"I like that idea." Thor nodded.

"There may still be some casualties," I said gently to Teharon.

Teharon sighed and hung his head, his long, straight hair falling like a curtain around his sad but beautiful turquoise eyes. His wide shoulders slumped, and he took Karni's hand as he nodded in acceptance. The most difficult part of seeing Teharon's reaction was that I knew I had once felt the same way but now, after years of fighting this war, I wasn't as sensitive to the possibility of human casualties. I didn't want them, but I wasn't naive enough to think that a plan should be tossed out because of the chance of humans dying. I had learned to look at the bigger picture.

"It's better than just assassinating them," Teharon said

quietly. "And at least I'll be there to help the wounded when it's all over."

I guess Teharon wasn't naive either, just sympathetic.

"But what about ISIS?" Blue asked. "Those are violent people, to begin with, and even if Torrent can unmake the magic influencing them, they'll still be angry men under attack. They're not just going to lay down their weapons and run away."

"And let's not forget that only one team will have the Godhunter," Brahma noted with a sardonic twist of his lips.

"So?" I shot back.

"So, you're the one who's able to kill Gods easily," Thor reminded me. "The rest of us have a harder time at it."

"Only extreme emotion makes it possible for us to kill each other," Blue added. "And we aren't nearly angry enough for that."

"But together, we'll have enough magic that it should make up for our lack of anger," Morpheus said reasonably. "I know you've all killed Gods before."

We went silent because everyone knew who Morpheus was referring to; his father.

"True enough," I whispered. "I think you'll handle things just fine without me. Besides, you'll have Torrent. He's even better than a Godhunter."

"I am?" Torrent looked baffled.

"You really don't understand what kind of power you hold with that unmaking thing, do you?" Artemis shook her head at him.

"But I don't really have a magic that's good in a fight." Torrent grimaced.

"What you've got is enough." Thor placed a hand on Torr's shoulder. "And you do well with hand-to-hand combat."

"All I can do is shift into a swan," Finn said. "And that's not at all helpful in a god fight."

"You can hold your own," I said to Finn, remembering the time he and his siblings killed a faerie who had cursed them.

"Yeah, I do all right." He chuckled.

"Well, I'm not afraid of facing another god without the Godhunter beside me." Hades took his wife's hand. "Persephone and I will go into the mountains with Torrent. Who's with us?"

"Let's go with them," Hekate said to Horus. "I want to see the mountains."

"In this cold?" I asked her. "I'm glad I'm staying here."

"One snowy mountain is the same as any other," Hekate immediately said to Horus. "Let's stay with the Godheater... I mean; the Godhunter."

"Whatever you want, Katie." Horus laughed.

"I'm going with you, of course," Artemis said to Torrent.

"Okay." Torrent's green eyes brightened as he smiled at his girl.

They were actually dressed for cold weather. Both of them had thick jackets, gloves, and ski caps on.

"How did you know to wear all that, by the way?" I asked them.

"It's February." Artemis gave me a *duh* face.

"She checked the weather on the Internet." Torrent grinned.

"And you didn't think to mention it to us?" I lifted a brow.

"No, I didn't." he shrugged. "You're Gods, I thought you had it covered."

"Torr, in the future, speak up." I rolled my eyes. "And you're a god too, by the way."

"More of a demigod, I think," Torr mused.

"Either way, you're one of us," Morpheus declared. "So, next time, share the info."

"You got it." Torrent smiled brightly.

We split up the rest of the Squad; Blue, Finn, Brahma, Morpheus, Mr. T, and Mrs. E would go with Hades, Persephone, Torrent, and Artemis while Teharon, Karni Mata, Horus, Kate, Thor, and Pan would go with me, Trevor, Kirill and Dave. Azrael had his own work to take care of so he wasn't there, but I thought we had enough gods that we'd be okay.

Chapter Twenty-Three

We were not okay.

Torrent had indeed been able to unmake the spell influencing the members of ISIS so we'd gone ahead and sent Teharon in to deal with the Afghan Police. He had managed to put most of them to sleep but then he'd been spotted and the remaining police had run off to warn their god. We rushed in to help Teharon and found ourselves in the middle of a gun fight. Except we didn't have any guns.

"Damn; we should have waited for Azrael," I growled as I crouched behind a crate and hid from rapid gunfire.

I'd probably be fine if I got hit by a few bullets but they had machine guns and if they managed to fire enough bullets at my neck, they could potentially behead me. Or they could obliterate my heart. I'm not sure if that would kill me but it would definitely sting a bit.

"Why do you think Azrael could have helped?" Trevor asked.

"Aren't his wings bulletproof?" I shot back.

"Several gods can be bulletproof," he said.

"What the hell does that mean?" I frowned over at him.

"Most gods have the ability to cast wards around themselves," Trevor explained. "Vervain, how do you not know this? I thought Thor taught you god magic?"

"Thor just taught me how to shield my mind," I grumbled. "He never said anything about shielding my body. I taught myself god magic from Ku's spellbook."

"I thought you'd figure it out on your own," Thor shouted over the gunfire at me. "Plus, it didn't seem necessary at the time."

"Does it seem necessary now?" I shouted back.

"Damn it all; can you do something about this, Teharon?" Thor asked the Mohawk god.

"Not from this distance," Teharon replied calmly.

"Can we get back to the bulletproof thing?" I huffed. "I shot Blue once and it just bounced off his chest. You could have told me then that it wasn't his villainous god superpower!"

"I didn't know you shot Blue," Thor rumbled. "You're a witch, Vervain, you can figure it out for yourself. It's just a tight ward laid over your skin. Visualize metal plating, just like the ward in your mind."

"Well, it's not as if I can practice it now," I muttered.

"And it's not even a sure thing that you'd be able to," Trevor added.

"Tima can do it," Kirill scoffed.

"It doesn't matter!" Horus yelled with extreme annoyance. "A ward could hold under a few bursts of bullets but it won't under this kind of an attack. If it did, I'd be out there already."

"Oh, please." Kate rolled her eyes. "We're gods."

She was sitting beside Horus, casually picking at her nails as pieces of wooden crate rained down around her. She stopped to brush some debris off her shoulder before looking up at us with a bored expression.

"What?" She huffed. "Throw some magic at them, you idiots. And if that doesn't work, I can open a path through the Aether that will let us out right behind them."

I grimaced, looking from Kirill to Trevor. We *were* idiots. Somehow, the gunfire had thrown us. It just wasn't something we dealt with very often. Most times when we fought against humans, they'd take one look at us and start to cower. Or run. It was a rare occurrence to have them pick up guns and start shooting. Rare enough to shock us and send us ducking for cover when we should have been throwing something back at them. That'll teach us for running in half-cocked *and* cocky.

Thunder rumbled as Thor held out his arms and lightning cracked through one of the dingy windows, straight into his glowing palm. He stood and cast the electricity across the room at our enemies. It burst into their makeshift shield of crates and tables, splintering it all while setting it on fire.

"Thor!" I shouted. "Remember that there could be explosives in here."

"Well, that's my magic," he grumbled as he hid behind the crates again. "What do you want me to do?" His massive shoulders hunched in as he sulked.

In response to Thor's outburst, Gish stood; giving us all a great view of a thick, chestnut-colored chest covered only by a sparkling rainbow stripe attached to his quiver. He glowered at us with his ponderous, warrior features and pulled a shiny arrow from the quiver on his back. Within seconds, the arrow came flying straight at Thor.

The crates Thor had been shielding himself with splintered apart as if the arrow had actually been a grenade. Thor, Karni Mata, and Teharon went flying back as debris shot out in all directions.

"Someone blast him!" Thor shouted as he rolled to his feet and helped Teharon get Karni behind the cover I was sharing with Trevor and Kirill.

"Just hold on." I held up a hand. "Let's think—"

"I got this," Pan said and flung his own magic over the pile of scrap metal he was hiding behind.

We all froze as Pan's magic hit and a group of men started to panic. Gunfire lessened and then stopped entirely as the unaffected men tried to calm their comrades. Gish disappeared behind a stack of crates with an angry shout. Then a horrible screaming began, and we all stood up to launch our own magical assaults. Trevor and Kirill leapt over our barricade, shifting as they went, and crossed the cluttered space separating us from Gish and his crew in moments. Soon more screaming was heard.

I felt the Moon rise within me as a cool energy filled my fingers. Every god magic was actually a collection of magics that were aspects of the whole. The moon magic had been slow to reveal itself to me, and I was convinced that there were facets to it which I still didn't know about, but what I had learned was worth the wait. There was Water Mastery; control over any amount of the stuff, be it a glassful or an ocean, Dark Dominion; which gave me control over nocturnal animals, Illusion; which is the ability to project any image I created out into the world, and Lunacy; which is actually another type of water manipulation. The human body is mostly composed of water, and I could exert a pull on that water, shifting it around until it drove a person mad. Which is exactly what I did to those men.

"Now, that's what I'm talking about!" Kate nodded in approval as she came to stand beside me and watch the chaos unfold.

"Well done," Horus agreed, his left eye glowing white. I assumed it was in response to my moon magic.

I pondered his reaction for a moment. Gods who held the power of the Sun usually felt drawn to me and when I used moon magic, it enhanced my allure. The fact that Horus didn't seem to feel an attraction was something I'd never considered before. I guess I thought of his lack of interest as a blessing and didn't want to look a gift Horus in the mouth. But now, I was curious.

Then Horus laid his hand on my shoulder and it all became clear.

A rush of power filled me, enhancing my own and burgeoning up my Moon until it once more burst from my hands to surge across the warehouse. Screaming turned into wailing as Trevor and Kirill raced back to us. They came to a stop at my side, both panting as they stared across the room in horror.

"What happened?" I asked as my limbs shook with the remnants of my super-charged magic.

"They're tearing each other to bits," Trevor whispered. "Gish is trying to stop them, but they began to attack him as well. He had to kill some of his own men."

I looked over at Horus, and he gave me a wicked grin.

"You don't hold any moon magic, do you?" I asked him.

Horus shook his head. "I was supposed to be a god of balance; Protection and War, Sun and Moon. But mainly, I was meant to help Re. I'm his right hand man, as it were." He indicated his right eye, which flashed gold briefly. "I can enhance his sun abilities, although I hold no sun magic of my own. Just as I can enhance moon abilities."

"Damn, Baby." Kate smirked. "And I'm a moon goddess. We're perfect for each other."

"You're a moon goddess too?" I asked her in surprise.

"Yep," she said. "Magic, Moon, Ghosts, Crossroads, and Necromancy; if it's Goth, I got it."

"Well, that makes sense." I looked over her piercings and purple hair.

"I detest that name." Horus rolled his eyes. "It has nothing to do with its source."

"Darling, please don't start that again." Kate grimaced.

"The Goths were a barbaric race who migrated from Scandinavia to Pomerania and then on to the Black Sea, where they ransacked and generally terrorized people. What does that have to do with the way you're dressed?"

"Wait." I blinked in surprise. "There's a place called Pomerania? Is that where those little dogs come from?"

"Focus!" Thor snarled at us before Horus could answer me (probably snidely).

The shrieking had faded to moans, and we all stared across the room to see that Gish was standing in a field of rubble and corpses. He stared at us with wide eyes, his body covered in blood and his chest heaving.

"Never mind; I got this," Thor growled as he strode by us.

We all followed Thor halfway across the room, stopping well before we reached Gish. No one wanted to go wading through dead bodies. Especially *those* dead bodies. I've seen a lot of gruesome things in my time but that sea of rendered flesh and ruptured organs had to be on my top ten most gory list.

Thor stepped over the corpses as if they were puddles, just minor obstacles in his path. Gish didn't move at all, just watched Thor approach with wide eyes. For a minute there, I thought Gish would be an easy conquest, that Thor would simply grab him and whisk him away.

Boy was I wrong.

Gish may have been surprised by the gore, but he wasn't standing still because he was horrified. On the contrary, he was absorbing all that delicious magic those sacrifices were giving him. His eyes closed briefly, and he sighed in delight... right before he smashed his fist into Thor's face. For the second time that day, Thor went sailing... and not in a boat. Nope, he sailed through the air on a straight course for our group, which had thoughtfully gathered together and made an easy target for Gish.

We lurched apart, several of us falling down completely in our haste to not be hit by the Thunder God, and Thor smashed into a pile of chairs. I scampered back to my feet and started forward, but Gish was already gone.

"Sons of Anarchy!" I shouted and stomped my foot. "And I didn't even get to use any of my lines."

Chapter Twenty-Four

Hades and his team hadn't caught any gods either but not due to distraction. Neither Qaus nor Disani had been at the mountain hideout. Hades' group did wipe out the facility and destroy all the weapons, as our group had done at our location, but with all the villainous gods on the run, it was obvious that this wasn't over.

Their team surprisingly didn't have as many human casualties as we had. Once the ISIS humans had seen what Gods could do, they had run off screaming. Blue had been smart enough to catch one of the humans for interrogation and so he'd at least come back with information on more ISIS hideouts. The man Blue interrogated didn't know all of the locations but still, the list was a long one. As Blue began to go over it, I fell back into a seat, overwhelmed by the magnitude of the task.

"That's a lot of places to clean out." I exhaled roughly as Teharon came over and gently laid a hand on my shoulder. I looked down and saw that I'd been shot. When had that happened?

"Allow me." Teharon waved a hand at the wound.

I could have healed it myself with fire magic, but I knew that look on Teharon's face. He needed to do something good; something positive to counteract the killing he'd just witnessed. I gave him a nod and his hands started to glow. A glance in the direction of my lovers showed me that they were fine;

any wounds they'd received had been healed during their shift back to human form. But I saw Trevor exchange a grateful nod with Teharon.

So, he'd noticed my wound and had sent Teharon over to heal it since I hadn't thought to do so myself. A little passive-aggressive, but I forgave the maneuver since it managed to accomplish two things at once; ease Teharon's mind and heal my shoulder. Trevor gave me a little smile and walked over with Kirill.

"We're going to take care of this." Trevor took my hand. "We've already made a huge step forward. They might not be able to recover."

"Oh, they'll recover." Hades grimaced. "At least on the side of ISIS. It's imperative that we find those other camps."

"If they spin this off as an ISIS attack here in Kabul," Torrent mused, "which I'm sure they will, then the Afghans will rally to the cause too. And if we end up killing more soldiers, we'll just be helping those stupid Rainbow Gods and their Water Goddess."

"She's not a water goddess," Blue began.

"It's a joke, Blue." I waved him down.

"I don't think this is a laughing matter." Blue frowned.

"No, the name is a—never mind." I sighed. "Torrent's right; we ended up killing too many humans today, despite our good intentions."

"We need to proceed more carefully," Thor said.

"I agree," Hades said grimly. "David, can you remain here and continue to keep a watch on things? We will of course pay for your stay."

"Dude, you're gonna foot the bill?" Dave grinned. "Yeah;

I'll stay as long as you want me to."

"We appreciate it," Hades said sincerely. "Then we can get on with finding the ISIS stockpiles."

"Hey, V, can't you go weredragon?" Hekate asked casually and totally off subject.

"Weredragon?" I lifted a brow.

"Like a dragon/human form," she clarified.

"Yeah." I frowned, wondering what she was getting at.

"Aren't your scales bulletproof?" She went on. "You could do that instead of worrying about a ward."

"Actually, I have no idea what my scales can hold up to," I mused. "Either way, there are weak spots that could be pierced. That's how my ancestors were killed. Well, that combined with magic."

"Oh, right," Kate said. "The dragonlances."

"That would be the weapon that murdered my family, yes," I said dryly.

"Sorry." Hekate grimaced. "That was a little insensitive."

"No, it's fine, really," I said. "My nerves are just shot."

"Just like your shoulder." Trevor gave me his *I-hate-it-when-you-get-hurt* look.

"Ve're all on edge after zat horror," Kirill said as he sat on the floor in front of me and leaned back against my legs.

I automatically started rubbing his shoulders.

"I don't think you should test your half-form in battle," Trevor sounded concerned. "Maybe start by testing it at home."

"Sure, I'll just shoot myself in the shoulder." I made a face at him. "I know I can take it."

"Not funny." Kirill turned to say.

"Well, how else do you test that theory?" I shrugged.

"Shoot edge of upper arm," Kirill said after some thought. "Least amount of damage."

"Okay." I gave a huffing laugh. "Wow, sometimes our conversations astound me."

"You and me both." Trevor grimaced.

"I think we're all in need of some R&R," I observed. "Time to get back to the Bat Cave. Maybe a few drinks will help clear our heads, and we'll be able to come up with a better plan."

"The *what* cave?" Horus frowned.

"Batman, darling." Kate shook her head at her boy-friend. "Really, what's wrong with you?" Then she looked over at me, "I swear; sometimes it's like living with a cretin."

"Marry her, Horus." I pointed at him imperiously.

"I intend to," Horus drawled, shocking us all.

All except Hekate, that is; who just smiled serenely and pulled off her glove, revealing a huge, sparkling, diamond ring.

Chapter Twenty-Five

After Horus dropped the bomb about his engagement to Hekate, we all decided to go out and celebrate. What better place to celebrate than Moonshine, where we could have the entire VIP floor to ourselves? So, that's where we went. And that's where we found the Four Horsemen of the Apocalypse.

I had no idea that I was married to one of them.

"Hey! I didn't know you were going to be here," I said to Azrael as I came out of the door to the Family Room, AKA the door which led to the overnight (actually over*day*) rooms for vampires to rent, and the tracing room. I went over to give him a kiss.

"Carus." Az smiled brightly and slid an arm around me. "Guys, this is my wife, Vervain. Vervain, these are some friends of mine from childhood."

"Childhood, eh?" I looked them over as the rest of our group filtered in.

"Sam?" Hekate came up to us and stared at one of the three men in surprise.

"Katie?"

The guy was tall and sleekly muscled like Azrael. Not crazy body builder muscles, but he was much bigger than the average man. His biceps stretched the sleeves of his black, Gods of War T-shirt. He had soft brown hair, cut in a short, modern style, and buff-colored skin. His eyes were hard to make out in the low light but as he came towards Kate, one of the twinkle lights in the nearby trees caught him just right, and I saw red. As in literally; his eyes were demon red.

Not a huge surprise. Az knew a lot of demons, having been raised in Hell. It made sense that these childhood friends would be demons too. It was just strange that I hadn't met these guys before. I'd been to Hell numerous times with Azrael, and I thought I'd met all of his friends.

"What are you doing here?" Kate asked Mr. Demon Eyes, I mean; Sam. Then her gaze shifted to Azrael and she nodded. "Oh, right. How long has it been since you four have hung out?"

"Even longer than it's been since I've seen you." Sam smiled and pulled Kate into a hug.

A hug which lasted a little too long. Horus cleared his throat, and Kate jerked away from Sam.

"Um, Horus, this is Samuel, my ex-boyfriend." Kate gave Horus an apologetic smile. "Sam, this is Horus, my fiance."

"Oh." Sam's face cleared with comprehension. "Sorry about that." He held out his hand to Horus. "Didn't mean to step on any toes. You're a lucky man. Congratulations."

"Thank you." Horus shook Sam's hand, and we all relaxed a little.

"Soooo." I looked around at the unknown faces as the rest of the God Squad started settling onto the faux hill seats around me. "You're Sam." I stuck out my hand at him. "Nice to meet you."

"Nice to meet you too." Sam gave me a grateful grin and eased away from his ex-girlfriend and her new fiance to shake my hand. "We were all shocked to hear that Azrael got hitched. Sorry we couldn't make it to the wedding, we were a little tied up." He cast a lamenting look at his friends.

"Did he tell you about our situation?" I asked, casting a quick glance at my winged husband.

"About your multiple husbands?" Sam lifted a brow. "Yeah; that's wild."

"Oh, good." I sighed and took a seat beside Az. "Cause these are my other husbands; Trevor and Kirill." I waved a hand at them.

"Oh, okay." Sam nodded to them as he returned to his seat. "Nice to meet you guys."

"Likewise." Trevor said as he sat on my other side

Kirill remained standing behind us.

"And these are the rest of the Horsemen." Azrael waved at the remaining men. "Ira and Thaddeus."

Ira was model thin, like female model thin. Gaunt, actually, but somehow he managed to look beautiful. He had white hair that fell to his chin in soft curls and tan skin as if he'd been sunbathing for weeks. His cheekbones stood out sharply beneath startling citrine eyes and his lips were as thin as his body. All in all, his was a hungry look. Like a starving predator.

Then there was Thaddeus. Blond hair, almost golden, swept back from a regal forehead. His eyes were green, like freshly formed leaves, and his skin was a healthy pinkish cream. He looked angelic instead of demonic and the pink bow tie he wore only added to the effect. There wasn't even a hint of menace about him. He was the dream boy; perfect for taking home to meet Mommy and Daddy.

"Hi," I said to them. "Wait... *Horsemen*?"

"You know that I'm the Angel of Death." Azrael looked at me as if he'd been caught in a secret that he hadn't known was secret.

"Death." I frowned and then felt my eyes go wide. "As in; He rides a pale horse, *that* Death?"

"Yes, Carus." Az smiled gently. "I'm sorry; I thought you knew."

"How could I?" I huffed. "There are other death angels."

"Yeah, but I'm kinda the big one," he said in his modest way.

"So, that would make you guys... ?" I looked over at Az's three *childhood* friends.

"War." Sam gave me a cocky grin as he settled back on his seat.

"You can never be too rich or too thin," Ira added.

"Famine?" I guessed, and he nodded. "And that would make you, Pestilence?" I asked Thaddeus with a doubtful look.

"Actually, the first horseman is the Antichrist." Thaddeus gave me a rueful smile. "Common mistake. Pestilence actually falls under Famine's domain."

"You're the Antichrist?" I gaped at him.

"That is amazingly cool!" Torrent swept around me and stuck out his hand to Thaddeus. "I'm Torrent and this is my girlfriend, Artemis." He nodded Artie, and she nodded serenely to the Antichrist.

"Nice to meet you." The Antichrist shook Torrent's hand. "Call me Ted."

"Ted, the Antichrist," Torrent said in awe as he headed back to his seat. "This is surreal."

"Says the god born of Internet magic combined with

god magic." Artemis followed Torr.

"Yeah, but he's the Antichrist," Torrent whispered dramatically to her. "Do you know how many movies he's in?"

"Not him personally." Artemis laughed.

"I'm married to one of the Four Horsemen of the Apocalypse." I tried to process it.

"The Horsemen ride again!" Sam shouted, holding up his drink.

"The Horsemen!" The other three, including Azrael, shouted back and clicked Sam's drink with their own.

"And they're frat boys," I said in my this-can't-be-happening-tone as I looked over at Trevor for support, but he was grinning in delight. "Okay. Well, we're actually celebrating Kate and Horus' engagement so you boys have perfect timing. Trevor, can you ask one of the waiters to bring up a few bottles of champagne?"

"Sure, Minn Elska." Trevor kissed my forehead and headed over to the railing to shout down at one of the froekn waitstaff.

"Right, I caught that." Azrael smiled over at Horus and Hekate. "Congratulations, you two."

"Thank you, we're very happy." Horus seemed to be loosening up now that it was becoming apparent that Sam wasn't about to whisk Kate away from him.

"You guys gotta come to the wedding," Katie said to the Horsemen, and Horus stiffened back up immediately.

"Um, I'm going to go check on that champagne." I jumped up before the Horsemen could reply to Kate's invite.

I hurried over to the railing, where Trevor had just finished shouting his order down, and grabbed Trevor's arm.

"This could go very badly," I whispered to him.

"Yeah, I got that." Trevor looked back over at the group.

Kate, Pan, Torrent, Morpheus, and Artemis seemed calm enough but the rest of the Squad looked nervous, especially Horus. Not exactly what we needed after the day we'd had.

Trevor headed over to Az, casting an, "I'll take care of it," back at me over his shoulder.

I was about to head back myself when a golden shimmer from the bottom floor caught my eye. I frowned and looked closer. It was Re, dressed in jeans and a black collared shirt. His skin gleamed in the low light, and he looked amazing... as usual. Every woman—and quite a few men—on the lower level followed his progress across the dance floor with their hungry stares and there was more than one who tried to intercept him as he passed by, but his determined pace kept him going; straight to the stairs which led to me.

"Oh, no way," I whispered. "Talk about bad timing."

I headed towards the stairs to cut Re off as celebratory shouting erupted behind me. I glanced back to see the Horsemen surging to their feet and then waving to the Squad as they headed my way. What now? I froze, unsure whether to go down and confront Re or wait for the Horsemen who were giving me that look people give you when they're coming over to speak to you.

I took too long and the decision was made for me.

"What are you doing standing here, Carus?" Azrael asked as they reached me.

"Um, I... where are you guys going?" I asked instead of answering.

"Trevor suggested we use the Wild Room as a party place, that way we can get as crazy as we like. He said if there were any froekn in there, he didn't think they'd mind." Az grinned and the Horsemen behind him mirrored it.

Well played, Trevor.

"We might lure some women in with us but don't worry"—Sam gave me a wink—"I'll make sure Death doesn't do anything he'll regret."

"As if she has anything to worry about." Ted rolled his eyes. "I could count the number of women I've seen him with on one hand."

"On one finger." Ira chuckled. "Honestly, Az, we wondered if you were gay."

"I've been with other women." Azrael shot me an uncomfortable glance.

I'm not sure if he was uncomfortable because he was mentioning other women or because he didn't want me to think he'd been a virgin when we'd met.

"Okay, enough with trying to embarrass my husband," I chided the Horsemen of the Apocalypse. "Go have fun. It was nice to meet you. Maybe you can come over to Pride Palace for a barbecue or something."

"None for me." Ira sniffed disdainfully.

"Oh, right... uh," I stammered, and they all laughed.

"He's just teasing, Carus." Azrael gave me a quick peck on the cheek. "He has a crazy fast metabolism. Just because he's Famine, it doesn't mean he has to starve."

"Oh, good." I chuckled.

"Vervain," Re's sexy voice slid over me.

Something inside my chest fluttered with happiness as I simultaneously cringed to see Azrael's shocked reaction to

Re's presence.

"What the *hell* are you doing here?!" Azrael's wings came out in full Angel of Death glory, and his buddies automatically had his back; all three of them displaying their feathers like a bunch of angry peacocks.

It was actually damn impressive; Azrael's star-sprinkled midnight feathers against a background of Ted's brilliant white, Ira's golden brown, and Sam's blood red wings. I gaped at them, barely hearing Re's response.

"I'm here for her." Re wasn't at all cowed by the feathered intimidation fan but then he *was* kinda a big deal in Egypt.

"All right, all right, Flyboys." I held up my hands and waved the winged wonders back. "Don't go all Horsemen on him until I hear what he has to say."

"Does that mean *we* get to hear what he has to say?" Ted smiled wickedly. "Cause I don't like the looks of this guy."

"Can't handle it when someone's prettier than you, Prince Charming?" Re shot back.

"Enough!" I growled in my dragon voice, and everyone went quiet, even the group behind us. "Yeah, that's right, you're waking up a sleeping dragon. Now, don't you think it's best to just walk away and let her settle back down?"

"All right, Carus. I trust that you can handle this but if you need help kicking this idiot out, I'm sure the Squad will be more than happy to assist."

Azrael's wings disappeared, but he made sure to lay a long, hot kiss on me before he left. My hands clung to his shoulders as he pulled back, and he gave me a sexy grin and another quick peck.

As Az walked by Re, he snapped, "Don't make me come

back up here and kick your ass."

"Or me," Ted added as he followed his friend down-stairs.

"What he said." Sam nodded.

Ira just smiled at Re maliciously.

"Nice friends your husband has." Re grimaced.

"Yeah; I just found out that I'm married to one of the Horsemen." I rolled my eyes and gestured to the side, where the second floor continued in a narrow strip along the wall. The thin balcony led to another VIP lounge at the opposite end of the club and that's where I intended to take this poten-tially loud conversation.

"Horsemen?" Re frowned as he followed me. "As in the Christian Apocalypse riders?"

"That would be Azrael and his drinking buddies, yes." I waved Trevor back when I saw him start to approach us. He narrowed his wolfy eyes at Re but sat back down. "This way." I led Re past the row of regular tables that lined the narrow por-tion of the balcony and then took him into a small meadow.

A wide expanse of fake, grassy carpet covered the ware-house's metal balcony and over it were hills for seats and boulders for tables. Fake trees spotted the area and from them hung little lanterns, giving off a gentle glow. Statues of fairies and forest creatures had been set around as decorations, some even hanging in the trees, and music wafted up to us. Thank-fully, no one was playing on the stage directly below us or this would have been a really bad location to talk. As it was, I was starting to doubt my decision to bring Re there. It was a little too cozy, too romantic, and too secluded.

But then it had been built to be so. Trevor had wanted a little make-out spot for us and although I could still see him across the way, he'd positioned the trees in this section to form a sort of screen and it would be difficult for him to see us. I hoped he didn't think I'd chosen this spot because of that.

"What did you want to say?" I turned to find Re sprawled out on one of the wide hills in a enticing pose. "Seriously?" I huffed. "Can you at least sit up nicely and pretend that you're not here to seduce me?"

"You're the one who led me to your little love grove." Re grimaced as he sat up. "I thought you wanted to have sex."

"No; I don't want to have sex," I growled. "I thought I made that clear when I walked out on you and your multi-limbed lover."

"Lala," he purred, "just sit down. Durga is not my lover... anymore."

"Oh, hell no." I shook my finger at him. "You don't get to do that. We had a great time, and I admit, I was really starting to fall for you, but you went and ruined it." I held up my hand when he started to talk. "I get it. I totally understand. I just wish you had made yourself more clear in the beginning instead of wasting both of our time."

"In what way could what we shared ever be considered a waste of time?" He went serious.

"In the way that my finding a new lover is vitally important to not only my well being but that of my entire Pride as well as that of my husbands." I went to stand before him. "I don't have time to waste on casual love affairs. I need someone that I can fall in love with for good. Someone who's going to be a partner to me and a supportive member of my family. You have your own family and your own way of living. That's wonderful and as your friend, I'm happy for you but, unfortunately, it means that you won't fit into my life."

"I think I fit rather well." Re stood.

I started to argue, but he kissed me into silence.

I had to hand it to him; the man knew how to kiss. Re could go from wild to tender to simmering in moments, keeping me from settling on one emotion long enough to regain my senses. When he finally finished, I couldn't remember what I was going to say.

"This is why I'm here." Re laid his forehead briefly against mine. "I don't feel this with anyone else. Just one kiss, and I'm left with shaking knees; threatening to take me to the ground to beg you to come home with me."

"What?" I whispered in shock. And there I was, thinking that I was the one being manipulated by his expertise.

"I can't let go of this," he admitted. "Even if it means letting go of everything else."

"I need you to be very clear now, Re." I used all of my willpower to back away from him. "I've had a horrible day, a very long and very *bloody* day, and it's hard for me to think straight right now. So, just, please, spell it out for me."

"I want you bad enough to give in to your conditions," Re declared. "I won't try to bring anyone else into our bed, and I won't sleep with anyone but you. At least until we decide if we want this for good. I'm not to the point of forever yet but it's definitely been taken off the impossible list."

"Fair enough," I whispered and held out my arms.

Re filled them in seconds, giving me a replay of that crazy kiss. I felt as if I were falling; my life rolling up and down as insane as the Lunacy I carried inside me. I didn't know where this ride was going but, for the moment, I didn't want it to stop. So, I'd simply scream in delight and hold both arms up in the air while I fell.

Chapter Twenty-Six

"Tell me about this long and bloody day," Re urged after we simmered down to cuddling on a hill.

"Oh, you don't want to know." I sighed and snuggled deeper against his chest. "It's God Squad drama; we uncovered yet another plot to manipulate humans into war."

"Well, now I really want to know." He angled his head to see my face. "Who's doing the plotting?"

"A goddess named Disani and two gods; Gish and Qaus," I said. "They're trying to escalate the war in Afghanistan into pure annihilation. We went in and destroyed a lot of their weapons and two bases of operation, but we ended up killing quite a few humans, which ended up empowering the Gods, just as they'd wanted."

"Not good," he said.

"No kidding," I grumbled. "But we did the best we could. It's hard to think when bullets are raining down on you."

"Why? You're Gods. Bullets won't hurt you as long as you have a ward up. Unless you're not powerful enough to cast a personal ward?" He looked at me askance.

"I didn't know about personal wards," I huffed.

"No." He chuckled. "How did you not know? You've been in lots of battles."

"Mostly with other gods." I sighed. "This is the first time I've been shot at with machine guns."

"Hmm," he mused. "Yes, that would be disconcerting. And a ward wouldn't last long against rapid fire anyway. Still, you have magic and that overcomes any man-made weapon."

"Hekate pointed that out," I said.

"She's a slick one; never folds under pressure," he observed.

"She's engaged to Horus," I added. "We're here to celebrate."

"Really?" Re sat up straight, taking me with him. "Then we should be over there, celebrating with them."

"Yes, we should." I got up and held a hand down to him. He looked from my hand to me with a grimace and got up on his own. "Oh, it's like that, huh?" I chuckled. "Can't take a hand up from a woman?"

"Not from anyone." Re sniffed and offered me his arm. "I'm the Sun God—"

"Re," I finished for him. "Yes, I've heard."

"Do you think I'm a narcissist?" He asked in a musing way.

"I *know* you're a narcissist," I confirmed. "I'm just not sure if it's entirely your fault."

"But is it narcissistic if it's true?" He cocked his head at me.

"Oh, why do I even like you?" I dropped his arm and gave him an annoyed face.

"Because I'm the Sun—"

"God, Re," I growled. "Yeah, I got that." I shook my head

and walked away.

"Lala," he whined but somehow it was still sexy. Then he caught up with me and took my arm back, wrapping it over his imperiously. "There's nothing wrong with being confident."

"Oh, honey"—I chuckled—"you passed confident centuries ago."

"Well, as one does," he said stiffly. "I was one of the oldest Atlanteans who escaped the fall and the only member of the High Twenty who made it to shore."

"The rulers of Atlantis?" I stopped and gaped at him. "You were one of the High Twenty?"

"See, now that's a proper response." He smiled smugly.

"You helped destroy Atlantis?" I hissed and pushed him back into a table.

He fell on it with a surprised huff.

"It was an accident." Re stood and frowned at me. "It's not as if we set out to obliterate the greatest civilization there ever was."

"Does Thor know?" I glanced over to where my friends were partying it up. "Horus? They must. Why didn't they tell me?"

"Because they know that I punish myself enough for it," Re confessed, his whole demeanor changing suddenly. The arrogant mask fell, and I saw the anguish hiding beneath. He exhaled roughly and went on in a somber voice full of regret, "We were foolish. We just kept reaching for power, more and more magic. We thought we'd found a path to the source; a way to tap into powers beyond anything we'd ever dreamed. We'd be able to sustain all life on Atlantis, not just those of the Council and our families."

"That's right." I frowned. "Most gods didn't get immortality until they started receiving sacrifice from humans."

"Most Atlanteans lived lifespans of two-hundred years or so." Re nodded. "Except for the High Twenty. As I mentioned, we'd found a way to connect with a potent magical source, and we'd been siphoning off some of that energy to sustain ourselves and our families. But we weren't sure what prolonged exposure to pure magic would do to physical bodies. So, we used ourselves as test subjects, like human scientists do with animals."

"But you didn't just experiment on yourselves," I whispered. "You did it to your children." I was horrified.

"No." Re held up a hand. "We tested ourselves first and then gave it to our families."

"But you weren't certain enough to give it to the rest of Atlantis?" I narrowed my eyes at him.

"We didn't have a way of siphoning off enough to give to everyone." He closed his eyes briefly. "Which is why we tried to enlarge the portal."

"And instead, you destroyed it." I held a hand to my mouth.

"It became unstable," Re confirmed. "And there was nothing we could do. We had to evacuate."

"You didn't tell everyone though, did you?" I gaped at him. "That's why most Atlanteans died."

"There wasn't enough ships to carry us all." Re swallowed convulsively, suddenly looking very tired. "We had to make the choice of saving ourselves and those we loved or causing a panic that might end up killing everyone."

"Leaders have to make hard decisions." I clenched my jaw. "But, Re, that's..."

"Reprehensible?" Re gave a grim chuckle. "Yes, Vervain, I know. It was an evil thing to do; to destroy Atlantis and escape with my family instead of warning the city. I've lived with the guilt of it and paid for my deeds in blood."

"Lusaset," I whispered.

"I had just climbed aboard our ship with most of my family when the first explosion rocked Atlantis," he whispered. "Lusaset had gone to find our daughters, who were visiting friends. They had to fight their way through confused crowds to get to the docks. By the time they arrived, the people of Atlantis had figured out what was happening and who was responsible."

"They attacked her," I guessed, and he nodded, his jaw clenching.

"They were right there," his voice broke as his eyes filled with tears. "Maybe thirty yards away from me. So close, but I couldn't reach them in time. Lusaset held back the crowd with sheer willpower and magic so that Sekhmet and Bastet could reach me. I tried to help her," his voice cracked, and I pulled him against me. He sobbed into my shoulder, "I tried to help her. I tried."

"I know." I stroked his hair gently. "I know you did. You saved your children and that's what she would have wanted."

Re sniffed back the tears and pulled slowly away from me, swiping at his eyes. When he finally looked at me, his golden stare was full of ancient agony. How many years had he tortured himself over his mistakes? How many times had he replayed the memory of Lusaset's death in his head? Had his living without love been more than just a tribute to his wife?

"Re." I laid a hand against his cheek, and he struggled to smile.

"Horus' sisters were with his lover, Yeasha. He was in-tent on warning his friends so he said he'd fetch the girls on the way to Odin's house and come right back." Re glanced over at his grandson and sighed. "But after Lusaset was killed, we couldn't wait any longer. We had to leave, but Isis and Osiris refused to go without their children. They ran into the mob, and I was sure I'd never see any of them again."

"But they lived." I took his hand.

"Yes, they did," Re said softly. "They made it to Odin's home and found Horus sobbing in Thor's arms."

"What happened to Yeasha and his sister's?" I asked, though I wasn't sure I wanted to know.

"When Horus reached Yeasha's home, he found it on fire." Re swallowed hard. "Someone had trapped the girls inside with Yeasha's parents and burned them all alive."

"Why?" I was horrified. "Why them?"

"Yeasha's mother was also a member of the High Twenty." Re's eyes closed briefly.

"So, even after that horrible sight, Horus found the strength to go and warn his friends." I cast a glance at Horus, feeling both admiration and sympathy for him.

"And Odin saved him for it; him and his parents." Re's jaw clenched. "Horus holds himself responsible for the deaths of his sisters and Yeasha but really, he should blame me."

"No, he shouldn't, Re." I took his hand.

"I, at the very least, should have done more to stop his parents," Re confessed. "But that mob; it was so thick, people were falling into the sea. And my Lusaset was gone. I had no choice but to set sail and save the rest of my family."

"Then it's not your fault." I squeezed his hand gently.

"It is, and you know it," he said softly. "But, as I said, I've paid the price for my folly, and I've tried to make up for it by creating a great dynasty to protect my family."

"Then maybe it's time to let go of the guilt," I suggested.

"Maybe." Re began to smile. "I think I could be ready to live again."

"Good." I slid into his arms and pressed a kiss into the column of his throat before I backed away and offered him my hand. "Now, let's go wish your grandson a happy marriage. He deserves that."

"He does." Re took my hand and went back to the group of gods with me.

"So, you've made up, then?" Trevor asked as we approached.

"Yes, things are as they should be," Re confirmed.

"Ve'll see." Kirill stared hard at Re, his deep sapphire eyes as dark as sable in the shadows.

"We've worked things out." I held up my hands. "But this is Horus and Kate's party. Let's not take attention away from them."

"The Horsemen have already done that," Horus griped.

"They're gone now." Kate slapped his shoulder. "And all because you're a big jealous idiot. Get over yourself; I'm marrying you, remember?"

"Yes, I recall something of the proposal." Horus grinned wickedly at Hekate and slid his hand around her waist, pulling her onto his lap.

Now, there was a side of Horus I'd never seen before.

"Awkward," I teased as I took a seat beside Trevor.

"Says the woman surrounded by three of her lovers,"

Kate shot back.

"Touché." I held my hands up in surrender as Kirill once more settled at my feet so I could continue his massage.

Re stiffened beside me, and I shot him a look. Would this be too much for him? I needed to know so I kept massaging Kirill as if nothing were wrong. Re took a deep breath and made a visible effort to relax himself, finally giving me a nod. Okay, so it would take some time but maybe he could get used to it. Until then, I'd try to be less affectionate with my husbands around Re and try to just ease him into things. It was the least I could do when he was willing to meet my conditions. If he did get to the point where he was willing to commit himself, we could all spend the night together and the lioness magic would take care of any remaining issues he had.

"Congratulations, Horus." Re waved a hand towards Horus. "I'm thrilled that you've found someone to love."

"Thank you." Horus looked from me to his grandfather and this time, I really did feel awkward.

"What; I don't get congratulated?" Hekate asked.

"No." Re blinked. "That's not appropriate. To you, I say; best wishes."

"I know." Kate smirked. "It's just that V looked a little uncomfortable sitting there with you while you congratulated your great, great, great, great grandson on his engagement so I thought I'd ease some of the tension."

"There are only two greats," I mumbled. "But thank you."

"No prob." She laughed. "Oh, let it go, V; he's wildly gorgeous. Just roll with it. Hell; roll with it, on it, around it, do whatever you can with it. I'm sure it's wonderful." Then she dropped her voice to a whisper and leaned forward to ask, "Is it gold like the rest of him?"

"Hekate," I groaned as Re preened, and Horus glared at his fiance. "You're going to make his ego worse than it already is."

"Nyet, impossible," Kirill said dryly.

"Valid," I agreed and grimaced.

"I feel as if I should be offended by that but I'm not." Re leaned back on the hill, spreading his arms out behind me. He accidentally brushed Trevor's arm and pulled back as if he'd been burned.

"A little homophobic. Are we?" Trevor leaned forward and smiled wickedly at Re.

"Oh, no," I whispered. "Don't, Trev."

"What?" He blinked innocently at me.

"They're not... they don't... *do they*?" Re looked from Kirill to Trevor in shock as Trevor laid his hand casually on Kirill's shoulder and then started to play with Kirill's hair.

"Nyet," Kirill huffed as he pushed away Trevor's hand. "But he likes messing vith people. Don't encourage him."

"Oh." Re sighed and relaxed back.

"I told you." I smirked at Re. "I don't share, not even with other men."

"Greedy much?" Hekate mumbled.

"Thank you!" Re waved his hands expressively at Kate. "I mean really; shouldn't I at least be entitled... to..." he trailed off as he saw the nasty look Trevor, Kirill, and I were all sending him. "No, I guess I'm not. All right, all right already. I'm drinking the Kool-Aid. She's worth it, I get it."

"Thank you." I beamed at him and slid my hand over his

knee.

"Damn straight she is," Trevor grumbled and put his hand on my thigh. "And you're lucky she even wants you."

"Honey-Eyes," I chided.

"Oh, please, for the love of all the Egyptian Gods, stop," Horus begged. "I can't watch this."

"Oh, please *don't* stop," Pan added with glee.

"Son of my blood," Re spoke in a deeply serious tone as he leaned toward Horus. "You will cease this immaturity this very instant."

We all went silent and watched Horus get lectured by his grandfather.

"Grandpa," Horus whined.

"Enough!" Re slashed his hand through the air. "I give you my most heartfelt blessing on your union. I'm truly over-joyed that you have found happiness after all this time. Now, I expect you to feel the same for me."

"Of course, I want you to be happy." Horus sighed. "I know you haven't been."

"For as long as you." Re nodded. "Now, here we are, both of us on the verge of finally being at peace, and you disparage my joy as well as belittle it. You try to turn it into something dirty or shameful but, for me, it's miraculous."

"I..." Horus' eyes started to shine as he swallowed roughly. "My deepest apologies."

"Accepted," Re said immediately. He stood and went over to Horus, pulling him up into a hug. "I love you, you're more son to me than grandson, and I rejoice that you've finally cast aside the garments of mourning and embraced life again."

"I'm happy for you too," Horus said as Re pulled away. "I truly am, it's just been a bit of a shock."

"There are times when your head will be at war with your heart," Re said gently. "When you think one way is best but you *feel* as if you should go in another direction. You'll have to choose what path to follow; that of reason or of love. I don't want to live without love anymore so I'm choosing the path that my heart wants me to take."

"Then I will support your decision." Horus nodded and looked over at me. "Vervain is a good woman, and she's become a dear friend to me. I wish you both the best."

If we'd all been shocked before after Horus said that, we were completely dumbfounded.

"Damn, Horus," Pan spoke into the silence. "I thought I was your bestie."

That broke through everyone's shock, and we all started laughing. Re came back to sit beside me and take my hand. I smiled up at him like a teenager with her first crush. I knew he was more than a pretty face, I wouldn't be falling for him if he wasn't, but that speech, combined with his earlier confession, had revealed aspects of Re to me that I hadn't even suspected existed. Aspects which made him so much more beautiful.

"I knew you loved me, Bird-Man." I finally transferred my attention back to Horus.

"Don't get too excited, Vervain." Horus sniffed disdainfully. "I'm engaged, remember? You won't be adding me to your lovers."

"How will I ever survive?" I rolled my eyes.

Chapter Twenty-Seven

That night I went home with my husbands. I needed to spend some quality time with them, and I wanted to give Re some space to adjust. It's easy to give in to your desires and make a rash decision you'll come to later regret. If I pushed things now, I might end up right back where we started, and I didn't want to be Re's regret.

Azrael stayed out with his buddies so it was just Trevor and Kirill with me. I may have mentioned how I don't sleep with more than one of my men at a time very often, but that's not entirely true. Trevor and Kirill shared well, so well that it seemed as if they were one entity sometimes. I didn't consider being with them to be a threesome. Strange, but true. I guess I wasn't as traditional as I'd like to believe.

When Trevor and Kirill laid me down between them and slid their hands over me, it became a graceful dance. A dance that we knew all the moves to but which changed every time. And every time, my heart sped up as we began. Every time, I wondered what new pleasure we'd find together.

"I love you," Trevor murmured just before he kissed me.

Wolf musk in my nose and whiskey on my tongue. Trevor had been drinking but his flavor came through the remnants of alcohol to leave me reeling as if I had been the one imbibing.

"Slow or fast?" Kirill asked as he kissed his way from one

of my breasts to the other. "Rough or gentle?"

"A little of both," I purred as I spread my legs wider.

Each man had a hand between my legs; Kirill rubbed me slowly while Trevor pumped his finger into me.

"Good," Kirill rumbled then licked the valley between my breasts thoroughly before he pulled me down the bed. "Hard first."

My lion straddled me and slid his cock between my breasts as he pushed them tightly together. Trevor chuckled as he crawled behind Kirill and settled between my legs. As I bent my head to lick the flushed tip of Kirill's cock as it emerged from between my breasts, I felt Trevor's breath on my sex. Kirill slid a pillow behind my head to lift me and angle me forward before he began a furious pumping; his cock slipping into my mouth with every thrust. I moaned and licked at him as Trevor began licking me.

The sounds of slick flesh and wet mouths echoed around me, spurring on my arousal. Trevor's tongue danced over me as his fingers started sinking inside; easing me open. I was nearly that plateau of pleasure when Trevor jumped to his knees, lifted my hips, and slammed home. He was inches away from Kirill, but they instinctively knew where each other was and fell into the same rhythm. My body trembled beneath them; overrun by ecstasy.

"Let's put her on her knees," Kirill said over his shoulder to Trevor.

Trevor grunted a response and slid out of me.

Then I was being moved; repositioned to their requirements. This was a favorite pose for them; me on my hands and knees with one of them in my mouth and one in my sex. Not that I was complaining. Hey, if it works. And damn did it work. I groaned around the silky skin of Kirill's shaft as he slid it past my lips. Then I balanced myself on one hand so I could massage his balls and stroke the sensitive skin just beyond them. Kirill roared and surged deeper down my throat; his hands going to my face to bracket it.

Behind me, Trevor had my ass in his hands, spreading it wide while he pushed slowly in and out of me. Even with them contradicting each other's tempo, it felt wonderful. Maybe because of it; the sensation of Kirill's cock plunging into my mouth rapidly while Trevor lazily ground into me made my head spin. Then Trevor reached around my waist and began to rub my clit. I cried out around Kirill, and he groaned from the vibration.

"Zat's it, Tima," Kirill growled. "Suck me just like zat."

I moaned over him again and tightened my lips as I rubbed the base of him with my hand. Kirill cried out, tensed, and started to come. He held my face tightly as he gave one last thrust; his cock filling my mouth. Only my hand at the base of his shaft kept him from choking me as he emptied into me. Then he shivered and slid slowly out of my mouth to fall to the bed before me. Kirill ended up horizontal to me; his belly in front of my face, and I was instantly shoved onto it.

Kirill laughed and held me to himself as Trevor began a more savage impaling. I moaned, and Kirill slid himself down so that he could hold me and kiss me while Trevor went wild. Kirill stroked my hair back from my face gently and then eased himself beneath my torso. I straightened my arms and braced myself against Trevor's savage slams while Kirill went back to sucking at my nipples; one of his favorite things to do. Some nights we'd lie on the couch together, and Kirill would sprawl across me and casually lick and suck at my breasts while we watched TV; just that for hours while I went wet beneath him. The man knew his way around a breast. Just thinking about it made me hot, but with him beneath me, working his magic, and Trevor's froekn cock filling my sex, it wasn't long before I was screaming again.

This time, Trevor shouted with me.

When the roar of rapture faded into delicious after-shocks, we snuggled together, sighed away the trauma of battle, and drifted off to sleep.

I was glad I'd had that night with them because the next day, Re began an aggressive plan of seduction. He took me out every day and kept me in every night. It got to the point where my husbands started complaining, and I had to make a schedule to be home at least two nights a week to give them some attention.

Re was relentless, taking me all over the world for endless romantic interludes and lavishing expensive gifts on me. It was wonderful, of course, but a little overwhelming. The moments I treasured most were the ones we spent lying together, talking about things that didn't really matter. You know; the normal way people get comfortable with each other and truly get to know one another. Funny how it really isn't about knowing all the details of a person's life or their family, it's the small things. Like if they prefer coffee or tea and how they take it. Do they snore? Do they have to make the bed in the morning or do they not see the point? Things like that help us acclimate to each other. And they matter more than we think. They help us to get comfortable enough to fall in love.

Falling in love with Re was like diving into a cold lake on a hot day. At first, it's shocking but the more you languish in it, the more comfortable it gets. I simply woke up one morning and found the water to be the perfect temperature. I rolled over and saw Re's face pressed into the pillow beside me, one arm slung carelessly over me, his cheek squished up endearingly, and just felt pure love for him.

Re opened his eyes and smiled softly as if he could feel

the shift in me. A hand stroking my hair and a gentle kiss on my lips; it was the way I wanted to start each day. I sighed into Re's kiss and when he pulled back, he shifted up, pulling me against his chest.

"You called my name in your sleep," he said in concern.

"Did I?" I whispered.

"Is everything all right?"

"It's too right." I sighed. "I never want to leave this bed."

"I'd be okay with that." He smiled wickedly.

"I love you," I said without meaning to. The words just tumbled out.

His eyes widened, and I tensed. Maybe it was too soon. Maybe I should laugh and take it back.

"I love you too, Lala," Re said then he kissed me and my heart relaxed into the love.

"Being with you is unlike anything I've ever known," I confessed. "You're arrogant and then humble, wild and then sweet, careless and then profound. Make up your damn mind," I teased.

"I think I have." Re pulled me from bed and spun me around. I couldn't help giggling. "I want this," he said as he lowered me down. "I want *us*, forever."

"Take a little more time to be sure," I said gently. "When you are, you can spend the night at Pride Palace."

"To let the lioness magic take care of my jealousy?" Re went serious.

"It sounds horrid but it will make things easier on you." I watched him carefully. "You don't have to do it if you don't want to. It's your choice."

"Is it?" He frowned.

"Re?" I asked, immediately wary.

"I want you to do something for me." He set glowing golden eyes on me. "Before I make this decision, I need one more thing from you."

"What?" I pulled out of his arms.

"Your trust." Re took my hand and led me back to bed. "I want you to let me try something new with you."

"What do you want to try?" I was instantly wary.

"Nothing painful or disgusting." He held up his hands and laughed. "But I want you to trust me enough to just say yes without knowing."

"No chains?" I asked.

"Do you trust me?" He shot back.

"Yes," I whispered.

Re smiled and went to the alcove. I swallowed past my dry throat as he opened a box, but then I gave a relieved sigh when he merely pulled out a length of black silk. He strode over to me and lifted the silk to my face. I started to stop him, but he gave me a stern look, and I dropped my hands.

"I want you to focus on feeling," he whispered in my ear as he tied the silk over my eyes. "What do you feel?"

"Nervous," I admitted.

"And now?" He laughed a little as he started to slide my panties down.

"The tug of fabric," I said.

"And now?" His breath rasped over my thighs as he stood, his fingers gliding lightly over my skin.

"Fingertips on flesh," I whispered.

"Keep feeling, Lala," Re said against my lips as he pulled up the snug tank top I'd slept in.

Re backed away as he tugged it over my head and there were a few panic-filled moments when I stood alone. Then warm skin pressed against mine.

I sighed as Re just stood there, holding me gently and letting me feel him as he grew more and more excited. Then he lifted me and settled me back on the bed but this time, I noticed the smooth weave of the luxurious cotton sheets and the way it cooled my overheated flesh. The pillow cradled my head and the light scent of burning frankincense wafted up from it. I sighed and snuggled in.

But then Re took my wrist and began wrapping something around it. I shot up and grabbed at him.

"Relax." He took my hands in his and held them still. "It's just the silk draperies around the bed. They're not chains. You can break them in an instant if you wanted to."

"Then why use them on me?" I asked.

"Because I want you to willingly give up control." His cheek slid against mine as he spoke. "I want you to believe in me and my desire for you. To know that everything I do with you will only bring us both pleasure."

Well, damn, what can a girl say to that?

I didn't say anything, just laid back down and let him have my wrist. Re went back to wrapping it with silk. Snug but not tight. Then he did the same to the rest of my limbs. I was spread out across that round mattress, feeling like a virgin waiting for a dragon to eat her. Except I was the dragon, wasn't I? I suddenly relaxed, confident that nothing would happen that I didn't want to happen. If it did, I'd set Re's beautiful ass on fire.

The thought made me smile.

"That's better." Re's hand trailed over my arm. "Enjoy this, just focus on the sensations."

He continued to wrap the silk around each of my wrists and ankles. Circling the bed, he bound each one once before moving to the next. Over and over, he kept wrapping until my body began to lift off the mattress. I frowned as it started to become uncomfortable. My back was drooping and my limbs straining with the weight. I also had to keep my head lifted, which was going to be an issue for my neck.

"Re," I groaned.

"I know." He squeezed my thigh. "Give me a moment."

His hands went beneath me, and I realized that he was tying even more lengths of silk under me; one group knotted beneath my lower back, one beneath my shoulder blades, and one under my waist. Then a final length stretched beneath my neck gently, my hair pulled back to hang over it. I was suspended comfortably in the air and it felt amazing. I could grasp the silk in my hands and adjust my body, so I didn't feel constant pressure in any one place. And every time I moved, I'd swing gently.

"You look beautiful," his voice was back in my ear, his hand on my waist. "Your hair is pooling on the sheets below you and your muscles are tightening and releasing in a symphony of seduction."

My breath trembled out of me.

"In fact, I think I want you to see this."

The tie around my face slid away, and I got a full view of my body stretched out above Re's bed. I looked up and saw the bed curtains strained tightly in their golden hooks. The silk swaths looked more like ribbons now, and I was reminded briefly of those acrobats in Cirque du Soleil who dance around long veils hanging from the ceiling. This was going to be a different type of dance.

"Just one more thing." Re hurried back to the alcove and over to the ribbons that hung there.

He chose two of them and pulled them off their hooks. I saw that they had clips on the ends of them, like the kind people use when they go mountain climbing. He fastened one of them onto one of the gold loops set into the sun beneath the bed. Then he tied the other end of the ribbon to my ankle, pulling it tight so that my leg stretched out to the side. I inhaled sharply as he repeated the process on my other ankle. My legs were as wide apart as they could get.

"Perfect," Re said as he climbed up on the bed and settled himself on his knees between my legs. "Now, you'll see what giving me control will bring you." He smiled wickedly and lowered his mouth to me.

His hot tongue split my sex and laid fully against me. Then he drew it up slowly, keeping his eyes on me, and covered my clit with his mouth when he reached the top. His hand went around my thighs to pull me closer, and then he released me to slide back. The ties on my ankles kept me from going too far. He kept up that rocking motion as he kissed, nibbled, sucked, and licked every inch of my sex until I could feel the pleasure dripping off me.

Then Re moved slowly around my body; caressing and kissing as he made his way to my head. He positioned himself behind me and slid the silk further down my neck so that my head hung back. I licked my lips eagerly as he angled the head of his cock toward me. Then he was sliding over my tongue, his hands on my breasts, massaging them and pinching my nipples as he used them to pull me onto himself. His balls rubbed against my forehead with every thrust, his musk filling my nostrils, and I only sucked him harder, licked him more furiously. Finally, Re pulled away from me and bent down to kiss me tenderly.

"That was lovely," Re said as he repositioned the silk to hold my neck. Then he wrapped the black silk blindfold over my eyes again. "Now, I'm going to fuck you, Lala."

I shivered, but he got off the bed, and I heard him moving away. I bit my lip to keep from asking him what he was doing. I heard a clatter and then he was back. His hand slid up my leg and then casually slid into my sex. I was just beginning to relax when something cool and hard pressed against my opening.

"Re?" I asked in shock.

"You will enjoy this, I promise," he growled. "Trust me."

"Okay," I whispered.

That cold thing shipped inside me and began a slow plunging. Re worked it deep, deeper than most men could have gone, and I writhed against it. My sex clenched over the unyielding thing and tingles spread out over my skin. The strange sensation was becoming addictive.

"That's it," he purred. "Work yourself on my glass cock, Lala. Let me see your pussy move in a way I can't when I fuck you myself. Let me watch you take it deep and grind down even further."

His thumb rubbed my clit tenaciously and my thighs trembled as I began to come. But then he slid the phallus out of my sex and moved it to my ass. I clenched up and pulled away from him.

"No, Re," I growled.

"Lala," he said gently. "Just give it a chance."

"No," I said adamantly. "I don't want that."

"Can I at least rub the outside?" He cajoled with a teasing tone. "Come now, Lala, there is nothing about you that is shameful. Let me touch you. I know how to make your body sing."

I forced myself to relax, and he rubbed the wet tip of the glass phallus against my other hole. As he did, he slid his real cock into me, and I cried out, my whole body clenching. It caused me to pull in the phallus a tiny bit, but I was already coming, and I couldn't bring myself to shout a denial him. Re began pumping ferociously; my body swinging out and then back onto him until he grabbed my hip with one hand and held me still. The whole time, he rubbed that other place, circling it with the glass and just dipping the tiniest bit in and out of me. Finally, he tossed it aside and started slamming into me.

"I'm willing to give up all other women for you, Lala," Re panted. "But I have been doing this too long; I am who I forced myself to become, and I have needs. I need you to be my partner in this; in my search for pleasure. I need to know that you will trust that whatever I do to you, it will be done out of love and with your delight in mind."

Re bent over me, hugging me tightly as he kissed me and kept driving himself into me.

"If I ask you to bend over, I want you to rip your panties off and do it eagerly," he whispered in my ear. "When I say I'm going to fuck you, I want you to shiver just as you did tonight. I want my words alone to make you wet. I want you to spread your legs and trust that whatever I fuck you with—be it a glass cock, a thick candle, or my own flesh—I will give you the most sublime pleasure that you've ever felt."

Re pulled away the blindfold and eased back to surge into me steadily; his hands around my thighs for leverage. He looked more powerful than I'd ever seen him; golden eyes glowing and hair wild. His chest gleamed with sweat and gold. His biceps bulged and the muscles in his flat stomach curled with every slam of his hips. He stared at me possessively but also with the deepest, most wild love.

"And I want you to demand the same from me," he growled. "I want you to walk into my home as if you belong here, because you do belong here. I want you to tell me you're going to fuck me as if I belong to you, because I do belong to you. I want to get hard from hearing those words on your lips and know that whatever you do to me, I will enjoy it because I trust you, and I know you want me to feel as much pleasure as you do."

"Re," I whispered brokenly.

"Will you do that for me, Lala? Will you truly be my woman?"

His body brought mine over, and I screamed my answer as I came, "Yes!"

That single word drove Re into his own completion, and he cried out with one word, just as I had.

"Vervain!"

That was just the beginning. In the hours of weightless pleasure that followed, I not only saw the light where Re's naughty needs were concerned, but I also literally saw Re light up with ecstasy. His sun magic brought forth my moon, and we swung suspended in desire until the restraints became too much, and I needed to touch him. I tore down the silk, and we tangled ourselves in ribbons and love.

Chapter Twenty-Eight

"What should we do today?" Re asked as he pulled a torn piece of silk from my hair.

"I thought we could visit my house in Hawaii," I suggested and then chewed my lip.

Would the great Sun God enjoy my tiny, three bedroom house?

"I think I'd like that. I'll get to see how you lived before you became a goddess," he kissed the tip of my nose.

"Before I became the Godhunter." I laughed. "Yeah, it's not all that impressive but it would just be the two of us. I thought I could cook us dinner."

"I'm even more intrigued." He got up and headed for his closet.

Re had a closet just as big as mine. I had laughed in delight the first time he'd opened the nondescript door next to his naughty nook and led me into the lavish dressing room. It was so strange to find a guy who loved clothes as much as I did but who also happened to be straight. It seemed utterly impossible. But then, that was Re; utterly impossible.

I went into the closet after him. He had cleared a rack for me so I could bring some clothes over. We helped each other dress, getting those hard to reach closures it's always nice to have an extra pair of hands for. Then he brushed my hair; one of his favorite things to do in the morning, though it still felt strange to me.

My husbands brushed my hair all the time but not like Re. With them it was sexy and loving, a sweet gesture that I enjoyed. With Re, it was primping. He liked to see how shiny he could get my hair, how perfect he could make the curls; how beautiful he could make me. It was more about his pleasure than mine. I felt like his doll sometimes and at other times, I felt as if I wasn't pretty enough for him. But I let him do as he liked; as we often do for those we love. It was just hair brushing after all.

When he had me presentable enough, we traced to my home in Hawaii, and I drove us to the grocery store since my fridge was pretty bare. I visited Hawaii maybe once a month now, sometimes even less than that. I used to bring Nick to give my tabby cat a chance to roam the human world for a little while. But ever since Azrael had started feeding Nick manna to prolong his life, it seemed as if Nick was happier at Pride Palace. So, I didn't bother bringing him anymore. The less he had to travel through the Aether, the better.

I was surprised to find that grocery shopping with Re was fun. It was such a mundane task, but he made it into an adventure. Every aisle was an opportunity to find new flavors, every person who passed presented an chance to be adored. He was almost ridiculous in his appeal to both sexes and definitely ridiculous in the way he lapped up all the attention. I laughed at him, more than once, and he began to laugh at himself.

"I'm glad you can finally see how silly you are," I commented as I put a wedge of Brie into the cart.

"Silly?" He puffed out his chest and flicked back his hair. "I am glorious."

"*Vain*glorious maybe," I huffed.

"That too." He grinned wider.

"Ta-da," I mimicked Zariel and held my arms out to present him. "It's the Sun God, Re."

"Yes, yes." Re smoothed the chocolate colored hair at his temples. "I am he."

"You are full of it, is what you are," I said.

"Excuse me?" A woman came up behind Re and tapped his shoulder.

"Yes?" He turned around with an expectant smile.

"Where did you get the gold shimmer dust?" She asked blandly.

"Excuse me?" His smile turned to confusion as I began to chuckle.

"The powder you've dusted yourself with." She motioned at his shiny skin. "And do you do parties? A friend of mine is getting married, and I have to find a dancer for the bachelorette party."

"Pardon me?" Re gaped at her, and I lost it.

I laughed so hard that I started to cry.

"Oh, I'm sorry!" She held up her hands. "I thought you had to be a stripper, guys don't usually coat themselves in glitter."

"I know, right?" I commiserated with her. "I once asked him if he was the God of Chippendales."

"Oh, thank goodness; I was about to be so embarrassed." She giggled. "Here I was, thinking you're a stripper when you're just gay."

I couldn't breathe for a few seconds, that's how funny Re's expression was.

"I am not, nor have I ever been, a lover of men," Re said with great effrontery.

"There's nothing to be ashamed of," the woman huffed. "I'm a lesbian. You should just come out of the closet. People are much more accepting these days."

I doubled over with laughter.

"I am not gay!" Re shouted, earning everyone's attention.

"Methinks he protests too much," I mumbled and then giggled some more.

"Okay, okay." She held up her hands. "In your own time. But I still would like to know where you buy your cosmetics."

"It is not cosmetics!" He exclaimed. "This is my skin!"

"I'm so sorry. He's had a rough day." I grabbed Re and our cart and pushed them both away as the poor woman stared after us in confusion. "What's wrong with you?" I hissed at him. "You can't tell a human that your skin is naturally dusted with gold. They'll either think you're joking or that you're insane."

"Normally, they simply think I'm beautiful," he mumbled.

"Oh, she thought you were pretty all right." I chuckled.

"Can we never speak of this again?" He sighed.

"Oh, no, we're speaking of this." I shook my head. "Every time you start getting all *I am the Sun God, Re,* I'm gonna be like; remember that time when the lesbian asked you where you buy your cosmetics?"

"Lala, please," he beseeched me. "Have some mercy."

"Nope." I grinned smugly. "Just call me Lala the Merciless from now on."

"Oh, why do I love you?" He rolled his eyes.

"Because I am Lala the Merciless!" I declared dramatically.

"Truer words have never been spoken," he muttered.

Chapter Twenty-Nine

"This is quite lovely," Re said as he explored my house. "Small but lovely."

"Well, we can't all start out with palaces." I rolled my eyes.

"Of course not," he said magnanimously, and I rolled my eyes again.

"The bed has definite possibilities." He slid a hand over the carved walls of my Chinese wedding bed.

"You have no idea." I smiled, thinking of all the good times I'd had in it with my husbands. Then I looked up and saw his face. I lost the smile immediately. "Sorry."

"It's all right." He sighed and moved away from the bed.

"No; I really am." I went over and took his hand to lead him out of the bedroom. "You've been trying hard to make this work, and I need to at least be considerate of your feelings."

"That would be nice," he agreed.

"Come on, I'll show you my art room." I took him into the room I used as my art studio.

It had been awhile since I'd had a chance to paint and there was a fine layer of dust on some of my supplies. I looked over the canvases leaning in groups against the walls and the careless spread of paint tubes over my work table and sighed. I picked up a brush and stroked the bristles lovingly. I used to treasure my paintbrushes more than my jewelry. But that was before Gods started giving me gifts.

"You miss it," he made it a statement.

"Yeah; I don't have a lot of free time to paint anymore," I said. "My art dealer calls every once in awhile, checking if, by some miracle, I have a new piece to sell." I shook my head. "But I never do."

"The curse of multiple lovers," Re observed.

"The curse of being the Godhunter," I corrected. "Even without my husbands my time would be taken up with godhunting. I used to try and make an effort to paint but now that I don't need the money, it's been pushed to the side as an extravagance. I hardly even get to see my human friends anymore."

"Life is about extravagance." Re slid his hands around my waist. "Without it, living becomes mediocre, too bland to even swallow. You must fill as many moments as you can with flavor so that the spice holds you over till your next bite."

"You're making me hungry," I teased.

"I'm serious, Lala," he chided.

"I have a lot of extravagance in my life," I assured him. "More than any woman has a right to. Don't worry about me getting bored or not being able to swallow." I gave him a naughty look, and he chuckled.

"Well, let's see how much more you can take." He went over to the CD player on the dresser near the door and pushed play. *Banks* started singing about love being a waiting game, and Re started to undress.

"What are you doing?" I blinked at him.

"I'm getting naked," he said matter-of-factly.

"Okay." I went with it. "Should I get naked too?"

"If that's how you like to paint." Re smiled lasciviously.

"You want me to paint you?" I gaped at him.

"You *don't* want to paint me?" He lifted a brow.

"Oh, sure, let's feed your ego some more," I huffed.

"My ego is rather hungry right now," he teased. "But I actually thought it might be a little sexy; having you paint me nude. I've never posed naked before."

"Never?" I lifted a brow.

"Why do you sound so surprised?"

"Really?" I gave him a bland look. "You're asking why?"

"I've had offers, of course." He shrugged as he slipped out of his pants, and I pushed down the lusty tingles that started filling my body.

"Of course." I looked away and cleared my throat.

When I looked back, Re was stretched out on the single bed Kirill used to sleep on. It made me frown a little and recall a flash of Kirill in a similar pose, his black hair surrounding him like a blanket. I swallowed hard and pushed the thought away. It wasn't fair to Re to be thinking about Kirill when I was with him. But I wasn't sure if it was fair to Kirill to have Re posing on his bed either. The thing was; Re looked really good there.

He was on his side, casually leaning on one arm with his legs angled artistically but not in any way concealing any-thing. It was all on full display; the glorious skin which turned his hairless chest into a golden sculpture, the elegant hands clenched in the sheets as if in passion, the curve of thick biceps, the sprinkling of blond hair on his forearms, the thick muscles in his thighs framing... well, I think that's enough to give you an idea of what I was dealing with.

I felt a shiver course over my skin as I picked up a canvas and set it on my easel. Re smiled sensuously as I chose a palette of cream, gold, and espresso, spiced with deep crimson and tempered with lavender. I laid brush to paint and was suddenly lost to my art. Re became a chorus of lines and curves, of tones and hues. Music filled my head as a dormant part of me took over my hands and captured Re on canvas.

I worked like a demon and hours later, I finally set my brush down and sighed. Re, who had been remarkably patient the entire time, stretched and got up. He strode over to me with a slick smile and reached out a hand to wipe my cheek. His hand came away streaked with burnt umber.

"You have never been more beautiful," Re whispered as he touched my hair and perused my paint-streaked dress.

I self-consciously touched the knot I'd twisted my long hair into. I always pulled my hair back when I painted. Strands were coming loose, and I must have looked horribly messy, something I would never have thought Re could find appealing. But he obviously did, his reaction was right there for me to see.

Then his hands were at the hem of my dress and his mouth was pressed against mine as he lifted my dress up. He pulled away briefly to yank it over my head and then returned to kissing me; wild and messy kissing, with teeth and grasping fingers. My underwear was gone in seconds and then we were on the floor, writhing in our discarded clothing as his unfinished but beautiful portrait watched us with a knowing grin.

Chapter Thirty

Hours later, we finally left the art room so I could cook us dinner. We ate in our underwear, laughing like teenagers as we devoured the food and chugged down two bottles of wine. We didn't even bother with the dining table but instead sprawled out on the floor and ate at the low Moroccan table in my living room. It was hedonistic and so very wonderful but before we made it to dessert, a shock wave hit the house, rattling the plate glass window in my living room.

"What in the world?" I stood up and started to head to the front door, but Re rushed in front of me and held his hand out as he stared towards the direction the boom had come from.

"Get dressed, Lala," he said as he padded toward the door in just his boxers.

I ran to the art room and yanked on my dress then snatched up Re's pants and brought them out to him. He was at the window, pulling the black-out curtains aside to peer into the yard.

"Here." I handed him his pants. "What is it?"

"A woman," Re said as he slid the pants on. "She's just standing there, staring at the house expectantly."

"Then I guess we should go and see what she wants," I muttered.

"Let me go first," he said gently.

"I can take care of myself," I said just as gently. "You must know that by now."

"It's not about the can." He kissed my cheek, opened the front door, and stepped outside to face the unknown threat.

"It's not about the can," I mimicked but inside my chest there was a little flutter of happiness.

All of my men were protective, but Re had made it into a romantic gesture. I followed him out with a little secret smile.

"Godhunter?" The woman was tall, with long black hair trailing in a straight but thick line to her waist. Bright green eyes seemed even more vivid against her dark skin. She was muscular and confident in her stance, dressed casually in jeans and a blue tank top.

"And you are?" I stepped up beside Re.

"I am the Death Goddess, Disani," she declared.

"You see?" I turned to Re. "Doesn't that sound annoying?"

"Yes, I understand now." Re grimaced. "Do I really sound that pompous?"

"Oh, yes," I assured him, and he grimaced deeper.

"I am here to finish our fight, Godhunter," Disani went on.

"Will the fight have natural fruit flavors infused in it?" I asked her, barely restraining my giggle.

"I... what?" She frowned.

"I assume you have some kind of water power with a name like that," I explained. "Are you sparkling or flat?"

"Is she insane?" Disani looked at Re.

"She is making light of your name," Re clarified. "It sounds like a manufacturer of bottled water; Dasani."

"That's..." She blinked. "What is *wrong* with you?"

"Definitely flat," I said to Re with distaste.

"I am hardly flat." Disani waved her hands violently at her muscular body.

"Where are your gays?" I went on relentlessly.

"What are you talking about now?" She huffed.

"Your rainbow sidekicks." I smiled. "Gish and Qaus; your gays."

"Gays?" She gaped at me. "Neither of them are gay."

"Then what's with the sash?" I waved my hand across my chest to mimic Gish's sling.

"Are you referring to the Rainbow Sling of Gish?" She asked disdainfully. "It's not a sash; it's an energy source."

"Oh, really?" I lifted my brows. "Thanks for the tip."

"You mongrel slu—"

"What about Qaus? He's the God of Rainbows. I mean, how obvious can you get? He's got to be gay," I cut her off.

That slut insult was old and boring. I wish my enemies would come up with new material.

"What do rainbows have to do with sexual orientation?" She fumed, on the verge of losing her damn mind.

I have that effect on people. It's part of my charm.

"The rainbow is a symbol of gay pride," Re explained calmly, though his lips were twitching.

It was kinda nice not to have to explain my own jokes.

"You two are out of your minds," she muttered. "Killing you will be a mercy."

"Yeah, about that." I looked around my neighborhood. The rumble had drawn people to their windows and we had acquired several witnesses. "We can't fight here." I waved toward the watching eyes. "If you don't mind, let's take this into the backyard."

"Sure," she grumbled in exasperation. "Why would I mind? It doesn't matter to me where you I kill you."

So, the Death Goddess, Disani, the Sun God, Re, and I walked in single file through my narrow side yard into the enclosed backyard to battle to the death.

"Stay away from the koi pond," I warned her with a firm finger pointed in her direction.

"Stay away from... oh, enough of this." She held her hands out and they began to fill with a dark mist.

"Hmm." I pondered her. "Death, huh? I probably don't want to get hit with that."

"Don't worry, the first strike will render you unconscious. Your death will be painless and quiet." She smirked and lifted her hands. "Utterly unremarkable, just as you deserve."

"Yours will not be," Re growled as he stepped before me. "You will die writhing in anguish and screaming for mercy. No one threatens those I love."

Re's face had set in harsh lines, his shoulders contracted into a menacing mass, and his palms filled with enough light to illuminate the entire yard. I'd never seen him so furious, sparks were actually exploding off his bare chest like solar flares as he bared his teeth at Disani in primal wrath. It was damn sexy, and I would have appreciated it more if he hadn't been in my way.

Before either I or Disani could do anything, a burst of searing light shot out from Re's hand and knocked Disani on her ass. I gaped at her burning chest as she rolled around in an effort to put out the fire. Well, damn, maybe I should sit this one out and just grab some marshmallows.

Then Disani flung her hand out towards Re, and he flew backwards. Tendrils of fog gathered around his arms and tightened like boa constrictors. Wherever they settled, Re began to bleed. I shouted his name and started to pull on my nine-pointed star. I didn't have time to be picky, any magic or combination thereof that my star wanted to use was fine with me. As I started forward, I saw Re flick his arms out wide and the dark snakes burst into flames. They blackened in seconds and burst apart. A shower of ash floated to the ground. Then he began to glow, brighter and brighter, until I had to shield my eyes.

Just as I was about to chance a peek, I felt a prick in my arm and a sleepy lethargy crept over me.

"Not again," I whined as the god drug Net shot through my veins and froze my magic.

My star faded and sunk back into my chest, submerged too deep for me to reach. I fell to my knees and dug my fingers into the soft grass, smiling at the sweet scent. There was shouting around me suddenly and a very bright light but then it all went utterly dark.

Chapter Thirty-One

I blinked awake and sighed. I felt wonderful, without a care in the world, but somewhere deep inside me I knew that I *should* care. It was just too difficult to hold onto the feeling. So, I let it go and gave into the relaxation. No magic meant no worries. I smiled blissfully and peered around me with casual curiosity.

I was in a luxurious room. Or maybe it was a tent. There was fabric everywhere; streaming over my head and draping down the walls. Then I caught the gleam of cream-colored marble just past the draperies. So; not a tent, just a draped room, kinda like my living room in Hawaii. There were even colorful lanterns hanging from the ceiling and lush carpets laid haphazardly across the floor. Potted palms stood near the walls and a few low, brass, Moroccan tables were set out, just like the one I'd had dinner on with Re.

Re. Oh, something had happened with Re. What was it? There was a woman and then fire. Or was it sunshine? It was too hard to focus. Every time I did, an uncomfortable feeling tried to rise inside me but then it was immediately doused in a fog of confusion which then turned into bliss. Maybe it would be better to let the past go and concentrate on the present. I took another look around.

I was lying on a huge pillow, possibly a mattress on the floor which was covered in pillows. Whatever, it didn't matter, it was really soft. Two men stood beside my low bed, looking down at me with stern expressions. The one on the right had deeply tanned skin which showed off his sparkling, multicolored eyes. The one on the left had even darker skin and more muscles than his friend; an obvious warrior. He was bare-chested, wearing only a pair of loose white pants. He also looked familiar. His angry face flashed in my mind, momentarily jolting me out of my languor. Then another wave of lethargy rose up, and I eased back into it.

"I know you." I pointed at the bigger man. "So, I think I know who you are too." I giggled and pointed at the other one. "It's Rainbow Brite and Rainbow Briter! Thank goodness I can finally use my jokes." I sighed in relief. "I'd hate for them to go to waste."

"Is this the affects of the drug?" The familiar guy asked the other.

Gish. That was the name of the guy I knew. So, this other guy must be...

"Qwas," I slurred. "No; that's not right. Cows. Cow-ass... no; that can't be it. Kass. Kiss-ass. Kissy-face. Kiss-my-ass! Wait..." I scrunched up my face in thought. Oh, but thinking; it was so hard to do.

"My name is Qaus," the man growled.

"Oh, like house with a K." I nodded sagely. "Just like he's Dish with a G. And you put dishes in houses, so Gish must be a top. Not a top like a toy but like in a gay couple; he's the one who goes on top. Cause he goes into the house with a K, get it?"

"Are you sure this is the Godhunter?" House-with-a-K asked Dish-with-a-G. "She's supposed to be some kind of seductress, but this woman—"

"I know, I know. I ain't nuthin' special," I cut him off. "And no; it's not lined in gold."

"What is she rambling about?" Qaus gaped at me.

"Wait, I think that was a double negative." I frowned and tried it again. "I'm not nothing special... no; that's still not right. I'm nothing special. Oh, there." I sighed. "I knew my words wouldn't fail me in the end."

"Who cares?" Gish was staring hard at me.

"I don't," I sang, "I feel too good to care. Carefree, that's me."

"How much did you give her?" Qaus asked Gish.

"Twice the usual dose." Gish shrugged. "She's a dragon. I wanted to be sure it worked."

"You fool!" Qaus snarled. "Now, we'll have to wait hours for her to regain her senses."

"So what?" Gish crossed his arms. "I got time."

"I didn't want to wait that long," Qaus muttered. "I guess I can start on her bonds. With her being a dragon, they'll have to be worked more subtly and much stronger than usual."

Qaus' hands began to fill with sparkling, rainbow light, and I giggled.

"I love the Gays!" I shouted and promptly passed out.

Chapter Thirty-Two

I came slowly out of the sluggish, honey-thick hell that was Net. My head felt tight, as if my brain had been battered and was now swollen; too big for my skull. Tingles raced through my nerves, bringing my senses back with a jaw-clenching rush. Like limbs that have been bloodless for too long and suddenly have circulation restored. I groaned and tried to lift my hand to my head but it was stuck in place. Oh, why was it so heavy?

Frowning, I looked down to see that I was strapped into a chair with glittering bands of striped, pastel light. Rainbows. I was bound by rainbows. Well, that was new. I strained against them with all of my strength but the bands only brightened and bulged just slightly. They were strong suckers. I shifted the tips of my fingers into claws and angled them toward the bands. That had no effect either. Oh, this was bad.

"Have you figured out that you can't cut rainbows?" Qaus walked up with a smug look.

We were in a large, marble-floored room that was completely bare of furniture other than the chair I sat on. The ceiling was domed, made from some kind of bone-colored stone, and was cut through with intricate designs. The sun shined through those lacy cut-outs and covered the floor with delicate patterns of light. A few tiny shafts of sunlight angled across my rainbow bindings, causing them to sparkle brilliantly.

"I have to say"—I smirked back at Gish—"these are the prettiest chains I've ever been put in. And Anubis had me in pure gold with this jackal head collar so that's saying a lot."

"Well, at least you have your wits back." Qaus stepped forward and set his hands on his hips. "Though I'm not sure it's much of an improvement."

I could clearly see the Arabian influence in his appearance now that I was more rational. He was a darkly handsome man with dramatic hollows and dips to his face. He had light eyes, which isn't totally unheard of for an Arab, but these were literally *light* eyes; as in eyes made of light. Rainbows to be exact. I thought I'd seen it all but those eyes were a first. They shifted through all the colors languorously as if they knew they were beautiful and wanted to give everyone time to admire each change. Narcissistic princess eyes, that's what they were... and the Rainbow Princess was seriously pissed off.

"All right, so we destroyed some of your weapons," I huffed. "But we also ended up killing humans for you. Didn't you get a burst of power from all the dead? You should be thanking me."

"How do you think I was able to make rainbows strong enough to hold the Godhunter?" His smirk widened. "Yes, you idiots gave us some extra power, but you also set us back years in our planning. If you hadn't interfered, we would have had enough magic to last us eternity."

"You already have enough to last you forever, don't you?" I frowned. "Thor told me once that Gods have enough energy to outlast the planet."

"*Some* gods," Qaus scoffed. "Our people have forgotten us. They're too wrapped up in war and their new god. A god who doesn't care at all about them."

"As if you would still care about them if they believed in

you but didn't sacrifice to you," I shot back. Then I mumbled, "Not that I'm on Jerry's side or anything."

"They *do* sacrifice to him," Qaus snarled. "How many wars do they fight in his name?"

"Is it really about him though? Or is it about power?" I mimicked Blue's observations.

"Regardless"—Qaus waved his hand—"he gets the dead."

"Does he?" I was a little surprised. "So, that's how Jerry keeps his throne."

"He's a slimy bastard but a smart one." Qaus nodded. "Very tricky; to head a pantheon and branch it off into three others."

"Christianity isn't a pantheon." I frowned.

"Isn't it?" He cocked his head at me. "Aren't you married to one of its numerous gods?"

"All right, I see your point." I gave him a grudging look of acceptance. "You know, I've never thought of that; how Christianity, Islam, and Judaism are all connected and so Jerry gets all of that devotion."

"He does have to share it with the entire Pantheon." Qaus shrugged.

"And all of Hell," I added.

"But these people are constantly killing each other so the flow is big enough to share," Qaus said enviously. "As I said, it was smart; ingenious actually. But then Jehovah wasn't the one to come up with the idea so I shouldn't give him all the credit."

"Let me guess; it was Lucifer's plan," I snickered.

"Yes, your father-in-law is the greatest tactician of all

the Gods," Qaus said reverently. "He even made sure that most of the sacrifices would go to him."

"Wait, what?" I frowned. "I thought Luke got most of the magic because humans believe more in the Devil than they do in God?"

"Yes, absolutely," he agreed. "But do you really think Lucifer Morningstar would help build a pantheon of that magnitude without having safeguarded his own interests?"

"No; I don't think he would," I said slowly. "So, you're telling me that Luke somehow worked out a way to take some of Jerry's power before it was distributed among the rest of the angels?"

"You think the war in Heaven was just about Holly?" Qaus laughed derisively. "It was because Jerry found out that not only was Luke sticking it to his wife, not only did Satan knock up the pure Holy Spirit and have a son with her, but the Morningstar had also forged a magical connection with Jehovah's own blood and made sure that no matter how much magic the God of the Israelites received, the God of Hell would receive more."

"Damn, that's brilliant," I breathed. "Note to self; don't piss off my father-in-law."

"He's not the god you need to worry about right now, Godhunter," Qaus sneered.

"Why do you guys always have to sneer in the same manner when you threaten me?" I sighed. "It gets a little old. Maybe try laughing maniacally next time. I don't think I've had anyone laugh mani—wait, maybe I have. Never mind, proceed."

"Don't you realize what I'm going to do to you?" He drew closer and narrowed his eyes at me. "I'm going to torture you slowly until you beg for death."

"Yeah; that's been said to me before too." I huffed out my breath with bored disdain. "And I've had to give this speech before. I don't think I want to go into all the gory details again. Suffice it to say; I've been tortured a lot... by the best torturers. You can't scare me."

"Then you're a fool," he growled. "Because you're trapped; trapped without any hope of escape or rescue. You're in the middle of the desert and bound with light. Even your dragon form can't save you now. Breathe fire if you like." He waved his hand out to indicate the stone room. "You won't hurt anything."

"Again; not all that impressive." I tried to shrug but could barely move my shoulders half an inch. Did I mention there was a wide rainbow band over my chest too? Then something he said registered. "Hold on... we're not even in the God Realm? You two kept me on Earth?" I chuckled. "Damn, you're dumb. I've met flying monkeys smarter than you."

"We have no need to hide in the God Realm," Qaus snapped. "My wards are stronger than they've ever been and they're concealing our location completely. Not even Gods can find us here."

"Okay," I said in my *dumb/duh* voice. You know; the one you use on people who are acting stupid and won't listen to you.

I wasn't about to tell them that not only could my men track me with my wedding band but that Dave had already found their little desert hideout when he trailed Disani. Which meant that the cavalry should be arriving at any moment. I just had to tough it out until they got there. No problem.

"If you're not scared of him, you should at least be scared of me," Gish announced as he strode into the room. "Your lover killed mine, and I intend to even the score."

"Re killed Disani?" I breathed a sigh of relief. I wasn't all that surprised but still, it was nice to know. "Thanks, that's good to hear."

"You fucking bitch," Gish growled and launched himself at me.

I blew a stream a fire at him but before it hit, a strong wind took it of course and it angled just to the side of Gish. I looked over at Qaus in surprise, and he smiled maliciously at me, right as Gish's fist connected with my face. Pain blossomed along my cheek as the crack of breaking bone echoed through my head and my vision went wonky for a moment. There was one second of blessed numbness before pain exploded in my skull. Still, this was the man who'd sent Thor flying. I should probably be thankful he hadn't taken my head off. That would have been difficult to recover from.

"You think you're going to frighten me with a punch?" I spat blood at Gish's feet and then adjusted my jaw back into place.

Head pain is the worst; you can't push it away like pain in other places. It's right there, too close to ignore. Like an annoying child shouting *Look at me! Look at me!* right in your face.

"I'm going to do so much more than just punch you," Gish vowed as he cracked his knuckles.

"Looks as if you've summoned the monster within the god," Qaus observed with a smirk. "Prepare for a violent introduction to the warrior god revered by the Nuristani."

"Monster?" I laughed even though my face was throbbing. "Don't you know who you're talking to? I was born of monsters. I am Queen of Monsters and their mother. I *love* them. Actually, I don't find them monstrous at all. But you would."

"I'm not afraid of dragons," Qaus scoffed. "I could bring

your kind down with an enchanted spear."

"You know nothing about my kind." I smiled serenely. "You don't know what I brought up from the darkness beneath the Fire Kingdom. And you don't know what true fear is."

"What's she talking about now?" Gish looked to Qaus. Yeah, he wasn't too bright, that one.

"I'm not sure," Qaus mused, looking intrigued in spite of himself.

"You don't know what real fear is until you sit in darkness so thick that it feels as if you've gone blind," I went on, and they went silent. "And you listen to sounds you've never heard before. Sounds that nonetheless hint at things with claws and teeth. The slide of something that leaves a trail of slime behind when it passes over the earth. The rustle of things which hunt from the air and rend flesh with razor sharp beaks. You think you're monsters? You're little boys, lacking even a costume to put on so you can growl at yourselves in the mirror. You would piss your pants and cry for your mommies if you ever met my faeries."

"She's out of her damn mind," Gish whispered.

"No; I don't think she is," Qaus murmured back. "Tell me more of these monstrous faeries, Godhunter. Illuminate me, if I am so ignorant."

"Look into your worst nightmares, and you'll find a glimmer of them there." I smiled proudly. I did so love my Hidden-Ones. "Then times that vision by ten—no; ten thousand— and you will have an idea of what the First-Born Fey are like."

"But you're not one of them." Qaus looked fascinated.

"No, I'm not a Hidden-One." I softened my smile. "Just their queen. Lucky enough to know them and be loved by them."

"Beloved of monsters," Qaus mused. "So, I guess we shall have to endeavor to be extra creative in our torture today." He looked at Gish and began to smile. "Fetch the bone saw."

"Who are the Nuristani, by the way?" I asked casually, even though the mention of a bone saw had rattled me a bit. "I thought you were an Afghani god."

"I am," Gish growled. "There is a Nuristan region of Afghanistan and that is where my people are from."

"Of course"—I rolled my eyes—"another *Stan*. Big surprise."

"Get the saw." Qaus shoved Gish away. "She's obviously stalling."

Gish sneered at Qaus but turned and headed out of the room. Just as my stomach began to clench, the building shook and the stone ceiling above us burst apart, raining down upon us. I ducked my head as debris pelted me, and the Rainbow Brothers hit the floor. Then I shook off the dust and looked up just in time to see an angel descend through the ceiling. Four angels, to be precise. And one sun god.

"And I looked, and behold a pale horse; and his name that sat on him was Death, and Hell followed with him," I murmured in awe.

Hell had indeed followed Azrael before, back when he'd rescued me from Heaven. But today, he had no need for a demon army because the Horsemen were riding at his side. The Horsemen and Re.

The Sun God, Re rode a beam of light down into the room, looking far more angelic than the Four Horsemen of the Apocalypse who surrounded him. Azrael was in his Death guise; his skeleton showing through his transparent skin and his eyes burning like stars in a night sky, dripping their acid tears. A menacing scythe extended before him, the angelic script along its vicious blade glowing bright blue to match the identical writing on Azrael's cheek. He wore bluejeans and silver bracers with thick black boots on his feet. Wings of darkness folded above him, their joints angled together to form the shape of a hood.

Beneath him galloped his pale horse, an animal I'd never laid eyes on before and one I would never forget now that I had. *Pale* was a poor description for this magnificent creature. It was creamy white, more like bone than snow, and shone as if it were polished smooth instead of sleekly furred. Its eyes matched Azrael's and its hooves glinted silver as if coated in metal.

War rode a fiery horse, its cinnabar hide sparking in the wind and trailing flames around its feet. The steed went well with War's crimson wings, as if both horse and wings had been drenched in blood. In War's thick hands he held a massive sword and a thick leather harness set with a gold medallion lay across his chest. Bracers covered his forearms and greaves covered his shins. Beneath that, he wore only red leather pants.

Famine looked almost emaciated, his body wrapped in shredded gray cloth. Beautiful brown wings rose up behind him, the only healthy aspect to his appearance; they caught the light and glowed gold along their edges. A pair of hungry eyes stared out of that famished face, as hungry as the sin-black beast beneath him. All of those wind-riding horses thumped the air with their hooves as if they were eager for battle, but Famine's mount foamed at the mouth and tore at the sky as if he were anticipating the taste of flesh and a full belly. Rib bones protruded from his hollowed stomach, mimicking the look of his rider. That rider held only a pair of scales, no weapons, but something about those silver plates unsettled me. They reminded me of the ones that sat in Duat; used only to weigh the hearts of humans.

The Antichrist looked like every human's idea of an angel. So beautiful, so pure, so ethereal that he didn't look real. His hair was windblown in a precise manner as if even the breeze bowed to his command. His green eyes seemed to be lit from within, shining out of his perfect, pale face like lasers looking for a victim. In his hands he held a red bow with an arrow notched and ready to shoot. Behind him rose a pair of folded wings, so white that they glowed; the perfect backdrop to his beauty. His horse matched his wings; mane, tail, hide, and even hooves all pure, glittering white while its large, round eyes were deep blue.

But the Antichrist wasn't the most beautiful of my saviors. No; the fairest of them all was the God amid the Angels. Sunlight made into man. Re shimmered in his shaft of golden light, that lowered him like some alien transport into the room. His skin shifted from dark to light as he descended and his golden eyes burned out of his face as if he wasn't just a sun god but actually the Sun made flesh.

Re was dressed in Egyptian armor; chest crossed by golden wings, a thick beaded collar draped over his shoulders, a short swathe of white gauze gathered around his hips, and a thick belt to hold the gauze in place. A sun adorned the center of the belt, its bottom rays forming a drape between his legs. Gold greaves adorned his shins and a thick band of gold circled one upper arm. Over his dark hair, a folded cowl of blue and gold stripes was topped with a gold crown. A red disc perched at the back of the crown with a golden snake encircling it; head lifted proudly at the apex. Re held a staff in his hand, and he pointed it straight at Qaus.

As the Horsemen and the Sun God touched the ground, werelions surged into the room along with the God Squad and an angry werewolf. But before anyone could attack, Re shot a shaft of fiery light into Qaus. The Arabian god started to scream as he burned.

Gish had enough time to settle into a fighting stance but that was all he managed before the Antichrist's arrow pierced his throat. He went down to his knees as Azrael rode up to him. One motion of his scythe, and the Angel of Death sent Gish's head sailing across the room. Yes, anger makes it easier for a god to kill another god. My husband was very, very angry. And he wasn't the only one.

Qaus continued to burn as a circle of growling gods and demigods surrounded him, but he fought back. Within the hazy heat of Re's magic, Qaus formed a liquid barrier, pulling on his weather magic to protect him. Unfortunately, all it did was boil and soon clouds of steam replaced the previous smoke. War dismounted and stepped forward with a raised sword, but Re stopped him with a hand on his shoulder. Sam nodded and backed away as Re stopped the burning attack.

Qaus moaned as pieces of bubbled skin slid off him. Blood and fluids dripped onto the stone floor yet somehow, he managed to open his eyes and glare at Re. But the Sun God didn't meet the vicious stare, he was too busy looking at me. After a thorough examination of my condition, he cast his gaze over to my husbands and waved them forward.

Azrael had his kill and seemed satisfied enough. He dismounted and led his horse past the prone Arabian god without a backwards glance. They came to stand beside me. Re joined them and he and Azrael laid their hands supportively on my shoulders. I would have reached up to them, but I was still bound by those stupid rainbows.

Kirill was in lion form, his black fur glinting blue in the light from the broken ceiling, and he padded toward Qaus silently. Trevor was half-shifted in his werewolf guise and although he could have been silent if he'd chosen to, he wasn't. He pounded across the stone, his claws clattering as a constant growling emanated from deep within his throat. A sudden howl announced his fury, and Kirill responded to it, launching himself forward with Trevor.

The kill was drawn out and several gods looked away from the carnage, but I forced myself to watch. They did this for me and the least I could do was respect their vengeance and acknowledge that it was merely a manifestation of their love. Yes, I know that sounds horrible and perhaps you think that violence should never be a part of love. But I'm a dragon, and I know the truth; love and violence are only a heartbeat apart. Losing one will lead you to the other and the stronger your love, the more bloody your wrath will be.

Qaus hadn't taken me from Trevor and Kirill; he hadn't destroyed their love, but he had tried to and it was the threat of loss that my husbands were responding to. They needed to do more than just kill him, they needed to feed their fury until it was full enough to step back behind the heartbeat and let love rule once more. So, I watched and respected their love. After all, I would have done the same for them.

I knew the exact moment that Qaus died and it wasn't because the screams had stopped. I think he passed out long before he passed away. It was the magic that clued me in. The rainbow bonds disappeared, and I fell forward out of the chair. Azrael and Re caught me before I landed, and I was laid gently back into the seat. Then Trevor was there, still in werewolf form and covered in blood.

"Minn Elska," he said softly, his voice a rough growl out of his werewolf throat. He laid a large, clawed paw on my injured cheek, and I hissed. "Teharon," he called over his shoulder.

Kirill came up beside me, back in his human form and gloriously naked. His ebony hair spilled down around me as he leaned over to nuzzle my uninjured cheek.

"It's okay." I pushed him back gently. "I got it. Just back away a little."

They eased back as I called forth my healing fire. All but Re, who was probably as fireproof as I. He held one of my hands as I put the other on my cheek. Flames licked upward from my fingertips, healing my skin instead of burning it. My broken jaw mended with a click and my vision went back to normal. The first thing I saw was the concern in Re's golden eyes.

"Lala," he whispered. "Are you all right?"

"Talk about making an entrance." I smiled and looked from him to the others clustering around me. "That was damn impressive. And you guys had perfect timing. They were just about to get creative in their torture."

"Creative?" Kirill's eyes narrowed.

"I may have taunted them a bit." I shrugged. "The words *bone* and *saw* were used."

"Tima." Kirill sighed. "Could you maybe not taunt gods who are about to torture you?"

"Come on." I rolled my eyes. "As if the Rainbow Twins could do anything to me that hasn't been done before. They didn't even last two minutes against you guys."

"Well, we did come in force." Finn smirked and waved at the gathering of Gods, Angels, and Shifters. "I'm a little bummed that I didn't get to do much beyond knock out a few humans."

"Knock out?" I lifted my brows.

"We learned our lesson." Hades grimaced. "The humans guarding this place are unconscious but alive."

"That's good to hear," I said but then slid a smile over toward my husbands. "Tracked me with my ring, did you?" I held up my gold wedding band that I'd enchanted with magic to alert us when one of us was in trouble... and to tell us exactly where they were. It had come in handy too many times to count.

"Yep," Trevor confirmed. "This was one of your best ideas." He held up his hand to show off his matching ring.

"Hey, Horsemen," I called over to Azrael's friends. "Thanks for lending a hand. Or should I say an arm-ageddon?"

"Carus," Azrael groaned and shook his head.

"Anytime you want an Apocalypse, we're at your service, my lady." War, I mean Sam, bowed and his horse bowed with him.

"We're always up for some action," Ted agreed with a wide grin. "I'm just thrilled that I got to fire my bow."

"It's been awhile." Ira nodded. "It felt good to fly in and rescue someone."

"Instead of just kill everything," Sam added.

"Tima?" Aidan had changed back to human form so he could speak.

Which meant he was as naked as Kirill, but shifters really don't care about that sort of thing. Of course, there were more than just shifters there, and I chuckled as I watched Horus slip his hand over Kate's ogling eyes.

"Aidan?" I lifted my brow at my lion.

"Shouldn't we celebrate?" He offered.

"Absolutely; party at our place," I said immediately, and everyone cheered.

Chapter Thirty-Three

"You look good in this." I flicked the metal wings crossing Re's chest.

"I know." Re smiled and pulled the elaborate headdress off, setting it on the floor beside him. "But thank you for noticing."

We were on the veranda, which was also a sort of permanently down drawbridge. It laid across the moat that surrounded Pride Palace. A moat that was connected to the pool nearby and which was now full of frolicking Intare instead of alligators... or whatever it was that one usually puts in moats. We had thick carpets laid over the veranda and several sitting areas with beautiful Victorian furniture. Re and I sat on the ground off to the side though, hanging our legs over the moat and having a private moment together.

"Thank you"—I took his hand—"for coming to my rescue."

"I was afraid," he admitted in a low tone. "I haven't felt that way in a long time."

"You did fine," I scoffed. "They didn't stand a chance."

"No, Lala." Re set his golden eyes on me. "I was afraid for you. When I killed Disani, I was enraged because she was threatening you. I got lost to the anger and burned her to ashes. Then I regained some calm and looked up to find you gone. I realized what had happened, that Disani had served as a distraction. This agony tore through me, crippling me. My heart constricted, my lungs wouldn't take in air, and my legs started to shake."

"Re, I'm so sorry you were worried." I squeezed his hand. "I know what that's like, feeling that panic."

"You don't understand." He pulled me into his side.

I laid my head against his chest and listened to his heart beating urgently.

"I was faced with the possibility that you were lost to me," he said. "That you were dead, and I would have to live through eternity without you. It was a bleak future that stretched before me, one which I now know I must avoid at all costs."

"Re, I'm so sorry."

"Stop, Vervain." Re angled my face up and kissed me. "Stop apologizing and just tell me that you'll be mine forever."

"I'll be yours forever," I whispered as I opened my eyes and looked up into Re's expectant face.

I blinked in confusion as I looked around the room. I was back in my own time, in Re's bed, which I now had intimate knowledge of. Oh, crap; I'd been seduced by my own memories. No, not memories really; they were a future that would never happen. And yet, I held it all in me now... as Re did.

"I love you, Lala." Re smiled as he lowered his face to mine.

"Wait." I slid hand between us and flinched away. "Just give me a second to get my bearings."

I sat up and slid from his grasp.

"Vervain," he growled and reached for me.

"How long was I out?" I demanded.

"You've only been here a couple of hours," he said soothingly. "They're probably not even missing you yet."

"If you think that, then you don't know my husbands... I mean; my fiances," I muttered as I tried to process what had happened.

I'd lived months in the space of a couple hours. How did that even work? I concentrated, trying to see if there were any missing pieces, if maybe I'd skipped parts. But no, they were all there. I may have fast forwarded through them, like when you scan a memory quickly in your head, but I hadn't skipped anything.

"My daughters have come up with an excuse for your absence, I'm sure." Re reached for me again. "Just relax and come here. Let me hold you, and you'll feel better."

"No!" I shouted, and he gaped at me. "Give me a second, Re."

"But you saw it all." Re scowled. "You did, didn't you? You just said you'd be mine forever."

"I was saying that in the memory." I shook my head. "I wasn't saying it to this you."

"I am *the same* me," he huffed. "You are that Vervain. You're mine; you already said you were."

"I *never* said I was." I shook my head and softened my tone. "That's a future that will never happen. It wasn't *meant* to."

"Look at me and tell me you don't love me!" Re snatched my hand and pulled me back to him. "Look at me!"

"I can't," I whispered miserably. "You don't understand what you've done. I'm not short a lover now and the only way

I'll bring a new man into my complicated life, is if I am in *absolute* need of him. I can't have you, Re. It's not right, not *fair* to my other lovers."

"Not fair?" He scowled. "This is love, of course it isn't fair. I don't care if you have an open seat at your table or not, I'm sitting down beside you, and we're going to share this feast."

"That was a little confusing." I blinked. "Are you hungry now, or is it just me? I didn't exactly get to finish my meal, and I am eating for two." I rubbed my belly.

"Vervain!" He shouted, making me flinch.

"I love you!" I shouted back, and he went silent. "Are you happy now? Is that what you wanted to hear? I love you, Re. You win. You've accomplished your goal. Bravo. Now, we can both be miserable because love is not enough!"

"Of course it is," he said calmly.

"Not when I have five other hearts to consider." I shook my head. "Think about what you're asking to be a part of. You'll be lover number six. Is that what you truly want?"

"What I want is you." His jaw clenched. "We can spend time together here, and I'll ignore the fact that I must share you."

"Denial isn't just a river in Egypt," I muttered.

"This is not a joke, Vervain," he growled.

"No, it's not. You've abducted me and forced me to relive things that will only bring me pain. What a romantic way to declare your love for me," I sneered. "Did you have to see our entire relationship or were you just given a glimpse? Because I saw every detail and it will haunt me forever."

"I relive them in my dreams," he whispered. "You went

through them in one shot; one long, single memory which you can now choose to push aside while I see you every night and will continue to do so. Every dream takes me back into your arms and makes me love you all over again. Each morning I wake up with fresh wounds in my aching heart. I can't live like this," his voice broke.

I automatically reached for him and hugged him tightly. Re wrapped his arms around me and laid his face against my neck. All I heard were his labored breaths, but I felt the liquid heat of his silent tears on my skin and my own heart broke along with his. I guess this was the price I had to pay for the life I was lucky enough to live. I loved Re now, but I also loved Trevor, and Kirill, and Azrael, and Odin, and Arach. I started to cry too. Penance for betraying the hearts that were so true to me. And perhaps a little for the love I'd have to let go.

"I'm so sorry, Re." I found myself repeating the things I'd be saying to him only moments before in my memories... my future... my false future... whatever. "I'm sorry to have made you a part of this. This is so unfair to you but it will be okay. I'll help you. There's no reason for us both to suffer." I called up my love magic and started to send it into him, to try and ease some of his pain.

Re jerked back and stared at me with horror-filled eyes. "What are you doing?"

"Just trying to ease your heartache," I said gently. "Let me take away some of the pain I caused."

"No!" He shouted. "No, Vervain! This is mine! *You* are mine! I'm not giving any of it up."

"All right, okay." I held up my hands in a placating way. "I'm not trying to take away the memories, just the hurt."

"You can take away the hurt by being with me." He stared at me as if he couldn't understand why being his lover was such a hard thing to do.

"It's just not possible," I said gently. "I'm so—"

"Stop saying you're sorry!" Re got up and stalked out of the room, slamming the door behind him. The click of a lock echoed through the massive chamber.

"Sorry," I finished in a whisper.

Chapter Thirty-Four

My stomach clenched, and I knew this was building up to becoming a repeat of my last abduction by an Egyptian god. I couldn't let that happen, especially not with Rian's birth so close. He shifted inside me as if he could sense my attention on him, and I set my hand over my belly.

"I know," I whispered. "We're *so* outta here."

I slipped my heels on and headed for the balcony. I know, not the best shoes for an escape, but I wasn't leaving them behind. They were Versace... as in the real deal, I didn't make them with magic. Thanks to my new memories, I knew where the tracing room was, but I couldn't risk breaking down the door and racing there. So, it was a good thing that those future memories had also provided me with a second option; the Watercourse. Re had said that it led straight into the Aether. If I could steal a boat and make my way past all of those gates, I could simply sail out of Duat.

I looked down at the steep drop from Re's balcony and realized that I'd have to fly. Fly! Duh, I could just fly over those pesky walls and straight to the end of the river. Take that, you tricksy Egyptian deities! I smiled and removed my shoes —didn't want to ruin them—so I could shift into my half-form—correction: weredragon form—leathery wings sprouting from my shoulders with a feeling very similar to a good back stretch. I sighed as scales lifted out of my skin and my fingers lengthened into claws. Rian stretched along with me, and

I wondered if he'd shifted too. Mind blown, I stood still for a moment and just stared out at the beautiful landscape.

The sight triggered a memory. They were all so fresh in my mind now but this one seemed special. This one I'd had before all of the others. It was given to me back in that future which would never be. The view from the balcony was only part of the swirling panorama I'd seen as I'd twirled in a circle. I had closed my eyes against the dizzying blur and fallen backwards, laughing; completely trusting in Re to catch me, and he had. When I opened my eyes, I saw his golden gaze.

"I love you, Lala," the words seemed to whisper in the breeze around me, and I cringed, claws cutting into the stone balustrade.

"I wish I could accept that love, Re." I sighed as I caught the whispering wind with my wings.

I lifted myself up with strong strokes of my dragon wings, watching the balcony fall away beneath my taloned feet and feeling that rush of happiness I always got when I flew. This was me, this demon-like form and this wild strength. Pieces of my true self that had been hidden before they'd even been allowed to emerge. For years my dragon had curled inside me, waiting with me in the Well of Souls until we'd finally been released. And even then, she'd waited, trapped until my visit to Faerie had finally freed her. Now, she was truly mine and so was the sky. I stretched my wings and soared, letting my heartache over Re fall away with the ground as I headed towards the walls separating the territories of Duat.

The feeling of flight is pure freedom. It's no wonder humans chase after it, creating all manner of unnatural wings. You can't be unhappy in the air. Not if you have confidence in your right to be there. Up in the sky, there are no limits, no boundaries, no chains or restrict—

I suddenly struck something solid, right above the

spear-tipped wall surrounding Re's territory, and I jolted back in alarm, almost dropping my shoes. I scowled at the glimmering space before me, knowing exactly what I'd hit. So much for no restrictions. It looked as if the Egyptian Gods were smarter than I'd given them credit for.

"Stupid ward," I grumbled as I hovered before it. "I guess I'm back to stealing a boat and fighting snakes. Maybe I can just charm them into letting me by. Where's a damn flute when you need one?"

I sighed and looked down toward the river. It was much darker here than at the palace, probably why I hadn't noticed the ward before I'd hit it. Full night seemed to have descended upon the land surrounding the river but the breath from the Guardians of the Gate—AKA the venom-spitting, fire-breathing, colossal cobras—lit up the river with eerie amber light. Not that I even needed light. I had great night vision, especially in my half-form. Still, it was there and it was more than enough to illuminate the boat that came sailing out of the first gate.

It was Re's soul boat, full of his followers and his magical hologram goddess. Heka would speak the proper words to open the gates and calm the guardians. Maybe I wouldn't have to become a snake charmer after all.

I swung around and angled towards the boat but hovered high out of sight while one of the six gods rowed over to collect the souls. After they reached the shore and started walking off towards their wonderful afterlife, I descended to the deck. Then I shifted back to human form and slid my shoes back on.

"What's up, Heka?" I asked the hologram who, of course, ignored me. I guess I hadn't said a trigger word.

We reached the gate, and Heka intoned something in Egyptian loudly. The snakes stopped their fire breathing and the wooden doors swung open to let us through on a rush of dammed up river water. I cast one last look at the shores of Re's territory as I was swept along into the next section of Aaru. Part of me was actually sad to see the last of it.

"Welcome to the Watercourse of the Only God, where Osiris is Lord."

"Yeah, I figured." I chuckled, and she went back to staring ahead.

There, in Osiris' territory, the sky lightened a bit and the forms of soaring statues were revealed on both banks. Egyptian Gods sat on carved thrones, staring out at us with their smooth stone eyes. In the center of the statues on the right bank, sat one which that larger and grander than the rest. Its throne was gigantic, set over a stream that poured into the river. The god sitting upon it stared out at the river with regal grace, one of those high Egyptian crowns on his head; that sort that looked like a tube with the front cut out and a bowling pin stuck in the center of it. The outer crown (the tube) was painted red and the bowling pin was white.

I tensed as I spotted a raft near the base of that grand statue. A god stood beside it. Probably that guy Akhabit, that Re had mentioned. He frowned at me but made no move towards the raft. I'm sure he realized that I didn't belong on the boat of souls but it didn't look as if he were going to do anything about it. Just like with humans, you could always count on laziness. Then again, maybe he was restricted by magic to only row out to Osiris' boat.

He'd no doubt report me to someone, but I couldn't worry about that. Plus, we were already approaching the next gate and the next set of snakes. I sighed in relief as Heka intoned the passwords, and the snakes pulled away. The narrow doors swung open, and I sailed out of Osiris' Kingdom, flowing into the next territory on another wave of water. Hopefully,

I'd be far downriver by the time anyone came looking for me.

"Welcome to the Living One of Forms," Heka stated, "where Sokar is Lord."

"That doesn't make sense," I muttered to her. Rian kicked inside me, and I chuckled. "My son agrees with me. Maybe it's one of those things lost in translation, Rian."

Then I got a good look at the territory. The sky had lightened a little more but this was a landscape that would have been better viewed in darkness. Dreary desert stretched as far as I could see. Just sand and more sand with huge snakes gliding across it. They had numerous heads and some even had stumpy legs, which should have made them look silly but instead, made them even more horrifying. Some snakes had wings and some had ridges on their heads but all of them spotted me at once. They hissed and roared at me as I floated past. I gave a low hiss back, and they all went still, sensing that I was more than I seemed.

"Huh," I huffed. "Monsters, he said. Dangerous, he said. This isn't so bad."

That's when the water dried up.

I gave a start as the water level dropped and the boat lowered steadily to an empty ravine where the water trickled down to nothing. We kept sliding down the sandy riverbed for a few minutes, through high rock embankments which caught the wind and made it howl. Then we came to a grinding stop and the boat began to lurch beneath me.

I spread my legs to steady myself and grabbed at a railing as the wood of the boat creaked and moaned. It shifted, smoothing first and then reforming into scales. The railing, the deck, and the cabin remained but the rest of the ship had gone as scaly as any dragon. Another lurch and a scraping sound announced the unraveling of a long tail behind me.

I turned just in time to see it settle in the sand. Then a hissing came from the front and a shimmering snake head rose up before me like the prow of a Viking ship. The snake opened its mouth to hiss once, revealing long fangs dripping with venom, and then settled its neck into a graceful curve.

"They sure do like their snakes here," I murmured as the body beneath my feet started undulating side to side, and we began to move forward once again. "Well, I'll be a dragon's mother." I gave a huffing laugh. "The adventure continues."

Ahead of us loomed another gate, this one seeming even bigger than the last, due to my perspective from the bottom of the ravine. The snakes reared above me, spewing fire and venom across the passage. But, once more, the hologram woman spoke her magic words, and the snakes eased back, closing their dangerous jaws and settling into peaceful coils. The doors slid open, and we slithered past them, the sound of scales on sand echoing off the wood.

"Welcome to Hidden," the hologram announced. "Where Sokar is Lord."

"What's hidden?" I looked over the new area we glided into. "And wasn't Sokar Lord of the last area? How come he gets two territories?"

The sky was even lighter there but it was appropriately gloomy since I was pretty sure that *Hidden* was code for *Hell*. The desert theme continued on but there was a little more character to this landscape. Hills created graceful curves and at the top of the ravine on my right, a massive structure stood. It was outlined in columns and rose up into the sky, where a pair of predator birds clung to it on either side. They cried out angrily at me and a flying snake undulated into view, swirling around the building as if he were guarding it.

"Another snake," I shook my head and looked away. "The Nagas would love it here. Then again, they're water snakes, and we just ran out of water."

There was nothing else really noteworthy to see until we rounded a bend. Then a mountain rose up on my left and the ravine walls shortened, allowing me a good view of the spectacle atop the sandy peak. A pair of sphinxes sat on the mountaintop, and I straightened in surprise when I saw them. These weren't statues but actual, real, live Sphinxes. I'd never seen one before and after all those damn snakes, I was even more interested in getting a good look.

The Sphinxes were part lion—the butt part—and part bird—the front part—with the head of a human man set atop. The stern male head had a pair of broad shoulders beneath it. Arms turned into avian legs, tipped in vicious claws, while the chest slid down into a lion belly. They had been sitting on their haunches, as lions do, but they went on high alert when they spotted me; standing up and turning to look at the serpent that coiled between them.

Of course, another snake. This one was winged and had three heads. Between his feathered wings, standing at the apex of the curve of his back, was a god. The God wore a skirt of white linen girded with a leather belt that had a loin-guard of leather strips down the front. On top of his thick shoulders, he had the head of a bird; golden brown feathers curving smoothly over the similarly colored skin of his sleekly muscled chest.

"Horus?" I frowned as I edged to the left side of the boat.

The falcon head turned sharply as if he'd heard me speak, and one bird eye focused on me. The God tapped one of the snake heads, and the beast sprung into the sky, swirling through the air as if it were gliding across sand. It landed on the riverbed beside my snake boat and the prow of my vessel hissed at it. All three heads of the flying snake hissed back.

"Silence!" The God shouted out of his bird beak, and the

snakes settled down immediately.

"You're not Horus," I accused him.

"Hawk, not falcon." He waved at his head with a graceful hand. "Common mistake."

"Who are you, then?" I peered at the golden amulet of a bird that he wore around his neck.

"I believe it would be more appropriate for you to answer that question first," he shot back. "You've invaded my territory."

"I'm just passing through," I insisted. "And my name is Vervain."

"Vervain," he mused as he shook his head like a dog shakes off water.

The feathers disappeared during that shake, revealing a striking face with a tall forehead. His short ebony hair was slicked back beneath a wide gold band. Although his dark eyes were human, they remained bird-sharp and continued to study me as I studied him. There were echoes of Horus in face; the angular nose and the regal lift of his brows. Was it the bird thing or were they related?

"Do you know Horus?" I asked him.

"Of course, I know him, but we only resemble each other because of our bird magic," he explained. "Are you the Godhunter? Is that why I recognize your name?"

"Yeah," I said and sighed. "Look, I'm just trying to get out of Duat—"

"Aaru," he corrected.

"Excuse me?" I lifted a brow.

"You're technically in Aaru," he explained. "It's a sub-territory of Duat. We are in Aaru, which is in Duat. Like a city within a state."

"Wonderful," I huffed. "Thank you for clearing that up. Now, I would like to get out of Aaru *and* Duat. So, if you don't mind, I'll just keep going down this river—"

"I *do* mind," he cut me off with an affronted tone. If he'd still had the bird head, I was pretty sure his feathers would have ruffled. "Do you know how often I get visitors?"

"Not very?" I asked with a whine.

"At least not any that I don't have to torture or throw into the boiling lake," he amended.

"Boiling lake, eh?" I gave him a grin. "I call that a Jacuzzi."

He blinked and then brightened. "Oh, yes, you're part dragon, aren't you?"

"I'm full dragon actually." I smiled bigger at his surprise. "And I'm fully goddess and fully human."

"So, that rumor is true?" His mouth hung open just a little.

"Yep; all three, one hundred percent," I nodded.

"That would make you three hundred percent," he pondered. "But no one can be three hundred percent; the very definition of one hundred percent is that it is complete. You cannot be *more* complete; that's impossible."

"It's not my physical body that's more complete." I shrugged. "It's my souls. I have three of them; each one is complete."

"Ah." He nodded. "I think I understand now."

"And now that you know my name..." I looked at him

pointedly.

"Oh, yes, pardon me." He gave me a bow, "I am Sokar, God of Those Who Are Buried."

"Nice to meet you." I cleared my throat. "So, I'd love to stay and chat, but I'm kind of under a time crunch." I rubbed my belly.

"Are you in labor?" His eyes widened.

"No. but it could be any day now," I explained. "I'm having a dragon-sidhe baby. and we're not sure how long the pregnancy will be for me."

"Well, you're safe with me. I've delivered several babies in my time." Sokar gestured at his winged snake. "Please, just a short visit. We can have tea. I insist, Godhunter. Besides, there's no need for you to continue through the countries of Aaru when I have a tracing room you can use... right after our tea."

"Oh, fine," I huffed and let him help me up onto his flying snake.

Chapter Thirty-Five

Tea in Hell. It wasn't the first time I'd been invited to an insane tea party. It wasn't even the first time that the role of the Mad Hatter had been played by an Egyptian god. Though now that I think of it, it may have been coffee that Anubis had served.

"How many lumps of sugar would you like?" Asked the Mad Hatter... er, I mean Sokar, God of Those Who Are Buried.

And what the hell did that mean? Or rather, what *in* Hell did that mean? Did he only rule over the entombed dead? And if he did, what about Osiris and his happy play-land a couple territories over? Didn't he get the buried dead? Weren't all Egyptians buried? I wasn't sure if I wanted to know, but I *was* sure that I didn't have the time to sit through a long lecture so I didn't ask. But it was hard to control the urge. I am, at heart, an inquisitive person.

"Well, one is too few and three is too many," I went with the *Alice in Wonderland* theme.

"So... *two* lumps?" Sokar lifted his brows at me as if I were the crazy one.

"No, three, of course," I huffed. "I always have too many." I frowned as my words hit on more truth than I'd intended.

"Indeed. I'd heard that about you." He chuckled and used a pair of tiny silver tongs to pick up three sugar cubes and put them in my cup. "Cream?"

"No, thank you." I accepted the delicate teacup and admired the deep blue designs on the thin china.

Sokar had gone all out. We were sitting at a long glass and gold table on his patio which overlooked his boiling lake. Steam rose from the bubbling surface and seeped into the landscape, turning it into a place of misty shapes and echoing murmurs. The moisture didn't reach us, but I could feel the heat and it relaxed my tight muscles even though my legs wanted to run. I took comfort in the fact that Sokar's tracing room was just down the hallway from us, and I could sprint there if I had to.

The house itself was technically a cave, though I think it would be a better description to say it was a palace set into the bottom of a mountain. We had entered through a small door at the base of the mountain he'd been sitting on earlier; the mountain guarded by his pet sphinxes. I didn't ask their names since they growled at me when we passed.

After that sandy facade, I'd expected a dreary and dismal home with torches set into stone walls, stuff like that. But Sokar had led me through an airy, bright, golden palace with dove-gray marble floors and gilded pillars soaring over our heads to the flat ceiling.

The furniture was grandly Medieval in tone, adorned with intricate carvings and upholstered in jeweled velvet and subtly patterned damask. Seating areas were defined by expansive plush rugs and tall pots of flowers posed around them for even more color. Sokar had led me straight through the luxuriant palace and out onto the patio, where he left me so he could personally prepare our tea. I guess the Sphinxes weren't trusted with the china.

I had wandered down the stone steps of his patio towards the lake and when I returned, I was presented with a view of the backside of the mountain. It was sliced away to reveal the columned levels of Sokar's palace; rising four stories up. Balconies jutted out from it, embraced by the foundational stone of the sandy mountain. I would have said it was formed from the mountain itself, like Castle Aithinne was, but the stone of the palace was different from that of the mountain; snowy white marble instead of beige rock. Veins of gold ran through the marble, gilded with even more gold in several places, making the whole palace glow and shimmer in the light of several braziers that lined the patio.

Then Sokar had returned with a tea cart and set the table while he hummed delightedly. He laid lacy doilies down first, upon which he placed silver trays. One was actually a three-tiered contraption which had a round plate at the bottom and then two on top, one to either side. It was full of little baby scones. Another plate held sandwiches cut into all sorts of shapes, and a third had pastry puffs in the form of swans. He also had two pots of tea because he simply couldn't decide on one, and a full service with cream and sugar. It was damn impressive on such short notice and taking into consideration the fact that he'd done it all himself. Sokar didn't have a bunch of servant souls running around like Re did. I guess they were too busy being tortured.

"Did you just have all of this sitting in the fridge, or what?" I asked as I reached for a scone.

Sokar had taken the seat on my right, allowing me to have the best view. He snatched up the triple tiered scone tray so he could present it to me in gentlemanly fashion. "Oh, I have a bit of magic." He shrugged.

"Tea-making magic?" I took a scone and then pointed at the pot of Devonshire cream.

"Creation magic." Sokar smiled and handed me the cream.

"Like Re?" I lifted a brow.

"I was a very important god once," he reminisced. "The Egyptians counted on me for a good harvest and to watch over their cattle, not just guard them in the Netherworld. I was a creator god, though not as powerful as Re, and I became a patron to all goldsmiths." He waved a hand toward his gilded palace.

"Oh, I get it now," I said. "So, how are you connected to Re?" I asked it casually but internally, I was worried. "You're not one of his many relatives, are you?"

"No." He smiled wide. "I'm one of the few gods he recruited into his pantheon. I'm an original from Atlantis, along with my brother Ptah."

"Ptah is your brother?" I blinked. "That's interesting."

"Do you know him?"

"No, but I was recently commenting on how similar his name sounded to Re's." I laughed.

"Oh, well he's married to Re's daughter; Sekhmet." Sokar went still when he saw my face. "What is it?"

"Sekhmet and Bastet were the ones who tricked me into coming to Aaru." I grimaced, wondering how much I should tell Sokar.

"They tricked you?" He chuckled. "What did they do; push you through the gates?"

"Actually, yes," I grumbled, and he laughed harder.

"Those girls are mischievous." He shook his head.

"Mischievous?" I lifted a brow. "That's putting it lightly."

"Well, it's not as if they were trying to kill you." He bit

into a sandwich and then paused. "Were they? Because if they were, they did a poor job of it."

"No, they weren't trying to kill me." I sighed. "I was at a Ball in Duat, and they lured me away and pushed me through the portal."

"See?" He shrugged. "They were just having a bit of fun."

"With a pregnant woman?" I shot back, and he frowned.

"Yes, I see your point," he said. "I shall have a talk with them."

"No, don't bother." I waved it away and realized I was famished. I never got to finish the dinner Re had promised me, and I'd been through a lot since then. I started piling food on my plate.

"Swan puff?" Sokar offered me the tray of swan pastries.

"Sure." I took two. "What was that building I saw just before the curve in the river?" I asked before I bit the swan's head off. "It had a couple of birds hanging on it and a big snake flying around it. It looked important."

"Yes, that would be Khepera's house." He rolled his eyes. "He likes to think he's important, and he especially likes others to think so."

"But he's not?" I lifted a brow.

"He's the God of Resurrection," Sokar explained. "The Egyptians believe that he resurrects Re every night on his journey through Aaru."

"Oh, right; Re told me about his nightly sail." I nodded. "He didn't mention any resurrection, though."

"He's the Sun," Sokar went further into it. "So, at night, Re dies and journeys through Aaru on the Mesektet, his funeral boat. He is supposed to pass through twelve countries, which represent the twelve hours of night, during which he is resurrected by Khepera. He also 'fights Apep.'" Sokar made the quote fingers. "But even in the myth, he isn't the one who actually conquers Apep since he's actually still dead, waiting to be resurrected."

"Then who kills Apep?" I asked, suddenly enthralled with the story.

"A bunch of people." Sokar shrugged as if he didn't care, but I could see that he was thrilled to have sparked my interest. "Isis is sometimes there, depending on who tells it. But that's besides the point. Re makes his journey and is reborn to rise in the morning."

"So, the only person Khepera resurrects is Re?" I asked.

"Ah, you're quick," he said. "Now you see why I say he only thinks he's important. Khepera's a god of resurrection who doesn't actually resurrect anyone, and he calls himself the Soul of the Universe, but he's not in charge of any souls. We don't have access to a well of souls here or anything like that. Khepera just sits in his palace and waits for Re to notice him. He won't even come over and play Cribbage with me," Sokar huffed.

"What about this Apep?" I asked. "Re mentioned that he's a snake-shifter."

"Oh, yes," Sokar said. "He lives right across the lake from me. But he's rather solitary as well. Once in awhile he'll come over for a night of revelry but that doesn't happen very often."

"A night of revelry, huh?" I smiled, wondering what this god thought of as revelry.

"He likes to throw people into the lake with me," he said, and I sobered.

"Oh, how nice." I smiled brightly. And now back to our

scheduled programming of; *Sokar's Crazy Tea Party*. "You guys should get out more often."

"Out of Aaru?" He mused. "Maybe we should."

I could have smacked myself for that one. I'd just told the crazies to leave their asylum and go take a walk-about around the Human Realm. Splendid, Vervain.

"As in maybe you should go and visit Anubis," I tried to recover. "He had a party tonight. Why didn't you attend?"

"Oh, I don't like the pressure of a big party," he said. "I feel awkward."

"You should cook something to bring with you," I suggested. "It might make you feel more comfortable if you have something to offer beyond conversation."

"You know, you're right," he perked up. "I think that would make me more comfortable. Oh, it's been so lovely talking to you, Vervain. I hate to have to end this."

"Me too," I said politely. "It's a shame that I have to get going."

"About that." Sokar looked guilty and when he glanced behind me, I knew I'd made a huge mistake.

I turned just as a fist came smashing into my face, sending me straight out of my seat and down to the floor.

"Be careful, she's pregnant!" I heard Bastet's worried voice but when I looked up, it was to see a man's face looming above me.

It was a familiar face, though a lot had happened since I'd seen it last and it took me a second to remember. Ptah, Sekhmet's husband... and Sokar's brother. I almost groaned. How stupid could I be? The guy probably notified Ptah while he was plating swan puffs.

I jumped to my feet and faced off with the angry deity. He was even taller than I remembered, wiry but elegant. Malachite eyes narrowed at me, set in a stern face with a hard line for a mouth. He had dark skin and shoulder-length hair but it was pulled back in a severe ponytail, and I realized that he was still dressed for the Ball. So, Re had been telling the truth, not much time had passed since my push into Aaru.

"Ptah-da!" I exclaimed.

"Is she bonkers?" Ptah paused to glance at his wife.

"All the best people are." I smirked.

"I'm not sure." Sekhmet frowned. "I suppose she could have lost her mind here. Or perhaps you hit her hard enough to do damage."

"Hey, you!" I pointed at Sekhmet. "I want my ring back."

"I gave it to my father," she growled. "If you hadn't left him heartbroken, crying all over the place like some silly teenage boy, he would have given it back to you!"

"I didn't mean to hurt Re," I huffed. "All of his memories are from a future which will never happen. It's not as if I did this to him on purpose. And; *ow*, by the way," I said to Ptah. "Did you really need to punch me?"

"He did, and he's going to do a lot more than that!" Claws popped out of Sekhmet's fingers as she spoke.

"What; I broke your father's heart so now you're gonna break mine?" I grimaced.

"Something like that," Ptah agreed. "Though I intend to behead you as well."

"You said we weren't going to kill her!" Bastet cried. "She's carrying a child."

"What do I care for this bitch's brat?" Ptah sneered.

"This child is the only hope for the the Dragon-Sidhe race," I snarled. "He's a prince and his father is King of the Fire Kingdom of Faerie."

"Still not impressed." Sekhmet shrugged. "My father created an entire pantheon."

"You mean he tricked humans into giving him enough power to live forever then a *faerie* showed him how to create this." I waved a hand to indicate Aaru. "Or have you all forgotten that none of you knew how to make your own realm until the Fey taught you?"

"She's right, Ptah." Bastet laid a hand on his shoulder. "Leave her alone. Dad will get over this."

"Not happening," Ptah said resolutely.

"We do owe the Fey," Bastet tried again. "And we don't want them seeking retribution for the death of their pregnant queen."

Sekhmet paused and looked back at her sister. It was the first time I'd seen her worried, and I admit that it gave me the warm fuzzies.

"They'll never reach us here," Ptah scoffed.

"You have no idea what the Fey are capable of," I bluffed.

He was right but the wrath of a dragon king could be a difficult thing to avoid.

"Enough talking," Ptah growled and stepped forward.

"Brother, I must protest." Sokar laid a hand on Ptah's arm. "I don't think Re would want her harmed, and I don't condone violence against an unborn child who is completely innocent of his mother's crimes."

"Re gave us a home," Ptah ground out. "He helped make us Gods and then he gave me his blessing to marry his daughter. He is both brother and father to me, and I will not see his pain unavenged."

"Wow, you need to get a massage or take a vicodin or something." I shook my head.

"You're dead," he said simply and came at me.

I jumped out of his way and began to shift. He wanted to play? Fine. Maybe I didn't have my ring, and I couldn't flee to another time, but I was still a dragon-sidhe among several other things. I had lots of ways of defending myself but the dragon bit was the most flashy, and I was pretty sure this guy would respond well to flashy.

Bastet, Sekhmet, and Sokar all drew back as my perspective shifted and lifted. The shreds of my gown fluttered down around me, and I spared just the tiniest moment to lament the loss of my Versace heels. But soon, I loomed above the Egyptian Gods, my throat filling with an itching burn. My beasts surged into my star-covered heart and the cry that erupted from my throat was a combined roar of dragon, lion, and wolf emphasized with a spray of flames. I stomped one paw down and the glass table rattled, several things rolling off it to smash on the stone floor.

"You're a loyal man and for that, I'll excuse the punch," I growled. "But threatening my child is an unforgivable act. Now I will be the one seeking vengeance."

I brought the fire forth again, this time aiming it directly at Ptah, but as I did, Ptah pulled a thick scepter from an inner pocket of his jacket and pointed the looped end at me. Bars ran through its length horizontally, down from the ankh adorning its top, leaving just enough space for Ptah to hold it. It looked unwieldy and impractical but it worked. Boy did it work.

Before the fire hit him, the scepter emitted a pulse like a

sound wave and covered Ptah in a protective shield. My flames raged over an invisible dome but couldn't break through to him. I stopped to take another breath and reassess. Maybe I could just step on him.

"I would put that down, if I were you," Trevor's voice was like silk on my soul; it made me sigh in relief.

I looked to my left and saw him coming around the corner of the mountain with Kirill, Azrael, Odin, Anubis, the God Squad, and all of my Intare. Play the bugles because the cavalry had arrived.

"Hey, Honey-Eyes," I said with a dragon smile.

"Hey, yourself." He smiled back. "Sorry it took us so long. We had to track you to the Gates of Aaru and then Odin insisted on going home for reinforcements."

"It's better to be prepared," Odin grumbled, making me smile.

It was so good to be back in this timeline where he was still himself and still mine.

"How did you guys even get here?" I chuckled.

"We followed your trail down the river." Trevor held up his hand with his gold ring on it.

"Doggy paddled." Kirill smirked at Trevor and then looked to his right. "Sorry 'bout snakes."

That's when I saw Re.

Re stood among the Lions looking rather embarrassed. He nodded to Kirill and then looked up to give me a sad smile. Re held up my ring as if it were a peace offering. I was just about to say something to him when Ptah lost his damn mind.

"Vengeance cannot be denied!" Ptah cried and pointed his weird scepter at me.

I roared and started to charge him when a blast of light beamed out of the rod and struck me in the chest. Chaos went off around me, with several cries of *No!* echoing in my ears. I saw my men running for me and among them was Re, his face filled with horror.

Pain blossomed within my chest as the light went straight into my star. Turning, shifting, writhing, the nine spokes of my star spun. They spun in ways they shouldn't have, ways that pulled them away from each other. Light trailed between the trinities like pulled taffy, trying its best to keep them bonded. But it was useless; I screamed as all the pieces that made up my triple being were ripped apart. Not just the three trinities but every spoke.

I was dying, I knew it, and the only thing I could think was; please let my son survive this. Let them cut him from my dead body if they have to. I don't care, just let him live. Sparks went off inside my head and pain blinded me to reason. I fell to the ground as my souls splintered, faltering under the vicious assault. As separate entities, they may have survived within me but this was no gentle parting. It was closer to tearing conjoined twins apart; you could do it, but you'd probably kill them. My conjoined soul twins were being severed, and I knew they wouldn't survive the hemorrhaging that would surely follow.

But then something stirred within my belly and magic blossomed; a magic that was not my own. My magics were too busy dying along with my souls; withering and screeching inside me. This new power pulled the invading energy away from my heart and took it into itself. I screamed again but this time in denial. My body shifted back to human as I clutched at my belly.

"Rian!" I cried as the attack pierced my child's heart. "My baby," I moaned as pain shot through my body and my limbs began to tremble with a shock wave of sound; a backlash of energy rippling out from unborn child.

Scream after scream rushed out of my throat as a tearing sensation filled my stomach. But it wasn't my body being torn, it was his; my son's tiny body. I wrapped myself around him as others surrounded me and held me. Beyond that, I didn't know what was happening, and I didn't care. All I could see was the body within me; the little form of my son being severed. Not just his body but his soul. Ptah's scepter was splitting him in half, from soul to cells, and there was nothing I could do to stop it.

I was crying hysterically by the time I felt Rian recover and begin to heal. My sobs slowed into stunned disbelief as I sensed that my child had made it through the severing. Somehow, Rian had survived. Not only that but he'd also saved us both. I whimpered in relief and held him as best I could, through the barrier of my own flesh. My son had become a hero before he'd even been born and although I was proud of him, I was also horrified that I'd been complicit in forcing him into that role. It was my fault that my baby had to man up and save us.

Then crippling pain rippled through my womb and water gushed between my legs.

"She's going into labor," I heard someone say.

"My ring," I gasped and held out my hand. "I need the Ring of Remembrance."

"Tima!" Kirill's tear-streaked face was above me, his eyes wide and panicked.

"I'm okay, and Rian's okay. We just need to get to Faerie," I whispered, even though I knew it wasn't true.

Something felt wrong inside me; something beyond the pain of childbirth. But I didn't want to worry them, I just needed to get to Faerie as fast as possible.

"We'll follow you," Trevor declared. "Don't worry about coming home for me, we'll go straight to Faerie from here."

"It's been almost two months since I've been back there." I touched his face gently.

Trevor knew what that meant; that I'd have to wait that same amount of time for him to appear in Faerie. Which meant it would be two months before I saw the rest of my men. If I made it through this birth that is.

"Then you'll have two months with your son and his father," Trevor whispered and leaned down to kiss me. "Hopefully, that will be enough time for you to adjust to the idea of returning with us."

And leaving Rian behind.

I knew what motherhood would mean for me. That even though my child would never feel the lack of my presence, I would be without him for weeks or possibly even months at a time. I had thought that it might be a good thing, a break from the stress of a crying baby and all that, but now, faced with his birth, I didn't like the idea of leaving my son.

"It vill be all right." Kirill leaned in to kiss me as another round of pain rocked through my body. I groaned into his mouth, and he pulled back in concern.

"I'm okay," I reassured them again. "And I love you. I love all both so much."

"Tima?" Kirill's face went even more panicked.

"I need my ring," I insisted. "Right now. Who has it?"

"Lala." Re knelt down beside me, covering me with his jacket as Trevor eased back a little. Then Re took my hand and slid my ring back onto my finger. "I've behaved like a lunatic."

"Lunatic," I mused. "Do you know that word means

moon-sick?"

"Then perhaps I shall be a lunatic forever." He kissed my cheek. "Please forgive me. I acted out of love."

"You're already forgiven, Sun God, Re." I smiled as I faded into the past, back to the last time I'd left Faerie.

Chapter Thirty-Six

"There you are." Arach smiled as I reformed in our bedroom but then he saw me and rushed forward. "Vervain? Where's the rest of your clothes?"

"I'm having the baby," I whispered past the pain as Re's jacket slipped from my fingers. "And he's a month early."

"Right." Arach looked scared, but he acted with confident calm; helping me to the bed and adjusting a pillow behind me so that I was angled properly. Then he covered me with a sheet before he ran to the door and called for Isleen.

When Isleen appeared, Arach sent her to fetch Laise, a leanan-sidhe midwife. Laise appeared just as the cramping was getting worse, and she came forward quickly to lay her hands on my clenching belly. A warm yellow glow emanated from her fingers and seeped into my stomach, easing the pain immediately. I sighed in relief, though the wrongness still filled my chest. At least I didn't hurt anymore.

"Thank you." I touched one of the hands she still had on my belly.

"It's my honor to assist you in our prince's birth." Laise smiled wide.

She was nearly as excited to see my son as I was. Laise was the woman who'd designed the nursery for us... and who I'd once mistakenly thought was having an affair with my husband.

"Rian just saved my life," I said to Arach and then swallowed hard past the lump of guilt in my throat. "Again."

"That future never happened and won't ever happen." Arach took my hand as Laise folded back the sheet at the foot of the bed so she could check on my dilation.

"But he did save me in this time," I insisted. "I was just attacked, and he took the magic into himself. I thought he was going to die."

A tear slid down my cheek, and Arach clutched me sideways against his chest, murmuring gently as he stroked my hair.

"But he's all right?" Arach finally asked.

"He's fine," I confirmed. "But Arach, I—"

"And he wants to come out," Laise interrupted. "When you feel your body tensing, you must push, my Queen."

And so I did. I pushed and although I shouldn't have felt any pain, and I didn't down below, my chest seemed to explode. I screamed as my vision went spotty and shifted inward to find my shattered star. Ptah's scepter had already done its damage when Rian had come to my rescue. By refocusing Ptah's attack, Rian had saved my star from being completely destroyed, which would have destroyed my souls, my beasts, and my magics. But he hadn't stopped it from separating. Now, those broken spokes were bursting apart from each other with my straining movements, each one trying to find its own place inside me.

What has happened?! Faerie screamed inside my head.

I couldn't even form a thought, all I could do was scream again as my body was attacked by nine arrows of starlight while it simultaneously tried to give birth. I could vaguely feel Arach's hand clenching over mine and hear his strangled cries in my ears. Someone else, Laise I think, was full out bawling, and Arach stopped whimpering to shout at her, but I couldn't focus on the words.

Who has done this? Faerie went on. *How? Vervain? Vervain you have to focus. Your souls have been severed from each other, they are in the most torment and the most jeopardy. See to them first.*

"What does that mean?" I bit out past the pain.

Calm them, find a place for each of them, she guided me. *They must be in your center, give them each a spot around your heart but be specific; feel the place where each one should go and command them to go there! Do it now!*

I did as she bade, mentally seeking a spot around my heart and then feeling it, sensing which soul needed to live there. Instinctively, I felt that they'd originally each had their own spot inside my chest. The star had connected them but not actually forged them into one. That was its purpose after all, to keep everything inside me together, balanced and united but still separate. Now, the scales had been thrown off kilter, and I needed to balance them.

There, just to the right of my heart, that's where my human soul needed to be. I commanded it to go there and felt it obediently slide into place, giving me a slice of peace. I inhaled deeply, suddenly able to concentrate better, and let my body handle the work of childbirth as I focused mentally on where to put my god soul. It went to the left, where it had always been, evidently. One spot remained, right above my heart, and my fey essence slid into its place without my urging. Once there, it seemed to rule the other two. Well, it was my original soul after all.

I sighed and opened my eyes.

"Vervain?" Arach cried immediately.

"It's not over yet," I ground out, "but I'll be okay."

"Vervain!" He shouted as I closed my eyes again.

"Just take care of our son." I squeezed his hand and bore down as I focused inward again. "I'm going to be all right."

Yes, you will, Faerie sounded much calmer. *The hardest part is over. Now, you must dominate your beasts. Show them who is alpha and who they must obey if they want to live within you.*

I sighed. I'd been here before; wrangling magical beasts into submission. It wasn't an easy task, but I was at least familiar with it. I didn't mess around this time, trying to cajole them into peace. I roared at them; snarled and growled at them until I felt them roll over and bare their bellies. Then my lioness eased into the space beneath my goddess soul, my dragon went beneath my fey essence, and my wolf slipped under my human soul. That's right, gods damn it! I am the boss of me!

Very good. Faerie sighed. *Now, there's just your magic to contend with. This is more about conquering yourself than the energy. Just think about each magic and why you want it. You must remind the magic why you hold it and why it should remain with you. Calm yourself and provide a safe place for it.*

Calm. Right. I could feel my son emerging into this world, and I had to calm myself into welcoming my magic instead of him. Sure. I took a deep breath and pushed back my anger. The alpha approach wouldn't work with magic. Each one needed a different technique. Well, then again...

I snarled the lioness magic into submission before I reminded it of what we had accomplished for her lions. We had freed them, made them into a family, and chosen one for our lover. We had made the Pride into what it should have been all along. The Intare magic purred inside me and settled into place beside the lioness and my goddess soul.

Next came Love. I wooed it, showing it images of those we loved and those we had helped to find love. I used the magic to join and mend hearts, not conquer them. Together, we did great things and the sub-magics of Lust, Victory, and War were used only in support of Love's mission. A warm glow filled me and my butterflies burst forth, swirling happily inside my chest before going to roost beneath my fey essence. It should have surprised me that the butterflies chose to live beside the dragon but it didn't. It felt right.

Last came the Moon. This was the hardest. I didn't have as much history with the moon magic as I did with the others. It was a magic laced with the memories of another woman, and I'd had to box those memories up inside myself so they didn't take over my mind. This led to a certain amount of reserve between us. Well, it was time for that to end.

I called to it, urged it to choose me. Not because I held Atahensic's memories but because I was a good home for it. Ata was gone, but I could keep it safe. I could use it in new ways; powerful ways that Ata had never thought to employ. Like passing a piece of it on to my werewolf son one day. I could help it grow and flourish instead of simply die out as Ata had.

Magic wants to live so it wasn't a huge surprise to have it agree and settle with my wolf, beside my human soul. I sighed, at peace again, if not as complete as I once was. When I opened my eyes, it was to find that Arach had slid onto the bed behind me, his legs stretched out around mine and his arms over my rounded belly. He was crying, a rare thing indeed, with his cheek pressed tightly against mine.

"Arach," I whispered. "I told you I'd be all right."

"I know," he whispered back and angled my face so that he could kiss me. "But sometimes when you say that, you don't really mean it."

Well, he had me there.

"I'm okay now." I lifted my hand to his cheek and wiped away the wet trails. "I promise. The attack shattered my star, and I had to settle the pieces into new places."

"Are you sure you're all right?" He asked urgently.

She's fine, Faerie answered. *Though our futures are now uncertain.*

"Again?" I whined.

You need to find a way to reunite your star, Vervain, Faerie said solemnly. *It was your greatest strength, and you'll need it back before someone attempts to take advantage of your weakness.*

"We'll worry about that later," Arach growled.

"My Queen," Laise called to me from the end of the bed.

She was holding a swaddled baby who was way to quiet for my comfort, but Laise was smiling when she held him out to us so I relaxed. I thought that babies were supposed to come screaming into the world. Not my son. After all the chaos that had preceded his birth, he had emerged silent and calm.

Arach shifted out from behind me and took the little bundle from Laise. He smiled brilliantly as he held our child as if he were the most precious thing in the world. Arach angled the baby so I could see him and there he was, my son with Ull's beautiful blue eyes staring back at me. I instantly started to cry, holding my arms out to take him, but before Arach could bring him within my reach, my stomach tensed and Laise's hands clenched on my ankles.

"There's another child!" She exclaimed as she reached forward. "Bear down again, Queen Vervain."

Another child? Faerie was back to being worried.

I shot an astonished look at Arach, and he gaped back

at me. Then my body took control, and I began the process all over again, with my deliriously happy husband standing at my side cradling our first born. This second birth was much faster and soon, Laise was cleaning off yet another baby boy in a silver basin at her feet.

"A second prince!" Laise held him aloft and as soon as she did, the baby began to scream.

I gasped in shock, startled after the first calm delivery. This baby cried violently and shook his tiny fists as if he would take on the world. His cheeks were red and his eyes shut in squished up fury but then they suddenly shot open, and he saw me. I know, I know; babies aren't supposed to be able to see you, not like that, and definitely not right away. But my second-born son did. He focused on me as if he'd sensed where I'd be and his vivid, emerald, dragon eyes seemed to know exactly who I was.

"Bring him to me," I demanded before Arach could claim him.

Laise smiled and wrapped the newly calmed baby in a blanket before easing him into my arms. I stared at the child in fascination, and he stared back at me. There were tiny green scales on his pink cheeks and a tuft of soft crimson hair on his head. Arach reached out with his free hand and stroked that hair.

"How?" Arach whispered.

"The scepter." I laid my forehead briefly against the forehead of this surprise son of mine and felt the truth of it rock through me. "I felt the magic splitting me apart, tearing my three souls away from each other." I looked up at Arach, and his eyes widened. "Rian took that magic from me."

And because he wasn't yet born, he was able to allow himself to be split, Faerie said with wonder. *Split into his two souls... and then he instinctively used magic to form two bodies out of one.*

"One faerie body and one god." I looked from the obviously dragon-sidhe baby in my arms to the little god baby Arach held. "It looks as if our first born son needs a name, because I don't believe it should be Rian."

"You're holding Rian," Arach whispered and looked down at the solemn baby in his arms. "So, who do we have here?"

"Ull." I started to cry as I touched the hint of blond hair, barely visible on his soft head. "He's Ull."

Chapter Thirty-Seven

"You know we can't name him Ull," Arach said gently as we lay in bed later with the Twins. "It would be too hard on people. Plus, I don't like the name. It's more like the description of a sound than a name."

"You think that's bad?" I chuckled. "Thor's daughter is named Thrud."

"Ugh, damn Vikings." Arach made a disgusted face.

Arach had Rian now, and I could tell that he would favor him. He wouldn't be able to help it. Rian was truly his son; his full dragon-sidhe heir. While I suspected that the baby who held Ull's soul had been created from my body alone. A god soul inside a body formed instantly from a triple souled being. He was even more miraculous than the long-awaited heir to the Fire Throne.

"You know that he's probably not yours," I whispered.

"If not mine, then whose?" Arach narrowed his eyes at me.

He's hers, *you stupid lizard,* Faerie huffed. *The fey essence had your genetic material to use but the god soul did not. He made due with what he had; namely, Vervain.*

"Oh." Arach blinked down at the quiet baby in my arms. "He doesn't have your coloring though."

"Actually, I had blond hair and green eyes when I was

born." I smiled down at my son. "They both darkened as I got older."

"Really?" Arach asked in surprise.

"Everyone thought I was a boy because my hair was so pale that it was virtually invisible." I stroked the wispy strands on the baby's head. "So, my mother used to tape bows to my head."

"She'd tape them on?" Arach laughed as he looked back at the son he held.

"I didn't have enough hair to hold them." I shrugged.

Rian was growling at his father and every once in awhile, he'd get a hand free from his swaddling and bat at anything he could reach. He was a feisty one, no doubt. Which I guess wasn't all that surprising.

This one is definitely fey, Faerie said smugly. *You have your heir, Fire King.*

"I can take Ull back to the God Realm with me," I offered.

"No!" Arach said immediately and clutched at the baby with his free hand. "He's our first-born. *My* first-born son... and his name is not Ull."

"But I don't think he's a dragon-sidhe." I laid my hand over Arach's, and he let his slip away. "He can't rule, you know that. Rian will be in line for the throne."

"But he's still mine." Arach looked so confused.

Dragons, Faerie huffed. *So possessive.*

"If you'd like to be a father to him, I'd be very happy with that." I snuggled the baby against my face and breathed in his sweet amber scent. "But he will have others who will gladly fill that role for him, if you change your mind."

"He's still part fey," Arach asserted. "If you're his mother, then he's part dragon-sidhe."

"Perhaps." I shrugged. "But I don't think so."

"Why not?" Both Arach and Rian were staring at me with confused and slightly angry expressions.

"I think all the fey blood went to Rian, while this baby got only god DNA."

For once, I agree with you. Faerie sighed. *I sense no faerie essence in this baby.*

"Does that mean that Rian doesn't have any god blood in him and so he won't be born again if he ever dies?" Arach's jaw clenched.

"Yes, I think so," I whispered. "But neither will you. So, we'll just have to make sure that we protect you both."

"Yes, we shall," he said determinedly. "My son will be guarded by his parents." Then he looked over at the baby I was holding. "Both of my sons."

"Arach," I started again, but he cut me off.

"Fey or not, he *is* my son," Arach said firmly. "He is brother to Rian and of your body. He has no other father and so *I* am his father. We have been blessed with twin boys, A Thaisce, and I rejoice in it... in both of them."

"I love you," I said as he hugged us together, all three of us pressed against his chest.

"You stop my world," he whispered, but I wasn't sure who he was speaking to; me or our sons. Maybe he said it to all of us.

There you go, focusing on all the happy stuff when doom looms, Faerie grumbled.

"Faerie, can you shut the hell up for this one day please?" I snapped.

Yeah, all right, she muttered.

"What shall we name him?" I looked down at our first-born son, and he reached a tiny palm out to touch my cheek. "What's your name?"

"I'll let you have the honor of naming him." Arach kissed my forehead. "As long as it's not Ull."

I considered the baby's sweet face and just waited for something to come to me.

Might I suggest Alaric? A voice slid into my head, and I looked up in surprise. Not that it mattered, he wouldn't be there, not in a physical form anyway. Alaric was more of an incorporeal being since he was the Consciousness of the Void.

"Al?" I chuckled. "Faerie let you through?"

Not unaccompanied of course, she said. *We were on our way here, to give you our congratulations, when I felt your star burst, Vervain. So... congratulations. And to you as well, Arach.*

"Thanks for including me." Arach rolled his eyes.

Did you push those babies out? Faerie snapped

"You tell him!" I laughed.

"Must my role in this be eternally dismissed as inconsequential?" Arach grumbled. "I am the father, after all."

For one *child,* Faerie said snidely. *Vervain made that other baby all by herself.*

Oh, that was rough. Tell the guy, I feel for him, Al said to me, since Arach couldn't hear Al, only Faerie and I could.

"Al sympathizes with you," I said to Arach.

"Thank you, Alaric," Arach said stiffly.

Oh, you see? Al asked me. *He calls me Alaric. How difficult was that? Just two more syllables.*

"But I like Al," I said. "It's brief and to the point."

"We are not naming the child Al," Arach said. "I don't care that I said you could name him. I take it back."

"I wasn't going to." I shook my head. "I was just talking to Al about his name."

"Well, all right then," Arach mumbled.

"I would like something brief though," I mused. "Something without origin, something new for a child born in a new way."

Something brief and new. Faerie sighed. *What ridiculous guidelines for a name.*

Brevity is the soul of wit, Alaric defended me.

"Shakespeare, nice," I said. "Thanks, Al."

Oh, why did I just give you more reasons to call me that? he grumbled.

"Okay." I sighed dramatically. "If you hate it so much, I will endeavor to call you Alaric."

My goodness but you are feeling joyous today, little mother, Al, I mean Alaric, sounded pleased.

"Brevity," I mused. "I like the sound of it. How about Brevyn?"

"I actually don't hate that," Arach said with some surprise.

Neither do I, Faerie sounded even more shocked than my husband.

I like it! Alaric declared.

"Well, a king and the consciousnesses of two realms have all given their approval." I looked down at the little face with Ull's eyes. "What do you think? Do you like Brevyn?"

The baby cooed and gave me the gift of his first smile.

Chapter Thirty-Eight

Two months later, Arach and I had begun to get comfortable in our role as parents. We were, of course, lucky enough to have lots of help looking after the babies, and I would have even been able to sleep in, if it wasn't for having to nurse them. Not that I minded. In fact, I think I enjoyed these early mornings the best; sitting in my rocking chair at the nursery window as I held either Rian or Brevyn and fed them while the Sun rose over Faerie.

I admit that I thought a lot about Re during these vivid sunrises. I didn't know what to do for him, to help ease his pain. I didn't know what to do for my pain either, but I at least had an abundance of love to console myself with. I hated to think of Re alone in that golden bed. Or even worse... with numerous women who I'm sure could satisfy his body but would never satisfy his heart.

Then there was my heart, and I don't mean love. I had no idea how to mend the broken pieces of my star, and Faerie was getting more and more frantic. I understood her fear; there was a lump of it growing inside me too. Not because I missed the power but because I'd felt more real when the star was whole. I felt more complete and alive. It was this completion that had allowed my wolf to truly come forth, and I'd developed the ability to shift into wolf form.

Being a wolf with Trevor had been so sublime. It had been the one thing we'd been missing, something that had filled a void for him. As a froekn, he'd expected to bind himself to another wolf and have all the wonderful perks that such a union included. One of the basic perks was being able to run beneath the Moon with his mate. How was I going to tell him that we couldn't do that anymore?

And then there was Fenrir. The Froekn went on bi-monthly runs in Fenrir's territory and the first time Trevor had brought me with him, Fenrir had looked brokenhearted when he approached me to tell me that I couldn't join them since I didn't have a wolf form.

I had shifted into my white wolf, and Fenrir had just gawked at me, his mouth hanging open and his arms dangling loose at his sides. The Froekn had rushed forward, howling and yipping, rubbing against me to let me feel their love and de-light. I had truly become one of them. Then Fenrir let out a jubilant howl and shifted into a massive wolf. I still remember the way he pressed against my side and rubbed his face along mine. My heart had been as happy as his when I followed Fenrir into the forest with the rest of the Froekn.

I wouldn't have that now. But at least everything was calm inside me, settled into the proper places. I'd have time to figure out how to fix my star. And I'd get my wolf back. I'd run beneath the Moon with my family again.

I sighed and put Brevyn back into his crib. We'd been prepared for only one baby so there was only one glittering diamond, fireproof crib. A second crib had been hastily con-structed but it was more traditional; carved from wood in-stead of gemstone and made in a rectangular shape instead of circular like Rian's bowl shaped bed. Still, it was made by fae-ries so it couldn't help but have at least one unusual feature.

As opposed to a human crib, that stood on posts, Brevyn's crib hung from thick vines growing out of the ceiling. The Pixies liked to hang out in the foliage and sing to my son or entertain him with their antics. He was such a solemn child that I think it was hard for them to leave him be. They just wanted to make him smile... which they succeeded in doing every time, those little rascals. They didn't understand that just because he was quiet, it didn't mean he was sad.

Brevyn was actually a very happy baby. He just didn't have any of that newborn angst; the flailing confusion of learning this world for the first time. Brevyn was at peace. It took more to surprise him or upset him than it did Rian. Brevyn was already sure of himself and his environment. It made me wonder how much of Ull's memories had come through and were lying buried in that infant mind, just waiting for adulthood to bring them forth. Or maybe he wouldn't remember a thing, just have a sense of *knowing*. I personally knew how tricky past life memories could be.

Whatever happened with Brevyn, I'd be honest and answer all of his questions when the time came. I wanted him to know who he was and what he meant to so many people. I wanted him to have the foundation of his past life as a support for him, not a hindrance, and I fully intended to give him the chance to become whomever he wanted to be.

Rian, on the other hand, was never still. Not even when he slept. He was always moving about, making some kind of sound, whether it be crying, murbling (as I'd taken to calling the little grumbling noises he made), or just cooing. He too, was a happy baby but where his brother was calm and pensive, Rian was adventurous and ambitious. I know that's not a word normally used to describe a baby, but Rian seemed to be constantly after one thing or another and if it wasn't handed to him, he'd find a way to get it on his own. Which made him a big pain in my patootie.

At two months old, a human baby can't really get that far on its own. Maybe they can roll around but that's about it. Not my Rian. Evidently, dragon-sidhe babies developed quickly and although Rian was still the size of a two month old human baby, he had already discovered his dragon claws and the many things he could use them for. He loved scaling his scratching post especially. I'm sure you can imagine my shock when I went into the nursery one morning to find Rian smiling at me from his perch, high up on the floor-to-ceiling post. It was a little like walking into a horror flick; this dragon-eyed baby with his chubby little baby fingers half shifted into claws and grinning at me like the Cheshire Cat. If he hadn't been my son, I'd probably have run out of the room screaming. Then there was the fire thing.

Dragon-sidhe babies are a bit volatile when born, thus the diamond crib. Well, all that was good and fine when you're prepared for it. I'm fireproof too so I didn't mind when Rian hiccuped and ended up burping flames or threw a temper tantrum and roasted his mattress. However, Brevyn was not fireproof and so we had to put Brevyn's crib on one side of the large room and move Rian's from where it had been in the center, to the opposite wall. We couldn't have him burning his brother accidentally.

These issues had me concerned at first for Brevyn's safety. I'd considered taking him out of Faerie, despite Arach's protests, or at least moving him into another room. But then something happened to change my mind. I had laid them down on the changing table; Brevyn on one side and Rian on the other. As I bent to get some swaddling moss—absorbent stuff that lines faerie diapers—from its growing tray below, I accidentally caught the a corner of the boys' blanket with my shoulder and pulled it with me. Brevyn began to fall over the edge with the blanket. It really wasn't a big deal, I have fast reflexes, and I would have caught him. But before I could react, Rian reached out, tiny claws popping free of his fingers, and caught the edge of Brevyn's diaper. With a little pull that shouldn't have been possible for a baby, Rian yanked Brevyn back to safety.

I stood up and stared at that in shock. Rian would have had to have been watching over Brevyn that entire time to have reacted so quickly. And that reaction... how did he even reach Brevyn in time? He must have rolled, but I hadn't caught the movement. All I know is that Rian had suddenly been beside his brother, keeping him from danger with a big smile on his face as if it were all a fabulous game.

As I righted the blanket, Rian pulled his claws away and giggled at me. Brevyn hadn't made a sound, just looked serenely from his brother to me as if everything had happened just as he'd expected it to. On top of that, when I unwrapped Brevyn's diaper, I found that Rian hadn't left a single scratch on him. The control that would have taken, even in an adult, is substantial. That Rian did it instinctively as an infant, was astonishing.

That's when I became certain that separating them would be cruel. They were obviously very aware of each other and now I knew that Rian wouldn't hurt Brevyn, not on purpose and probably not on accident either. Not with that kind of awareness between them. The episode had brought up all kinds of new questions for me and some very startling theories. I didn't share them with Arach because I didn't want to scare him, and I wasn't sure he'd understand anyway. I'd held these babies inside me, and I knew them profoundly. I had connected with their mind when they'd been one being and just because that being had been split into two, it didn't change its original personality. That mind had been split just as its body had.

Their souls were complete *and* completely different, but they were like halves of the same whole. Or perhaps two sides of the same coin. They balanced each other because they'd once been one person. Rian got the ambition while Brevyn got the contentment. Rian was wild while Brevyn was calm. Action and Stillness. Risk and Stability. Dragon and God.

Their bond was probably even stronger than I realized. A birth like theirs gave the potential for infinite possibilities.

"What will you two be like when you get older?" I mused as I set Brevyn's cradle to rocking.

"Beautiful," Lissa, my favorite female pixie, said as she hung from one of the swinging vines and stared down at Brevyn. "And brave and kind. Just like their mother."

"You're buttering me up for something, aren't you?" I teased her as I went to check on the murbling Rian. He was fast asleep in his gently rotating crib but his upper lip curled up as he snarled and drew his blanket tighter around him. "Look at him, fighting even in his sleep."

"Probably protecting his brother," Lissa commented.

I may not have told Arach about my theories, but I had to tell him about the episode with Rian saving Brevyn. The dragon daddy had been so proud that he'd told the whole damn castle. So, comments like Lissa's had become common-place.

"I want one," Lissa murmured, and I turned to look at her in surprise.

"A baby?" I asked.

"Yes." she glanced up at me. "Felix and I are already try-ing."

Felix was Lissa's fiance and the whole Pixie community was gearing up for their wedding, which would probably be shortly after mine. The thought gave me a start. I'd been so fo-cused on the children, I'd forgotten that my other men would arrive any day now, and they'd soon become my husbands.

That made me a bit anxious. I was glad I didn't have to plan the ceremony because I had no idea how a wedding be-tween four men and one woman was going to work. Would it be like; *I do; to you and you and you and you*? That sounded like a Julie Andrews song. Sure, why not? Maybe we could just sing our vows and skip off over the Alps.

As I mused over musical matrimony, my current husband walked in. Arach stood just inside the doorway and put his fists on his hips, surveying the full nursery with obvious pride and massive male satisfaction. I rolled my eyes as Lissa giggled.

"Yeah, yeah." I went over and nudged his shoulder. "We did good. But remember that they're the ones who split into two. We can't take credit for that."

"We can take credit for creating such brilliant boys who were valiant even before their birth," he said proudly.

"Oh, here we go." I sighed as Arach strode over to Rian's crib and smiled at the little noises he was making.

"Don't wake him." I shook my finger at Arach. "I just got them down and if you wake him up, Brevyn will wake up too and the whole process will have to start all over again. My grandmother was right; twins are hell."

"The let it start again." He shot me a smile over his shoulder and then nodded toward the doorway. "They have family to meet."

"And I, at least, am well acquainted with Hell," Azrael's voice carried over to me.

I turned to see Trevor, Kirill, and Odin come walking into the room after Azrael. It was so strange to see them in Faerie that I didn't react for a second, just stood there gaping. Then they were wrapped around me, and I was laughing and hugging them. Funny how sometimes you don't know how much you've missed someone until they're standing right in front of you.

"You're not so fat anymore," Kirill observed with a smile. "Are you happy now?"

"That I don't look like a beached whale or that I have two sons?" I asked.

"*Two*?" Trevor pulled away from me and looked over to where Arach was posing proudly beside the diamond crib. "You didn't tell us there were two babies."

"I wanted to let her tell you." Arach waved his hand from Rian's cradle to Brevyn's. "And I will let her explain it all as well."

"Carus?" Azrael slid his hand to my cheek. "What happened to the baby?"

"So very much." I sighed and took a second to kiss Odin hello before I explained what I believed happened with my boys.

"So, this is truly Ull?" Odin was standing over Brevyn's cradle, and I was shocked to see that Brevyn was awake and staring up at Odin with a little smile. "My word, he even looks like Ull."

"His name is Brevyn now," I said but I also nodded. "We believe he's formed only of my cells, my blood."

"And Rian is fully dragon-sidhe?" Trevor edged over to Arach and a loud cry announced that Rian was awake.

"That he is," Arach said proudly as he scooped the wailing baby up and presented him to the other men.

"Good lungs." Kirill nodded in approval. Which had the odd effect of stopping Rian's screams.

Rian set his bright eyes on Kirill and sniffed twice. Then he held up his hand and popped out his claws. With a rapid movement, he clicked them in against each other. When Kirill did nothing in response to this, Rian smacked Arach's arm angrily and clicked his claws again.

"That means he wants you to come closer," I explained and gave Kirill a little push. "Go hold him."

"Vould you mind?" Kirill asked Arach.

"Not at all." Arach handed Rian over.

Kirill tried to hold Rian as one does a baby; on his back, cradling Rian's head in the crook of his arm. But Rian didn't want that. He wiggled so that he was chest to chest with Kirill, staring him straight in the eye. Then Rian cocked his head to the side and sniffed Kirill fully. Kirill laughed and leaned his head closer to the baby.

"You von't know my scent yet, but you remember my voice, don't you?" Kirill asked. "I used to talk to you vhen you vere inside your mama's stomach. I'm your Uncle Kirill."

Rian stopped sniffing and abruptly curled up on Kirill's chest. His little claws dug into Kirill's T-shirt, and he gave a huge sigh before settling back into sleep. Kirill looked up at all of us in amazement.

"He likes you," Lissa said from the vines behind me.

"I've only seen him do that with me and Vervain." Arach frowned.

"It's a memory from the womb." I went over and stroked Arach's arm soothingly. "Just as Kirill said. That's all it is. Kirill's voice is probably very comforting to Rian."

"And I think this guy must remember Odin," Azrael observed, and we looked over to see Odin holding Brevyn in the traditional manner; rocking him gently as if he'd held a baby a thousand times. Which I guess he had. Brevyn was also sleeping again.

"Well, I guess I don't have to worry about you guys getting along with the babies." I smiled and slid my arm around Arach's waist.

I knew Arach was trying hard to be gracious, and he deserved a little support for his efforts.

"This child isn't fey," Odin said as he stared down at Brevyn. "He should come back with us to the God Realm where he belongs."

Before I could say anything, Rian rolled in Kirill's arms and shifted into a little green dragon. His emerald scales shone like glass as he jumped from Kirill's startled grasp, and his wings opened with a crack of sound to soften his descent. His blanket and bits of torn diaper fell around him as he dropped to the floor on outstretched claws and ran for Odin, fangs bared as he inhaled in preparation to breathe fire.

"Rian!" I shouted and scooped him up.

His claws cut into my arms and the scent of blood seemed to drive him even more wild. I shifted into half-form as the sound of Brevyn's screaming was added to the chaos. Rian's claws scraped along my scales as he struggled to get free and attack Odin. Then a roar shook the room, and Rian was taken from me.

I looked over to see Arach slightly shifted; crimson scales outlining his face and going down the sides of his neck. His hands were transformed into claws and one of them held our son up to his face as he roared again. Arach's yellow eyes were bright and glowing, and his sharp incisors were bared in warning. Rian went limp; long neck drooping along with his tail and legs. His eyes lowered submissively to the floor, and he gave a little whimper.

"That's better." Arach sniffed and shifted back to normal as he placed the baby dragon down in his diamond crib. "I understand your anger, but I am King, and *I* will handle this."

Rian curled up and laid his head on the edge of the crib to warily watch his father. Brevyn was still crying, though he wasn't screaming anymore. He was doing that huffing sniff that signaled the end of tears. I shifted back to human and took Brevyn from Odin, giving my lover a chiding look. Then I turned and set myself between Odin and Arach.

"He only spoke aloud the thoughts I myself have had." I put Brevyn into Arach's arms, forcing him to concentrate on calming the baby instead of attacking my fiance. "He's not taking Brevyn anywhere."

"I obviously misunderstood how attached the brothers are to each other," Odin mumbled behind me.

"They were one person." I glanced back at Odin. "These are not your normal twins. This is one life which has been divided into two, and I think their psychic connection is only the beginning of what they'll share. They cannot be separated. At least not so soon."

"I agree." Odin held up his hands in surrender. "And I apologize." He leaned around me to address Arach. "I meant no harm. Honestly, I thought you'd prefer to not have a god baby around."

"He's my son and so that makes him fey," Arach growled and beside him, Rian lifted his head and angrily huffed out a puff of smoke. Brevyn let out a mewl, and Arach automatically began rocking him.

"But you need to understand that this boy has my grandson's soul in him." Odin gently eased me aside so he could face Arach. "And I *will* be a part of his life. A large part. I don't care if it's as his uncle or step-father or whatever he wishes to call me, but I will know him, and he will know me. He will know Thor, who was once father to him, and he will know all of those people who have loved him because we will not let any-thing or anyone keep him from us."

"Then he truly is a blessed child." Arach sighed and looked down at the suddenly quiet baby. "To be so loved can't be a bad thing."

"Exactly." I took Brevyn back gently and handed him to Trevor, who hadn't held one of the babies yet.

Trevor smiled broadly as he took the baby from me. Brevyn sighed and closed his eyes, once more content. Rian, however, was not. No one was paying attention to him and that just wouldn't do. He let out an unhappy yip, and I went to stand in front of his cradle, holding out my forearms for him to see. Unlike my lioness form, shifting from human to half-dragon didn't heal my wounds. I needed fire to do that. But first, Rian needed to understand what he'd done.

"See what you did to Mommy?" I put a wound right be-neath his nose, and Rian sniffed at it, then began to lick at it apologetically. "Remember this the next time you get upset. Power needs to be controlled or it becomes chaos."

Rian breathed out a stream of fire and healed my wounds, shocking us all. Then he rolled and shifted back into baby form, giggling at me as if he knew he was too cute to stay mad at. When I continued to glare at him, he began to whine and then, finally, to cry. Arach slid around me with a sigh and picked up Rian, taking him over to the changing table to put a new diaper on him.

"He's not old enough for that kind of treatment yet," Arach scowled at me as I came over with his swaddling blan-ket. "He doesn't understand."

"Oh, yes he does." I leveled a look at Rian, and he hid his face behind his hands. "Both of my sons understand me just fine."

"At least he made amends." Azrael came over to watch Arach wrap Rian in his blanket.

"That he did." The Fire King finished swaddling Rian and then handed him over to Azrael with a smile.

"You know, I love dragons," Azrael whispered to Rian, and the baby giggled in delight. "Maybe I can convince your Mommy to give me dragon sons too."

"No, we're having a pair of mischievous angels who will tend to behave more like devils." I grimaced. "It's our fate."

"Dragon children can be challenging but at heart, they are pack animals, and they will always bow to the will of their alpha," Arach said to Az. "I think your angelic twins will be more wild than my fey sons."

"Says the man who just told me not to lecture my children." I rolled my eyes.

"Don't lecture them, no," Arach agreed. "You must simply show them who's in charge. That's how you train a dragon."

There was a pause and then the whole room burst into laughter.

"What did I say?" Arach scowled, and we all laughed harder.

Chapter Thirty-Nine

Leaving my sons in Faerie was the hardest thing I've ever had to do. I kissed them both as they laid sleeping and then immediately burst into tears. The men didn't know what to do, floundering through hugs and reassurances that had no effect on me. Finally, Arach took me aside and put my face between his palms to stare at me sternly.

"We all have sacrificed things to be with you," he said, and I instantly stopped crying to stare at him in horror. "Now it's your turn to sacrifice for us. You're needed elsewhere right now and our children will never even know that you've gone. Even if they did sense your absence, I am here, and I promise you that nothing will hurt our sons while I still draw breath."

"Okay." I sniffed and rubbed at my face. "Okay. I'm sorry."

"You don't have to apologize." Trevor came up beside us and took over. "Maybe we could stay here with you a little longer."

"No." I shook my head. "Arach's right. I've made all of you a promise that you'd have the wedding you wanted after the babies were born. It's time to see that promise through. I'll be okay."

"You can come back everyday, A Thaisce," Arach said gently as he put his hands on my shoulders. "Just come home for a few minutes and then you can return to the God Realm.

Will that help?"

"I hadn't even thought of that." I brightened and the tension in the room eased considerably. "Thank you, Arach. That's a wonderful idea."

"Brilliant," Trevor agreed. "I was worried about you missing them."

"They'll barely have moved by the time you return." Arach kissed me goodbye. "And neither will I."

"Thank you." I sighed and then turned to the others. "I'm going to leave from here so I return to this moment, if that's okay?"

"Why don't you see us out first?" Odin offered. "I don't think it's wise for us to be here when you immediately return. Things could get strange."

"Good point," I agreed. "I'll see you out then."

I walked the men down to the castle entrance where a carriage was waiting for them. I hadn't known the exact day they'd arrive, but I'd had an idea. So, we'd posted guards near the Great Tree—which is the only tracing point in Faerie—to wait for them. I didn't want them to have to walk all the way to the Fire Kingdom alone.

The same carriage that had brought them to Castle Aithinne took them back to the tracing tree. There were four phookas pulling the coach and one in human form to drive it so I knew they'd get there safely. Not that my men were easy to kill but still, it was nice to know they had some fire faeries guarding them through Faerie. The Faerie Realm could be dangerous, even for Gods.

I went back up to the nursery to give Arach a more thorough goodbye kiss before I took another long look at my sons. Both of them were sleeping soundly now. Rian was back to murbling happily while Brevyn was completely silent as usual. I slid an arm around Arach's waist as we gazed down at Rian.

"That was his first complete shift," I said softly.

"And it was in defense of Brevyn," Arach added. "That says a lot. Honestly, I'm proud of him. Two months old and already a fighter."

"I figured you'd be proud of that." I gave a quiet chuckle. "But I already knew he was like his father so that didn't surprise me. I was just pleased by how beautiful he is in dragon form. Bright ivy eyes with dark emerald scales."

"The perfect camouflage for a forest beast." Arach grinned.

"That's the first time I've seen such a small dragon," I mused.

"He's magnificent," Arach's voice faltered, and I looked up at him in surprise.

"Are you *crying*?" I gaped at him.

"I never thought this day would come." He swiped at his eyes and took a deep breath as he turned to me. "Thank you, Vervain. He's perfect; everything I wanted and everything our kingdom needed. Beautiful and strong; an heir for the Fire Throne and a bringer of hope for our people. But you didn't stop there. You gave me a second miraculous child. A son who even destiny didn't expect. He's bound for glorious things, and I feel so honored to be his father."

"What do you mean; destiny didn't expect him?" I turned to look at Brevyn.

"Vervain, you've been to the future," Arach said gently. "Granted, it was one which was never meant to happen but you, Faerie, and Alaric all believed that your children were meant to be born. That they were destined to be. But now, Rian has changed all of that. His act of heroism has created a new life outside of the lines of Fate."

He's right, Faerie added gently. *Well done, King Arach. I was wondering who would figure that out first.*

"Well, you did mention that the future was now uncertain." Arach shrugged. "It didn't take extreme intelligence to figure out that Brevyn has no fate."

"Outside of Fate?" I started to smile. "That means that Ull is truly free in this life, doesn't it?"

Brevyn, Faerie corrected. *But yes, he's free of any ties to the future. Whether that will be good or bad, I simply don't know. I can see nothing for him. It was all Rian's path but now, that too has gone hazy.*

"Explain that," Arach growled.

By splitting himself, Rian has not only added a new life which was never meant to be, he has also altered his, Faerie said gently. *He is not the child he was supposed to be. Complete, yet divided. I don't know what consequences this will have upon his life. I still see a path for him, a future for the Dragon-Sidhe race, but now there are variables building. Threads are forming that were never there before.*

"But that's not a bad thing." I rubbed Arach's arm soothingly. "I don't know how many times I've lamented having a future planned out for me. I'm thrilled that my sons can choose their own way. This is a good. This is how life should be."

And most life is, Faerie agreed. *But those with great gifts require attention. If I'd left you to your own devices, you could have destroyed realms.*

"Now, that's a little extreme, isn't it?" I scoffed but neither Faerie nor Arach said anything. "Isn't it?" I asked again.

"Well, look at what almost happened here in Faerie." Arach cleared his throat. "Granted, that was more my fault than yours."

It wasn't about fault, Faerie said before I could add anything. *It was the wrong path and it's a perfect example of why I watch over you, Vervain. These babies have split a single path and now they forge ahead along that fork, into unknown territory. I can't help them. I can't guide them. I have no idea what to do.*

"Then I'll just have to raise them to not need your help," I said determinedly. "They'll be fine."

Oh, they will, will they? Faerie's voice lost its sympathy. *Well, think about this, Mrs. Smug Mother; your sons have either split their magic and halved its power or they've forced it into becoming stronger.*

"Like setting iron into the flames," Arach whispered.

Exactly, Faerie made an approving sound. *Trauma forces healing and in the case of magic, it sometimes forces change. Your sons may be more powerful than any realm is ready for.*

"I know my children," I said resolutely. "Pregnancy for me was more than just feeling life growing inside me. I connected with them, with all they felt and wanted. My sons are heroes, born with the instinct to protect, and I don't believe they will ever willingly endanger innocent lives."

All we can do is hope. Faerie sighed. *And I do. I hope these babies grow to become guardians and not conquerors.*

"I'd be happy with either." Arach smiled wickedly, and I smacked him in the chest.

Chapter Forty

I used my ring to take me home to Pride Palace and reformed in the middle of my bedroom. My stomach immediately clenched as I thought about how far away my sons were. I had a moment of extreme panic and had to breathe deeply to get it under control. I'd go back and see them in the morning and no time will have passed for them at all. It was going to be fine. I wouldn't miss a minute of my sons' childhoods.

Then I heard the voices that were carrying up to me from downstairs. Some kind of argument was going on, heated enough to echo up five floors. I sighed and trudged to the closet. I wanted to put on something more appropriate for this realm before I went down to face whatever drama was happening now.

I slid off the heavy velvet dress I'd been wearing and slid on a much lighter, blue, silk dress that only came to my knees. I sighed happily as I slid my hands over my slim waist. Goddess healing plus faerie regeneration had brought my pre-baby body back within a week. Don't hate me; I also have to deal with a baby that can shift into a little dragon, remember?

I slipped my feet into some comfy but cute Croc wedges and shifted them into a version of the gold Versaces I'd lost. They had the look I wanted but with the comfort of Crocs. I kinda liked them better than the originals. I smiled in satisfaction as I headed off to face the music. I had a feeling it was going to be more of a musical than just a single song. A whole

Broadway show full of dramatic performances. Why was I so sure? Because one of the voices I heard was Re's.

I'd thought a lot about him during the two months I'd spent in Faerie. Him and the future he'd shown me. Well, it wasn't the future anymore but you know what I mean. The thing was; Re wasn't the only problem I'd returned with. There was that whole thing with the Rainbow Gods and their Bottled Water Goddess.

In the memories, Rian had been around three. Had the future changed so much that Disani and her Rainbow Brites wouldn't go stirring up trouble in Afghanistan? Somehow, I didn't think altering my future would affect their intentions. Which meant that I'd have three years before I'd be facing them.

Now, the question became; should I make a preemptive strike? Should I pull a *Minority Report*; hunt down these Gods and kill them now, thereby saving the lives of all their victims? Or do I give them the benefit of the doubt like I was doing for Zariel? Maybe they wouldn't cause any trouble, in which case, they'd be innocent. Executing three gods on the chance that they might wreck havoc one day seemed a bit unfair to me. But if this was my chance to save the lives of all those humans who would die because of them, and I did nothing, I would never forgive myself.

"He forced his way into her heart!" I heard Odin shout, and I cringed as I stepped into the dining hall.

"I was in torment," Re defended himself. "I merely showed her why. You would have done the same."

"You, out of everyone here, should be the most understanding," I said to Odin as I stepped into the room.

Everyone went quiet and stared at me. Everyone being; Odin, Re, Trevor, Azrael, and Kirill. All my men and the one god who wanted to be added to their number.

"Vervain!" Re stood and stared at me as if he were mired in quicksand, and I was the only one with a rope.

"Minn Elska." Trevor sighed and came over to give me a kiss on the cheek. "This is going badly," he whispered in my ear.

"What do you mean by that?" Odin scowled at me.

"We had a past that I didn't fully remember, and you manipulated things so that I would." I held up my hand when Odin started to protest. "Don't insult my intelligence by saying you needed me to help you. You hoped that being around you would bring back my memories, Odin. That's why you asked me to help you with your *traitor issue.* I'm not condemning you for it, but I want you to see how hypocritical you sound now."

"She makes good point." Kirill nodded.

"Damn it, you're supposed to be on my side," Odin growled at Kirill.

"I'm on *Vervain's* side." Kirill strode over to me and kissed me quickly before rubbing his nose over mine and whispering, "As always."

"Damn shifty shifters," Odin grumbled.

"Just stop." I sighed and went to take a seat at the long, heavy, wooden table. Kirill and Trevor flanked me on my way there and then took the seats beside mine. "What exactly do you think you're arguing about?"

"Trevor called Re here to discuss the possibility of him becoming your lover," Odin huffed and resumed his seat at the head of the table. "We're about to get married, and he wants to bring in another man. I don't understand it."

"Do you?" I looked over to Trevor in shock.

"He would be a good man to have on our side." Trevor shrugged. "He has the whole Egyptian Pantheon available to him. That means that if we ever get into another situation like the one with the Hindu Gods, we'd have another army to back us."

"You're willing to share Vervain with another man just to get his army?" Odin glared at Trevor. "You're turning our woman into a whore."

"Easy now." I held up a hand when Trevor started to growl.

"We don't need the Egyptians," Odin snapped. "We have the entire Pride, the Norse Gods, the Froekn, and the God Squad."

"We don't call upon the Froekn if we don't have to," Azrael mused. "The Pride is strong but not as powerful as full Gods are, and who exactly can you call upon besides your sons and the Valkyries?"

"Valid." Kirill nodded as Odin transferred his glare to Az.

"You can call upon both Angels and Demons if you need to," Odin pointed out to Azrael.

"If I'm desperate, yes," Azrael agreed. "But I have to admit, there's a part of me that wants our family as strong as possible, and Re would make a good addition. Remember Alaric's warning; trouble is coming."

"We agreed to accept more lovers for Vervain if the need arose," Trevor said calmly.

"You're all insane!" Odin threw up his hands and sat back in his chair. "Trouble is always coming; it loves our woman."

"Odin, calm down." I held up my hand. "You haven't

heard what *I* want yet."

Odin immediately leaned forward and gave me his full attention. "I'm sorry, Vervain. You're right. We've proceeded under the assumption that you'd want a relationship with Re."

"Don't you?" Re set wide eyes on me from his seat across the table from me. "If they all agreed, wouldn't you want to be with me?"

"It's not about that," I said gently. "This aspect of my life has caused a lot of pain for people I love. It almost destroyed the Faerie Realm. I have to handle things more carefully from now on. I have to give myself rules and awhile back, I promised my lovers that there would be no one else unless the magic demanded it. There's been so many vows that I couldn't keep, but I'm going to do everything within my power to keep this one. I owe them that and, honestly, it's not a lot to give in light of what I already have."

"And what about me?" Re whispered. "Don't you care that you've done this? You brought these memories back to me and forced this love upon me as much as I forced you to share it. Shouldn't you take responsibility for that?"

"I do take responsibility for that." I swallowed hard. "I may not have intended it, but you're right; it's my fault. I did this to you, and I will regret it till the day I die. I hate that I hurt you; you've been such a good friend to me, and I repaid you with heartbreak. It's not fair but neither is bringing you into my life. If I let you go, you can get over this. You can move on and find someone else to love. Now that you know you're ready, you can start looking for it and open yourself up to love again. I can even help you." I lifted a hand, and he cringed back.

"Don't you dare, Vervain!" Re's jaw clenched. "I don't want your help finding my true love. I don't need it because you're sitting right there. You're the one I'm supposed to be with. I know it in my bones. No one else will ever make me happy."

"Re, that's a fantasy," I said gently. "It just feels like that now but in time, you'll see that I'm not that hard to get over. And in the end, you'll thank me that I let you go. You'll have a woman all to yourself, no sharing or setting up schedules to see her. She'll be entirely yours. Don't you want that?"

"I want you!" He slammed his fist down on the table, making me flinch. "I don't care about sharing or schedules. I care about you... about us."

I put my face in my hands and sighed. I wasn't prepared to handle this. I should have been. I should have been using all that time in Faerie to plan out how I should deal with Re. But I didn't and now I was lost.

"I release you from your promise," Kirill said, shocking everyone.

"What?" I lifted my face to gape at him.

"I release you." Kirill waved. "I vill not be zat vich holds you back from happiness. Vhat does it matter, one more lover? I know your heart, and I know my place in it. No one vill ever take zat from me. So, vhat matters more; having one less man around or having voman I love be happy?"

"Kirill, I *am* happy." I took his hand. "Amazingly and ridiculously happy."

"Tima." Kirill sighed. "I vant you to make zis choice vith your heart. Don't make me ze reason you deny him. I don't vant zat."

"You don't *vant zat*?!" I surprised them all with my anger. "You *are* the reason! All of you are the reason. That's called love. That's called a relationship. Commitment. I'm the reason you don't sleep with other women, and you are the reason I don't sleep with other men. It's not about want; it's about love and respect, and I will give you as much of both of them that I can. All of you."

"Every time I zink I'm past vhat Nyavirezi did to me, you do something to show me vhat love really is," Kirill whispered. "Zen I see zat zere are still parts of me vhich remain twisted by her."

"Not twisted." I gripped his hand tightly. "Confused or maybe ignorant. I'm sorry I yelled at you. I just want you to know that there are no lessers in this relationship. No one's happiness matters more than anothers. We are all equals here and every opinion matters. *Promises* matter."

"And this is why we're willing to share you." Azrael smiled serenely at me. "Because even though there are five of us, you make each of us feel as if we're the only one."

"Life for us can be complicated," I spoke softly as I looked at the amazing men around me. "But love is simple." I shifted my gaze to Re. "I do love you. But I fell in love with you in another time, and I have to leave our love there. I have to respect the relationships I already have and the boundaries we've put into place to maintain them. I want you, I admit that, but people fall in love every day and don't act on it. That's part of being in a commitment; wanting someone else but not acting on it because you already love the person you're with. If I had a normal life, and I was married to just one of these men, would you still be here, asking to be included in our life?"

Re exhaled roughly and rubbed a hand over his face. His shoulders were tight and his features closed down. It hurt to see him suffering, especially since it would be so easy to ask him to stay. To ask him to share my life and himself with me. How easy it would be to change everything. But I knew this one step could have disastrous effects. If I let Re into my life, my promise would be worthless and my limits would disappear. How many men would I stop at? Six? Seven? *Ten*? No, the magic was happy with five and so I must be too. And wasn't that the most ridiculous thing ever? How could I possibly whine about losing Re when I had Trevor, Kirill, Azrael, Odin, and Arach? No, I couldn't have Re too.

"I would probably try to seduce you and make you unfaithful to your husband," Re admitted as he looked back at me. "That's what I would do if you had a normal life. I would find a way to make you leave your husband and marry me. Is that selfish of me? Maybe, but I've never loved anyone as I love you, and I'm not going to give that up without a fight. If you were married to one man, I would do whatever it took to have you. But you don't have to leave anyone to be with me. I don't have to be that man who breaks up a woman's marriage. I don't have to be selfish or cruel, I simply have to be willing to share you and as much as I rebel against the thought, I've accepted it. I'd rather share than have nothing. So, why can't you, Vervain? Why can't you accept me when I'm willing to sacrifice so much for you?"

I just gaped at Re. All of my love and reasoning was confused by the question. I wanted limits. I wanted normal. I wanted true love. But my life wasn't normal and sometimes limits were meant to be stretched. So, there I was, circling back to the easy choice. Should you take love when it's offered, even if it turns you into a liar? If it hurts no one, should love be denied? But this *would* hurt someone. I looked over at Odin and saw that his jaw was clenched, his hands curled into fists on his lap.

Odin may be all right with the other men, the lioness magic took care of that, but he wasn't a pack animal like Trevor or Kirill, or a loner who'd lived without love as Azrael had. Odin ruled Asgard. He'd been married, once to me, and had several women devoted purely to him. He has a whole flock of Valkyries who fly to his hand when he beckons. He wasn't a man who knew a lot about sharing, and I knew that if I took Re, Odin would suffer for it. It would wound him deeply... and that was something I would not do if I could help it.

"You may be willing, but they have already sacrificed to be with me." I waved my hand at my men and stopped to smile gently at Odin. "Odin died for me, and Azrael came very close to doing the same thing." I looked back at Re. "Do I repay them by taking more time away from them? By spreading myself thinner to be with you, just because you offer me more? Wouldn't that be cruel and selfish?"

"Lala," Re whispered.

"Please understand that this isn't about you or how I feel for you. This is about Odin." I looked back at Odin, and he smiled broadly at me. It was all I needed for my heart to warm and my resolve strengthen; for me to know that this was the right decision. I transferred my gaze to Trevor. "It's about Trevor"—I looked toward Kirill—"and Kirill." And then my gaze settled on Azrael. "It's about Azrael." Finally, I looked back at Re, filled with love for my men, and he flinched, seeing it clearly. "It's about Arach. I can't make it about you. They come first; they have to."

"I see that," Re said stiffly and stood. "And I hope that someday I'll understand it but for now, I'm hurt, Vervain. I'm angry and I'm hurt, and I need to not see you for awhile."

"Re," I called out to him as he walked away, and he stopped to look back at me over his shoulder. "Life is always a blessing, even if we're not allowed to be a part of it."

"That was unfair, Godhunter," he said softly. "And a bit cruel."

I was about to apologize when chaos erupted inside my chest.

Without the bond and control of my star, my beasts

were able to assert themselves more fully, and my lioness was doing just that. I hadn't even considered that she would love Re as much as I did, that she might not take kindly to letting him go. I'd always thought my dragon was the most possessive of my beasts, but I was wrong. So very wrong.

I screamed as she clawed inside me as if she could burst out of my chest and chase after Re. Everyone jumped up, and Re came racing back as I was violently tossed about and my chair toppled. I fell to the ground, rolling with each internal blow, crying out with each swipe of those invisible but vicious claws. It was a psychic attack, of course, I wasn't really being torn apart from within, but damn if it didn't feel like it.

Pain upon more pain. It became mind numbing, and I faded away from any other sensation, like that of all the concerned hands on me. I closed my eyes and retreated into my head, in an effort to confront my lioness. But that's what she'd been counting on. Immediately, flashes of memory played out like a movie on the screen of my mind. But they weren't my memories; these were the memories of my lioness. My Intare magic.

I knew the magic was alive, I even knew it was sentient. Hell, I've reasoned with it enough times to know that. But I didn't realize it could share its memories with me. And that's exactly what she did. She took me back to her beginning, to the time when her energy was first gathered and focused into the original lioness goddess; Nyavirezi.

The images came forward and sank into me until I wasn't just watching them, I was experiencing them. I saw the ground flying away beneath my paws, the sharp taste of blood in my mouth and the sweet scent of crushed grass in my nose. I was full, completely sated and on my way home... to my husband. I wanted the warmth of our fire and of his hands. I expected him to be inside, giving me time to shift back into human before I went within. But when our home came into view, I found him standing outside of it, waiting for me. He was holding a spear, and he came towards me waving it aggressively. I stopped, frozen in panic.

If it were anyone but him, I would have attacked, but I didn't. I chose instead to flee. My husband probably thought I was a real lioness, braving the human settlement to hunt. He was only trying to protect our home, as any man would. So, I turned swiftly in the tall grass and was about to run away when he called out to me.

"Nya, come here," he said with a voice full of rage.

He knew. How? Could I still run? Did I even want to? I was a goddess now, the people worshiped me. Bobingo would understand. He accepted sacrifice from the humans too, he knew it was changing us. He would understand; he must.

"I know it's you, Nyavirezi." Bobingo smacked the end of his spear into the hard earth. "What have you done?"

What had I done? I blinked, trying to think. I hadn't done anything wrong. I'd hunted as a lioness does, killing only animals, never humans. I'd run across the grasslands and basked in the sun. Simple pleasures. Where was the harm in that? I turned and looked at him in confusion.

"This is what you want me to be?" He asked angrily. "Some animal? Did you think I'd let the magic transform me into a lion, and we could rut like beasts?"

I cringed. My lioness heart saw nothing wrong with being a beast or glorying in it.

"I am master here, do you understand me?!" He shouted, shaking the spear at me. But then he came forward and crouched so he could sneer, "If I became a lion, do you know what I would do, Nya? I would be a true lion and create a Pride. I would take all the women I wanted and make you hunt for me, make you kill for me, while I feasted and fucked my way through life. That's what I'd do."

Anger rose in me, fierce and sudden. I held the lioness magic. It had chosen me first, not him. I gave it form and life. I was descended from a royal line of Atlanteans, unlike his common family. My blood was pure, and I was meant to rule. No one would take that from me. With a swift strike, I jumped up and closed my jaws around his neck. It was so easy. It took barely any movement at all to kill the man I'd once loved.

Then I felt a tingle on my skin, more magic trying to get inside me. Bobingo's magic. He had been on the cusp of godhood, just a step away from forming his own power. The irony was that I could feel the lion in it, the male counterpart to my lioness. Perhaps that was why he'd been so mad; I'd made the choice for both of us. I'd accepted the lioness and his infant magic had chosen to follow. Whatever had prompted Bobingo's anger, his magic didn't want to pay for his mistake. It wanted to live.

I decided to welcome it, to let it merge with mine and strengthen me so that I would never have to subject myself to another man's rule. I would be both lion and lioness. I would be the only goddess of my Pride. And I would be the one who feasted and fucked my way through life.

As the magic melded together, I licked my husband's blood from my lips and smiled.

"No!" I screamed as I came out of the horrible vision. "We are not that woman. We aren't her," I whimpered as my lioness began to roar inside me. "Stop!" I gasped for air as she cut into me again. I guess she disagreed.

"Vervain!" Someone was shouting my name in a hoarse voice that sounded as if it had been shouting for quite awhile. "Vervain, tell us what's happening!"

I opened my eyes and saw Trevor, his honey-colored

eyes tight with worry. He didn't know, none of them knew about my star yet. I needed to tell them, needed to explain why I was losing control of my lioness. But I couldn't breathe. Those claws just kept digging into me, pain shooting out from my core. I realized that this pain wouldn't kill me. It was all just a stimulation of my brain. Which meant that it could go on forever. Just as Iktomi had done to me. How horrible that I was now doing it to myself.

"What's happening to her?" I recognized that voice and so did my lioness. He was one of ours; Aidan. Ours. Just like Re.

"Re," I breathed and everyone went still.

"I'm here, Lala." A warm hand took mine, and I opened my eyes to see Re's eyes above me, so close in color to Trevor's but with that metallic gleam instead of a warm glow. "What can I do?" And those eyes were worried... no, scared. He was terrified.

"I..." I looked around at all the anxious faces.

Kirill, Azrael, and Odin were all pressed close to me while Trevor held me in his lap, and behind them were my lions. I screamed again as my lioness clawed at my chest.

"I'm sorry, Odin," I sobbed as tears streaked down my face.

"It's all right, love," Odin whispered and took my other hand. "Whatever you need to do, do it."

"I love you." I swallowed hard and then turned to look at Re. "But I love you too."

I let go of Odin so I could reach for Re's face and pull him down to me. His eyes lit with hope and then his mouth was on mine, calming my raging beast as he brought forth another storm inside me. Mine. Yes, he was mine. I ruled the grasslands. I took the best cuts of meat and the best mates. I decided who stayed and who left. This queendom is mine.

The pain eased and the rage reduced to a simmer. I had my hands at Re's shoulders, digging into them as I growled low in my throat and bit at his lips. He responded with equal vigor, pulling me tightly to his chest and positioning me across his lap. It was just what she needed, and the lioness began to purr inside me, content at last.

I pulled away from Re suddenly as I pushed my lioness instincts down. Instincts that I now knew were more than just a lioness. They were both lion and lioness. Creator and destroyer, provider and protector, king *and* queen. It was a lot to take in but maybe now that I understood it, I could learn to control it better. I could prevent anything like this from ever happening again.

"I rule," I whispered as I looked up into Re's face.

"Vervain?" He frowned. His eyes were glazed with passion and his lips swollen from my kiss.

"It was the lioness." I sighed and eased off his lap.

"Tima, are you all right?" Fallon called out to me.

"I'm fine, everyone," I reassured them, and the Pride visibly relaxed. "Go back to whatever you were doing. I'm okay, but I need to talk to my men now."

"Yes, Tima." Fallon nodded and ushered everyone else out.

"Carus." Azrael helped me to my feet. "You're saying that your lioness was hurting you?"

"She wants Re. She was tearing me up inside for letting him go." I glanced at the Sun God, expecting to see a smug look on his face but all I saw was pain. "Why aren't you happy about that?" I asked him.

"*She* wants me," he said and sighed. "Not you."

"You're a moron." Odin shook his head.

"Excuse me?" Re growled.

"They *both* want you," Odin snapped as he got in Re's face. "Woman and beast. It's just that the woman has more sense than the animal."

"Vhat's done is done." Kirill laid a hand on Odin's shoulder.

"I'm so sorry, Odin." I took his hand. "I know this bothered you the most. I didn't want to do this."

"I know." He turned away from Re and pulled me into a hug. "Your safety is more important to me than my ego. You know that."

"But your happiness is important to me," I whispered back. "I brought you back because I can't live without you, my Sweet Raven."

"I'll be happy as long as I have you," Odin said softly. "But he's not being added to the wedding."

"No, he's not," I agreed, a huge weight lifting from my chest. Then I looked at the others. "Are the rest of you still okay with Re?"

"I think it would be best if he didn't move in," Trevor said reasonably.

"I don't want to move in." Re frowned at Trevor but then focused on me. "Are you saying that we're giving this a shot, Vervain?"

"I'm saying that I'll be yours forever. If that's what you still want." I held a hand out to Re, and he used it to pull me into an embrace.

"It's about damn time," Re whispered right before he kissed me.

Chapter Forty-One

My new relationship with Re was taking a slow start. We had agreed that he would remain in his home, and I would visit him there but those visits had been limited. Wedding plans were going full throttle and it seemed as if I woke every morning to a new schedule of events that had been made without my input or approval. Well, I did give my men complete control over the wedding so I guess I only had myself to blame for that. But who knew there was so much to be done just to get married?

Because it was finally decided that the wedding would be held in my territory and due to the simple fact that I was the bride, even though I wasn't in control, I still had to be involved with most of the preparations. For example; my territory magic was needed to transform things into party necessities. I made a rock into a massive white tent, sticks into seating, and blades of grass into a rose garden. Why decorate with cut flowers when you can make them grow wherever you want?

So, the aisle was lined in arches covered in white roses, and the seating was luxurious damask cushioned couches. I controlled the weather in my territory too so I didn't have to worry about a sudden rainstorm. At the back of the tent, I created a raised dais so everyone—and there would be thousands of guests evidently—would be able to see us exchange vows. The dais wasn't wood but shaped soil, with a gentle ramp sloping down from its center. I'd chosen soil instead of wood so I could grow even more white roses over an arch big enough to cover all five of us.

I was so nervous about the ceremony. I'd had private commitment ceremonies with my men before but this would be all of us, in front of our friends and family. My mother would be there, though she was my only family member who would. This was my life and I wasn't ashamed of the choices I'd made but the thought of my grandmother seeing me marry four men at once made my throat go dry. So we had told Grandma that I was getting married to Trevor in Africa, knowing full well that Grandma wouldn't want to make the trip. Trevor was the only one with a human identity and so he was the only one I could legally marry. Why Africa? Because my family would obviously want to see some wedding pictures and the landscape around Pride Palace was definitely African.

Azrael's entire family would be at the wedding, including his half-brother Jesus (AKA J-Man), and all of the Demons of Hell. I wasn't worried about them, they were actually great at parties and most had perfectly normal looking faces they could wear. The Froekn however, could get wild, and they would also be in attendance along with Trevor's father; Fenrir, and Fenrir's wife, Emma. Then there was Odin's family, which included our sons; Vali and Vidar, who would be walking me down the aisle. There was also the Valkyries, as well as several Norse gods I'd never met. I'd have to change the wards after the wedding, just to be safe.

The only one of my men who didn't have family, in the traditional sense of the word, was Kirill. Still, the Pride was his family and they would, of course, all be there. Then there was the full flock of Thunderbirds, several angels, Salem the dragon, a slew of Greek gods, a nest of nagas, and even a few of my human friends.

So, to accommodate all of our guests, the party would

be both inside and outside of Pride Palace; with a buffet table set up in the dining hall and seats spread about everywhere. The Dark Horses and Roar would provide the entertainment, there would be a bar near the pool, and Zariel would be my flower girl. Oh, yes, and Satan would be conducting the ceremony.

Back at Pronovias, Andre had been gleefully shocked at how fast I'd gotten my pre-baby body back, and he'd whispered to me that he hadn't truly believed I would make it in time. Then he asked me what wonder pill I'd taken to make it possible. I told him it was magic, and he had giggled like a little girl.

My trousseau had been ready and waiting for me, but I had to return later for my wedding dress which was being fit to my exact measurements. It was a good thing too, because it turns out that *trousseau* is French for *a crap load of stuff* and the wedding dress alone would be packed in a box taller than me. Andre offered to have it all delivered but, of course, that wasn't possible.

So, we'd lugged home the numerous boxes which held Venetian lace underwear, silk stockings, a garter belt, frilly garters (why did I need a garter belt then?), cream-colored silk high heels, a robe, a silk nightgown, a handkerchief, a pair of silk boxers for the groom (no one told Andre there were four grooms so I had to whip up three more), a cocktail dress for the reception, a bottle of perfume, and my veil. I had changed my mind and decided to go with the matching veil after all— it wasn't as if I couldn't handle the weight of all those crystals —so the veil's box was nearly as big as the one for the dress. Insert big sigh here.

It had all gone by so fast and now, I sat at my little kitchen table, having my morning tea, on my wedding day. I stared at the massive box holding my wedding dress but my mind was elsewhere, in Faerie to be exact, with my infant sons. I was heading back there for a quick visit right after I finished my tea.

My men had restricted themselves to some empty bedrooms downstairs, all of them agreeing that we didn't want to press our luck by seeing each other before the ceremony. So, I was alone for a few minutes. At least until Holly arrived with my mother and my bridesmaids. My bridesmaids being Samantha, Sommer, Krystal, and Persephone. Sommer and Krystal are human so a couple of intare were going to pick them up (trace them here from Hawaii) along with Tristan and Jackson, my other human guests.

I set my empty tea cup down and smiled in anticipation of seeing my sons. Then I asked my ring to take me back to Faerie, to the last moment I'd left, and I was pulled back through time and the realms to emerge right in front of Rian's crib. He was sleeping again. I had put them down for a nap the last time I'd left Faerie, but I didn't want to let them sleep today. It was my wedding day after all and if my sons couldn't be there, I at least wanted to spend some time with them first.

"So, it's today then?" Arach asked from behind me.

I turned, realizing that I was wearing my wedding underwear; bra, panties, garter belt, stockings, and little blue garter beneath my silk robe. I slid a hand over my legs self-consciously and gave him a small smile.

"Yeah," I whispered.

Arach hadn't taken the news of Re very well and now, I felt a little awkward around him.

"You look beautiful already." He slid forward and gave me a kiss. "I'd marry you just like this."

"You're already married to me." I laid my head on his chest in relief. It looked as if he'd gotten over his anger. "And this outfit would be highly inappropriate for a wedding."

"I'd marry you again," he said and sighed. "In fact"—he pulled away and got down on one knee—"Vervain Lavine, mother of my children, Queen of Fire, will you be my wife?"

"Arach?" I frowned, completely confused.

"When you married me, you weren't yourself," he explained. "You weren't yourself when I proposed either. I want to marry *you*, with your full understanding and agreement. I want you to experience our commitment as you should have."

"Arach"—I smiled and got down on the soft carpet with him—"we may not have had the most traditional ceremony and perhaps I wasn't in full possession of my memories, but I was still me. I remember every second of it and it was beautiful. I will never forget the way you dropped to your knees and vowed that you had nothing else to live for but me and my love. You proved the truth of your vow in that horrible future, didn't you? You swore to be mine forever in front of all the monarchs of Faerie, and I don't want to tarnish that memory by trying to replace it."

"You don't?" He blinked in surprise.

"You tricked me." I nodded. "It was a nasty move on your part, Dragon King. But that's our story and it has evolved and altered from deception into trust and from base carnality into love. Our marriage is real. There's no going back to change the path that has brought us here, and I wouldn't even if I could. Our story. Our way. *Our* love."

"A Thaisce," he whispered and pulled me into a hug. "You're right; our life is perfect the way it is."

"But what if I'm not a good mother?" I said it to his chest, where I didn't have to see his face or his reaction to my words. It was a safe place for me, there against his heart. I knew I could say anything, and Arach would make it all right.

"That's not possible." His hand went to the top of my

head and he started to stroke my hair soothingly.

"Of course, it's possible," I began to admit all of my doubts to him, doubts which Faerie's words had doubled. "I could make them too arrogant or too soft. Or I could make them too fierce. I did that to Vero." I pulled back to look at Arach with wide eyes. "In that wrong future, I made Vero jaded. I made him almost bitter and too harsh. I don't want to do that to my children."

"Then you won't, Vervain" he said gently. "You came back to change that future. That means nothing in it is certain. Vero doesn't have to be that way and neither do our sons. We'll raise them to be both strong and happy. To take every day as the gift it is. We can do that. We can give our children whatever we want them to have."

"What if we give too much? What if we make them self-centered and demanding?" I knew I was getting ridiculous, but I couldn't stop myself. There was this awful tingling going through my limbs, an instinct to run, but in this case I couldn't run. I could only sit there and panic.

"Vervain, stop," he said as he took my upper arms in his hands. "We have each other, remember? You will be my mirror, and I will be yours. If something goes badly with one of us, the other will reflect it, and we'll be able to change. I promise you that."

"No." I put my hand to his chest. "I should be making that promise because it was I who broke it. I failed you. That's why the future went wrong. I will never fail you again."

"I know you won't." Arach smiled confidently. "But I will try my best to not need such action from you. I will limit my dreams for our family to the boundaries of our kingdom."

"Thank you." I slid back into our hug.

A little cry from Brevyn had us pulling apart to smile at

each other. I gave Arach a quick kiss and then stood to check on my son. Brevyn rolled over and opened his eyes, looking up at me with Ull's beautiful stare as Arach came up behind me and put his arms around my waist.

"He just went down," Arach said. "I'm surprised he woke up already."

"He knows I want to see him before I go back." I leaned over and picked Brevyn up. "Don't you, Brevyn?"

My son laid his little palm on my cheek and stared at me solemnly. It felt significant, more than a casual touch, so I stared back just as intensely. A flash of light filled my mind and then it turned into the flames of a raging fire. I inhaled sharply as the fire consumed my vision and sent warmth surging through my limbs. Then the flames died down and an image appeared; two boys holding hands. One had red hair and Rian's green eyes while the other was dark-haired with Brevyn's blue stare.

The children smiled at me and pointed off into the distance at something. I turned and saw Arach in dragon form, flying above the Weeping Woods in the Fire Kingdom. When I looked back, Rian had shifted into an emerald dragon, and Brevyn was climbing on his back. I felt myself shifting into a dragon as well, and as Rian took them into the sky, I followed. My heart soared as we did, our family flying together through the fey sky.

A Dread of Dragons.

Then Rian roared, flames bursting from his mouth and trailing back over Brevyn. Instead of being burned, Brevyn laughed and trailed his fingers in the fire as if it tickled. He was immune to the flames!

Then the vision faded, and I was left staring at the baby in my arms once more. I gave a happy sob and laid my forehead against my son's. Arach was tense behind me but this was a special moment between Brevyn and I, and I wanted to cherish it before I shared it with Arach.

"Thank you," I whispered to Brevyn. How perfect, that my first wedding present should come from my son. Finally, I turned to look at Arach. "Faerie may not be able to see our sons' paths now, but Brevyn can."

"What do you mean by that?" Arach laid a concerned hand against Brevyn's cheek and stared down into his sleepy face.

"He has the gift of sight." I smiled widely. "And he just gave me a glimpse into our future. Our boys will be fine. They don't need Faerie to look after them. They're going to look after each other."

"Oh, Vervain." Arach sighed and pulled us into a hug. "That's wonderful."

"And Brevyn's fireproof, Arach." I laughed. "All of our worry was for nothing."

"How is that possible?" Arach trailed a finger over Brevyn's cheek.

"I don't know," I shook my head. "It could be a side effect of the separation. Perhaps Brevyn got a bit of Rian's fire. It's not unheard of for a god to be fireproof either. It could just be that Brevyn's magic centers around fire. Oh, and he'll have my dark hair when he gets older too."

"If Brevyn got fire immunity, what did Rian get?" Arach turned to look at our other son.

Almost as if he sensed our attention, Rian stirred and started to grumble. I handed Brevyn off to his father so I could pick up my other son. I settled Rian into the crook of my arm and took him back to where Arach was settling into a chair with Brevyn. I sat in the rocker beside him, and Rian shifted so he could lay his head on my chest. I stroked the soft crimson hair on his head and looked up at Arach.

"Whatever gifts he has," I whispered, "I'm certain he'll use them well."

"Yes." Arach smiled serenely. "I believe you're right. But not to worry. If he doesn't, I'll show him the error of his ways."

"Meaning you'll kick his ass?" I lifted a brow.

"Precisely." Arach nodded, and Rian gave a low whine.

Chapter Forty-Two

I returned home just as the intercom buzzed, and Fallon's voice came through to tell me that the ladies were on their way up. I smiled and set out the coffee pot next to the pot of tea I'd made. I had some breakfast snacks for them too because I knew it was going to be a long morning. All of it was laid out on the glass top of one of my jewelry cases in the middle of my dressing room.

They had to come up in two groups because they wouldn't all fit into the cage elevator with all of their stuff. Each woman had her dress along with a box of make-up and accessories. But they all made it up quickly enough and soon we were giggling through dirty jokes while we did each other's hair and make-up.

"I'm so glad I got out of having a bachelorette party," I announced. "You guys should have seen Holly's. It was both shocking and humbling. I never want to see Gello dance again."

"Holly made Jello dance?" Krystal gaped at the Holy Spirit. "What did you do, put it on your head?"

"No, Gello is the name of a demon." I chuckled.

"Shut up!" Sommer said in disbelief.

"That's her name," Holly confirmed. "Gello with a G. And she kind of jiggles like gelatin too."

"She does," I said dryly. "And it makes you hate her so much."

"But you're the one marrying four amazing men," Samantha pointed out.

"Well, Jello tastes good but it doesn't exactly satisfy, now does it?" My mom said smugly.

"Mom!" I laughed.

"You're damned straight!" my human friend, Krystal fist bumped my mother.

Hours more of such talk ensued, interspersed with breaks for food and lots of cocktails. We quickly moved beyond the coffee and tea into mimosas and then straight champagne. It was a good thing my goddess healing abilities burned off alcohol so fast or I'd be stumbling down the aisle.

"Holy cow!" Persephone exclaimed as she tried to pull my wedding dress out of its box. "This thing must weigh sixty pounds."

"I think it's like thirty-five, but yeah." I went over to help her. "It's all the crystals. The veil is heavy too." I waved a hand at the long box laid out on one of the tables.

"You're going to have to take the elevator down all by yourself," Sam observed.

"Probably." I grimaced.

"But you'll look amazing," Sephy breathed as the dress was revealed.

Boy did it sparkle nice in the soft light of the dressing room. The radiating, spiked bands of crystal beads caught the light and cast rainbows all over the carpet. Tulle and silk chiffon shushed its way over to me with Persephone's help and it took three more women to get me into the thing.

"It's good that you'll have multiple men to get you out of this," Krystal commented.

"I don't think getting her *out* of the dress will be a problem for them." Sephy giggled.

"Okay, enough already." I laughed as they fastened the heavy garment on me.

I ran my hands over the crystal covered waist and glided forward to look at myself in the full length mirror. Layered skirts tried to flare out beneath the weight of the thousands of crystals but they just couldn't manage it. So, it wasn't Cinderella-full but it was still an impressive amount of skirt. The color had been specially ordered; a combination of colors really. It went from deep blue around my waist to peacock green, then honey gold, and, finally, an opalescent diamond. The colors of my soon to be husbands' eyes. It made a glorious display; the deep blue making my waist seem smaller while the lighter colors gave fullness where it was best to be full. The radiating bands covered the long sleeves too, with sapphire around my elbows and the other colors expanding out from there.

My mother came up behind me and settled the veil over my hair. I'd gone with long trailing curls but there was a braid that swept back over both of my ears to attach the veil to. She smiled at my reflection as she settled the heavy drape, with its looser spaced lines of crystals, on my head. It formed a sort of cap, gathering at my nape before falling free, and it reminded me of veils from the 1920's. There was nothing to drape over my face, and I kinda loved that. It felt symbolic, as if I was walking into this marriage with open eyes, nothing to impede my vision.

"I'm sorry that more of the family couldn't be here," my mom whispered. "But I'm so happy that I am."

"Me too." I took her hand and squeezed it a moment.

"I have gifts from your fiances." Holly came up beside us, holding a large, blue velvet box.

She opened it to reveal a collection of jewelry done in the same colors as my dress. Diamonds, sapphires, and emeralds were all set in twenty-four carat gold. There was a tiara, a trailing necklace, a bracelet, and a pair of earrings. Holly lifted the tiara out of the box and handed it to my mother.

"The tiara is from Azrael." Holly smiled as her eyes went misty.

"Thank you." I touched my mom's hand before she could put the tiara on. "Why don't you let Holly do that?"

Mom smiled and nodded, handing the tiara back to Holly while she took the box. Holly gave me a huge grin and came forward. She laid the tiara right at the edge of my veil, setting the cap of it firmly into place. A tear trickled out of her eye, and I leaned forward to give her a hug.

"Thank you for allowing me to be a part of this," she whispered to me.

"Of course," I whispered back. "We're going to be family."

"I'll finally have a daughter." She smiled and swiped at her eyes. "I'm so proud of Azrael, he made a good choice."

"Thank you, Holly." I smiled but then went stern. "But don't you dare make me cry and ruin this make-up."

We all laughed and the rest of the jewelry was put on without any waterworks. The earrings from Odin, the bracelet from Kirill, and, finally, the necklace from Trevor. I slid on my silk heels and took a deep breath.

"Let's do this."

Chapter Forty-Three

I stood at the end of the drawbridge/veranda with a racing heart, watching Zariel cast white rose petals on the path before me. She looked darling in a fluffy pale blue dress with multicolored crystals sprinkled over it. Gods and Shifter stood on both sides of the aisle she pranced down; so many of them that they stretched out past the boundary of the tent. A sea of glamorous people from all ethnicities. Some wore modern clothes and some wore more traditional costumes. Some were quite tall and some, quite muscular, while some had wings rising above their shoulders. But they were all smiling as they watched Zariel pass by, her dark curls bouncing around her happy face.

I looked at the sloping rise at the front of the tent, where Zariel's mother; Samantha, was urging her daughter towards her and the waiting bridesmaids. Across from the bridesmaids stood the groomsmen, only one for each groom. Trevor had chosen Hades, Kirill had Fallon, Azrael had Cid, and Odin had Thor. It was odd to have my ex-boyfriend serving as groomsman to my future husband—who also happened to be his father—but Odin's other sons were already walking me down the aisle.

"Are you ready, Mom?" Vali asked.

Vidar, who was known as The Silent One, stayed true to his name and simply watched me, waiting for me to give him a sign. It just so happened that I was more than ready and with perfect timing too, because that's when Roar began to play the "Wedding March." All eyes turned to me as my sons escorted me down the stairs and along the god-bordered aisle.

I set my stare on the smiling faces of my men, waiting between the bridesmaids and groomsmen. They were stunning and my stomach clenched, wondering why they were mine and how I'd managed to get to this moment, where they stood before a host of Gods, waiting to tell everyone how much we loved each other. I may have been a traditional girl at heart, and I may still believe that marriage should be between two people, but I was so thankful that for me, it wasn't. There, walking towards my men, I admitted that I wanted this. I wanted all of them, and I wouldn't have changed a second of my life if it meant giving them up.

My sons and I walked up the slope onto the dais, and Luke came forward to ask who gave me into marriage. As outdated as the question was, it still touched my heart to have Vidar and Vali say together, "We and her mother do." They kissed my cheek and stepped back to take the seats reserved for them in the front row, between my mom and Azrael's. They carefully avoided my long train, which flowed down the ramp behind me.

Sitting beside my mother was Re, looking magnificent in an elegant black suit and golden tie. He gave me a wicked wink, and I gave him a sweet smile in return. It should have felt strange to have him there, sitting beside my mother as I married four men, but all I felt was joy. He wasn't alone in his palace, heartbroken and bitter. He was there, supporting me as I committed myself to other men. And I found that humbling instead of strange. I turned around and passed my large bouquet of jasmine and roses to Samantha before I stepped forward to stand with four of the greatest loves of my life.

We hadn't practiced this so I had no idea what was going to happen next. The men had wanted it to be a surprise. So, I stood there waiting for Luke to begin, hoping I wouldn't botch anything up in front of all those witnesses. The men looked amazing in their black tuxedos, with ties that matched the colors of their eyes, and they smiled at me in a way that had me wondering what they were up to.

"We are gathered here today to celebrate the unique bond between these five people," Luke began, and I felt my heart slow down to normal.

It didn't matter if I said something wrong or messed things up the way I always did. These men loved me anyway. They had done all of this for me. They had asked for this marriage, and they weren't going to back out at the last second. They were mine, even before the vows were spoken, and that was the most peaceful thought I could have.

"How lucky are they to have found each other?" Luke went on. "In this crazy existence we all share, with magic and war striving to tear us apart, they have triumphed. They have made the magic work *for* them instead of against them. They've taken a power intended to subjugate and formed it into an alliance. They've turned pain and blood into love and family. And now, they stand before all of you, their *numerous*"—he paused to smile, and the crowd chuckled—"friends and family members. To declare that they will continue to triumph and continue to love each other for all of time."

I felt my lips tighten and start to tremble. *No, don't you cry!* Ugh, maybe getting married right after having babies wasn't such a good idea. Damn baby hormones! I was going to ruin this after all, blubbering so bad that they'd have to stop the ceremony. Then I looked over and saw their beautiful, smiling faces; each of them staring at me as if I were the only woman in existence. The tears dried before they had a chance to fall as the weight of what I had filled me. This moment was beyond tears, beyond anything but bone-deep gratitude and sublime, awe-filled silence.

"The men have prepared their vows, and they will speak them now to Vervain," Luke said to everyone.

At least I'd been told to prepare my own vows so I was ready for that. But nothing could have prepared me for what happened next.

The men stood in a semi-circle before me, and Trevor pulled a ring from his pocket. About a week ago, they'd asked for my gold band, the one bonded to the bands that each of them wore; the ring that had led them to me in Aaru. I'd given it to them without question. So, I wasn't surprised to see Trevor with it now in his hands. What surprised me was that there was now a diamond set into the band.

"We wanted you to have a ring which represented all of us," Trevor said as he held the ring up for me to see. "So, we each donated some of our hair, and Luke transformed it into this diamond. If you look closely, it's cut with a star pattern to represent you."

"It's beautiful," I whispered as I stared into the brilliant cut diamond.

"Ve have committed ourselves to you individually," Kirill went on. "But today ve vill all bond ourselves together."

"One force united," Azrael added, "to defend you and each other."

"Love for you has forged an alliance between us." Odin held out a hand to me and placed their four gold rings into my palm. "But now, it has become so much more than that. So, our marriage vows must not only be to you but also to each other."

The men put their hands on each other's shoulders, leaving Odin and Azrael on the ends, to finish the circle by touching my shoulders. I blinked and clutched the gold bands in my hand, not sure what to do next.

"I bind my life to yours," they all intoned, not just to me but to each other. "My magic will magnify your magic and my strength will reinforce your strength. I will be your shield and your sword. I will stand beside you against all enemies and if you fall, I will avenge you. I vow my fidelity to you above all others, for all of eternity. We are more than blood, we are one."

"Carus"—Azrael took my hand as the others took a step back—"you have been the greatest love of my life since the moment I touched your soul. That love hasn't been smooth and there have been days when I've tried to deny it but today, I vow that I'll never deny it again. That from here forward, I will do whatever it takes to keep us together. You are my life and nothing will ever separate us, not even Death himself." He smiled as light laughter circled the tent.

Az stepped back and Kirill stepped forward.

"Tima." Kirill smiled gently at me and then his jaw clenched and his eyes watered.

"Kirill." I clutched at his hands.

"Vervain." He took a deep breath and started again as a single tear trickled down his cheek. "You saved my life and zen you saved my heart. You showed me vhat love truly is, and you continue to do so every day. I have no one to pray to but you, my only goddess. So, here is my prayer; zank you for loving me. You gave me a home and a family, and I vould give you my heart in return but it has always been yours, from moment you cried over my chained paw and zen tore zose chains away. So, instead, I give you my promise; to never take my heart back. To trust you vith it forever and to take care of yours in return."

"Kirill," I whispered, and I would have wiped the tear from his cheek, but he stepped back so that Trevor could step forward.

"Minn Elska"—Trevor took my hand—"I stumbled into loving you. I gave you blood, and you gave me mercy. I gave you my life, and you gave it back to me without a moment's hesitation. From that second on, I was yours. These vows today have already been settled between us. Under the Moon and before my Valdyr, I have declared my bond to you. But today, I swear upon more than moonlight. I swear upon my breath and blood, upon my bones and honor, that were the Froekn bond to fail and fade away, I would still be yours forever, and I would still wither and die without you."

Trevor released my hand and stepped back. I was trying desperately to stay calm and not rush into their arms but it was getting difficult. Then Odin stepped forward.

"Vervain"—Odin took my hand—"I've loved you through lifetimes. I've watched you bear my children, and I've watched you die. I've fought against time and magic to bring you back to me and still, I almost lost you to my own folly. I vow that will never happen again. You will come first in my thoughts as you already do in my heart. I promise that every decision I make will not be made without first considering you. You are, and ever will be, the truest, most pure love I've ever known."

"Now, please bring the ring forward." Luke held a hand out to rest of the men.

The others stepped forward to join Odin. Trevor took the diamond ring and placed it on my finger. The other men placed their hands over his to guide him. The ring slipped on and glinted up at me.

"Please repeat after me," Luke said solemnly. "With this ring, we thee wed."

"With this ring, we thee wed," they intoned as one.

"Now, Vervain"—Luke looked at me—"you may say

your vows."

"It's hard to follow all that," I grumbled, and the gathering of Gods laughed. "But I'll try my best." I smiled at my men and held my hands out to them. Azrael and Kirill took my left hand while Trevor and Odin shared the right. "I hoped that someday I would be lucky enough to find one man to love; one man to bind my life to. But here I am with four. Four loves of such overwhelming power and beauty that I can't always comprehend how one woman could be so blessed to have them all."

I squeezed their hands and paused to smile at them, basking in our love and the moment that was all about us. Then I threw away the rest of the vows I had planned and went with my heart. It was how I've always handled things with them and it seemed appropriate to give my vows in the same manner.

"You say that I've touched your soul"—I stared into Azrael's brilliant eyes, gone diamond bright, a moment before looking to Kirill—"that I've saved your life"—I transferred my gaze to Trevor—"that I gave you love in exchange for blood"—I finally settled my eyes on Odin's brilliant peacock colored irises—"and that my love is pure."

I stepped back a little so that I could see them all easier.

"But you've all touched *my* soul. Each one of you has saved my life, given me your blood *and* love, as well as offered up your lives for mine; what can be more pure than that?" I shook my head in awe. "So, what can I vow to you? What can I possibly say that encompasses all I feel for you; all I want to give you and be for you? I could tell you that I'd slay dragons for you, but *I am* the dragon. I could say that I would give you the stars, but you already own my heart and the star that resides there."

I paused a moment as I remembered that my star was

broken but then pushed the thought aside. This wasn't the time for fear.

"Minn Elska?" Trevor frowned and started to come forward, but I shook my head, and he settled back into place.

"I could tell you that I'd die for you, but I already live for you, and that's a much harder thing to do. As cliché as it sounds, there are no words which could ever describe how much you've changed me and enriched my life. To even attempt to speak them feels like a betrayal of what we have. So, instead of trying to explain what you already know is between us, I'll speak simply. I love you. I love each of you more than dragons and stars and life itself. There is no life without you in it. I promise I will always love you. I will always put that love first and put you first in my heart, my life, and my arms."

"Well said." Luke nodded. "Now, if you will place the rings on their fingers?"

I slid a ring on each of their fingers and then took their hands again.

"Repeat after me, Vervain," Luke said. "With these rings, I thee wed."

"With these rings, I thee wed," I said.

"Then in the power vested in me by all of humanity"—Luke paused to smile broadly—"I declare you to be husbands and wife."

The entire gathering cheered and the sound was loud enough to make me cringe but still, I smiled as the men leaned toward me expectantly.

"You may kiss your bride!" Luke declared over the cheering.

And they did. Four sweet kisses that changed me forever.

Chapter Forty-Four

Pride Palace had seen parties before. Being related to the Werewolves insured that those events had been some ragers too. But this party was beyond anything my territory had ever witnessed. It lasted late into the night, lighting the landscape with torches and magic, filling it with laughter and love.

I transformed some of the seats within the tent into a large dance floor and the rest into dining sets. Roar was first on stage, which was the raised portion of earth we'd given our vows on. They rocked the tent with their rumbling music, and the Gods celebrated my multiple nuptials with some wild dance moves. The Thunderbirds, in particular, were crowd favorites; twirling in tribal circles with their feathered capes outstretched.

Inside the palace, fairy wine and Duat champagne flowed, and the Gods did their best to overcome their rapid healing and get drunk. The powerful drinks helped, and I saw several jolly gods and goddesses stumbling around the halls. One god, in particular, had no problem with getting inebriated. Silenus was a friend of Dionysus, who was also a fun guy to have at parties, and he was the only god I knew who could get drunk with ease.

"Whoa, Silenus, are you okay?" I grabbed him before he fell into a potted palm.

I had just come out of the elevator, having gone up to

my bedroom to change into the short, white, cocktail dress Provonias had so thoughtfully provided. It was a simpler version of my wedding gown; strapless and covered with the same pattern of radiating, multicolored crystals. A lot sleeker and a lot lighter.

"I'm finnnsh..." Silenus slurred, his horse ears twitching and his hooves clacking on the floorboards as he tried to right himself. His tail swished out and slapped me across the shins.

"You're a fish or you're Finnish?" I asked, giving the offending tail a harsh glare.

"He says he's fine." Dionysus chuckled as he came up to us with his wife, Ariadne. "You have to know how to speak drunkard."

"Ah." I laughed and released Silenus into Dionysus' hands. "How's the party going?"

"Fantastic," Ariadne answered. "I haven't had so much fun since we last visited Greece."

"That was a good time," Dionysus agreed. "Come on, Sil." He corralled Silenus. "Let's leave the bride alone."

"No, wait!" Silenus suddenly grabbed me and his voice went clear. "I have something to tell you, Godhunter."

"No, no, no!" I tried to pull out of his grasp, but he was strong like a... well, like a horse. "No prophecies today, Silenus! Don't you dare ruin my wedding."

"Silenus!" Dionysus shook him, but the Horse God couldn't be stopped.

"Beware of false futures," Silenus intoned dramatically, and as he did, he gained the attention of all who were passing by, including two of my new husbands; Kirill and Trevor. They came rushing over to stand behind me as Silenus went on, "They will lure you into action which should not be taken. Let the threads of Fate lie untouched or they shall tangle." Silenus blinked and then stumbled, releasing my wrist. "Whatch I say thish time?" He looked up at Dionysus.

"I have no idea." Dionysus looked from him to me in horror. "I'm so sorry, Vervain. I hope that wasn't as bad as it sounded."

"Actually"—I blinked in surprise—"I don't think it was."

"Vervain?" Trevor asked. "Do you know what he meant by that?"

"In the memories Re showed me," I explained. "The memories of a *false future*," I used Silenus' words, "we had some trouble with a few gods, and I was considering hunting them before they caused that trouble again."

"Sounds as if that's not such a good idea," Artemis said from the side, and I looked over to see her and Torrent staring at me in concern.

"And that's really good to know." I nodded. "I was stressing out about it. Thanks, Silenus." I rubbed his shoulder gently. "You've actually eased my mind and saved three lives."

"I dish?" He blinked at me.

"You dish." I nodded.

"You did good!" Dionysus patted him. "This calls for a drink!"

"A drink!" Silenus perked up and spoke as clearly as he had during the prophecy.

"Have as much as you want," I offered generously.

"Thanksh, Goshdunter." Silenus waved as Dionysus and Ariadne led him off.

"Are you certain that's what it meant?" Torrent still

looked concerned.

"What else could it be?" I shrugged.

"I don't know." Torr sighed. "But prophecies are tricky things."

"It doesn't matter." I shook my head. "I want to believe that's what it meant because I don't want to have to think about any other option. Not today at least."

"That's totally understandable," Artemis said as she elbowed Torrent in the side.

"Oh." Torr shot a look at his girlfriend. "Okay, yeah, sure."

"But if you decide you want some help later," Artemis went on, "you could always ask the Fates. I mean Silenus did mention threads."

"That's true," I mused. "Thanks, Artemis. I'll think about it."

"Hey, did you guys see my grandpa?" Morph asked as he walked up. "I thought I heard him just now."

"Your grandpa?" I frowned.

"He went that way." Artemis pointed off in the direction that Silenus had stumbled.

"Thanks." Morpheus smiled and raced off.

"Silenus is Morpheus' grandfather?" I was astounded.

"No." Artemis laughed. "Dionysus is." She cocked her head at me. "You didn't know?"

"No, I didn't," I admitted and then had a horrible thought. "Was Hypnos Dionysus' son?"

"No, Pasithea is his daughter," Artemis explained. "She's from an affair he had with Hera."

"Hera!" I gaped at Artie. "You're kidding me."

"Nope." She laughed. "I know, it's hard to believe that Hera would ever have sex with Di but that was before she met Zeus."

"Damn," I huffed.

"Where do you think Pasithea got her talent for making potions from?" Artemis grinned.

"Potions." I frowned as Re walked up. "You!" I pointed at him in accusation.

"What?" He blinked in shock and looked around at the others for some clue as to what he'd done.

They just shrugged at him.

"You drugged me with Net!" I narrowed my eyes at him. "And I've just remembered that you said something about Pasithea taking poppy seeds out of the Underworld."

"What?" Artemis gaped at Re.

"So?" Re huffed.

"So, we've gone through great pains to try and destroy Net," Trevor growled. "And all this time you've known that Pasithea is still making it?"

"Well, I didn't know you were a bunch of Narcs," Re huffed. "What's your problem with Net?"

"Um, it's been used to abduct me and almost kill me a few times." I looked pointedly at him. "And it's just an all around bad thing to have out there."

"Oh, I see." Re sighed. "Just go talk to Dionysus; she's staying with him."

"She's what?" I gaped at him.

"What's the problem now?" Re held up his hands in frustration.

"Ve have had trouble vith her recently," Kirill said democratically. "She tried to kill Vervain."

"She what?" Re snarled.

"Oh, *now* you're mad?" Trevor shook his head.

"I'll take care of Pasithea," Re promised.

"Let's just stop." I held up my hands and took a deep breath. "I don't want to get into this tonight. We can talk about Pasithea and Net and prophecies later." But then I saw Azrael walking up to us with Ted. "What are you doing here?" I pointed at the Antichrist in accusation.

"Um, I was invited." Ted looked at Azrael in confusion.

"Have you met?" Azrael glanced back and forth between us.

"Yeah." I cleared my throat. "It was in the future that never will be."

"The what?" Ted's eyes went wide.

"The future Vervain changed," Az said to Ted. "I just told you about it."

"Oh, right." Ted gave me a grin. "Well done."

"You didn't come to our wedding in that future," I explained. "You and the rest of the Horsemen couldn't make it. And, by the way, thanks a lot for telling me you're *that* Death, Azrael."

"He is?" Trevor lifted his brows. "As in; *on a pale horse?*"

"How did you guys not know this?" Azrael shook his head.

"Zere are plenty of death angels," Kirill said.

"Thank you." I nodded to Kirill.

"Well, I don't know why we didn't attend the wedding in that future, but we're all here now," Ted said. "Ira and Sam are dying to meet you. Get it?" Ted elbowed Azrael in the side. "Dying. And you're Death."

"Yeah, I get it." Azrael rolled his eyes.

"They can meet her later," Trevor said.

"Da," Kirill said. "Now, ve dance."

"Our first dance as a married couple." Trevor grinned.

"A married sextuple," Kirill corrected, and everyone gaped at him. "Vhat? A sextuplet is six, so sextuple is like couple except vith six people."

"It just sounded kinda dirty, man." Ted chuckled.

"Da, zat's point." Kirill shook his head. "It's funny *and* true."

"Technically, with Arach in Faerie, we're only a quintuple," Azrael corrected.

"Perhaps," Kirill agreed. "But zat is not as funny. Plus, Re is here, zat makes us still a sextuple."

"All right, all right." I laughed. "How are we going to do this first dance, my quadruple of husbands?"

"We drew straws." Odin held his hand out to me. "I got the first pass."

"First pass?" I lifted a brow as he escorted me outside, over the veranda and down to the tent.

"You'll see," Trevor called out from behind us.

As we entered the tent, people stopped to congratulate us but the Dark Horses was on stage and Rain, the lead singer, spotted us and called us forward.

"They're here, everyone," Rain said after he stopped the music. "So, let's clear a space for the first dance."

Gods parted and a circular area appeared before the stage. I gave Rain a big smile as Odin led me to the center of it. My new and old husband took my waist in one hand and my right hand in his other. Arach and I attended a lot of Balls in Faerie so I was very comfortable with traditional dancing. I guess it was about to come in handy.

The Dark Horses started playing a slow song, not a waltz or anything like that, just a sweet romantic ballad that they'd wrote for our wedding. It was beautiful, with lyrics like; *love with wings and lions and kings,* and; *no one can define my heart but you.* Odin led me around the circle as if we were dancing to Mozart and it was so damn sexy. I laughed as he twirled me around and released me... right into Trevor's waiting arms.

It went on like that, a different style of dancing with each man, ending with a twirl that sent me spinning to my next partner. It was thrilling, and I wasn't the only one who thought so. The crowd cheered with every new man and called out encouragement to the men with each new style of dance. Trevor's was a little wild, full of dramatic lifts ending with brief kisses. Kirill's was proper but very masculine, he was definitely leading me, with strong movements of his arms and occasional stomps of his feet. I finished with Azrael, who outdid them all by releasing his wings and lifting me up in the air to twirl above everyone.

At the end of the song, I tried to walk off the dance floor, but Trevor was suddenly holding my hand again. He pulled me up onto the stage with him and let go of me so he could pick up an acoustic guitar. I gave him a confused look as Rain gave me a wink and stepped away from the mic. Trevor settled the guitar over his chest and took my hand once more to ease me up beside him at the mic stand.

"I apologize in advance for putting you all through this," Trevor said into the microphone. "But it's my wedding so suck it up." He paused for the laughter to die down and then looked over at me. "I wish I had the talent to write you a love song, but I don't, I barely have the talent to sing one. So, I'm going to have to make due with a song I found that says everything I want to say."

Trevor set his hands to the guitar strings and shocked me by playing it beautifully. Then he started to sing and shocked me even more. His voice was rich and deep, with that sort of masculine vibration that flies into your chest and makes you shiver.

Trevor's voice carried over the crowd, but they faded away for me. It was only us there on that stage. I recognized the song immediately; "I will Follow You Into the Dark" by Death Cab for Cutie. A bittersweet love song, but Trevor was right; it suited us perfectly. I teared up in seconds, knowing what was coming but still unprepared for my reaction. The words were perfect for us, describing a life and love so wonderful that death wouldn't be anything for us to fear. We would face it together, as we did everything else, and beyond it, we'd find each other again.

Trevor stared at me as he sang, and I sobbed like a little girl. He blinked his honey-eyes and tears overflowed them to trickle down his cheeks.

By the time Trevor finished the song, I was a mess. Thank goodness I'd had the forethought to wear waterproof mascara so at least I didn't have black streaks running down my cheeks, but I was sure my nose was as red as Rudolph's. Trevor handed the guitar to Rain without even looking at him. He kept his eyes on me and as soon as his arms were free, I went into them. We shared a tear-soaked kiss as the crowd cheered.

"All right, all of you deadly deities," Rain was on the mic again. "It's cake cutting time!"

Trevor led me back to my other grooms, and we led our guests over to the veranda, where the wedding cake, and all four groom's cakes had been put out on display. I fed my four husbands little bites of cake and then cringed through the possibility of getting cake all over my face, four times. Not one of them did it, and I breathed a sigh of relief until suddenly, all four of them ganged up on me with fresh bits of cake, and smashed them all over my face at once. I had so much cake on my face, I couldn't even open my eyes, and they had to lead me off to the bathroom to wash up. That was the one bad part of being in a relationship with five men; they outnumbered you.

"It's delicious!" I declared, to the delight of the crowd, as I was led away, licking my lips.

And I knew that life would be just as sweet now that we had taken the final step and bound ourselves together.

Chapter Forty-Five

My husbands would be taking me on separate honeymoons, but our first night as men and wife would be spent in our home; together.

At the end of the evening, we waved goodbye to our guests as we went up in our golden elevator to the top floor of Pride Palace. The elevator door opened onto a corridor scattered with rose petals. I laughed in delight and followed the trail into the bedroom with my grooms close behind me. The petals led me out into the Butterfly Garden where strings of light hung in the trees to guide me to the very center. There, beneath the moonlight, a chiffon canopy had been erected. Under the canopy, an enormous bed draped in white linens and puffy pillows waited.

I stopped in front of the bed, admiring the twinkle lights woven around the canopy above it and the scattered rose petals on the sheets. The combination of amber bulbs and moonlight made the perfect glow. Just enough to see by but not glaring. Before I could turn to tell my new husbands how much I loved the little love bower they'd made me, their hands slid over me from behind.

"It's beautiful," I whispered as my dress fell away.

"It will be even more so as soon as you're lying naked across it," Azrael said with a grin.

The men carried me to the bed together and then descended.

"Stop!" I declared, and they all paused. "Take off your clothes before you get into bed with me," I said imperiously. "I don't want to deal with all of that." I waved at their suits.

The men grinned at each other and then hurried out of their clothes as I posed on the pillows in my expensive underwear. Trevor made it to me first, and I eagerly accepted his kiss as his hands slid over my silk bra and undid the clasp. He tossed it away and replaced it with his hands. The other three made it to me around the same time; Azrael slipping in beside me, across from Trevor while Odin and Kirill started removing the rest of my underwear; stockings slid slowly away and then garter belt, and, finally, my panties.

When I turned away from Trevor to kiss Azrael, Trevor lowered his mouth to my breast. Odin's hand strayed up to the other breast to massage it as Trevor sucked greedily on me. I moaned into Azrael's kiss, his hands sliding through my hair, before I reached for Odin and began kissing him.

Kirill settled between my thighs, but I stopped him with a hand beneath his chin and then broke my kiss with Odin.

"I want a kiss from each of my husbands before we move on to other things," I said to Kirill.

"I vas going to kiss you, Tima," he purred and stroked my sex gently. "Just not on your mouth."

I moaned and reached for Kirill. The other men eased back so I could have my Kirill kiss. Each of them kissed me differently; Trevor with wild abandon, Azrael with sweet tenderness, Odin with talented passion, and Kirill with possessive awe. I treasured each experience but when I eased back from Kirill's kiss, I had even more to delight in.

Four beautiful bodies bathed in moonlight. Thick

muscles, broad shoulders, and hardened sex. They stared at me with luminous eyes full of love and touched me with hands full of passion. Kirill sank back between my legs and nuzzled his face against my sex before he started licking me with long, lazy passes of his tongue. I moaned as Odin held one of my knees up and out to the side as Trevor grabbed the other. Azrael moved back so Odin and Trevor could each claim a breast, and their hot tongues began licking and flicking my nipples in two different ways.

"Az, move the pillows and help me get my head over the edge," I said.

Azrael's eyes widened as he realized what I was suggesting. The other men helped me move up the bed as Az tossed the pillows aside and went to kneel behind me on the grass. When I angled my head over the edge, it thrust my breasts upward and moved my legs even further apart, making Kirill, Odin, and Trevor groan. Then Azrael slid his length in my mouth and groaned along with them.

I reached down my sides and stroked Trevor and Odin's cocks; enjoying the feel of having two different members in my hands. Odin's a little thicker while Trevor's was longer. I tightened my lips around Azrael's erection and ground my sex up into Kirill's mouth. Kirill's solid shaft soon replaced his lips, and his steady thrusting shoved me back onto Azrael. Trevor's hand slipped down to rub my clit as Kirill's pace increased, and I screamed out around Azrael's cock.

"That's so fucking beautiful," Odin groaned as his hand swept up my throat and helped to push me onto Azrael.

"Suck him hard, Tima," Kirill growled. "I come soon. Your tight pussy is too much for me. So fucking tight."

I bucked against Kirill as I sucked Azrael in, and soon, Azrael tensed and exploded in my mouth. I drank him down as Kirill followed quickly after; one last thrust sending him deep inside me to fill me with heat. Azrael moved away and sprawled in the grass, one arm on the edge of the mattress to watch me as Kirill did a similar maneuver to relinquish the bed and his wife to her other husbands.

"Mouth or pussy?" Odin asked Trevor.

"I want her pussy," Trevor said.

"Good." Odin grinned.

"Yeah; I saw you watching her suck Az," Trevor teased.

"Fine, but I'm moving onto my hands and knees," I said. "My neck is getting sore."

The men laughed as they helped me up the bed and positioned me between them. Odin stroked the hair back from my face while Trevor spread my legs and eased his cock into me.

"Give me a second here," Odin growled at Trevor.

"Hell, no," Trevor snarled back as he started a rapid pace immediately. "I've been waiting all night for this. I'm fucking my wife beneath the Moon as I was meant to. No more waiting."

"Odin," I moaned as Trevor drove himself deep. "Put that beautiful cock in my mouth."

"As my lady wife commands," Odin purred.

My husband offered me the silken hard length of him, and I slipped my lips around the plump head and let Trevor's slamming motion push me onto it. I moaned at the delicious taste and scent of Odin; laying my tongue hard against the underside to stroke him and lick him before I tightened my lips around him. Trevor and Odin worked out a rhythm between them, and I sank into it as the desire compounded inside me. Along with it came Lust and Love; my magic. My skin began to glow red and the haze spread out to Odin and Trevor.

Kirill and Azrael slipped back onto the bed and began stroking my sides and breasts so that the magic extended to them.

It built up and shot out to the men then back into me, over and over until I came in a screaming surge and the magic shattered around us into millions of glittering pieces. Trevor and Odin came with it; shouting out their pleasure as the lust dust settled over all of us. We fell back onto the bed, and I moaned as Love called them all to me. My husbands settled in around me; Odin and Trevor against my sides, with my arms around them, while Kirill and Azrael spread my legs and laid their heads on my thighs. Love brightened and spread, pulsing through all of us like a heartbeat, and bestowed her blessing on our union.

My magic had given us a wedding gift.

But Lust hadn't quite finished with us. It had sent Trevor and Odin into completion but had brought Kirill and Azrael back to rampant readiness. As I snuggled and sighed between Odin and Trevor, Azrael and Kirill started stroking my sex back into aching need. They suddenly pulled me down the bed between them, away from Odin and Trevor, who grumbled good-naturedly, and Azrael thrust himself inside me while Kirill settled himself between my ass cheeks. They ground me between them; filling me and surrounding me in passion with the fading glow of Love's blessing still upon our skin.

My star may be broken, but nothing could stop the magic of love. Nothing could stop *our* love. Not in this time or any other. No one was ever going to take them from me. Not them or my golden-eyed sun god. I pity anyone who tries.

Keep reading for a sneak peek into the next book in The Godhunter Series:

My Soul to Take

Now available on Amazon:

https://amzn.to/2I263ln

Chapter One

I appeared in my bedroom at Pride Palace with a smile on my face. I was beginning to adjust to leaving my sons in Faerie and now I could do so without anxiety or tears. That didn't mean I enjoyed leaving them there while I came back to the God Realm to spend some time with my new husbands. But now I could at least enjoy the time I spent with my children and hold that memory close until I went back.

Faerie was an idyllic place for me now; a sanctuary of love and peace. Ever since the birth of my twin sons, Brevyn and Rian, the Faerie Realm had been quiet. There were no stirrings of war or rumors of vicious plots. No crazy faeries tried to kill me or anyone I loved. The Fire Kingdom was in a bubble of bliss, enjoying the security of having their heir and a happy royal family. There hadn't even been any village disputes to mediate. It was perfect.

The God Realm was a different matter entirely.

I'd had a bit of a break on my honeymoons. I hadn't known it but my husbands had each planned a separate honeymoon for me. So I went to a villa in Florence with Azrael, a castle in Scotland with Trevor, a posh hotel in Paris with Kirill, and on a Mediterranean cruise with Odin (courtesy of Thor, who actually owns a line of cruise ships... guess which one).

The honeymoons were fabulous and decadent and maybe a bit naughty, just as honeymoons should be. I've now had sex in so many beautiful (and sometimes public) places that I couldn't think of a single new scene for romance. That should be depressing, the thought that there was nowhere I could go for a passionate rendezvous that wasn't similar to one I'd been to before. But it's pretty hard to be depressed when you've got five incredible husbands and one sexy sun god lover. I figured we could just look on it as a challenge.

Unfortunately, as soon as I returned home from all of my love-basking honeymoons, the reality of being the Godhunter returned. The God Squad wanted details of my trip down future-memory lane. Not because they were a bunch of pervs but because they'd heard about my run in with Qaus, Gish, and Disani. Even though I'd decided not to hunt these gods, based on Silenus' prophecy, the Squad still thought we should keep tabs on them. They also thought I should go see the Fates and make sure the prophecy was what I thought it was. Finally, they wanted to discuss Pasithea and her fresh crop of poppies. We knew exactly where she was but there was a slight problem with getting to her since she was staying with her father, Dionysus.

Then there was my Intare and all the drama they stirred up on a daily basis. I was placing more and more responsibility on them and I think they're starting to mature past the frat boy stage but it's taking awhile. So, just as in the Fire Kingdom, I was in charge of settling disputes. Unlike the Fire Kingdom though, these disputes were usually ridiculous and often included Aidan. I swear, that lion loved making trouble. I had started calling him the Instigator.

So even though I was smiling from my visit with Brevyn and Rian, I lost that smile when an urgent voice crackled through my bedroom intercom.

"Tima, are you there?" It was Fallon and he was upset, which was a very bad sign.

I crossed the room and reached the intercom in three

seconds, "I'm here."

"We have a visitor," the words formed an ice cube in my belly. What fresh Hell was this?

"Who is it?" I asked warily.

"It's Yemanja," Fallon whispered.

Yemanja. I blinked in surprise. I hadn't seen the Vodou lwa in years. The last time was on a beach in Hawaii. I'd been with Thor and she had warned us that I was in danger. It was actually the second time she'd tried to protect me. The first had been when I was a child and had fallen off a boat. She'd saved me from drowning, though I hadn't known who or what she was at the time. Basically, I owed her.

"Send her up," I said into the speaker.

"Right away, Tima," Fallon replied.

"What's going on?" Trevor came down the stairs from his tower bedroom, looking as delicious as ever, even though he was only dressed in jeans and a T-shirt. A T-shirt which read; *Definition of Animal Magnetism:* followed by an arrow pointing up at his face.

"Ain't that the truth," I smiled at his shirt and he chuckled as he came forward to give me a kiss.

"You gonna answer my question or make me guess?" Trevor pulled back a little but kept his arms around me.

"Yemanja is here," I answered him. "I don't know why but she's on her way up."

"She is in fact, here already," Yemanja said from the doorway.

She looked a lot different from the last time I'd seen her but then she didn't have an ocean handy to clothe herself with. Instead, she wore a turquoise silk dress which skimmed over her lush body almost as slickly as the water had. The color was vibrant against her dark skin. Her crown was gone but she didn't need it, she looked like a queen as she walked toward me on high heels coated in sparkling crystals.

"Come in, it's good to see you," I hurried over to her and reached out to shake her hand but she surprised me by giving me a hug.

"It's good to see you too, Vervain," she stroked my hair lovingly. "You look beautiful, motherhood suits you."

"You heard about that, huh?" I smiled.

"Would you like something to drink?" Trevor offered. "Coffee, tea, water?"

"A glass of cool water would be wonderful," she nodded to him. "And congratulations on your recent nuptials." We both thanked her before she went on. "I would have been at the wedding but I've had some trouble within the Vodou community."

"What's going on?" I asked immediately as I ushered her to a seat at our little kitchen table.

"People are being murdered, Vervain," she said gravely as she took a seat and set her intense, dark stare on me. "*My* people. And I don't know who's behind it."

"I'll help you of course," I gave her hand a pat. "I owe you that much at the very least. Tell me what's happening."

"It began with just one death," she frowned. "A loyal servant of mine died and I went to her, to help her soul move past the gates and into the Waters of Ginen."

"The Waters of Ginen?" I'd never really understood how the Vodou religion worked and as much as the timing was inappropriate, I was still curious.

I knew Vodou was based on a belief that there was one god but he was too busy to handle petty human issues, so the lwa, who were kind of like angels, were there to look after humans. The belief was that lwas were once humans who had achieved greatness in life and so, upon death, were elevated to this angelic status. Of course, I knew that lwas were never human at all, they were Atlanteans who took sacrifices to become god-like. But still, the Vodou religion was the one which came closest to the truth about the origins of the Atlanteans.

"The Waters of Ginen is a territory of the God Realm," Yemanja explained. "It's a type of purgatory where souls go to rest before being called back to Earth."

"Like reincarnation?" I asked.

"No, not at all," she shook her head. "In Vodou, it's believed that a human soul can be split into pieces. When you are reborn into humanity through an initiation ceremony, you take with you a jar which is bound to you, so that you may put a piece of your soul into it. Specifically, the gros bon ange, the part of your soul that carries of piece of Bon Dieu, the Good God, and can live on after death."

"Okay," I frowned. "So they have a jar to put their souls in?"

"A piece of them, yes," she nodded. "This is for times when their met tet, their personal lwa, wants to borrow their body. It's called being rode, like a horse. The gros bon ange goes into the pot de tet for safety until it can return to its body but there is always a connection between the individual and the pot de tet."

"The soul pot?" I lifted a brow.

"Literally; the head pot," she nodded. "This pot is very important but it is left on the altar in the oumphor, the church, and is guarded by a priest or priestess, known as a houngan if he's a male or a mambo if she's a woman. This is an act of trust between the initiate and their priest because the pot can be used to control a soul."

"Whoa, hold on," Trevor looked back at us from his spot at the counter, where he was brewing a pot of coffee. "You're saying that this pot can be used for mind control but these people just leave them on an altar in the care of some priest?"

I could understand Trevor's horror. As a bonded Froekn, he was very familiar with the idea of splitting his soul. But the split was only done during a Froekn binding ceremony and the piece of soul was given to the werewolf's mate. This not only bonded the couple but ensured that if one were to die, the other wouldn't suffer for long. They would soon follow their mate. I held a piece of Trevor's soul, though he didn't have a piece of mine.

"Yes," Yemanja nodded. "And there can be issues with that but normally, the priest or priestess is worthy of the trust."

"Normally?" I cocked my head.

"There are, of course, those humans who are lured by greed or power and abuse the trust put into them," Yemanja sighed. "These people are considered to be evil and are called bokors. They are the dark side of Vodou, the monsters that so many humans believe my people to be."

"Right," I understood monsters. "So you've got your villains, just like everyone else does, but let's get back to this death you were talking about. What happened to make it unusual?"

"Well, the soul I found was unsettled," Yemanja swallowed hard. "She said that her pot de tet had been stolen from the oumphor and that a bokor had murdered her shortly afterward. She believed he was the one who'd taken her pot and she feared that she'd be called back from Ginen early, before the traditional year and a day, and forced into a govi pot to serve the bokor."

"A govi pot?" Trevor asked as he set a cup of coffee down in front of me and put his own in front of his seat.

"Thank you," I whispered to him. He'd already put cream and sugar in it and it was perfect. Just like him. Oh, give me a break, I was still in the honeymoon phase.

"The pot de tet is made into a govi pot when a person dies," Yemanja has explained. "I'm sorry this is so complicated. I don't have to go into all of this if you'd rather just skip to the end."

"No," I waved her concern away. "I think I need to understand everything if I'm going to help. So, let's be clear... this govi pot would give an evil bokor power over a soul?"

"Yes," Yemanja said gravely. "A soul which he could summon to Earth to do whatever he bids of it."

"That sounds like trouble," I grimaced.

"I was concerned, to say the least," Yemanja nodded. "I instantly followed her connection to her pot de tet and discovered that she was right. The pot was within the hands of a bokor."

"Can't you take it back?" I asked.

"He is protected by great magic," Yemanja sighed. "And here's where it gets really troubling... there were more of him."

"What?" Trevor asked.

"He was just one of a large group of bokors who all seemed to have many pots in their possession," Yemanja stated grimly. "I could sense the taint in their living bodies and the misery in the enslaved souls."

"Sense?" I frowned.

"I couldn't get close to them," her jaw clenched. "As I mentioned, this bokor is protected. He lives within a community of these bokors and not only do they have strong wards in place but they are all under the protection of another lwa. There was nothing I could do but retreat."

"Sounds like this may be an issue for the God Squad," I observed and then glanced up to see Kirill come into the room from the hallway. "Hey, Honey," I paused to give him a kiss. "Have you met Yemanja?"

"Nyet," Kirill held his hand out to the lwa. "I am Vervain's husband, Kirill."

"Yes, I know," Yemanja smiled and shook his hand. "I'm Yemanja, Lwa of the Sea."

"It's pleasure to meet you," Kirill nodded and went to get himself a cup of coffee.

"Oh, the pleasure is mine," Yemanja gave him a quick smile. "But back to the souls, Vervain."

"The souls?" Kirill returned to the table with his coffee and took the seat between Yemanja and Trevor.

"I'll fill you in after," I waved a hand at him and he nodded. "Do you have any more information, Yemanja?"

"Yes," she ran an elegant hand through her long, ebony hair and then ended up nervously playing with the strings of silver beads around her neck. "I don't know if you know this but I am a cross-over deity. I am both a lwa of Haitian Vodou and an orisha of Santeria."

"No, I didn't know," I confirmed. "Are the Vodou lwas and the Santeria orishas like Roman and Greek gods?"

"Yes, it's very much like the Roman and Greek pantheons," she agreed. "We have similar religions and similar gods but most of our deities are separate individuals. I am one of the few who connect the two."

"Is the main god the same?" I thought about how I'd just discovered that Jerry held sway over the Christian, Jewish, and Islamic religions.

"Yes, our Bon Dieu is the same god," she grimaced. "And just as with Jehovah, Bon Dieu doesn't bother with humans much."

"Ah," I nodded. "So you can't go to him for help."

"No," she rolled her eyes. "He would tell me not to interfere, to let the humans determine their own fate. But I can't abandon my children to these evil doers, Vervain... and I come on behalf of several lwas."

"So this has happened to more than just you?" Trevor asked.

"Shango, Oshun, Erzulie Freda, and Erzulie Dantor," she listed. "I could go on and on. We've all lost people. All but a token few of us, including the Baron."

"Baron Samedi?" Kirill asked and I looked at him in surprise.

"Yes, the Baron of the Cemetery has not come forward to report any victims," Yemanja's jaw hardened.

"So you think he's behind this?" I concluded.

"It's possible," she closed her eyes briefly. "I don't want to believe it of him but I think he may be guilty. He doesn't have the highest morals to begin with and then he hangs out with that group of miscreants, the Gede."

"The Gede?" I lifted a brow.

"A family of lwa whom Baron Samedi leads," Yemanja

explained. "They can be kind but also very cruel. In fact, one of them is called the Master of Murderers."

"That doesn't sound good," I sighed.

"But isn't zere also Papa Gede?" Kirill asked.

"You know Vodou," Yemanja said with delight. "Yes, Papa is among them and he is said to never take a life before its time but he is rather outnumbered in that group and as fickle as the rest of them."

"So we need to talk to this Baron," I surmised.

"It would have to be done delicately," Yemanja frowned.

"How does one delicately accuse the Lord of the Graveyard of murdering and betraying his own people?" Trevor rolled his eyes.

"With tact," I smiled and my men groaned.

"Do you have tact, Godhunter?" Yemanja lifted a doubtful dark brow at me.

"Maybe we should send Hades," I sighed. "We'll have to talk to the God Squad anyway. Can you stay awhile, Yemanja? We have plenty of room for you."

"If you don't mind having a mermaid in your moat," she smiled.

"I don't mind at all," I chuckled. "As long as you don't mind being chased by a bunch of randy werelions."

"We'll just see how fast your cats can swim," she laughed.

Chapter Two

It turns out that my lions can swim pretty darn fast when properly motivated. So Yemanja had lots of social interaction to keep her entertained while I met with the God Squad. I would have invited her to the meeting but we needed to be able to speak freely. There were some things I didn't want non-squaders to know about. The fact that the Greek God of the Underworld could be a bit of a whiner was one of them.

"Why me?" Had been Hades' response to my suggestion that he be the one to approach Baron Samedi.

"I thought you might be the most tactful," I said as Kirill laughed.

"If you want tact, you should send Teharon," Hades smirked.

"But you're a god of the dead," Teharon pointed out. "You're the better choice."

"Is he really so bad that no one wants to go talk to him?" I asked in surprise.

"Yes," several gods said at once.

"I don't see why anyone needs to talk to him," Torrent mused as he played with Artemis' hand. "When we could just spy on him. Then you don't have to worry about his feelings or if he's lying."

"Spying on a god can be difficult. If they trace away, it's hard to follow them," I looked over to Azrael. He was probably the best suited for spying; what with his ability to make like a ghost and walk through walls while invisible.

"Unless you have the ability to unmake wards," Torrent shrugged.

Torrent had been created from Internet and god magic. It had given him a unique ability to un-make magic. He could see spells like computer code and just decode them. There wasn't a ward in any of the realms that could keep Torrent out. And this was another of those secrets I didn't want Yemanja hearing. A god who could destroy magic was a threat to everyone. So we thought it best to keep Torr's magic a secret for as long as possible.

"If we could combine you and Az together, we'd have the perfect spy," Finn mused in his Irish lilt. He'd been spending more time with his siblings lately and it always made his accent stronger.

"So send them out together," Horus rolled his eyes at the obviousness of the solution.

"You know, you don't have to sound like such an ass when you make suggestions," Horus' fiance Katie, aka Hekate, scowled at him in disapproval.

"Have I told you today what a wonderful choice you've made in a girlfriend?" I asked Horus as he scowled back at Katie.

"Twice," Horus snapped at me.

"Well, as we witches like to say; third times a charm," I chirped. "I applaud your wisdom in choosing Hekate."

"And I question yours," Horus said to Odin.

"Hey," I huffed as my men narrowed their eyes at Horus.

"Your gonna get your ass kicked one of these days, babe," Katie shook her head at Horus. "And I'm going to stand on the side and laugh at you. Possibly point and laugh."

"Thanks for the support," he smiled sweetly at her.

"Anytime," she kissed his cheek.

"What's with the attitude today?" I asked Horus. "I mean the *extra* attitude."

"Gothic Greek Vampires," Horus huffed.

"Pardon?" I blinked at him.

"The lamiai are not vampires," Katie rolled her eyes.

"That's what they call themselves," Hours shrugged.

"Not after Eztli gave them such a big...deal...about...it," Katie looked around the suddenly silent table. "What?"

"What about Eztli?" I pounced. "Was she with Blue? Is he all right? Why didn't you say anything?"

"Blue is fine," Horus held up his hands. "We didn't want to say anything because we know very little and we didn't want to worry you." He cast a sideways accusatory look at Kate.

"You can't expect me to keep a secret when you don't even tell me it's a secret," Kate huffed.

"Tell me what happened," I growled.

"My girls were out partying in Greece," Katie explained. "They went into Ichor, which is a known vampire hang-out, thinking that they'd be welcome."

"They weren't," Horus chuckled and Kate slapped his arm. "What? They weren't welcome. I was emphasizing your statement."

"No, they weren't welcome but you don't have to sound

so pleased about it," Katie glared at Horus and then looked back to me. "The vampires of Eztli's line seem to think they're different from my girls and as such, don't want to share their club."

"Eztli kicked them out," Horus said gleefully and got another slap for it. "What?!"

"She did," Katie nodded to me. "But it wasn't only her. Blue was there and he made it clear that not only was he with Eztli, they were allies."

"I like him so much more now," Horus smiled as he got another slap from Katie. "Cease with the physical abuse! Those women are harpies and you know it."

"No, they're lamiai," Katie corrected. "Harpies are completely different, which you know very well."

"They're blood-sucking, headache-inducing, obnoxious, uppity, mean girls!" Horus shouted and the room went silent.

"They're my friends," Katie narrowed his eyes at him.

"Yes, my darling," Hours kissed her cheek. "Your friends whom I dislike. There's nothing wrong with that. I'm entitled to my own opinion."

"I like *your* friends," she huffed.

"Because my friends are fabulous," Horus said snidely.

"We are?" Pan jumped on the comment. "Oh, buddy, I knew you loved me!"

"Except for Pan," Horus immediately amended with a straight face. "I have no idea how he got into the Squad."

"Uh-uh-uh," Pan shook his finger at the Falcon God. "No takebacksies."

"But Blue's okay?" I asked insistently.

"They said he looked well but that was months ago," Kate shrugged.

"We will tell you if there's any more Huitzilopochtli sightings," Horus sighed. "But can we get back to your Vodou problem?"

"Yeah all right," I grumbled, still a little butt-hurt that my friends had held out on me.

"I guess now's the time I should mention that I helped Blue out before the lamiai thing," Torrent muttered.

"Excuse me?" I gaped at Torrent.

"He asked me to break through some wards Eztli had up around an apartment in Paris," Torrent shrugged. "It wasn't a big deal. I just went with him and took down the wards, then I left."

"And you didn't think you should mention this to me?" I growled.

"I didn't think it was important," he gave me an apologetic look.

"Ugh," I rolled my eyes. "Fine. But in the future, I'd rather you keep me informed."

"Noted," Torrent nodded.

"I could go into his dreams," Morpheus offered, as if we hadn't strayed from our original topic.

"Blue's dreams?" Sara whispered to Brahma.

"Baron Samedi's," Brahma whispered back. "Remember; the whole reason we're here?"

"Oh right. Sometimes it's hard to follow along."

"You're telling me," Brahma commiserated.

I didn't let on to the fact that I'd been just as confused as Sara for a second. And halfway to accepting Morpheus' offer, thinking that he'd meant Blue. I couldn't help it, we hadn't seen nor heard from Blue in a long time and I was deeply concerned for my friend. Not to mention the fact that I'd been the one to encourage him to go after Eztli in the first place. If anything happened to Blue, I'd feel responsible.

"That won't be proof of anything," Pan shook his head and his curls flopped around his sweet elvish face. "Even were he to dream about these trapped souls, it doesn't mean that he was the one to trap them."

"But thank you for offering," Thor added.

"Perhaps we *should* just send out Torrent and Azrael as a team to spy on him," Mrs. E said.

"A scouting party is always a good way to start," her husband, Mr. T, nodded his agreement.

"Are you guys up for doing that?" I looked back and forth between Az and Torr. "Azrael can take you through walls with him, Torr, and you could get him into any god territory Samedi might trace into. It's a good idea."

"I'd love to," Torrent grinned and Az extended his fist for Torr to bump. "Team TorrAz."

"Why not AzTorr?" Azrael asked.

"Because it sounds like you're a butt-tearing team," Trevor chuckled.

"Valid," Az made a face.

"All right then, Team TorrAz" I rolled my eyes "Go and ask Yemanja where to find Samedi."

"I need to go find my fedora and trench coat first," Torrent jumped up excitedly. "You can't be a spy without the proper attire."

"At least he doesn't want to dress up like a ninja," Azrael grimaced as he followed Torrent out.

"Don't say that so-" Artie began but was cut off by Torrent.

"Oh, that's an awesome idea," Torrent's voice carried back to us. "I think I even have some throwing stars."

"Loud," Artemis finished.

Chapter Three

As I was leaving the dining hall, Katie grabbed me and pulled me aside. Horus was being harassed by Pan so he didn't even notice.

"I need to tell you something else about Blue," she whispered to me. "It may be nothing but since we told you about the other thing, I thought I should tell you about this."

"Okay."

"Libys said Blue, Eztli, and a bunch of vampires assaulted her in her home in Greece," Kate looked back at Horus to make sure he wasn't listening before she went on. "They thought Libys had been involved with an attack on one of Eztli's nightclubs; Infusions in New Orleans."

"Why would they think that?" I frowned. "Also; one of Eztli's clubs was attacked? And it wasn't by us?"

"They thought it was the lamiai because of that scene they caused in Ichor," Kate explained. "And yes, Infusions was blown up and all the little vampires inside were blown up with it. Then Pulse, her club in New York had the same thing happen to it."

"Damn," I breathed.

"Yeah," Kate grimaced. "Libys convinced them it wasn't her and then offered to investigate for them."

"And then?"

"Libys put up cameras at all of the clubs," Kate went on urgently. "She caught a glimpse of the bomber, actually they launched missiles from a van but never mind that," she went on as I gaped at her. "She wasn't able to identify the bomber but she did see something strange; Morrigan was at several of the clubs, watching them like a creepy stalker. She was even at Pulse when it was hit; standing across the street eating a hot dog."

"Morrigan?" I frowned. "You mean *the* Morrigan, the Triple Goddess of the Celts?"

"Yeah but she's not triple like Brighid and her sisters were," Katie grimaced. "She's triple like a shapeshifter. She can change into three different women and each one has their own mind and personality. Morrigan is one of the three and it was her who Libys saw."

"Talk about a multiple personality disorder," I blinked. "But Libys didn't think Morrigan had anything to do with the attack? Her being there during an attack seems rather coincidental."

"Morrigan assured Libys that it wasn't her," Katie sighed.

"Oh, well if she *assured* her," I rolled my eyes.

"No, you don't understand," Kate shook her head. "If the Morrigan had done this, any of them, they would have admitted to it gleefully. That's just the kind of women they are."

"So why was she there?"

"Libys doesn't know but she did find out something about Eztli and what Blue has been up to with her."

"Why didn't you tell me all this in there?" I jerked my thumb back towards the dining hall.

"I didn't say anything about this to Horus," she confessed. "I didn't want to upset him. He may swear that he hates my girls but it's a sibling rivalry kind of hate."

"I can punch my brother but if you do, I'll kick your ass?"

"Exactly," she smacked my arm in approval. "If he knew that Eztli and Blue had gone after Libys, even if they didn't hurt her, Horus would want revenge. Especially since Libys was innocent of their accusations."

"So tell me then," I got back to the subject at hand. "What has Blue been up to with Eztli?"

"Blue used the soma Brahma gave him and made Eztli a goddess," Kate quickened her words when she saw Horus start making his way over to us. "Eztli is now the Goddess of the Blood Moon."

"Well, hopefully she'll be happy now," I huffed.

"She's powerful, Vervain," Kate hissed. "She has a brand new magic and who knows what- hello, handsome," she broke off as Horus joined us.

"What are you two talking about?" Horus narrowed his silver and gold eyes at me.

"Blue," I confessed and Kate's eyes went wide with surprised betrayal. "I was pushing Kate for more info on him but she doesn't know anything else."

"Yeah," Katie looked relieved. "But, I like the way your friends take care of each other. Vervain is seriously worried about Blue."

"Katie," I looked at her in surprise. "We're *your* friends too. You're a part of the God Squad, which means you're a part of my family."

Hekate, Goddess of Magic, Crossroads, Ghosts, Necromancy, and the Moon, teared up and took my hand.

"Thank you," she whispered sincerely.

"Girl, you've had my back," I squeezed her hand. "How could you ever think that I wouldn't have yours?"

"It's a good thing my mascara is waterproof," she chuckled.

I laughed, thinking about the Hekate I'd met in the future that I'd altered. Not only had she been seriously different, she'd been engaged to Horus.

"It wasn't that funny," she frowned.

"No, it's just... oh, screw it, I'm going to tell you. It's not like you knowing would mess anything up," I shrugged.

"What?" She and Horus both started to look worried.

"Well, in that future that I went into..."

"Yes? What? What happened?" Horus demanded. "Did I die? Did Katie die? Did Katie kill me?"

"Kate was dressed conservatively," I confessed.

"Conservatively?" Katie asked like she didn't know what the word meant.

"Your piercings were gone, your make-up was subdued, and you were wearing slacks," I said with deep sympathy.

"Slacks?" She asked in a horrified tone.

"*Beige* slacks," I nodded.

Hekate screamed.

Pronunciation Guide

Aillidh: Ah-lee

Aodh: Ee

Aoife: Ee-fa

Arach: Air-roc

A Thaisce: uh-Hash-kuh ("my treasure" in Gaelic)

Bearach: BEH-ruck

Carus: Care-us ("beloved" in Latin)

Cian: Key-an

Craigor: Kraeg-or

Daoir: Daheer

Drachleen-sidhe: Druch-leen Shee

Eilidh: Ael-ee

Ellingran: El-ING-rawn

Estsanatlehi(Mrs E): Es-tan-AHT-lu-hee

Farinne-sidhe: Fare-nya Shee

Fionnuala: Finn-noo-lah

Fionnaghal: Fyoon-ghal-a

Froekn: Fro-kin

Gruach: Groo-ah

Huitzilopochtli: Weet-seal-oh-POACHED-lee

Intare: In-tar-ay ("lions" in Rwandan)

Kanaloa: Kah-nah-low-ah

Kirill: Key-reel

Khorosho: ho-roh-sho ("good" in Russian)

Leannan-sidhe: Lah-nan Shee

Lesya: L-SHY-aa

Meilyr: May-ler

Minn Elska: min L-skah ("my love" in Old Norse)

Nephthys: Nep-th-es

Nyavirezi: Nee-yah-veer-ez-ee

Peig: Paeg

Qaus: Kowse, like house with a K

Raiseala: Rash-uh-lah

Rian: Ree-An

Scotaidh: SCO-tee

Shehaquim: Shah-ha-keem

Tairhail: Tah-vel

Tima: Tee-mah ("heart" in Rwandan)

Tlaloc: T-la-lock

Tsohanoai (Mr. T): So-ha-noe-ayee

Zariel: Zare-ree-al

Glossary of Characters

This character list was requested by a reader (you wanted it, you got it, from the most important to the bit characters). It's a bit mind boggling so I suggest you only use it for reference when you're confused and I apologize for the amount of pages you'll have to skim past.

Aalish: (Alis) Queen of the Earth Kingdom.

Aba: Angel friend of Holly's.

Adele: Sabine's middle sister. Deceased.

Adriano: Lead guitarist for Dark Horses. Celtic horse-shifter.

Aednat: (Eye-nit) dragon-sidhe, Sabine's mother.

Aidan: Intare (were-lion) pain in Vervain's ass... and everyone else's for that matter.

Alder: Dark-sidhe of Sloth.

Amphitrite: Greek Goddess of the Sea, wife to Poseidon.

Angelica: Dark-sidhe of Fear.

Anna: Fire cat-sidhe, mother of Hunter.

Anubis: (Ah-new-biss) Egyptian God of the Dead. Lord of the werejackals. Son of Set and Nephthys, brother to Ma'at, great-great-grandson of Re.

Aodh: (Eee) Finn's brother, a Celtic swan-shifter.

Anjana: Haruman's mother.

Ananta: AKA Sesha Lord of the Nagas. Hindu.

Aphrodite: Greek Goddess of Love, Victory, War, and Sex. Married to Hephaestus. Lover to too many men to name. Deceased.

Apollo: Greek God of the Sun. Twin brother of Artemis.

Apsaras: Hindu female spirits of clouds and waters.

Arach: King of the Fire Kingdom. Married to Vervain, father of Brevyn and Rian.

Ares: Greek God of War. Married to Eris, lover of Aphrodite, son of Zeus and Hera. Deceased.

Ariadne: Dionysus' wife, mortal made goddess.

Armadal: fire fey leader of Misty Meadows.

Aruna: Hindu suparna, second born son of Vinata.

Artair: earth pixie turned fire pixie.

Artemis: Greek Goddess of the Hunt. Dating Torrent, member of God Squad.

Ash: Dark-sidhe of Pride.

Athena: Greek Goddess of Wisdom. Daughter of Zeus and Metis.

Azrael Morningstar: Archangel of Death. Son of Lucifer and Holly, brother to Jesus. Married to Vervain.

Badb: One of the three aspects of the Morrigan; the Washer at the Ford, the old seer.

Baron Kriminel: Vodou lwa of Criminals. Enforcer of the Gede.

Baron Samedi: (Baron Sah-meh-dee) Vodou lwa of the Graveyard. Married to Maman Brigitte, head of the Gede.

Bastet: Egyptian Goddess of War. Cat-shifter, daughter of Lusaset and Re, twin sister to Sekhmet.

Bearach: (Bare-rock) Imp.

Beryl: Drachleen-sidhe male.

Besa: (Bay-sah)Egyptian Spirit of the Corn, lives in Re's territory.

Brahma: (Brah-mah) Hindu God of Knowledge, member of God Squad. Married to Sarasvati.

Brave Gede: Vodou lwa, Guardian of the Graveyard, member of the Gede.

Breana: Queen of the Air Kingdom.

Bres: Half Formorian and half Tuatha Dé Dannan, Bres is the son of Eriu and Elatha and once husband to Brighid.

Brevyn: Vervain and Arach's son, twin brother to Rian, and holder of Ull's soul.

Brid: (Bride) Celtic Goddess of Prophecy and Learning, sister to Brighid and Brigit.

Brighid: (Bri-jed) Celtic Goddess of Healing. Dated Thor and betrayed him. Deceased.

Brigit: (Bri-jit) Celtic Goddess of Metal Work, sister to Brighid and Brid.

Burdock: Dark-sidhe of Suspicion.

Cahal: King of the Earth Kingdom.

Cailleach Bheur: (Coyluck Bear) Celtic Goddess of Winter. The counterpart to Brighid.

Cait: (Kate) Brownie female working in the Dark Court.

Caitir: (Kate-teer) Fire-sidhe friend of Vervain's, lives in Misty Meadows.

Calamus: Dark-sidhe of Stubbornness.

Campe: Greek drakaina (she-dragon) of Tartarus.

Cassiel: (Cass-see-L) Archangel of Solitude, Ruler of 7th Heaven.

Celandine: Dark-sidhe of Loneliness.

Cerebus: (Sare-ah-bus) Greek Hound God, dog-shifter.

Cernunnos: (Sir-nah-noose) Horned God of the Celts.

Charon: (Care-ron) Greek Ferryman of the Underworld.

Cian: (Key-an) High King of Faerie, married to Meara.

Ciaran: (Kee-ah-rawn) Leanan-sidhe healer.

Cid: (Sid) Warden of Ice Block One, demon, and close friend of Lucifer.

Conn: Finn's twin brother, a Celtic swan-shifter.

Constantin: Drummer for Dark Horses, a Celtic horse-shifter.

Cora: Earth pixie turned fire pixie, Artair's wife.

Craigor: (Krayg-ore) Air-sidhe father of Aradia.

Dagda: Son of Elatha and Danu. Celtic God of Earth.

Dahlia: dark-sidhe of Vengeance, mother of Zinnia.

Damiana: Dark-sidhe of Envy.

Danal: Knight of the House of Air, first fey to find Vervain in Faerie.

Daoir: (Dah-here) Hidden-One baby boy, son of Taog and Fionnaghal.

Darius: Intare (werelion) Lieutenant. One of the first lions Vervain met. Dating Lorna.

Deirdre: (Deer-drah) Hidden-One baby girl, daughter of Taog and Fionnaghal.

Diarmad: (Dyeer-muht) Earth pixie turned fire pixie

Diarmat: (deer-mit) goblin.

Dionysus: (Die-oh-nie-sus) Greek God of Grapes, married to Ariadne, father of Pasithea, grandfather to Morpheus.

Disani: (Dee-sah-knee)Goddess of the Kafir. Vervain calls her Bottled Water Goddess.

Dominic: Future angel son of Azrael and Vervain.

Dughall: (Dew-gull) Fire cat-sidhe.

Dwarves of Nidavellir: Norse gods who live in Nidavellir, they're talented metal smiths.

Elatha: Formorian king, previously prince. Celtic God of the Sun. Father to Bres and Dagda.

Elena: Vampire psychic and best friend to Eztli.

Emma Langston: Human rescued from Demeter. Married to Fenrir.

Epona: (Ee-Po-nah)Celtic Horse Goddess, dated Thor and was married to Constantin.

Estsanatlehi: (Es-tan-AHT-loo-hee) AKA Mrs E. Navajo Goddess of Change. Member of God Squad. Married to Mr. T, mother of Naye and Toby.

Eztli: (Ahtz-lee)Aztec vampire turned Goddess of the Blood Moon, married to Blue.

Fallon: AKA Bhekifa Lungani. Intare Lieutenant. Married to Samantha, father of Zariel.

Fand: water-sidhe foster mother to Lugh and wife of Manannan.

Fearghal: (FAR-rell) red cap captain.

Felix: Fire pixie dating Lissa.

Fenrir: (Fen-rear) Norse God of the Wolves, father of the Froekn, married to Emma.

Finn: AKA Fiachra MacLir. Swan-shifter, son of Lir, brother of Aodh and Fionnuala, twin brother to Conn.

Finnian: (Feh-knee-an) Dragon-sidhe, father to Sabine.

Fionnaghal: (Fee-oh-nah-gal) Hidden-One, married to Taog, mother of Mini V, Deirdre, and Daoir.

Fionn: (Fee-on) King of the Air Kingdom.

Fionnuala: (Fee-oh-new-ala) Finn's sister, a Celtic swan-shifter.

Freyr: Norse God of Fertility. Ruler of Alfheim, brother to Freya.

Freya: Norse Goddess of Cats, Love, Fertility, Marriage, and Prosperity.

Froekn: Werewolves. *Valiant* in Old Norse.

Gabriel: Archangel, God's Messenger, Ruler of 1st Heaven.

Gandharvas: Hindu male spirits of nature, usually part animal.

Garuda: Hindu suparna, first born son of Vinata.

Gede Babaco: Papa Gede's brother.

Gede Nibo: (Geh-day Knee-bow) Vodou intermediary between the living and the dead. A member of the Gede.

Gello: (Jello) Female demon, Holly's best friend.

Gersemi: Freya's daughter.

Gish: (dish with a G)Afghani God of War, carries a rainbow quiver.

Granuaile: (Graw-knee-ah-wail) Fire-sidhe nanny to Vervain's twins.

Green Men: Celtic demi-gods of nature, they hang out with Cernunnos.

Gruach: (Groo-ah) water-sidhe who's dating Kanaloa.

Guirmean: (Goo-rah-man) King of the Water Kingdom, father of Morgan.

Hades: Greek God of the Underworld. Married to Persephone. Member of the God Squad.

Hanuman: Hindu Monkey God. Dated Rhiannon.

Hawthorn: Dark-Sidhe of Scorn.

Hel: Norse Goddess of the Dead. Ruler of Niflheim (Norse territory for the dead who died outside of battle). Sister to Fenrir.

Hekate: Greek Goddess of Magic. Engaged to Horus. Member of the God Squad.

Helene: Sabine's youngest sister. Deceased.

Hera: Greek Goddess of Women and Marriage. Married to Zeus. Mother to Ares, Hebe, Hephaestus, and Pasithea (by Dionysus).

Hermes: Greek Messenger God. Father of Pan.

Holly: AKA The Holy Spirit. Mother of Azrael and Jesus, married to Lucifer.

Horus: Egyptian God of the Sun and Moon, War, and the Sky. Engaged to Hekate. Member of the God Squad. Son of Isis and Osiris, father of Ithy, great great grandson of Re.

Huitzilopochtli: (Weet-seal-oh-POACHED-lee) AKA Blue. Aztec God of War and the Sun. Vampire God. Member of the God Squad. Married to Eztli.

Hypnos: Greek God of Sleep, married to Pasithea, father to Morpheus, Phobetor, and Phantasus. Deceased.

Hunter: cat-sidhe toddler, son of Roarke and Anna.

Iain: (Ee-an) Fire cat-sidhe.

Iktomi: Lakota Spider God. Father of Torrent. Deceased.

Ilario: (Ee-lar-ree-oh)Guitarist for Dark Horses, a Celtic horse-shifter.

Intare: African demi-gods, werelions. A list of various Intare includes: Lucian, Jared, Ryan, Aaron, Kevin, George, Dexter, Ethan, Christopher, Timothy, David, Troy, Wren, and Alexander. The deceased lions who live with Anubis in Duat are: Rick, Hamish, Alan, and Noel.

Ira: AKA Famine, Horseman of the Apocalypse.

Isidore: Sabine's oldest human sister. Deceased.

Isleen: (Is-lean) Leanan-sidhe chatelaine for the House of Fire.

Isis: (Eye-sus) Egyptian Goddess of Magic. Daughter of Geb and Nut, wife to Osiris, mother of Horus, and twin sister of Nephthys. Great-granddaughter of Re.

Jade: drachleen-sidhe female.

Jambavant: Hindu King of the Rikshas(werebears).

Jerry: AKA Jehova, the Christian, Muslim, and Jewish God.

Jesus: AKA The J-Man, Christian God, son of Holly and Jerry, and Guardian of the GRAYEL.

Juniper: Dark-sidhe of Apathy.

Kadru: Hindu Mother of the Nagas.

Kaitlin: Human girlfriend of Ull's, ate an apple of immortality to wait for him.

Kali: Hindu Goddess of Empowerment. Married to Shiva.

Kanaloa: (Kah-nah-low-ah) Hawaiian God of the Ocean. Squid-shifter. Dating Gruach (water-sidhe).

Karni-Mata: Hindu Goddess of Rats. Dating Teharon. Member of the God Squad.

Katrina: Farinne-sidhe.

Kirill Alexeyevich: Intare Ganza, married to Vervain.

Kuan-Ti: (Kwahn-tee) Chinese General turned God of War. Friends with Blue.

Laise: (Lash-ah) Leanan-sidhe who designs the nursery.

Lamiai, The: (Lah-me-eye) Greek vampiric demi-goddesses who hang with Hekate.

Laurell: Dark-sidhe of Weakness.

Leto: Greek daughter of the Titans. Mother to Artemis and Apollo.

Lesya: (Lay-shah) Future daughter of Vervain and Kirill. Lioness-shifter.

Liatris: Queen of the House of Darkness, married to Rowan, mother of Sinnea and Baidhen.

Lir: Celtic king turned god, father of Finn, Conn, Aodh, and Fionnuala.

Lissa: fire pixie.

Loki: Trickster God of the Norse. Fenrir's father. Shapeshifter.

Lorna: Water-sidhe, mother of Morgan.

Lucifer Morningstar: AKA Satan etc. (I'm not listing all his names). Father of Azrael and married to Holly.

Lugh Mac Cein: Celtic God of Skill, Crafts, Arts, Oaths, Truth, and Law.

Lusaset: (Lew-sah-set)Egyptian Primal Goddess, Re's wife. Deceased.

Ma'at: (Mah-aht)Egyptian Goddess of Justice. Daughter of Set and Nephthys, sister of Anubis, Re's great-great-granddaughter.

Mace: Dark-sidhe of Anger.

Macha: (Mock-uh) One of the three aspects of the Morrigan. Fury incarnate. The red-haired goddess of Fire, Victory, Protection, and Fertility.

Machatan: (Mah-cah-tan)Cherubim who looks like a Harley wheel.

Mairi: (Mah-ree) fire cat-sidhe.

Maman Brigitte: Vodou lwa of Crosses and Gravestones. Wife of Baron Samedi.

Manannan Mac Lir: (Ma-nah-nahn) Celtic God of the Sea, foster father to Lugh. Guardian of the Celtic Otherworld, and ferryman to the souls of the dead.

Mandrake: Dark-sidhe of Jealousy.

Marasa: Vodou twin lwas, members of the Gede.

Meara: (Meer-ah) High Queen of Faerie, married to Cian.

Meilyr: (May-leer) Imp.

Michael: Archangel and Ruler of the 4th Heaven.

Mimir: Norse Giant God of Wisdom. Taught Odin how to bring back Sabine's soul. Dating Isleen.

Moirai, The: AKA The Fates. Lachesis the Alotter, Clotho the Spinner, and Atropos the Unturnable.

Morgan: Prince of the Water Kingdom, son of Guirmean and Lorna.

Morpheus: Greek God of Dreams, one of the three Oneiroi, son of Hypnos and Pasithea, brother to Phantasus and Phobetor. Member of the God Squad.

Morrigan: (More-ri-gahn) One of the three aspects of the Morrigan. The Great Queen or Phantom Queen. Battle Crow.

Morvran: (More-v'ran)Celtic God of War. Deceased.

Nala: Hindu were-monkey leader.

Nagas: Hindu snake-shifters.

Nainsidh: (Nan-she) Bean-nighe woman who gives Vervain a prophecy.

Nayenezgani: AKA Naye. Navajo God of War. Twin brother of Tobadzistsini. Son of Mr. T and Mrs. E, married to Atahensic (deceased). Father of Teharon and Tawiskaron.

Neala: Phooka mother who's married to Righ.

Nemesis: Greek Goddess of Revenge.

Nephthys: (Nehp-sis) Egyptian Goddess of Mourning. Daughter of Nut and Geb, wife of Set, mother to Ma'at and Anubis, great-granddaughter of Re.

Nepra: (Neh-prah)Egyptian Spirit of the Corn, lives in Re's territory.

Nora: Phooka turned into first water phooka, engaged to King Guirmean. Daughter of Albion and Sonasag

Nuada: (New-ah-dah)Celtic God of Healing, has a silver arm.

Odin: AKA The Allfather, AKA Oathbreaker. Norse God of the Occult. Married to Sabine in the past, now married to Vervain. Father of Thor, Balder, Vidar, and Vali. Member of the God Squad. Has two ravens; Hugin and Munin, and two wolves; Geri and Freki.

Oran: (Ah-ran) Fire cat-sidhe.

Osiris: Egyptian God of the Afterlife. Married to Isis, father of Horus.

Pan: Greek God of Nature. Member of the God Squad.

Papa Gede: (Papa Geh-day) Vodou lwa, member of the Gede.

Pasithea: Greek Goddess of Relaxation. Married to Hypnos, mother of Morpheus, Phobetor, and Phantasus. Creator of Net.

Pele: Hawaiian Goddess of the Volcano.

Persephone: (Per-sef-oh-knee) Greek Goddess of Spring. Married to Hades. Member of the God Squad. AKA Bunny-Nose.

Phantasus: (Fan-tah-sus)One of the three Oneiroi, Greek God of Illusion. Brother to Morpheus and Phobetor, son of Pasithea and Hypnos. Deceased.

Phobetor: (For-bet-tore) Greek God of Nightmares. One of the three Oneiroi. Son of Hypnos and Pasithea, brother to Morpheus and Phantasus.

Poseidon: Greek God of the Sea. Married to Amphitrite.

Ptah: (Pa-tah) Egyptian Creator God. Married to Sekhmet,

father of Nefertem.

Qaus: (Kow-sus)Arabian Weather God associated with rainbows.

Rainieri: (Rain-nee-er-ree) AKA Rain, lead singer for Dark Horses, a Celtic horse-shifter.

Raphael: Archangel of Healing, Ruler of the 2nd Heaven.

Re: Egyptian God of the Sun. Vervain's boyfriend. Father of Sekhmet, Bastet, and Shu, was married to Lusaset (deceased).

Rebecca: Human sorceress and necromancer. Deceased.

Rhiannon: Celtic Goddess of Horses. Dated Constantin and Hanuman.

Rian: (Ree-an) Vervain and Arach's son, twin to Brevyn.

Rikshas: Hindu bear-shifters. Demi-gods.

Rind: (Rin-d) Norse Giantess, mother of Vali.

Roarke: (Roar-k) King of the Fire Cat-Sidhe, father to Hunter.

Rosemary: Dark-sidhe of Greed.

Rowan: King of the House of Darkness, married to Liatris, father of Sinnea and Baidhen.

Rue: Dark-sidhe of Hunger, father of Zinnia.

Sabine: Vervain's name in her past life when she was married to Odin.

Samael: Archangel of Death (Yes, there's more than one) and Ruler of the 5th Heaven.

Samantha: Froekn(werewolf) married to Fallon and one of Vervain's best friends. Mother of Zariel.

Samara: Future daughter of Vervain and Arach. Dragon-sidhe and Princess of Fire.

Samuel: AKA War, Horseman of the Apocalypse.

Sarama: Hindu Goddess of Dogs, Bitch of Heaven.

Sarasvati: (Sare-ras-vah-tee) AKA Sara. Hindu Goddess of Knowledge. Married to Brahma. Member of the God Squad.

Sekhmet: (Seck-met) Egyptian Warrior Goddess of Healing: Lioness-shifter, daughter of Lusaset and Re, twin of Bastet, mother of Nefertem.

Scotaidh: (Sco-tee) Imp.

Sebastian: Future angel son of Azrael and Vervain.

Senna: Dark-sidhe of Malice.

Silenus: Greek God of Prophecy. Drunkard. Companion to Dionysus.

Siuna: (Sh'ooh-nah) Female fire pixie dating Diarmad.

Snarl: Ellingran faerie male.

Sokar: (So-car) Egyptian God of the Buried. Brother to Ptah, resides in Aaru.

Suparnas: Hindu falcon-shifters.

Tagas: (Tah-gahs) Angel of Music.

Taog: (Took) Hidden-One who's married to Fionnaghal, father of Mini V, Deidre, and Daoir.

Taraghlan: (Tare-ah-gawn) Air-sidhe.

Tawiskaron: (Tah-wisk-kah-ron) Mohawk Demon God of Darkness. Teharon's twin brother and son of Nayenezgani and Atahensic. Deceased.

Teharon: (Teh-hah-ron) Mohawk Creator God of Healing. Son of Naye and Atahensic, twin brother of Tawiskaron. Dating Karni-Mata. Member of the God Squad.

Tefnut: (Teff-newt) Egyptian Goddess of Moisture, wife of Shu, mother of Nut.

Tepu-yn: (Teh-poo-in) Egyptian Spirit of the Corn, resides in Re's territory.

Thaddeus: AKA Ted, Antichrist, Horseman of the Apocalypse.

Thor: Norse God of Storms. Son of Odin and Iord, brother to Vali, Vidar, and Balder. Prince and Guardian of Asgard. Member of the God Squad.

Thoth: (Toth) Egyptian God of Knowledge.

Thrud: Norse Goddess of War. Thor and Sif's daughter, brother to Ull.

Thunderbirds: Native American bird-shifters.

Tobadzistsini: AKA Toby. Navajo God of Darkness. Son of Mr T and Mrs E, twin brother of Naye.

Torrent: Demi-god creation of Iktomi. Made of god magic and Internet magic. Dating Artemis and member of the God Squad.

Trevor: AKA VéulfR, AKA Honey-Eyes. Froekn Prince and Heir Apparent. First born son of Fenrir. Married to Vervain.

Trillium: Dark-sidhe of Obsession.

TryggulfR: AKA Ty, Froekn(werewolf) 3rd son of Fenrir, Brother to Trevor and UnnúlfR.

Tsohanoai: (So-ha-noe-ayee) AKA Mr T. Navajo God of the Sun. Married to Mrs E, father to Naye and Toby. Member of the God Squad.

Ull: (uh-LL) Viking God of Justice. Son of Sif and stepson to Thor. Deceased.

Una: (Oooh-nah) Fire cat-sidhe.

UnnúlfR: Froekn (werewolf), 2nd son of Fenrir, brother to Trevor and Ty.

Vali: Norse God of Archery and Hunting. Son of Odin and Rind, adopted son of Sabine, brother to Vidar, Thor, and Balder.

Valkyries: Odin's warrior goddesses. They include Brynhildr (Brin-hill-da), Eir (Air), Herja (Her-yah), and Kara.

Vampires: This pertains mainly to the Aztec strain, children of Blue and Eztli. They include: Ajax, William, Alexandra, and Jason.

Vanaras: Hindu were-monkeys. Demi-gods.

Vayu: Hindu God of Air. Father of Hanuman.

Vero: Future son of Trevor and Vervain. God of Moon and Wolves, Froekn (werewolf).

Vervain: main character- the Godhunter. Also a Hidden-One child called Mini V for the sake of clarity, daughter of Taog and Fionnaghal.

Vidar: Norse God of Vengeance and Silence. Son of Odin and Sabine, brother to Vali, Thor, and Balder.

Vinata: Hindu Mother of Suparnas.

Violet: Dark-sidhe of Heartache.

Xi Wang Mu: (See-wang-moo) Chinese Mother Goddess. Dating Kuan-Ti.

Yarrow: Dark-sidhe of Exploitation.

Yemanja: (Yay-mahn-yah) Vodou lwa (low-ah) of the Sea. Also Santerian orisha (La Sirene) of the Sea.

Zachariel: (Zah-care-ree-all) Archangel of Healing.

Zariel: First Intare (lion-shifter) ever born. Daughter of Fallon and Samantha.

Zeus: Greek God of the Sky. Married to Hera, father of Athena, Artemis, and Apollo.

Zinnia: Baby dark-sidhe born to Dahlia and Rue.

Michelle Hoffman, thank you for your support, your encouragement, your hours of editing, and your boundless friendship; this book is for you.

Subscribe to Amy's Newsletter
and get a free gift:

http://google.us11.list-manage.com/sub-
scribe?
u=398603e0fc6b3876340e37356&id=3abd32e
dce

About the Author

Amy Sumida is the Internationally Acclaimed author of the Award-Winning Godhunter Series, the fantasy paranormal Twilight Court Series, the Beyond the Godhunter Series, the music-oriented paranormal Spellsinger Series, and several short stories. Her books have been translated into several languages, have made it to the top sellers list on Amazon numerous times, and the first book in her Spellsinger Series won a publishing contract with Kindle Press.

She was born and raised in Hawaii, and brings her unique island perspective to all of her books. She doesn't believe in using pen names, saving the fiction for her stories. She's know for her kick-ass heroines who always have a witty comeback ready, and her strong, supporting male characters who manage to be sensitive and alpha all at once.

Author Information

If you enjoyed this book, please let the author know by leaving a review. Reviews help her sell more books and keep her writing.

For information on new releases, detailed character descriptions, and an in-depth look into the worlds of Godhunter and the Twilight Court, check out Amy's website;

http://www.amysumida.com/

Sign up for her newsletter and receive a free gift: http://google.us11.list-manage.com/subscribe?u=398603e0fc6b3876340e37356&id=3abd32edce

You can also find her on facebook at:

https://www.facebook.com/AmySumidaAuthor/

or

https://www.facebook.com/groups/1536008099761461/

Follow her on Bookbub to get news on latest releases: https://www.bookbub.com/authors/amy-sumida

On Twitter under @Ashstarte

On Goodreads:

https://www.goodreads.com/author/show/7200339.Amy_Sumida

On Instagram:https://www.instagram.com/ashstarte/

On Tumblr: http://vervainlavine.tumblr.com/

And you can find her entire collection of books on her Amazon Author Page:

https://www.amazon.com/-/e/B00BVUWW9K

Printed in Great Britain
by Amazon

72624381R00241